# BY JANE S. FANCHER

**WARNER BOOKS**

A Time Warner Company

WARNER BOOKS EDITION

Copyright © 1991 by Jane S. Fancher
All rights reserved.

Questar® is a registered trademark of Warner Books, Inc.

Cover design by Don Puckey
Cover illustration by Barclay Shaw

Warner Books, Inc.
666 Fifth Avenue
New York, NY 10103

A Time Warner Company

Printed in the United States of America

First Printing: October, 1991

10 9 8 7 6 5 4 3 2 1

# SPIRITS
# OF SPACE

*       *       *

"Hononomii—can you *call* Dena Cocheta?"

A breath of a whisper, "Yes . . ." His eyes misted.
". . . yesss . . ."

Cantrell signed to TJ: *Link up! Trace it!* She turned
the prisoner's chair toward the desk. "Here,
Hononomii, here's the keyboard."

His fingers flickered rapidly over the keys. At a
choked sound from TJ, she looked up to the screen
where the coded keystrokes should be echoing. It
was blank.

Abruptly, a deep, young voice came over the
system: *"Dena Cocheta. De'ninaah."*

Hononomii called out: *"Nayati! Nayati Hatawa?"*

From the system: *"Hono? Hono? Where the hell are
you?"*

And Hononomii, his voice near breaking: *"Nayati?
Shin'niilhi! Hodeeshtal . . . Hodeeshtal!"*

And the system: *"Oh dear God, Hono, forgive—"*
Silence.

Cantrell hit the com connect. "Dammit, Chet! Get
them back!"

*"Admiral? Get who back? No transmission has left the
ship in the last two hours!"*

She got up, never taking her eyes off the prisoner,
who'd lapsed back into catalepsy. "If there was no
transmission, then what the hell were we just
listening to?"

The preliminaries were over, the remnants of the appetizers removed. Good friends, good food and a pleasant buzz well underway from the best wine to touch her palate in over two years.

The waiter arrived with the recommended shalimba filets, and Loren Cantrell closed her eyes to savor the aroma. As host of the small party, she received hers last, which gave her nose ample time to prepare her tastebuds.

The waiter's presence passed behind her and she controlled her reflexes with less effort than it had required two glasses of wine ago. He positioned the plate in front of her—filet at lower left, the seven-vegetable crescent an artistic curve above. She smiled. The waiter smiled back. A cool *Thank you*, met a warmer *You're very welcome, admiral*, and she laughed.

It was an old game, one the young man played to perfection. He'd get his tip; he was an excellent waiter. But style and a good—personality—wouldn't lower it.

With an impish grin and a wink, he gathered up his tray and stand and glided back to the kitchen, nonchalantly avoiding collision with an outbound dessert. He disappeared behind intricately carved panels, and Cantrell turned back to her companions to find the two females in the party gazing at the panels with equal appreciation. Don looked—resigned.

Smothering amusement behind her glass, she sipped her wine, set it down, and was reaching for her fork when her personal pager buzzed in her ear.

"Damn." If she didn't have the implant, she could ignore it. As it was . . . She held up her hand, forestalling questions as she tapped a query, listened for the encoded response.

—Station Security Com: Albion consul/Stat: Kurt—

"I don't believe this! Kyla, Don, Sharon—excuse me a moment. I've got to find a Secure Line. —Please don't wait for me. I've no idea how long this will take. No sense in all our dinners going cold." And with a final, longing glance at the filet: "So help me, if this is anything short of intergalactic war, Kurt Eckersley may not survive the night."

A roar went up in the Security Club bar as the ball shot through the pocket. Dead center: a three-pointer, no question.

The revised score flashed on the screen. TJ Briggs leaned back in his chair, licked foam from his upper lip, and smirked at the security officers crowding up behind him.

"One more, gentle-folk, and it's mine—all mine. Thought the old man would be out of touch, didn't you? That's why God invented the 'Net. I've seen all the games. No way those academy kids can beat Joharan's lot. And it's their serve now."

The red-head sharing his chair leaned her elbows on the table, rested her chin glumly in her hand. "Yeah, Teej, but who would have thought a bunch of belt-miners' brats could beat Vandereaux's Best? Let alone by thirty points."

Briggs twisted to grab a handful of popcorn and grinned at her. "You ever watch miners' rug-rats in ZeroG? You've got to—"

A buzz in his ear. No! They wouldn't. *Couldn't!*

A second roar from the crowd unfortunately failed to drown out a second signal, this one persistent enough to wake the dead.

If the corpse happened to be one TJ Briggs.

Desperately hoping for a replay, he queried the System with discreet taps at the implant. On the bar's vid screen, a foul being reviewed—and in his ear a goddamned Priority call from Old Man Morley in Central Security.

*"Shit!"* he growled, then yelled, "Look out, troops, I'm coming through! —Terry, I need a 'Line. Now!''

Another uproar in the bar: whether from colleagues outraged at him or at something on the screen, Briggs didn't know and didn't dare take time to inquire. He stepped from his chair to the tabletop, then over the crowd, fellow officers lending shoulders and hands as stepping-stones.

By the time he reached the floor, the barkeep had the back room cleared and a Security Line standing-by.

Alexis Fonteccio carefully lifted the top layer of pasta. Steam rose: at least it was hot.

She sniffed hopefully—

—and let the pasta fall.

She'd hoped—she'd truly hoped she would find something somewhere in the much-vaunted Vandereaux Station which wouldn't make her gag. This—purported lasagne—was not it. She suspected that their "imported chef" had indeed been imported—from the seagoing salt processors of Venezia. No wonder stationers got such strange notions about Recons: no Venezian—not even Cousin Michaelino—would eat this garbage.

A managerial inquiry tapped into the electro-menu roused a form display:

> **Regret unavailable at this time.**
> **Please log complaint for queued review.**
> **For complaint list, enter L.**

With a sigh and a sip of mediocre red, Lexi leaned her chin on her hand and replaced the inquiry with the Bracketball game. Tiny players bounced in random (to her eyes) chaos across the screen. Another button displayed the score:

TJ should be happy. One more goal and she reckoned the pot was his.

She chewed half-heartedly on a bread-stick that tasted of stale plastic and wondered how to forego the rest of her leave. Three months stuck on Vandereaux Station while *Cetacean* and her crew were off doing outer-system maneuvers was not her idea of a good time. But Adm. Cantrell had insisted her personal staff get the same time off as herself, and she personally had not had the heart to tell her commanding officer she'd rather scrub pots in *Cetacean's* galley than spend a week in this hive of NeoDarwinists.

Lexi stuck the plastic breadstick into the plastic lasagne, pushed the plastic plate across the plastic table, signed the plastic register chit and tossed it in the plastic cashier-slot on her way out the plastic door.

"Hold it right there!"

Unmistakable, that Tone. She curbed hostility before turning back. A real-live HB: 'Cashier,' according to his name tag. "Yes?"

"What's the problem?" Low and brisk inquiry from a third party. 'Manager,' *his* name tag read. Funny thing—not so 'unavailable' as advertised.

The cashier held up the chit. "She's Recon, sir."

The manager eyed the signature, eyed Lexi up and down. She turned so her *Cetacean* patch and the security badge were clearly visible. The Look didn't change.

Maybe it was the way she walked.

Not a word spoken. None necessary. She handed them a ten-credit piece: cash; they handed her the change, *less* a tip for nonexistent service: *The Green Olive* 'employed' electronic menus and robotic servos.

Lexi turned her back on the *Olive's* plastic people and headed aimlessly down the row of so-called ethnic restaurants, working her way slowly through the crowd, side-stepping noisy children and pulling a drunk from the path of a speeding VipCab. Garish colors and raucous music assaulted her senses from all sides. Men and women in ill-fitting replicas of ancient clothing styles accosted passers-by, enthusiastically urging them to try a 'new taste sensation.'

Busy place. Ironic: Vandereaux, undisputed center of the Separatist movement, boasted the largest, most elaborate EthnoStrip of any station in the Nexus ComNet Alliance. —But then, what better way to reinforce your own sense of superiority than by sporting a parody of a parody of a Reconstruction of the Real Thing?

And she had three months of this to look forward to.

She could, she supposed, get a downworld passage, but somehow she doubted it would be any different there. The entire Vandereaux system was too old—and too completely in Councillor Shapoorian's pocket—to give a visiting Ethnic Reconstructionist anything but an ulcer, and while the admiral kept including her in Councillor Eckersley's plans for downworld excursions, tours of CentralSec and Capitol Station, Lexi foresaw nothing but an endless repetition of tonight.

At times, Adm. Cantrell had the most incredibly naive notions how far she could bend the system.

The change from the ten covered a hot dog and chips from a stand. Mustard was extra. She splurged, smothered the Mystery Meat into edibility and headed down-rim in quest of a phone.

With luck, the admiral would understand.

*"Dammit, Eckersley! You owe me for this!"* Tiny pinpoints of light bounced from Cantrell's beaded blouse to her dark fist as it struck the *Embassy* manager's desk. "My first leave in over two years and you pull me away from a kilocred meal because a goddamn computer *hiccuped?* Send in the fucking maintenance crew!"

*"Loren, please, trust me on this."*

The councillor's voice sounded strained even through the damping effects of a temporarily Secured phone line. *Good,* Cantrell thought sourly. She'd pulled him out of a meeting—*damned* if she'd take a message like that from a secretary—and now he wanted to get back to his important cronies?

Let him sweat.

"Trust you, Kurt? After you've just cancelled three months of plans? Three months of plans *you* made? And *you* promised me? You do make trust difficult."

*"Loren, my dear, old friend—"*

"Watch who you're calling dear—or old, *Councillor.*"

*"You know I didn't mean it like that. Loren, I need you on this one. —Dammit, yes! I'm coming! —Listen. Just get over to AcStat. Danislav will explain everything."*

"AcStat?" A quick evaluation of local possibilities. "The *Academy?* What does Vandereaux Academy have to do with a RecRun? Who the hell's Danislav?"

*"For God's sake, didn't that secretary of mine explain anything?"*

"Don't try to put it off on her, Eckersley. She said Records clarification and I said Get you! Now, who's Danislav?"

*"Dean of 'Net Studies over at Vandereaux. And this is in addition to the RecRun. The reason I want you to go . . . There's a paper, one supposedly without published precedence. The student who found it will be going with you to—"*

" 'Published *precedence'*? Good—God. You're sending *Cetacean* on a Bug Chase! —Forget it, Eckersley. I resign. That's it."

*"Loren! I don't have time for this!"*

"Make time, Eckersley."

*"Look. It's not so much who's responsible for the theory —personally, I think it's a lot of hoopla over nothing. It's the student, Stephen Ridenour. This boy is special. The brief on him is waiting for you in the AcStat admin office. Take a look at it. You'll understand after your meeting with Danislav. Trust me. You'll like HuteNamid—"*

"HuteNamid? —Is *that* where we're going, Kurt?"

*Didn't I just say that?"*

A breath. A second, while her heart rate slowed. Deliberate relaxation of her fist, one finger at a time, before she said softly, "I may forgive you for this yet, Kurt. —Good enough. I'll go talk to this Danislav. See you in a subjective year or so, —old friend."

A faint: *"Dammit, Loren, what—"*

The receiver clicked into the old-fashioned cradle.

She couldn't believe she was letting Council get away with it again. At least all the other too-fast turnarounds had been justifiable: interCorps emergencies *were* her so-called specialty. This time . . .

Confusion on the 'Net DataBase an 'emergency situation'? Hardly, though most people in the ComNet Alliance would disagree with her. Most people *believed* the hype about the Instantaneously Available (excepting certain 'space-time deformations' —or the whim of the local SysOps) Miracle-of-Modern-Science 'Net. Most believed its Nexus-Space-permeating data cache never ever (like the ancient elephant some satirist had dredged up to represent it) forgot; they actually *believed* that from the moment the 'Net had gone up seventy years ago, every entry into that NSpace resident memory was pure—inviolate—absolutely, physically unchangeable.

Those who knew the ComNet system *really* knew it, knew better. Sometimes (in very minor ways, of course) data got—scrambled. Somehow. A subspace twitch, a pion or two confused . . .

The damn thing got a belly-ache from too many addenda and hiccuped, *that* was what. And because of a computer's indigestion, her extremely weary crew got their leave cancelled and *Cetacean*, one of the most specialized starships in Central Security's fleet, got dispatched to a frontier world on the edge of the known universe to ask for original hard copy to straighten out a half dozen words in some useless file. . . .

A second call: this time to Central Security, with a request for TJ to meet her in front of the SecClub Bar on her way to pick up the Academy Clone—she hadn't the stomach to face a dripping-wet-behind-the-ears student alone.

Student, hell. This Ridenour was a 'Net Authority Del d'Bugger, no more, no less. You got a good idea? You'd damned well better tell the whole universe exactly where it came from, particularly if you were one of the SciCorps Researchers living on taxpayers' credit. Otherwise, you got a 'NetAT-appointed Special Investigator—a Del d'Bugger—going through your notes to attribute sources and straighten out the record (*and* the royalties). If the omission was innocent, no problem. You just wrote formal apologies and promised you'd never *ever* do it again—and paid for the InterLinks programmer assigned to straighten out the 'NetDataBase records.

But heaven couldn't help you if you were caught faking sources or data. There had been no few cases of researchers busted clear out of the Corps forever for that—*after* paying for the InterLinks programmer's services.

And those were the researchers the 'NetAT *liked*.

Still, Eckersley had said It's not the paper, it's the student. *He'd* better *be special, Kurt Eckersley.*

A third call, to order an in-station cab and special shuttle to Vandereaux Academy—damned if she'd wait for commercial transport—then she released the 'Line and vacated the *Embassy* restaurant manager's office, resisting the temptation to key a Security Override into the state-of-the-art lock and call in an audit. She'd love to know how much of the very expensive upported furnishings had been 'expensed.'

Considering the static the manager had given her when she'd requested a Secure Line—the *gall*, demanding a full BioScan . . . —As though anyone could get through the Security Operator *without* proper access.

God, she hated incompetence.


"What do you mean you can't tell me where she's gone? What do your records say?"

*"I'm sorry, Ms. Fonteccio—"*

"That's *Sergeant* Fonteccio!"

*"Yes, —quite. The admiral's orders are under Security Two. You, ma'am, are a Five. I suggest you call your duty desk."*

Keeping her frustration from her voice, Lexi thanked the fool in Morley's office and called *Cetacean's* onboard hotline this time, on the off-chance Morley's fool knew something.

And got the same—helpful—*recorded* message . . .

*"Cetacean is under emergency recall. Shore leave is cancelled. All personnel report immediately to gate H-41B. Repeat: all leaves are cancelled. No exceptions."*

. . . which had caused her to call CentralSec in the first place. She hung up and headed for gate H-41B.

The admiral's arrival at the SecClub entrance coincided with the loudest roar yet from inside. Briggs winced as he climbed into the AutoCab. Foul? or goal? Why, oh, *why* had the Vandereaux coach called that last minute time out?

The 'Cab's acceleration pressed him back in his seat; he looked across to Cantrell—

—and whistled. "Shee-it, woman, you could'a warned me. A bit under-dressed, aren't I?"

"Don't press your luck, TJ. Did you get hold of Lexi?"

"Couldn't. Left a message at the gate. Admiral, we've *got* to get her that G3 personal."

"Tell me about it. However, after this *jaunt* we're taking, Eckersley's going to owe me plenty. Lexi's security upgrade will be a roll in ZG and you'll be able to whisper sweet nothings into her skull to your heart's content. —Did Morley explain what's happening?"

"Not much. Really, Boss-lady, *Cetacean* on a RecRun is a bit much, even as a favor to Eckersley. Why doesn't the 'NetAT send its own people in?"

"Hell if I know. Maybe the 'NetAT's pilots are on strike again. Kurt muttered something about an 'emergency situation,' and to give him the benefit, it *could* be Security sensitive records involved. Maybe something got transed that shouldn't have."

"Still doesn't justify *our* going."

The cab jolted to a halt at the Security Terminal. Cantrell didn't wait for the attendant's assistance. She shoved the door open with an elegantly sandaled foot and was half-way to the waiting bubblecar before he caught her up.

The Boss-lady was pissed.

Terse instructions to the controller as they boarded, and acceleration hit before they'd settled their safety straps.

The Boss-lady was definitely pissed.

Stars surrounded them as the bubblecar burst free of the SuperCon track and began its coast toward Academy Station. His scalp prickled as the sudden lack of gravity attacked thinning hair. Funny: he never used to hate ZeroG.

"Why AcStat, Loren?"

Her preoccupied scowl eased. Dark eyes flickered toward him. "We're picking up a passenger. A *student* passenger. According to Kurt, it'll all make sense after I talk with the Dean of 'Net Studies over at the Academy."

He put on his best *I'm confused* look.

Cantrell smiled grimly. "*Cetacean* is also on a Del d'Bug run." She held up her hand as he opened his mouth. "And before you say anything, Kurt insists I not draw any conclusions about this Ridenour kid until *after* I talk with Danislav."

"Ridenour." He knew that name from . . . "*Stephen* Ridenour?"

"I think that's the name. Why?"

"Vandereaux Academy's Fifth-level all-around that wracked up his arm—two—three years ago?"

She stared at him as though she couldn't believe what she was hearing. "TJ, *I* don't know. Why, for God's sake? What difference does it make?"

He shrugged. "None. Just wondered. He was a damned fine gymnast. A shame Vandereaux lost him off the team. I've often wondered—"

"TJ." Her voice was dangerously soft. "Ask me if I care."

He grinned. "*Do* you care, Boss-lady?"

She shook her head. Mouthed *No*, then said, "Did Morley tell you where we're headed?"

His grin widened. "Ask me if I care."

"No, I won't ask—because you don't know the right answer. Believe me, you *want* to know. —It's HuteNamid."

He felt the grin fade, felt his jaw drop. "Does Corlaney know you're coming?"

She shrugged.

The grin returned tenfold. "This should be good. Have I the admiral's permission to sell tickets?"

## ii

*Cetacean's* shuttle gate assignment had changed.

Lexi arrived at G-35A out of breath and out of patience, only to have twenty fellow *Cetacean* Security personnel accost her the moment she cleared the scanners. She held up both hands. "Look, guys, I have no idea. All I've heard is the same recording you got."

Protests from all around. A dozen arms pointing toward the message monitor:

**A. FONTECCIO: URGENT**.

She extricated herself and worked her way through the crowded lobby to the gate steward's desk.

"I'm Sgt. Alexis Fonteccio. You have a message for me?"

The Look. She saw It coming and flipped her ID out before he had time to ask. He checked it, ran it through the scanner—twice—scowled and insisted on an awkward and embarrassing implant scan before reluctantly handing her a sealed envelope.

**Vandereaux Academy Admin.**

 **Stat.**

 **TJ.**

*That's it, Teej? How? Why? When? And with what reinforcements?*

She said to the steward, "I need to call the Central Security offices. May I use your phone, please?"

"That line has to stay free for emergency use."

She smiled sweetly. "This *is* an emergency."

The steward looked up from his vidmag article. "Hardly."

Same sweet smile, same sweet tone: "It will be once I break your arm. Now may I use the phone?"

A page drifted to the plush carpet. Victor Danislav leaned over to pick it up, grunted as he straightened, made an issue of carefully tucking the age-yellowed paper into place. His round face was still flushed when he finally faced her and extended the battered notebook with both hands.

Cantrell leaned forward to accept, stifled irritation as the man's colorless gaze focussed somewhat below her face. She sat back, settling the blouse with a subtle twitch of her shoulders.

She had no patience with fools easily swayed by cleavage.

Danislav shifted in his chair and cleared his throat. "Take care of it, admiral. As far as I know, there is no copy."

Fragile sheets filled with childish script; she scanned at random, increasingly impatient. So far the man had told her less than Kurt Eckersley. The file on this Ridenour held nothing more than test scores and psychological evaluations, the former meaning nothing outside academia, the latter not exactly encouraging. Now, Danislav was insisting she read this asocial academy brat's diary . . .

A name caught her eye. An unrecognizable word or two. She flipped to the beginning and read with greater care—after searching the first quarter of the book for a page she *could* read.

"The boy is Recon?"

A surprised blink: he'd expected her to know.

She scanned further. Felt a coldness in her gut as she realized:

"From Rostov-on-Don." She shot another glance at him without lifting her head, intercepted a nervous twitch, a different shifting of weight. "How long has he been here?"

But he replied calmly enough, "About ten years."

'About'? Hardly a time for approximations. How long before the Quarantine? What was Danislav's clearance? *Dammit, Kurt Eckersley, you might have warned me!*

"Part of the general pullout?" she asked, cautious reference to the GP version.

"You and I both know better, admiral."

"Has the Rostov investigation team seen this?"

"Their experts examined it—afterward—" Casual. Perhaps *too* casual. "And I suppose it *is* in *their* records, if they want it, but I doubt they found anything meaningful. He was far too young when he left to have been privy to any of the system's—alleged peculiarities—"

"That's a matter of opinion." She allowed a hint of irritation through.

"Yes, of course." A strategic retrenchment. "But the daily life of a Reconstructionist child is boring at best—"

She shrugged. His attention wavered again as that movement sent a strap off her shoulder. She left it there.

"I doubt the child found it so."

He cleared his throat. "But still, a slower-paced life, I'm sure you'll agree." He crossed his arms on the desk and looked earnest. "Let me be frank with you, admiral. I argued against Council's decision—"

"What decision?"

"To send Stephen on this mission."

"Council? Del d'Bugging is 'NetAT business."

He winced. "Source Verification, please. —But, yes, normally, it is. However, certain political factions have followed Stephen's progress with some interest for several years. Those interested parties decided to take a hand in his career. I argued. I was overruled."

"I fail to understand your reservations. Council's eager for him to get established and pay his own way. The 'Net Authority evidently feels he's a useful asset on this trip. It's a major break for such a young man. A chance to establish himself this early in his career—"

"Early in his career? He hasn't even graduated yet! Admin threw re-tests at him cold just last week! *No* one gets retested. They pass or they fail. Early graduation . . . The whole damned *Council's* going to have to approve it. This blatant favoritism . . . It's unforgivable!"

"You think he's not ready?"

"Of course he's not ready. The 'NetAT looked only at his NAP scores, not . . ." Bitterness crept into his voice—

—bitterness she prodded. "Not?"

"The 'NetAT MasterProgs didn't give a damn about him until the results of his 'NetAT Aptitude and Performance exams hit their desks. Then they *insisted* on changing his course of study. Insisted he be directed into PreDesign—put a damned foolish boy into a damned awkward position— Have you any idea how many applicants make it into the 'NetAT's Design program? And of those, how many survive the apprenticeship?"

She shook her head. Sore point for the man. *Extremely* sore point.

"Two—*maybe* three—a year get in. From the whole fu—" His mouth clamped shut and he sat back, breathing hard, fighting for composure. "Of those who are accepted, *maybe* a third achieve Designer certification."

"What happens to the others?"

"What will happen to Stephen, now they've interfered in his life. One wrong move and he's out. Not only of Design, but of any meaningful occupation in the field. He'll know too damn much and nowhere near enough. They got his hopes up, and now they want to send him out cold into an arena he hasn't a chance in hell of surviving. That's why I'm giving you the diary. I hope it will help you to understand the boy. Help you to deal with any problems—"

"You anticipate there will be? Problems, that is?"

"I don't know. Stephen's a wildcard right now. I wish we had a few more years with him here, but . . ."

"But you don't."

The straightest look yet. "No. We don't."

*"I'm sorry, sergeant, but SpecOp Briggs left no clearance for appropriation of a security vehicle. The commercial shuttle leaves in five minutes. May I suggest you stop wasting time and get on it?"*

*"Mille grazie,"* Lexi said sweetly to Morley's fool-on-the-phone. *"Porco meticcio apolide."*

*"Certainly, Sgt. Fonteccio. Glad I could help. Goodbye."*

"Thank you," Lexi said, surrendering the phone to the gate steward, still with that plastered smile. If she didn't get out of here, her face would crack.

She pushed her way back to the entrance, closing her ears to the insistent voices around her. She was going to get to Vandereaux Academy if she had to rent an EV-suit to do it.

And when she did get there, one TJ Briggs was going to die.

Cantrell said quietly, "You insist Ridenour's not ready. Council thinks otherwise. Council says you'll brief me on him. But I'm not getting what Council expects. —Am I?"

A frontal when the man was expecting a flank. A momentary regroup; then Danislav's intensity eased to a practiced, disarming smile. "Say, rather, I'm giving you somewhat more than Council expects. I'm simply trying to smooth over potential rough spots for a child I've worked closely with for over ten years. That's quite an investment on my part. I'd hate to see it destroyed by too early a cultivation."

" 'Too early'—how?"

"The child's been researching a *thesis* when others, his age and older, are still studying the basics.'' Easy slip into the role of Concerned Student Advisor.

''Why?''

''A Review Board decision. *I* opposed pushing him at the time, and my opinion hasn't changed. Certainly the boy was showing some aptitude for program design, but he was bounding ahead—independent studies, hit and miss—until his Mentor couldn't track him. He threw himself completely outside its assessment boundaries, *not* because he knew so much, but because what little he did know didn't make operational sense. You don't *solve* a problem like that by encouraging his flights of fancy, you damnwell go back to the basics and fill in the gaps. But the Board disagreed. The *Board* felt the thesis was a means of focussing that energy as well as presenting him to the 'NetAT for application.''

Convolution upon convolution: ''I thought you said the 'Net-AT was already interested in him.''

''Certainly, insofar as they wanted him to enter *our* PreDesign track. That doesn't mean they would automatically accept him into *their* program. It's a common request, rarely followed up. The paper was the Board's way of regaining their acceptance committee's attention.''

''And how did you want to—focus that energy?''

''Initially, a paper seemed a good idea: a *paper*, not a graduate-level thesis. Force him to slow up, to concentrate on his weakest area, not go off half-cocked into theory. It was not an attempt to opt him past the rest of his classes. Graduate him now, and who knows what he'll miss?''

''If your interactional can't find the gaps in his learning, they can't be very broad gaps, can they?''

''I didn't say the Mentor couldn't find the gaps. The boy's bright, but he's no damned genius.'' Concerned Student Advisor was slipping badly. ''Those aptitude scores were a fluke—just like his Vandereaux entrance exams.''

''You're sure of that?''

''Damn right, I'm sure. Either a fluke, or a cheat—but the latter *would* require a genius. His second year here, we had to put that Recon-brat into spec just to *pass*. We don't *have* 'special' children here, admiral; we can't afford them—there are too many brilliant ones fighting for space—but there was no damn place to put him. Rostov was gone. —You want to know why *I* think he had to retake those exams last week? Because they found out he doesn't know spit, and since they're forced to give him that degree because of some *arrangement* with Eckersley, they're *praying* he'll do better the second time around!''

He broke off, breathing heavily. She ignored his passion and flipped the pages of the diary. ''Does Ridenour know why he's being sent?''

Danislav seemed to catch himself, at least the Administrator mask settled into place. ''He's being sent, admiral, —as I've already told you—as your technical advisor on a 'Net glitch. I'm told the fallout is quite real. You'll receive further information on that from a Council representative. —*I've* not been advised as to the precise nature of that glitch. I'm not, after all, a part of the 'Net Authority.''

''So you said, Danislav. Is that the *only* reason?''

A twinge of irritation deepened the furrows in Danislav's brow. But she didn't give a damn about his offended pride. She didn't give a damn about that glitch. That glitch wasn't Kurt's reason for sending *Cetacean* to HuteNamid.

Danislav said, ''Stephen's research turned up a certain—'' A distasteful lift of his lip. ''—paper from HuteNamid: a work that could vaguely be construed as dealing in 'Net design theory that *Stephen* feels bears on the merit of his thesis. Unfortunately, the foolish boy brought it to me *after* sending in a formal change of thesis topic to the 'NetAT. Had he brought it to me first, I could have ended this—*fiasco* before it began.''

''Why?''

''Because the author of the work is one Jonathan Wesley Smith, and we *do* know him. He was another student who showed great promise in design. He might well have gone all the way to Master Programmer. Instead, he pulled a—practical joke—on his academy's base-system which barred him from RealTime Programming for life.''

''For a *joke?*''

''The 'NetAT doesn't have a sense of humor in that department. When you're on the 'NetAT's DProg track, break the rules and you're out—*and* under a security flag for the rest of your life: the Alliance simply cannot afford individuals with questionable judgment programming in the 'Net. The 'NetAT is out to get Smith's hide, make no doubt about it, and they're sacrificing Stephen to get him.''

"No doubt." She wished the man would stop making a modicum of sense. Her gut said he was a Shapoorianite. As such, he should be eating Recon lambs for breakfast every day.

Danislav continued smoothly. "Smith's paper is years old, has no attribution of sources, no peer review—again, not surprising considering Smith's conduct at Vandereaux—but he doesn't claim it's new, makes no attempt to promote it as such. That's how it escaped challenge until Stephen cited it as a source."

"Smith graduated from here?"

"I didn't say that. He attended for a time. He attained his degrees elsewhere."

"In?"

*"DataTracking."* She lifted her brows at Danislav's vehemence, and he continued in a milder tone. "The point is, admiral, the 'NetAT *knows* Smith, and Stephen's thesis change, his analysis of Smith's paper, and Smith's background had them checking into everything Smith had ever touched. They found a data fallout associated with Smith's local Corps—certainly not that extraordinary, but the coincidence suggested to some there should be a closer investigation. Somehow, the matter came to Council's attention and Councillor Eckersley had the notion to send Stephen. He's offered the boy a position if he does well on this assignment. Why, and doing what, I have no idea."

"In your *professional* opinion, is Smith a threat? Are the two problems connected?"

Danislav shook his head. "Oh, there were suspicions in the 'Net Authority, but—I've read that paper, admiral. It's worthless. Same as all Smith's overblown notions. —No, Smith is not my concern. HuteNamid is."

"The *planet?*"

"It's a Recon world, admiral. Contact with Reconstructionists at this critical point in Stephen's life—even remotely—might not be a good thing."

Shapoorian's Genetic Memory crap: the Dean was afraid of 'recontaminating' the boy's 'instincts.' They'd achieve nothing but useless argument on that subject. "And how did this—" She patted the book lying in her lap. "—come to be in *your* hands?"

Danislav tapped the desk top with his fingertips and rose, paced to his office door and back. "Stephen was injured—some years ago. An accident, you understand. I found that book in the corridor where it happened. That diary was *all* he brought with him from—that place—but he never asked about it.''

''No doubt it was an accident?''

''He never claimed otherwise.''

''Sufficient grounds for a probe?''

''He reacts to Deprivil and I refused to let the psychs play exotic chemical games with that mind.''

Translation: this Ridenour kid wasn't worth the hassle. But: ''*You* refused?''

''As his advisor. His sponsor. *In loco parentis*.''

Justification: a Recon child with a Shapoorianite for a guardian. If giving this kid a chance to escape Danislav's clutches *wasn't* Kurt's motivation, it damnwell ought to be.

She probed carefully. ''What are you trying to tell me, Dr. Danislav?''

Danislav clasped his hands behind his back, staring at his desk top. ''I'm afraid, admiral. Afraid Stephen might blow out there where he has no advisor, no one sensitive to his—particular needs.'' He was silent a moment; then his head rose, the tension vanished in an almost-smile. ''As I recall, you yourself, have nominated Recon students to the academies. . . . Not Vandereaux, of course, but some of the others.''

A moment's doubt . . .

Perhaps not bigotry. Perhaps, in this political hotseat, a necessary caution. ''None of mine got through.''

''But consider how you would feel: Vandereaux is the life *I* gave him. The first Recon student ever admitted to an academy—to *Vandereaux*, no less—and I'm responsible for it.''

. . . Doubt vanished: the slime was back, trying to impress her.

She wasn't. Impressed. ''Why *did* you sponsor him?''

''To see whether or not a Recon child could benefit from an academy education. I really thought for a while he was going to manage it. But, much as I hate to admit it, it looks as though something of Shapoorian's position is correct: Stephen has the brains—possibly even an extraordinary intelligence—but, socially speaking, *psychologically* speaking, he's just too different. I told you we had to bring in specialists just to get him through those early years. The psychs couldn't figure it. It took the neural-netters to realize the boy *sees* things wrong, and by then it was too late. We tried putting him in the VR tanks, but virtual reality is only *real* if you engram it early. By the time Ridenour got here, his neural pathways were already so interlaced with his own skewed cosmology, we could never sort out the chaff. Deprivil might have helped, but as I said, he can't handle Dep—we found that out the hard way.'' A discreet shudder. "Have you ever had to clean up vomit in ZG?''

*Try blood and brains in the controls of a pod gone random-vectoral at high-v, doctor.* She tapped a slow fingertip rhythm on the chair arm. ''Did the other students know about him?''

''There were rumors.'' Danislav slid back down behind his desk. ''He *was* different when he first came. But the details of his transfer are top security, and it's unlikely he confided in any of the students.''

''Why?''

''For one thing, he was told to keep the secret—for obvious reasons. Secondly, Stephen wasn't exactly popular when he first came in; no new student is. Unfortunately, while physically somewhat undersized, he was older than most entry-level students—''

''*How* old?''

Shifting gaze. Shifting body: the good doctor was squirming. The Good Doctor didn't know. The Good Doctor said, ''Nine . . . ten—but that's really quite irrelevant. The social bonding within his study group had already taken place, and you've *seen* his records. I had *no idea*, of course, when I agreed to sponsor him—''

''Of course. —So why *did* you sponsor the boy, Danislav?''

''I—'' More squirming. ''Family, mostly. His mother was a distant relation. She made the request. Evidently the family was having difficulty with him not fitting in. Not terribly surprising: Recon parents couldn't possibly keep ahead of him. But frankly, my sponsorship was mostly gesture at the time. I never imagined the Acceptance Committee would approve his application. As I said, his scores were good—quite good—but why they should decide in favor of Stephen and reject others with better—''

They'd been through this before. Gathering up the reports, transcripts, passports, and various other papers that defined Stephen Ridenour, she stuffed them into their packet and stood up, declaring an end to the interview.

Danislav preceded her to the door, prevented its opening with a touch on the wall. "One more thing, admiral: two months ago, Stephen knew what he was and where he was going. Then, all this—Smith's paper, the councillor's offer—and all of a sudden he's nearing the edge again, and this time I'm in no position to help him."

Cantrell frowned. "Again?"

Danislav didn't answer. His voice was cold as he released the door and held out his hand. "Goodbye, admiral, and—good luck."

She tucked the diary and the packet securely under one arm, took Danislav's hand in a firm grip—felt perverse satisfaction when he winced and flexed the hand after. She said drily, "Don't worry, doctor, I'll have my eye on him every moment. —Goodbye."

She turned on her heel and left.

Normally Lexi loved the transparent bubblecars—in her view, the only truly unique pleasure the stations had to offer. But the beauty of the surrounding stars on this particular coast between Vandereaux Station-main and Academy Station was somewhat—marred. The game was over. Vandereaux had *not* won. And the last *commercial* shuttle before AcStat curfew was full of Vandereaux—students.

". . . that Josh Hainert can't hit a three meter hole from the inside!" A slightly inebriated voice from the rear.

"That's not what Tonya says!" A matching slur from the front.

"Awww, how would she know?" Drunk number one: definitely dense.

"Trust me!"

General laughter became a cheer as the shuttle slipped into the AcStat decel track with a bone-jarring lurch and an abrupt return of gravity.

The pilot must have bet on Vandereaux.

The seatbelt sign winked out and auto-restraints retracted. The snoring alumnus, who'd been bobbing gently next to her during the inter-station coast, fell against her shoulder, wedging her against the bubblecar's side. Lexi endeavored to ignore him, endeavored not to see, hear—or smell. The air circulation system was completely out-matched.

She hated beer. Passionately.

"Hey, Beejee!" A slurred call from the front of the car. "What'v'ya got t'say *now* 'bout scummy miners?"

The individual slumped in the seat opposite scowled. He tipped up the travel mug he'd carried aboard—sneering openly at the *no drinks* sign—and drained the last of the beer from it. Then he lurched up and hurled it at his interrogator.

*Not a friendly throw, that*, she thought, and winced as the silver mug rang off the wall. That sucker was expensive: she'd had to pass on a less elaborate one only two hours ago.

Throwing himself back into his seat, the sulky 'Beejee' growled, "Same as before the game: they're barely one step up the evolutionary scale from Recons. Sure the assholes won. What else have they got to do out in the belt but practice sticking things in holes?"

*Must be a quote from one of his classes*, Lexi thought, listening for the mug's final position. *How to Win Friends 101*.

The shuttle paused momentarily for the 'lock; renewed acceleration sent the mug rolling down the aisle between the seats. 'Beejee' made no move to pick it up. *Maybe I should rescue it. TJ won't notice a dent or two*.

"What about the 'Buster-boy, Bijan?" A lighter, equally drunken voice, this time from the rearmost seat. "You including him in that category?"

'Buster-boy. As in planet-buster. As in Recon. Singular and specific.

The scowl deepened. A lip curled. Someone from the seat behind Lexi called, "Careful, Sandy. Got to watch old Bijan's blood pressure."

—Poor sod. She wondered how he got associated with this lot.

"Aw, screw Bijan's blood pressure," said the voice from the rear of the shuttle. "And scuh-rew B—" Hiccup. "—eejan!"

"Jeez, Sandy, shut up!"

Bijan's companion began active distractions, but he pushed her off angrily and twisted around to direct that scowl over the top of his seat.

"Care to repeat that, Sandini?"

Just what she wanted tonight, a drunken bigot on the way home from a collegiate slaughter. She eased the snoring alumnus off her shoulder and he flopped over into the lap of an equally oblivious soulmate.

"Yeah. You bet." Sandini swayed to his feet, brushing off the hands of those who tried to stop him. He was tall, slender, with red hair in elaborate waves down his back: no match for Bijan. He slipped down the aisle with only a stagger or two, and stood with one hand on the seat back, looking down a long nose at Bijan. "I'm tired of your crap, Shapsy-baby. The fact is, the 'buster-boy proved you wrong, for all your efforts to the contrary. He's *Doctor* 'Buster-boy now, whether you—like it—or—not."

*Dr.* Buster-boy?

"He's no doctor yet, Sandini," Bijan growled.

A wave of a heavily be-ringed hand. "A mere formality, my dear. A mere formality. *I've* seen his test scores." Sandini leaned on the back of Bijan's seat, tilted his head to one side and ran his hand along Bijan's clenched jaw. "Not only is he already a Doctor of ComNet Science, my love, he is also three years younger than your charming self, and tonight, he leaves on his—maiden—voyage."

Muscle bunched under Bijan's tailored jacket.

Lexi planted both feet on the transport's deck. *TJ, you're going to die.*

Sandini turned back to his seat, cool as you please. "Don't worry overmuch, though, Shapsy. Most of these trips take two—even three—years. Perhaps by the time Cantrell returns, you'll have graduated and your *mama* can arrange—"

With a roar, Bijan sprang—

—faster than she'd expected: he'd nearly cleared the back of his seat before she captured a handful of his jacket. A shift of her weight. He staggered back, fell into the space she'd just vacated, dislodging the two alumni, who slipped to the floor without waking.

Everyone froze. Silent. How nice.

Two students who were holding Sandini released him at her glance. She sensed Bijan moving and said, "I wouldn't advise it, young sir. I sincerely would not advise it."

"And who the hell are you to tell me what to do?"

A thin smile. "Security." Softly, gently. "*Cetacean* Security."

"The hell you are," Bijan spat. "You're a damned 'buster, woman. No way a Recon bitch makes Security."

Make that Winning Friends 1501: this lad was a grad student. Still with the smile: "Would you care to argue the matter, sir?"

He glowered at her a moment, then, his upper lip wrinkling, "You're not worth the trouble. Probably are. I wouldn't put anything past that Recon-fucking Can—"

"I suggest, young man, you consider the rest of your phrase very carefully. It is, of course, quite possible that I might not take exception to your evaluation of my commanding officer. —On the other hand, I might."

He shut up.

*TJ, you—are a dead man.*

A brief passage in the TransTube—commercial, this time —carried them halfway around Academy Station rim, from plush opulence to a starkly utilitarian, 'less distracting environment for the students.'

He'd seen livelier crypts.

Briggs sighed and plopped into a chair, wishing Cantrell would hurry up. He was bored, and the crypt gave him the space-heaves. It wasn't only the Interiors by Torquemada & deSade; it was the whole damned at-ti-tude of the place. He'd never been inside one of these government academies before; now he understood why so many of the researchers they produced were loonier than Virtual Space miners.

Everything was grey. Not blue-grey, not brown-grey, just grey-grey. After the first two minutes, he found himself staring at his cuff's red braid just to be sure his cones—or was it rods?—were still functional.

Worse, the people were grey: the uniformed youngsters moving quietly through the corridors, the sober academicians passing through this waiting area to offices beyond. The receptionist even had silver hair (purposely: he couldn't be over thirty) and wore a black and gray suit: probably considered the overall effect aesthetic.

Bored with his sleeve, he found himself studying that thick coiffure, and when the suspense grew too strong: "That your own hair?"

Mr. Receptionist jumped, looked from his desk monitor to the door and back, a pathetically confused search for the source of the question. Naturally: the door hadn't opened: Mr. Receptionist was taught to recept.

Briggs grinned and waved a hand. Receptionist met his look, blushed (nice artsy-red contrast to the gray) and touched his hair with one self-conscious hand. Then his chin raised, his hand dropped, and he said through his nose, "Is there something you required, sir?"

"Oh, no." Another close-lipped smile. "Just trying to be friendly."

Receptionist frowned. "Then, if you don't mind . . ." And turned back to his monitor.

Briggs shrugged, and returned to mentally redesigning the room.

Good thing Lexi hadn't shown yet. The place would give her nightmares for a week.

Made you wonder about the Reconstructionists' efforts to get their kids into these places. If they were all this glum, you'd think Mum and Dad would be happy to keep junior at home; and if an academy education weren't the only ticket into the ThinkTanks and the bulk of the prime civilian career positions, he supposed they would.

The door through which Mr. Receptionist had recepted Cantrell slid open, and from that opening: "I'm terribly sorry, admiral. If Mr. Ridenour returns, I'll *personally* see he gets the proper directive."

Mr. Receptionist started to his feet, checked, and sank back behind his counter. Wise move. Compared to her present mood, the admiral's exit from Danislav's office had been cheerful.

He followed her silently from the administration offices and down the corridor to the shuttle tube. While they waited for the next car to arrive, he asked, "Well, where's the kid?"

"Someone—" A disgusted, over-the-shoulder snap. "—told him to meet us at the shuttle gate."

"And did that someone tell him our gate's been changed to G-35A?"

The incoming shuttle alert flashed. Cantrell cast a dark look over her shoulder and said shortly, "No."

The car coasted to a stop in front of them. The door slid open. From an office doorway down the corridor, someone shouted: *"What happened?"*

And from inside the car: *"They killed us!"*

They stepped hurriedly out of the way as a cascade of Vandereaux Vagabonds tumbled through the door (amazingly active for corpses) and disappeared down the corridor as rapidly as they'd appeared in the first place. In their wake:

*"What score?"*

Briggs held his breath.

*"Don't ask!"*

He let go the air in a sighing huff and ducked his head to enter the shuttle on Cantrell's sandaled heels. On the far side of the car, shoulders propped against the wall, arms crossed . . .

"Hi, Lex," he said. "Where've you been?"

# iii

If Cantrell weren't in a murdering frame of mind, the look Lexi gave her partner, his instinctive duck and catch, might have amused her. Instead, she threw herself into the nearest seat and demanded,

"Is this thing clean?"

TJ sobered immediately, tucked the silver mug into his lap, and touched the scanner on his wrist once . . . twice. . . . "It is now."

"Good." She hit the com-connect on the armrest. "Priority override, express to Vandereaux Station. Decel G35. Cantrell: SOA-371-A."

A moment's wait as the com analyzed her voice pattern and request, then flashed green. "Lexi, this is need-to-know. SecThree and better."

Lexi shifted uneasily. Cantrell noted that, knew Lexi hated overrides—hated the idea that *her* screwup with this secured information would reflect not on her, but on her CO—but since Lexi wasn't likely to get an upgrade in the next thirty seconds, it was too damned bad. If she'd ever needed her Recon advisor's peculiar talents, it was going to be in dealing with this academic misfit.

She briefed them on the gist of their assignment, leaving that tidbit for later. Stephen Ridenour's breeding was *not* a subject she wanted to broach outside their own security.

"I must admit," Lexi said, finally, "I'm confused. Are the records clarification and this paper related?"

"Not that anyone's cared to admit—yet. Eckersley said Go talk with Danislav, but Danislav knows nothing specific about the glitch: that explanation is coming from a Council rep. Why it's a *Council* rep and not a 'NetAT rep, I don't know: I'm *assuming* it's protocol, since *Cetacean's* assignments come through the Council. When and where this rep is to meet us, I don't know: I'm *assuming* it will be at the gate—hopefully before our scheduled departure. —Needless to say, I'm certain the 'NetAT would be extremely happy if the 'Net's little hiccup proved out as a tekkie glitch and Ridenour could prove the Smith paper a complete fizzle with no useful purposes and less precedent.''

Briggs said: "So Ridenour really *is* coming along as the 'Net Authority's Del d'Bug man.''

"TJ, I should wash your mouth out!"

He grinned. "Choose the right solvent and I won't even argue.''

"Well, for God's sake don't say it to his face, got me?"

"Yes *sir*, admiral, sir!" TJ said, sparking a reluctant grin out of her.

Lexi asked, "Is there some special reason not to use the term to this Ridenour?"

"Not just him. Any researcher. Officially, he's a 'Source Verification Specialist,' but SVS or DdB, researchers hate 'em.''

"Why? No *honest* researcher should object to verifying his resources and numbers—''

"But to one deliberately claiming credit for other people's ideas," TJ cut in, "the Del d'Bugger is the taxman himself. He's literally going to take money from their pockets. Possibly even their job and reputation.''

"And the honest ones must lose sleep at night wondering which minuscule reference they forgot to footnote," Cantrell said. "Anonymous tips from unknown enemies have prompted many a research audit.''

"But Ridenour knows his assignment, doesn't he?" Lexi persisted. "That's what he is. Is there some reason he'd be *particularly* sensitive about that word?"

"Embarrassment, for one," Cantrell said. "It's the sort of job only the most hard-assed—or the most desperate—individuals handle.''

"And why would this young genius be so desperate?" TJ asked.

"I'd rather wait—" Then she noticed Lexi staring down the length of the shuttle, an oddly pensive look on her face. "—Lexi?"

Lexi turned that Look on her. "He's Recon, isn't he, admiral?"

She nodded. "How'd you guess?"

"Just—something the students said." And in an undervoice directed toward the window: "Poor sod."

So. That answered one question: Ridenour's fellow students were not entirely oblivious.

TJ asked: "How did he get into Vandereaux?"

"I'm not certain. *I* didn't know about him. He was under Dean Danislav's sponsorship. On the records, he's stationer. His transfer to Vandereaux was SecOne: name change, false background—the works."

"What planet?"

Damned if she wanted to go into that now. "Later, Teej, we're here. —Why don't these things ever stall when you need them to? —Release their system and let's go see if the kid's found his way home."

The kid hadn't. In disgust, she called Station Security from the gate steward's desk and reported the situation. Let them worry about it.

"Admiral?" TJ's voice, requesting her attention. The obsequious gate steward's gaze slipped past her and he blanched, muttered something about checking a schedule, and hurried through a door behind his podium.

Curious. She turned to where Lexi and TJ flanked a woman who was, without question, the Council representative. From her close-cropped hair to her expensively shod feet, she stood out among station functionaries by her very inconspicuousness.

Likely her thinking was equally unique. *Couldn't Eckersley have done better than this?* she wondered. He had any number of class acts onstaff back at Ptolemy. Here at Vandereaux—lord, the predictability quotient was higher than ever.

She held out her hand, recalled a name from the written brief: "Irene Meeker?"

The tight smile Meeker returned stretched muscles that, from the accompanying grimace, hadn't been used in half a century. She grasped Cantrell's hand in a limp, cold grip, then gestured toward a door marked *Private.* "If you please, admiral."

She raised an eyebrow at TJ and Lexi, and with a slight jerk of her head, started for the door, knowing they would follow.

"One moment, admiral."

A stop. A slow turn to the presumptuous rep, and with what she considered admirable calm: "Yes, Ms. Meeker?"

The woman didn't blink. "This is a security *three* meeting, Adm. Cantrell." With a significant glance toward Lexi.

"Fonteccio is my Recon advisor."

"The information I have for you has no connection with the IndiCorps on HuteNamid. Ms. Fonteccio stays here."

"*Ms*. Meeker, my ship runs quite differently than your office. I have need of certain resources you cannot—possibly—comprehend. Councillor Eckersley understands my situation: he'll back me completely. *Sgt*. Fonteccio comes with us."

"Councillor Eckersley's opinion does not affect me, admiral. I represent Councillor Shapoorian."

Cantrell exchanged a frowning look at TJ . . . directed an apologetic one toward Lexi. "Very well, Meeker. I haven't time to argue with you. But I guarantee Council will hear about this. I have no patience with bureaucratic stupidity—particularly where it compromises my efficiency. —Fonteccio, wait for us here. And keep your eye out for Dr. Ridenour—"

"Excuse me, admiral. *Mr*. Ridenour's standing has yet to be determined."

"Briggs, you come with us," she continued, ignoring the interruption. Then she turned to the Shapoorianite. "—Any argument with *his* rating, Ms. Meeker?"

"Certainly not, admiral." The rep sounded almost cheerful as she started for the private room.

Cantrell said in an undertone to TJ as he fell in beside her, "Do me a favor?"

"Anything, Boss-lady."

"Don't let me throttle her *before* we get the full story out of her."

His thin mouth twitched. "Sure thing."

From the door behind the steward's desk, the steward's blond head protruded. He scanned the lobby, and jerked immediately back inside.

"What did you do to that poor sod?" she asked TJ.

"Moi? Not a thing, Boss-lady. Never met him before."

The blond head made another brief appearance. Exceedingly strange. Cantrell shook her head and preceded TJ into the conference room.

* * *

Curiouser and curiouser. Not only Eckersley taking a personal hand, but Shapoorian, as well. . . . *Eccolá*.

Lexi leaned against the gate steward's desk, disgusted but resigned. She'd learned not to let a flunky's inflexibility bother her—much. If it were any other councillor, they could have called Eckersley's office and cleared her presence in that room, but trying to make headway against one of Shapoorian's crowd in this district wasn't even worth the trouble.

According to Shapoorian, no ethnic Reconstructionist could be trusted with highlevel securities since (also according to Shapoorian) a Recon's special association with his home world gave him an irreconcilable Conflict of Interest. How that differed from Shapoorian's own bias, which invariably tilted Council's decisions to benefit Vandereaux system—and specifically the conglomerate with which she had quite properly relinquished all connections upon her election—was of course a mystery to a mere Recon from watery Venezia, while (also of course) Shapoorian's *former* company's research grants couldn't possibly inspire certain highly-visible psychologists, economists, neuralnetters, and even a bioengineer or two, to corroborate her controversial views.

A tap on her arm: Eddie Bernstein, ComTech2, with a plastic cup of bubbly. Someone had 'accidentally' cracked a seal. Couldn't waste it, now could we?

She grinned, but declined. Not in the mood. Not without knowing what was happening in that room marked *Private*. Eddie sighed, made a crack about depressing Recon sense of doo-tie and drifted away.

As if any of her fellow crew members would do differently, knowing the circumstances.

Damn, she loved them. . . . Sometimes she wondered where she'd be right now if Cantrell hadn't signed her on. Dead, most likely. Luckily for her, Cantrell had won that one—and a very young, very stupid Lexi Fonteccio had discovered the sobering reality behind heroic gestures.

Because while Shapoorian's 'experts' were bought and paid for, it *was* true that the indigenes—particularly the Recon indigenes—were drifting toward independence in increasingly violent movements like Venezia's Julian rebellion, of which she'd been a part. But what choice did Shapoorian's crowd leave them?

Once-upon, the Recons must have seemed God-sent to the terraforming IndiCorps desperately searching for permanent colonists—particularly large groups already organized and with a strong inclination to develop planetside colonies. But after the initial enthusiastic surge, the well of human resource had dried up. Not surprising: not many people willingly put their heads in a noose.

Because those colonists begat children—*lots* of children—kids, the same as she'd been, with a strong sense of pride in their heritage. But also like her, many thousands grew up with the same fascination which had driven humanity into space in the first place. They wanted offworld again, now that there was a definite homeworld to be from.

But the chains which held *Recons* to the ground were political, not physical, and infinitely more difficult to sever. What had started as simple correspondence networks between spacefaring families of similar ethnic groups, had widened, found itself leaders, planets to colonize—and a Cause. A Cause which made them Politically Significant to people like Shapoorian.

Because with the ComNet Transition and its associated severance of ties with Earth, the Recons had become the repository for the Unique in humanity, the last defense against the sociopolitical homogeneity for which Shapoorian's party had fought when they led the push for Severence nearly a century ago. Others had followed the Separatists for their own reasons—valid ones: by its very nature, there could be no partial users of the 'NetDB, and when Earth argued the terms, their access had to be deleted—but that it would put the Separatists so solidly in power . . . that, no one could have anticipated.

On the record, the hatemongers were careful; Recons were *not* inferior, they simply shared—ties—with old Earth, which 'inhibited their adaptation to life in space'; unspecified biochemical traits made them more inclined toward unspecified medical ailments linked to a non-gravitied environment. Spacers, the NeoDarwinists' *HomoSpatialis*, had a different 'genetic complex' suited to life outside GravityWells, never mind the only ZG most 'spacers' ever encountered was the shuttle-coast between stations.

Shapoorian's pet scientific 'authorities' extended the theory to mental limitations, claiming those without the proper GeneComp had certain 'spatial misperceptions' and 'orientation problems,' which led to 'psychological disorders' in space. Humans who chose to return to GravityWells were simply unable to comprehend the 'vastly complex cosmology' of MultiDimensional NexusNet science.

In other words, compared to spacers, Recons rated somewhere around *HomoErectus*.

And a whole segment of the human population who'd never seen the bottom side of a cloud, let alone weathered a storm, were ready to believe in their own Evolutionarily-given superiority.

At least Ptolemy's Councillor Eckersley was willing to speak against Shapoorian on the Council itself, but it seemed to Lexi that, even in her short time in space, public opinion had swung increasingly toward Shapoorian's views. And Eckersley couldn't last forever—

—One never knew about Shapoorian.

The door marked *Private* slid open. Shapoorian's rep slipped out and slithered her way through the crowd, and TJ appeared in the doorway, signalling Lexi to join them with a lift of one finger.

"Disappearing data?" Lexi couldn't believe she was hearing correctly. "A whole person? As in *gone?* As in *off the 'Net?* I thought that was impossible."

"Supposedly it is." Cantrell seemed perfectly serious.

"Just one person?"

"Two that we know of," TJ replied from his side of the document-strewn table. Security documents. *Not* on file on the 'Net. Maybe not on the Secured Line Transmission. "Both researchers. How many others is one of the things we hope to find out."

"How did they discover the—" How did you refer to something that couldn't happen? "—dropouts?"

"In the general investigation of this notorious Smith's postgraduate production, a piece of an archived file the balance of which was not on the 'Net put them onto the problem. Follow-up got no information, period, on one Barbra Liu. No personal files, no professional; nothing. Council's hardcopy SciCorps register showed them what researchers *should* appear on HuteNamid records, which turned up William Bennett's absence. As far as the experts can tell, the glitch is confined to HuteNamid files, but the error glitched outward, somehow got *through* the 'Net and *into* local RealTime memory files.''

"But you *can't* . . ." Lexi shut her mouth. Fast. This went way beyond SecFive. You didn't talk about the 'Net losing things. You didn't ask the question she'd been about to ask.

"The 'Net does things," Cantrell said carefully, "for reasons you have to ask somebody who understands NSpace communications better than I do; and even then you won't get a straight answer. Personally, I don't think *they* really know. Officially, we're not assuming it goes beyond HuteNamid."

"But it already has, admiral," TJ objected.

"Quite," Cantrell said drily.

The file fallout could well explain why the Council had released a SecOne StarShip on this particular RecRun, but:

"What about Smith's paper, admiral?" Lexi asked, her earlier question suddenly achieving far greater significance. "What's it about? Does it have anything to do with the glitch?"

Cantrell shrugged, scattering a bead-glitter throughout the small conference room. "Meeker never mentioned it. Danislav seems to have determined it's worthless; perhaps Council agrees. Obviously, this Ridenour kid thinks it's valid. As for the 'Net Authority . . . who knows what the 'NetAT thinks?"

"The 'NetAT's been all *too* retiring in this for my taste," TJ growled.

A second scattering glitter. "They're never prone to overt participation."

"But why in hell are they sending this green kid? We're not talking ordinary RecRun here. What's wrong with an experienced *secured* 'NetTech? Hell, what do we pay Chet that big salary for? He's one of the 'NetAT's own. He could—"

"He's backup, for sure. But Chet's also very much on Record—both his association with the 'NetAT and *Cetacean*. Maybe that's why we're being sent."

"Ridenour's handling it, but Chet's the real rep?"

"Maybe. And maybe the 'NetAT doesn't take the whole problem any more seriously than Danislav does. *He* calls Smith a prankster and Ridenour a gullible fool. He says Ridenour's off-course entirely."

"Then Danislav's the fool. If Ridenour's off-course, why the Council's involvement? Why *Cetacean?*"

"Could the 'NetAT have engineered the whole thing?" Lexi ventured. "Maybe created the glitch? Maybe even steered Ridenour toward Smith's paper?"

"They *could* have," TJ said, "but, why?"

Good question. She had no answer, but Cantrell did:

"Ridenour."

"What about him?" TJ asked.

"Kurt called him 'special.' *Danislav* implied he's not exactly swift—in fact, made a point of it. Say Kurt knows something Danislav isn't admitting. Say this Ridenour's really a wiz-kid. Right now, Danislav controls him, legally and psychologically. Maybe the 'NetAT wants him free and this is a way to bust him out. It's like Kurt: if all goes well, create a position for the boy—give a bright Recon kid a break: maybe even help get him into the 'NetAT program, if it ends up that's what the kid wants." She laughed humorlessly. "That'd give Shapoorian a seizure, now, wouldn't it? The 'NetAT's one entity she *can't* control. And a Recon DProg? Does boggle the mind."

TJ said: "Or it could be Kurt's just getting old and sees a chance to *win* one against Mialla Shapoorian. —So we're going to have to trust a *kid's* judgement in this whole damnable mess to make Eckersley *look* good?"

" 'Bout have to, won't we? past a certain point? We've got Chet—he'll keep tabs on Ridenour as well as anyone can, but any good 'NetTech's got an effective security clearance higher than God. If one goes bad—"

"—You better shoot him," TJ said; and Lexi thought: *Fast.*

Cantrell nodded grimly. "It's worth making real good friends with this Ridenour. Help him have a pleasant trip."

TJ said, "Wonder how much Council really thinks it knows."

"Council has to rely on the 'NetTechs, ultimately," Cantrell said. "Ultimately, so do we. So we *don't* use them for target practice *before* we know what they've done to the 'Net."

TJ said, "I'd like to know why Eckersley never mentioned this kid before."

"I'd like to know the same thing. I'll tell you, it doesn't do a whole helluva lot for my confidence in anything *else* Eckersley's done and said over the years. I *thought* we were on the same side." The admiral rose and handed a security packet to Lexi while TJ gathered the reports from the table. "Read up. If

Danislav's right and that kid *is* unstable because of his background, you're likely to be our best hope of gluing him back together if he blows."

She opened the packet, saw the diary within. "Ridenour's?" Cantrell nodded.

"Admiral, if his background is SecOne, does he know that *we* know he's Recon? I mean, if the students knew . . ."

"Good question." Cantrell frowned. "Hell, don't mention it until *he* does."

"What's his official story?" Lexi asked.

"According to Danislav, Del d'Buggers usually approach the researcher in question very quietly. Legalities. Officially, Ridenour's along as *Cetacean's* tech advisor and as a possible transfer to the HuteNamid 'Tank. Ostensibly, he's along to check out the facilities, to see whether he wants to join that team. Since he's in Smith's field, that will allow him to approach Smith discreetly. Smith gave *no* cites whatsoever in his paper: he *must* be expecting questions."

"Does Ridenour know about the missing records?"

"At a *student's* security level? Unless he's deeper in this than we've been told, he doesn't know anything yet about *missing* records. Not even Danislav knows that. Just 'discrepancies' and that only as a cover story for his investigation of Smith's paper."

TJ said slowly, "If Ridenour lives in this universe, he sure doesn't think transporting *him* is *our* only reason for going. Eventually, this *kid* is going is going to start asking Lexi's question, isn't he? Maybe start to think his cover's *not* a contrived story and maybe understanding a whole lot more than we're going to figure. Academies don't just hand out doctorates to twenty-year-olds; the 'NetAT doesn't take personal interest in just any student 'Tech. Danislov called *Smith* 'Designer material.' Get Ridenour and Smith together and we don't know what in hell's going to shake out."

Cantrell nodded. "I don't discount the possibility that our wizkid—if he ever makes it here—might just find a connection between that paper and the fallouts once he gets with Smith: I don't believe in coincidence on this scale. If it's a prank, it's damned unfunny. No, if that kid's legitimately what they want for the 'NetAT, that brain *lives* in NSpace, and we'd better hope he wants whatever bribe Kurt offered real bad."

"Maybe we'll luck out," TJ said. "Maybe he's one of those

that can't match his own socks, and we won't have to worry about his motives.''

''I don't care if he wears his socks on his *head*, we keep on our *toes* dealing with him. —As for why *Cetacean*: we're on a training run and this RecRun is an opportunity to do some mechanical shakedown. We *don't* say 'erased files.' That can't happen. On Shapoorian's personal orders it can't.''

''Yeah,'' TJ said. ''Right.''

The lounge outside the security room was packed now to overflowing. *Cetacean* bridge crew were draped on chairs and in each other's laps in varying degrees of inebriation, surrounded by bags of purchases which absolutely *had* to be hand-carried aboard. (Heaven forbid they should trust their precious new toys to the cargo crew, who would only see them safely crated and painlessly transported to *Cetacean*.)

Cantrell shuddered to imagine the chaos which must reign at the ZG transfer tubes where the bulk of *Cetacean*'s personnel were gathering. The rotating shore-leave meant eighty percent of her crew were wandering Vandereaux Station-Main or any of its six subsidiaries, all of them being tracked down, their leaves cut short, and the lostlings herded back aboard. They all had beepers installed in their heads, but some became amazingly hard of hearing under certain—recreational conditions.

For some, like herself and her personal staff, leave had just begun, and only the crew now onboard had had their full, promised, two weeks.

They were going to be such a happy ship.

Suddenly, from down-rim, the irritating chime of an AutoCab on an emergency run. People and carriers scattered in all directions as the blinking light atop the vehicle drew closer. And closer. And lurched to a halt at gate G-35A.

''Why did I suspect as much?'' TJ muttered at her shoulder.

Out of the cab, perfectly composed, apparently oblivious to the havoc he'd created, stepped a slender, dark-haired young man. Definitely *not* the awkward, painfully-out-of-place Recon she'd been led to expect. Every hair and every creased seam was very much *in* place. The kid was as identifiably Academy as Meeker had been Council.

''Good God.'' Another TJ mutter as the Academy Clone cast a cool glance around the lounge, and the AutoCab released two enormous suitcases (and a *trunk?*) to a RoboPort. "What does he think we are? A cargo hauler?" And as the young man's gaze fell on them: "If he dressed himself this morning, we're in deep shit."

Ridenour—it *had* to be him—started toward them, the RoboPort at his polished heels.

"What do you mean?" Lexi's murmur from her other side.

"Adm. Cantrell?" The fashion plate's voice was silky-smooth, his accent pure A-ca-de-my. He held out a perfectly manicured hand. "I'm Stephen Ridenour."

And TJ, in a voice meant only for Lexi and herself: "His socks match."

i

"Do you mind if we switch to topside view, admiral?"

Loren Cantrell shifted her gaze from the planet floating in the air of her private quarters to the young man seated opposite her.

"Any particular reason?"

A refined shrug of well-shaped shoulders beneath a tailored dinner jacket, a tapering, manicured fingertip tracing the edge of a wineglass, eyes downcast: Stephen Ridenour was about to lie.

That was unusual.

"Not really. I just . . . prefer stars."

"I'd've thought you'd be tired of them by now. We've had a steady diet of them for weeks."

Pale eyes lifted: strange eyes which reflected every color in that floating planetary image. They'd given her chills once; now she waited curiously to see what color they'd assume next. "I never tire of space, admiral." His habitually low voice held a wistful note. "It's my home."

She leaned an elbow on the table, rested her chin on her knuckles. "I believe you mean that."

"That's an odd comment." A line appeared between his brows. A small, carefully calculated line: sufficient to imply genteel confusion without disrupting the sculptured features. A passing, unkind thought imagined him practicing that expression before a mirror. "Why wouldn't I mean it?"

"I'd have thought HuteNamid . . ." A glance toward the holo above them ". . . was more your style."

"God, no!"

Calculation played no part in that exclamation or in his subsequent stammered apology. She'd expected to rouse some reaction from him—had, in fact, deliberately courted one—but his vehemence surprised her: another Unusual.

She keyed in the view change without further comment.

The planet faded out and layer upon layer of slowly rotating stars faded in, drifting silently through selected objects, momentarily eclipsed by others, dependent on Priority. The HoloImager had been an extravagance, but she'd never in ten years regretted the impulse.

In the 'distance,' HuteNamid's small maintenance station gleamed metallically in Etu's light. Considering the lack of facilities here, she was glad circumstances had given the crew at least a brief chance at Vandereaux Station. HuteNamid Station Alpha was little more than a fuel dump with vending machines, less appealing than *Cetacean's* own onboard facilities.

As for the CO, remembering a filet left cooling on an *Embassy* table, the CO's one real regret was not having been in Eckersley's office when the bill for that aborted dinner came through. Tours were easily relinquished; the chance for an uninterrupted meal was not. Particularly when one's companions at that meal were old and rarely seen friends.

Her current dinner companion, while neither old nor (as yet) what she would term a friend, was certainly decorative and generally pleasant—though preoccupied at the moment with his wineglass, and paying no attention whatsoever to the revised view.

"Better?"

He started, and his quick, self-conscious smile seemed almost shy. "Much. Thank you, m'lady."

She chuckled, honestly amused. "Stephen Ridenour, you're the only person I know who can use that term without sounding ridiculous. Wherever did you learn the trick? And don't try to tell me gallantry was a part of Vandereaux curriculum; I've met your dean."

The smile vanished. Heightened color unquestionably touched his flawless, pale skin. "Gallantry? You make me sound like an anachronism."

"Did I object? I merely remarked on a rather delightful—if somewhat unusual—mannerism."

But her qualification came too late. Academy-perfect manners surfaced with a vengeance, same as they'd held throughout the trip. Every time she encouraged hints of a unique charm in the boy, that charm shut down—*deliberate* cutoff, damn his good-looking hide. The only *hint* of spontaneity anyone had seen in him was in the gym—and even then, it was only when he thought no one was looking.

ShipCom signalled an incoming. Naturally: she was eating.

"Excuse me, Stephen." She touched the transmit button on the console in her chair arm. "Cantrell."

The AutoCom's carefully modulated voice issued from invisible speakers overhead: *"Admiral, I have an incoming from George M. Downey, HuteNamid Station Alpha. Will you accept?"*

"Relay message, 'Com."

A pause as the AutoCom interceded with the waiting stationer. Then: *"He requests special 'Net dispensation, admiral."*

She sighed, anticipating the next answer. "Purpose?"

Another pause.

*"To call his broker, admiral."*

"*Dammit!* —Scuze me, Stephen." That, as the lad practically jumped out of his skin. "But I knew it!—'Com, tell him the answer is the same as yesterday. Stocks do *not* qualify as an emergency! Put it in his report! Cantrell out."

"Who was that, admiral?" Stephen asked, a none-too-steady hand raising his wineglass to his lips.

"One of the more colorful locals over in the station. He's got some notion about major deals going through concerning one of the corporations he holds stock with, and, since I'm here, he expects me to let him put a direct call through to his broker."

"Personal calls of that sort would jam Accesses in a hurry." A polite smile followed by another sip, steadier this time. Pre-final nerves? Or something else? Hell of a time for cold feet. "I didn't realize you had Authority to Expedite, admiral. For private citizens, too?"

"One of my more troublesome insystem responsibilities. Sometimes deciding what constitutes an emergency isn't nearly so simple as with our Mr. Downey. Especially for the AutoCom. Downey's a station systems contractor. His company has a direct callcode and he thinks his company's Right to Access means his right to call his broker. He even offered one of my ComTechs a stock tip—hoping, I suppose, to influence my decision. God, sometimes I wish the 'Net had never been invented."

The po-lite smile twitched—"Trying to put me out of a job, admiral?"

"Not at all. Think how much fun you could have, writing programs to account for relativistic delays in stock values; just think what you could do with a relativistic futures market. Or legal system: a relativistic deeds and titles registry—there you go: you could invent a whole new definition of supply and demand."

—and broadened. "Like before the Transition? Thank you, anyway, admiral. I'll take NSpace."

*I'll bet you will*, she thought, registering that knowing smile. Chet Hamilton, head of *Cetacean's* Security Communications, had been watching Stephen Ridenour. Chet had personally monitored every time Stephen touched a keyboard. According to Chet, Ridenour's actions on *Cetacean's* system had been exemplary, so far.

They'd also been damned slick. *Chet* said, Watch him.

She attempted a delicate probe: "A 'NetTech doesn't have to go through an Access vendor or a traffic manager to call his broker, does he?"

The smile crystallized around the edges. "Theoretically, no, I suppose. But in actuality, since *you* are the one with AtoE, I'd need to access your personal files to manage it. Without your cooperation—or some means of duping your BioData—it's impossible." An elegant shrug. "I'm not a designer, admiral. I'm taught to program the 'Net, yes, but my job's to infiltrate existing data and locate specific information, or to search for the source of error and then create a fix for it." His voice wavered, steadied between one breath and the next. "I'm little more than a glorified DeOp. The program designers are a whole different field, and only the 'NetAT's MasterProgs have the keys to the CNOS itself.''

So *he* said. *Danislav* had said, *When the 'NetAT saw those test scores . . .*

Danislav also said Stephen Ridenour was looking to enter that elite group of programmers. *Stephen* had never mentioned that ambition—or any other—to her. This kid was bright. Brighter than Danislav had led her to believe.

He was also very, very careful.

"I'm just curious," she said. "Theoretically speaking, could you crack the market datastream?"

"No, I couldn't." Flatly. Then, smooth delivery restored: "Besides, why would I want to?"

Break the law with little or no possibility of getting caught—except, possibly, by another programmer? Tap directly into the RealTime of the market? Inject small addenda to Real-Time data while it was flowing? Or reach right into the machinery of government and add a law or two?

Danislav had said, *Out there where he has no advisor . . .*

Stephen had done just fine, out where he had no advisor. Smooth. Composed—until tonight.

"I've got everything I need . . ." Stephen was saying.

One thing she was certain of after several weeks in Ridenour's company: Danislav hadn't the brains to *understand* Stephen Ridenour—

". . . breaking the law would compromise—everything. That's foolish. And I'm not a fool, admiral. . . ."

—let alone advise him.

She took a breath, thought: *I never said you were, boy.* Fortunately, Stephen Ridenour lacked a true sense of adventure.

". . . Why do you ask?"

She hoped.

"Curiosity." She took a leisurely sip of wine. "Are you ready for your meeting with Dr. Smith tomorrow?"

Polite smile turned rueful. "Theoretically, yes. In actuality, I fear not."

"I'm sure you'll do fine, Dr. Ridenour."

The smile vanished abruptly. His eyes dropped. This time, the flush was decided.

"Chin up, Stephen," she chided. "You've got your degree; be proud of it!"

His eyes flickered up, revealing bitterness and a hint of anxiety. "*What* degree? The Board still hasn't decided—" A momentary pause, bitterness turning hopeful: "Or, have you heard . . . ?"

"No, Stephen, I haven't." She was honestly regretful: this was the first hint of concern the boy had shown. "But don't worry. Your *doctoral* standing isn't in question. The Vandereaux Board of Regents wouldn't dare lie about that—or change its mind at this late date."

The fingertip traced the rim of the glass again. Stephen said nothing: not denying her observations—

—not acknowledging them, either.

"Careless of me," she said, keeping her tone casual. "I should have been using your title all along. Gotten you used to hearing it. It wouldn't do for Wesley Smith to observe any discomfiture on your part regarding your credentials. Your rating may have been rushed through, but it's no less valid than his for that expediency."

"When it comes. *If* it comes—"

"It will."

"—his will still be ten years *more* valid than mine, *and* with the most revolutionary concept in 'Net history to its credit."

"Which, as I understand, crossed *your undergraduate* thesis work."

"But—"

"Stephen, —Dr. Ridenour, —only you, in all the Nexus ComNet Alliance, recognized the significance of that paper. Remember that fact. Engrave it into your soul, if—"

The signal light blinked again and she acknowledged: "Cantrell. Go ahead, 'Com."

"*Admiral, I have a Priority Two call from the Escort Team. Will you accept it?*"

Not the AutoCom this time: Chet down in Security Communications. She glanced at Stephen: P2 definitely excluded him. Looking decidedly relieved, he raised his glass in a silent toast, drained it, and quietly slipped out the door.

She touched the transmit: "Go ahead, Chet."

A moment later, from the planetside escort team: "*Admiral?*"

"I'm here, Lt. Buchanan. Is our Line secured?"

"*Yes, admiral. We got it synched this morning.*"

"Then go ahead, Buck."

*"We have a problem, sir. At the Science Complex. While we were waiting for Smith to return—"*

"He showed up, then?"

*"Nossir. Still missing."*

"Go ahead."

*"I questioned the 'Tank secretary regarding the Subjects as you requested. She denied knowing them. I double checked her system, but found nothing."*

She'd suspected as much when their records didn't show up on the system dump.

"Anything else?" This was hardly P2-caliber information.

*"Yessir. Helmond and I left Calhern at the SciComp offices and headed across the Complex to the libraries—thought I'd check for their names in any of the hardcopy material. . . ."*

Hardcopy. And her colleagues wondered why she kept so many Recons on staff. "Did you find anything?"

*"Never got the chance.There was a large group in the central plaza—a mixed group, admiral. Researchers and Recons."*

"Not totally unknown. Could account for why their Civil complaint records are so uncommonly clean. —Go on."

*"They invited us to sit and join them. We exchanged bits of information—the usual pleasantries, family and such; they seemed exceedingly interested in my own background. I encouraged it. Eventually I was able to work in some questions about Bennett and Liu. They said they knew no such persons. But one little girl—she appeared to know the researchers—thought her friends were joking. She was sitting on Helmond's lap and couldn't see the signals her elders were sending her. The governor's son apparently decided to—create a diversion."*

"What kind of diversion?"

*"He attacked me, armed with the biggest damn—excuse me, sir—knife I've ever seen."*

Good—God. "Anyone hurt?"

*"Bent. But nothing broken. —I'm okay, too."*

"Where is the boy now?"

*"In custody."*

"Get him up here. The sooner we get his depo on tape, the better for everyone."

*"His father is resisting the transfer."*

"Put him on."

*"Yessir."*

While Buchanan retrieved the governor, she pushed the dinner dishes to one side and punched the coffee brewer.

A hot-headed indigene attacking Alliance Security wasn't unknown. Her credentials and empowerments allowed her to balance local policies and needs with Alliance requirements, and in that capacity she had seen uncommon situations. But the indigene governor's son doing the attacking—that *was* a new one.

According to Lexi's meticulous notes, in the fifty-odd years since HuteNamid's colonization, indigene/spacer relations had been unusually quiet and remarkably free of the schisms that notoriously plagued Recon worlds. HuteNamid was a pastoral paradise. Nothing violent happened here.

And now, less than two days after system-entry, *Cetacean* personnel had a major incident involving the indigene governor?

Dammitall!

The coffee pot was half-filled, and Buchanan was back on line.

*"Admiral?"*

"I'm here, lieutenant."

*"Go ahead, governor."*

*"Adm. Cantrell?"* The governor's deep voice vibrated the glassware on the table.

"Yes, governor. I'd say it's a pleasure, excepting present circumstances. Officer Buchanan tells me you're objecting to the transfer of an Alliance Security detainee."

*"I am, admiral."* The glassware stayed steady this time, Chet adjusting the gain manually: the SecLine lacked the AutoCom's self-modification capacity.

"Are we talking privilege? The law is quite clear in such cases, sir. If—"

*"Perhaps the law requires adjustment, —sir."*

"Governor, I understand your personal concern in this . . ."

*"My concern, admiral, is for the forcible removal of a Tunican citizen from his planet and his interrogation not only in a hostile, alien enviroment, but also without the presence of his peers."*

"Your son may be a citizen of Tunica, but he's a citizen of Alliance first. I've the legal right—the *duty* to your son's own rights as an Alliance citizen—to bring him up here to give his deposition under probe, the same as the others. It's for his own protection, sir: you haven't the facilities, and my failure to secure depositions close to the event would seriously jeopardize his defense and my personnel's civil rights. If you need clarification of the law—''

*"Your law is not in question, admiral. As a member of our society, Hononomii has the right to be heard, and if necessary disciplined, by our Tribal Council."*

"For internal matters only, sir, as I'm sure you realize. This involves an Alliance Security officer's guilt or innocence on charges more serious than those against your son. There are always allowances given a colonial; there are none given Security personnel. I have no latitude to dismiss this incident without an investigation. That means depositions from both sides.''

*"As you will, admiral. Your assurances—and my protest—are now on official record. You would do well to remember that. Goodbye, admiral."*

Now, what could he mean by that? A steadying sip of coffee, then: "Lt. Buchanan?"

*"Yessir!"*

"Get you, your men, and the arrestee up here immediately. The Smith problem can wait."

*"Yessir! Buchanan out."*

"Com-off!" She leaned back, closing her eyes as she cradled the coffee mug between her palms and inhaled the fragrant steam.

The Murphy-factor was definitely high in this assignment. Two days insystem, and they were already three behind schedule. Quite an accomplishment for an assignment which should be routine. Possibly a record for screw-ups.

Not exactly one she cared to include in her next 'Net report. She tapped the call button.

"Briggs," she said shortly, and sipped her coffee as the 'Com traced and alerted TJ.

*"Briggs."*

"Something's come up, Teej. Are you free?"

*"You bet, Boss-lady. Lexi, too?"*

"Let her sleep. She was up all night getting that 'Tank production analysis ready. I'll need you both soon enough."

*"You sound serious."*

"Just get your butt down here."

*"Yessir! Right away, admiral, sir!"*

Which meant, if he was in his quarters, about thirty seconds. Chuckling, she cut the connection and moved over to the couch, coffee mug in hand. TJ popped through the door, not bothering to signal his arrival, and she waved him toward the coffee. He checked out the leftovers, and with a satisfied murmur snagged a roll out of a warming basket. Topping off the large silver mug he'd brought along—half coffee and half (she shuddered) sugar—he joined her on the couch.

"Okay, Boss-lady, what's up?"

"I can't believe you drink that without gagging. —I just got a call from Buck. Apparently the famous HuteNamid interCorps cooperation doesn't extend to Alliance Council representatives. Things aren't going well down there."

"With the records check? What's 'interCorps cooperation' have to do with that? It's SciCorps, and they should expect a records clarification once in a while; everyone gets—"

"Buchanan was attacked this afternoon while he was asking questions about Smith and the two missing Researchers."

"Attacked? By whom?"

"The governor's son. —With a knife."

"Good lord."

"Precisely. Buck took the young man into custody. They're on their way up now. *Not*, however, before Papa registered Official Objections to Sonny's incarceration."

TJ's brow knit sharply. "Official record? Bit of heavy muscle under the circumstances, isn't it? Governor's taking a chance."

"Heavy, indeed. I want some answers—*before* I send Stephen down there."

"Before you . . . Is Smith still playing hide-and-seek? I thought you cleared with him last night."

"So did I. He seemed perfectly amenable to coming up here. —Dammit, young Ridenour comes halfway across Alliance space for this conference and the good doctor disappears! No apology. No reason. Nothing. It's not as though Ridenour's request is unusual: wanting to talk to a local 'Tank member in his own field is a reasonable first step!"

"Not having had much experience with these things . . ." A wry Briggs-dig at their assignment: "Wouldn't a potential transfer normally go *downworld* to check out the facilities? Maybe he's guessed what Ridenour is. Did Ridenour talk to him?"

"Smith talked. *Stephen* barely said Hi-how-are-you."

"Ridenour? *Shy?* Since when?"

She was not so amused as she might have been. Not after

Stephen's performance at dinner. "Actually, the 'shy' routine seemed to—amuse Smith. I offered excuses: Stephen's youth, his inexperience in non-academy situations . . . Basically, I implied he's scared spitless, getting cold feet about a world drop and a new environment, and it would help matters if Dr. Smith would come up and meet with him one on one. Break the ice, so to speak."

TJ grunted. "And Smith bought that?"

"Seemed to. No reason not, really."

Another grunt. "You really planning on sending the kid down after him?"

"If the mountain won't come to Mohammed . . ."

"You could wait. Give Smith a chance to show."

"Give him time to raise suspicions."

"A day? Two? Maybe the man has a hangover!"

She shrugged. "No reason to delay. —Lord, TJ, you're the one who's been complaining about our wasting time here."

TJ took a long swig of coffee and sat for a moment swirling the last of it around the bottom. *Probably trying for another mouthful of sugar*, she thought, getting up to refill her own.

From behind her, TJ asked, "Did you ever really intend to bring Smith up here?"

"Of course I did. Why wouldn't I? Dr. Ridenour obviously prefers not to go down there."

"Isn't that really the point? Ridenour's your own dream come true—except for one small flaw."

She twisted around. "Now, wait just a—"

"Am I wrong?"

She wished she could deny his implications, but he was right, damn him. He knew her too well. He'd been a friend when they were both wet-behind-the-ears trainees, and was one of the few people left in the Alliance who dared give her a straight answer.

He kept her sane.

She sighed.

He kept her honest.

"No, you're not. Stephen could be a helluva spokesman for the Recon movement if he comes out of this smelling good. —In the 'NetAT, no less, if they're on the level."

"You don't know that, Loren, and no one can *make* the 'NetAT accept anyone, assuming that is Eckersley's plan. What if the kid doesn't want to be a 'spokesman for the movement'?

How do you know he even considers Recons his people anymore? He's been away a long time. And *his* people are gone. Long gone. Recons don't think of themselves as unified with anything but their own culture anyway. That's why they're Recons, for God's sake. They don't *want* unification. They don't *want* homogenization. That's why they go onto planets and cut each other's throats over things outsiders don't understand.''

She propped against the table, cradling her coffee cup between suddenly cold hands. "That's almost profound, TJ. —But it's not that, not totally. I admit I thought, at first, we'd taken on an academy clone, but every once in a while, I catch a hint of Zivon Ryevanishov. Either way, he can't be hurt by a bit of exposure to non-academy thinking processes. I suspect he's sensitive as hell about his Recon background. Can't say I blame him: it's his whole career on the line and he's getting the jitters. Could be he's afraid it's going to come out in the meeting and undermine his credibility—which it could: Smith was Academy, too. *Vandereaux* Academy, once upon a time. But if Smith won't come up to the ship—we haven't much choice, have we? Stephen's got to go down there.''

"Alone?"

"Naturally not. I rather cherish my job—and my neck—thank you.''

## ii

Stephen one-handed the RotaRing as he shot by, timing a twist so that momentum carried him in a smooth arc around the virtually frictionless universal joint. He closed his eyes and let his body swing in perfectly rhythmic rotations.

God, it was wonderful!

Some uncounted rotations later, he released his hold, still without opening his eyes, and flew across the room, knowing his vector to the millimeter. He counted to the rhythm of the room and on the fourth beat opened his eyes and reached with both hands to catch the curved side of the five-bar. He laughed aloud as his toes hit the cushioned wall, absorbing momentum, changing his vector.

*Take that, Dr. Phillips!*

He bounced back and forth between the vector walls surrounding the five-bar, challenging himself, making each pass more complicated than the last, choosing rec-pads totally at random.

He'd forgotten how much sheer fun the ZeroG gym could be, and *Cetacean's* was the liveliest he'd ever been in, strong and predictable, like the heartbeat of the massive vehicle surrounding it. The equipment was in ideal condition, the spring in the walls exquisitely calibrated: you could pick your colorblock and know the exact recoil to expect . . .

In the middle of a triple-twist Rolani with a half turn on the rip, applause echoed through the supposedly empty cavity. He missed his catch; a toe hooked on the ripple bar, sending him in an uncontrolled tumble out into the middle of the gym. The accolade ended as abruptly as it had started, and someone shouted his name.

He ignored it. Heard instead Coach Devon's calm voice. *Don't panic! Panic wastes energy. Blows thinking.* He concentrated on his vector, spotted the RotaRing—just out of reach. A twist put his foot to the wall in place of his head—one of the high recoil pads. He used that rebound, plus a kick-off, to aim a controlled attitude dive toward a catch-ring beyond the main entrance.

As he passed that opening, a half-seen arm reached out and snagged him. He shouted *No!* but the arm kept its hold and somehow cushioned his bounce off the wall. He grabbed for his would-be rescuer and together they spun to a halt at the end of a magne-tether.

Breathing hard, his heart racing, he blinked his eyes clear of sweat and discovered his deliverer was none other than the admiral's own bodyguard, Sgt. Fonteccio. He blushed violently and did his best to avoid her gaze—not easy, floating nose to nose.

She caught her own breath, grinned at him, said, "Sorry 'bout that."

He said on a—damn he *was* out of shape—breath, "Hardly your fault, was it, Sgt. Fonteccio? It was my foot caught the bar, not yours."

"After I was stupid enough to startle you. But that was quite a demonstration."

He blushed again, not knowing what to say. "I was the stupid one, sergeant. No way I should have let so minor a sound disrupt my focus.'' He met her smiling eyes then. ''My old coach would have had my hide.''

''Call it even on stupidity, eh?'' She winked. ''And it's Lexi to my friends, Stephen. You ready to go in?''

He nodded. She turned off the mags and tugged the line, starting them in a gentle drift toward the entrance as the 'tether reeled them in.

An over the speakers announcement called her to the admiral's office and she tugged again, harder this time. A moment later they were in the corridor, the 'tether coiled into its chamber.

Lexi released him with a See you later, then dived down the corridor for the lift, whipping neatly around and through the opening with a one-hand to the door 'ring. The hand waved at him, then disappeared, narrowly escaping the closing panel.

He stared after her, bewildered. This wasn't the first time she'd appeared to save him from his own stupidity, although in general the rescues were rather less dramatic. How did she know? And why did she bother?

She was the admiral's bodyguard: he understood that. And Recon, which he didn't understand.

He didn't know why she bothered—

The light above the elevator shaft flashed green; the door slid open.

—but he was increasingly thankful for her quiet interventions.

He shook his brain clear of progwuzzles and tapped easily off the ledge and toward the lift. He hesitated at fifth-level, then got out, forcing the twist in his gut to leave.

He reached under his sweats and tightened the shoulder brace with a touch: the greater G here would put an altogether different strain on it, and he'd best take precautions. That shortness of breath in ZG was a warning: he was out of shape—

—and this was no time to get careless.

Even in the diffuse light of this low-sensory area, the long blade glittered: twenty-five centimeters of razor-sharp HuteNa-mid steel with an intricately carved and inlaid hilt. Well balanced, though not for throwing: its designer had had more—personal—contact in mind.

And somehow Cantrell doubted it had gutted many fish.

A com alert from TJ. She asked: "Have you completed the room-check and alerted Dr. Mo?"

*"Yes, admiral."*

"Soon as she's ready, bring him on up."

She sat behind the desk to wait. A simple desk, as all the decor here was simple: subtle colors, deep carpet, sound-dulling acoustics—all designed to set a subject at ease and minimize sensory input for a psych-probe case. The Quiet Room's constant monitoring fed directly into the *Cetacean's* Security files, and echoed to another special read-only storage under constant-scatter tamper-proofing not even Chet's staff could alter. Stress-monitored testimony in this room, in those few critical hours before witnesses' short-term memory passed to subjective recall, was the kind of documentation the dismissal of felony charges had damned well better have on file for the Justice Bureau.

And after Buck's depo, she *wanted* those charges dismissed. She wanted two good Security personnel cleared, the governor's son off her ship, and the whole damned screw-up off her desk. She didn't like the speed with which foreign presence had drawn fire (a qualifying glance at the knife) so to speak, when nothing they were doing should even involve the indigenes.

She wanted the why of it. Quietly, and without asking any questions that might be grounds for carrying this further.

A message response flashed on the console: Stephen, returning her page at last. She cursed his timing under her breath, hit the acknowledge button with her fist and looked up—

—to a blank screen.

"Stephen?" *Dammit, boy, what're you hiding?* "Turn on your damned vid!"

*"Vid, please, 'com."* She sensed startlement in his tone and in the face that faded in from the blackness; read guilt in the boyish duck of his head.

*Damn right, I'm mad, kid. Pull a stunt like that— How many times do you have to be warned?* "Where the hell've you been?"

An uncharacteristically shy smile. Atonement? *Forget it, kid.* She thought. *Time you straightened up your act.*

"The library, then the gym, admiral. I'm terribly sorry. I heard the shuttle arrival . . . Is Dr. Smith here? Shall I come—"

"Never mind. I've news for you. You have a reprieve."

"A . . . Why? *What's happened?*"

"Calm down!" Damned if she'd mince words with him now. No matter he suddenly looked his youth. No matter his reactions suddenly puzzled. Not with TJ showing up any moment with yet another troublesome—and knife-wielding—youngster. "I didn't mean to break it to you like this, but if you *will* disappear—!"

*"I'm sorry, admiral. I forgot to—"*

"Well, dammit, don't do it again or I'll have a beeper plugged into your head and you'll auto-record like everyone else! Right now I haven't time for amenities. Something else came up. It appears as though it'll be a day or so before Dr. Smith arrives, so you can relax."

*"But I—"* He faltered, then with forced calm: *"Yes, ma'am. Is there any way I can help expedite the situation?"*

*Good lad.* "No. I'll keep you posted. Cantrell out."

*"Good ni—"* TJ's announcement of their imminent arrival sounded in her ear and she cut the connection.

"—admiral."

Stephen stared at the now-blank wall until water trickled a cold path down his neck: commonplace reality intruding on the chaos that used to be his mind. The chill continued down his back and he shivered, uncomfortably aware, of a sudden, of his shirt clinging damply. He pulled it off, took a half-hearted swipe at his head, then flung the towel around his neck to catch the drips.

Habit honed by a decade of academy life carefully folded the brace into its case and tucked it into its drawer in the bathroom. The same habit placed his anti-stat shoes neatly under the desk and draped the shirt over the chair back to dry, incipient wrinkles carefully smoothed away. Pulling on a thick robe, he leaned back against the pillows, rubbing his hair vigorously with the towel.

He'd had a headful of shampoo when he'd heard the 'lock hydraulics operating. On the chance Dr. Smith had decided to come up early, worried that he might miss a call from Adm. Cantrell, he'd paused only to rinse, then rushed back to his room, dripping all the way.

And still missed Cantrell's call.

He sat up, wadded the towel and tossed it in the general direction of the laundry tube. Leaning his elbows on his knees, he kneaded his neck and shoulder muscles, stretching his head down and back, fighting a losing battle against tension, and felt his hair curl crazily against his fingers. *It'll stand straight up in the morning*, he thought absently. But then, what difference would it make? He could look like a VRT junkie, for all it would matter.

*You have a reprieve . . .*

He didn't *want* a reprieve. He buried his face in his hands, rubbing his temples hard, willing the dull throb away.

It didn't leave.

All day and most of the evening in the library, disk after disk, file after file (the *Cetacean* had a phenomenal store of RealTime datadisks—files not even Vandereaux had in house) scanning for misLinked files (every researcher's nightmare) hoping for some last minute insight, some ultimate bit of brilliancy—

—It was worse than cramming for finals.

And an equal waste of time: he either knew his business or he didn't.

*And that's the whole problem in a nutshell, isn't it, Ridenour?* He chuckled ruefully and dropped his head into his crossed arms, shutting out the light, knowing he'd go through it all over again whenever Cantrell decided to bring Smith aboard. Because, the admiral's protestations of confidence aside, *he* knew that the degree Council had promised him was only to legitimize his presence here, an award necessary not because anyone at the 'NetAT took his report seriously, but because 'NetAT regulations required investigation of *every* reference lapse on the 'Net. Danislav had told him as much when he'd tried to dissuade him from accepting Council's offer.

Dissuade? Hell. Danislav had called him a fool—and worse—several times over. And Danislav should know. Danislav knew all his scores and ratings from the last ten years—along with every other Vandereaux student's. But a fictitious doctorate? Would they really go that far? And once granted, could they take it away?

No matter he thought he'd aced those finals—they'd still called him in for a second go-round. Danislav had his theory for *that* too. And someday, Danislav would know the reason, but *he* wouldn't. Not so long as Danislav held the keys to his files and refused to pass those keys to him.

He'd learned very early in his academic career that Sandini's quarterly Mentor Ratings Comparison in the green-wing showers did not include him. But he'd never really cared about where he stood with other students, past and present. Mostly he'd have been content with the knowledge that the next call to the Registrar's office was not to be his last.

There'd probably been a time he hadn't worried about such things, but he couldn't remember it. He dimly recalled his first weeks at Vandereaux and discovering a terminal that was his alone and could go everywhere with him—just plug it into the wall and the Library was there. He didn't recall any problems early on, but that memory was probably a lie, too—so many of the old ones were—and the Mentor had been editing those files even then, using his entrance exams as a baseline.

Then had come the psychs. The psych-wing memories were real—he knew that:

*("No! I don't want—"*

*("It doesn't matter what you want, boy. We can't have that mop fouling the readings.")*

He remembered hands holding him still while they shaved his head, though he couldn't believe it had been necessary—surely he'd been taught better manners than that—so that part of the memory was probably a lie, too.

But the VRTs were real, he'd seen them used often enough since. Had even used them himself, a time or two—

—under threat of expulsion. Hour after hour of *being* an electron, a black hole, of skipping across the contours of NSpace—

—of throwing up all over the inside of the 'Tank. He'd lost count of the number of times he'd had to clean it up before they believed him about the Dep. And without the Deprivil, he was just too old—so they said, and after an endless series of tests.

The NeuNetters said his 'pathways were too interlaced,' the PsychTechs taught him Compensation Techniques. Lord, he'd known all the buzzwords (and a host of others no ten-year-old should understand), but none of them had made any real difference. Bottom line was, he saw things differently—wrong, so they said—and that limited how much he could learn.

So they said. He'd resented it at the time—hated the specs and their tests. Eventually, they taught him games that helped him survive—barely. But those Games left him with Questions. He'd ask those questions of his computer, and the Mentor would respond with strange pictures and short sentences which only confused him more. He found refuge in the purity of mathematics, but gave rote, meaningless responses to everything else.

In desperation, he'd finally taken those Questions to his human professors—so often they began changing their office hours, though they denied that was the case. Eventually, one had finally sent a message to him via the Mentor:

*(Ridenour. GOTO A:*
*("You have no idea what you're asking! There's no way to answer that at your level!"*
*(And/Or B:*
*("You'll never need to know—so forget it!")*

It had bothered him at the time, but he understood now, so it didn't matter.

Much.

And they hadn't screwed him purposely.

Probably.

A moment's smugness; he wallowed in that feeling for a moment before shoving it aside. He couldn't afford overconfidence. Not until he knew the results of those finals. But damned if he hadn't cracked the code.

He'd found the key the day he'd asked Dr. Phillips' temporarily abandoned computer the same question he'd asked his own and received an altogether different answer—one that made *sense* even if many of the words were new.

From the first, the Mentor had been editing its responses, using his entrance exams for a baseline, trying to present material in its most understandable form for his particular mind. But when the Interactive had tried to form itself to follow his logic structure, between his early non-academy training and his own 'twisted neural pathways,' the poor thing had gotten so confused it hadn't a chance in hell of communicating to him.

And if not for those endless sessions with the head-thumpers and NeuNetters, if not for their buzzwords and their Games, he'd probably never have known.

He'd wiped that info-req off the system as best he could, but Dr. Phillips must have realized what he'd done. If not then, his subsequent piggybacking into her accesses *must* have shown up. But for some reason, she'd never reported him.

Probably she was waiting for him to fry himself totally. Though maybe not. She had a sense of humor—he could tell from the way her Mentor chided 'her' about 'naiveté' and 'encroaching senility.' He'd probably pulled her baseline down a good five points in that handful of sessions.

But he hadn't fried himself—or her. He'd been very very careful, only using her access to ask questions—he didn't care about the security stuff, and only until he understood *how* to pose *his* Mentor questions that would upgrade his own accesses—which it wouldn't do until he convinced it he knew what he was asking—which meant knowing the right 'NetSci buzzwords.

He started chuckling into the moist darkness of re-breathed air. He'd learned more about feedback programming in that one week than in the balance of his academic career.

He'd hated the psychs and the NeuNetters once, resented their assessments and their Games. He felt differently now; he still hated them, but the resentment was gone. Maybe someday he'd even tell them how he'd done it. Maybe someday, he'd thank them.

Maybe.

Once the Mentor understood him, the overall picture began to emerge, and past a certain point, you got to read papers *as they were written*—without the Mentor's interface. The profs still called him lazy and gave him more out-of-class than anyone else, but he didn't mind; it was all a part of the total picture, and the more you understood, the more sense it made. . . .

. . . He hoped. The NAPs had been his first challenge of that understanding; and out of those had come his change of program. He didn't know why—*everyone* got shuffled after those tests.

The NAP tests, the change of program, and retests on his finals; Smith's paper, the 'NetAT's interest and Eckersley's offer . . .

And still no—what did they call it?—*Sheepskin?*

He threw himself back against the pillows, bashing his skull against the wall, renewing the throb with a vengeance. He chuckled again, for want of anything better, and curled around a pillow, burying his face away from the light.

*Damn right I question my credentials, Adm. Cantrell. 'Dr. Ridenour' indeed. Hell, I had a hard enough time getting used to 'Stephen'!*

Hononomii Tyeewapi might look as Old Earth Amerind as the Alliance genetic pool could produce nowadays, or he might not:

the 'Net contained lies, and the facts resided in bits and pieces in records that old. But while much might have been lost across forty lightyears and after two centuries, one could believe something authentic had come together in this young man—from the proud lift of the chin to the beaded leather on his feet.

The young Recon stood quietly under Cantrell's silent scrutiny—a deliberate test of his nerves while taking in the well-muscled torso, the little details of stance and balance a trained fighter unconsciously released—and likewise silent through the formalities of introductions and the explanations of procedures.

Finally: "You understand, Hononomii Tyeewapi, this hearing can result in your being held on felony charges of assault with intent to kill, *or* in charges of provocation being filed against the arresting officer."

Tyeewapi stared through her.

"Or it can result in a declaration of misunderstanding—a clash of cultures—and a new beginning for us all. Wouldn't that be preferable?"

Silence. For all the evidence, he hadn't comprehended a word she said.

The transcript indicated otherwise.

"You *are* Sakiimagan Tyeewapi's son, are you not?"

Still no answer.

"All right, young man, I'm duly impressed with your . . . inscrutability. However, you *are* answering. Instruments are recording and this is a court proceeding. You might prefer to have your own explanation on record. Lt. Buchanan has already given his—under sedation: that's mandatory for our personnel. Given your youth and your colonial status, I have a certain latitude to dismiss charges without that step, *if* you can answer questions and satisfy our monitors—and me—of your reasons. Your planetary constitution may be a factor in my ruling, but Alliance law and Alliance rights apply in this hearing." She took a breath: the rest was more formula, for the record. "This is a discovery proceeding. It can lead to dismissal or to the filing of felony charges that will place you in detention pending examination and possible treatment at a regional psychological facility. For the record, do you intend to cooperate with this hearing? —And, *in camera*, young sir, don't fuck with me. We both know you understand, and life will be ever so much more pleasant if you say yes."

The corner of his mouth twitched slightly. She sighed openly and said, "I suggest you answer, son. You're not helping your case in the least."

Still without looking at her, he said, "I have heard nothing yet which requires verification, admiral, other than—possibly—my parentage. And *that* is available in the 'Net." Finally his eyes met hers. ". . . Is it not?"

She felt her mouth similarly twitch. "I could learn to like you, boy. If I make my questions to the point, would you condescend to give us simple, straight answers?"

"Possibly." She lifted an eyebrow. His lips twitched. "Probably."

Cautious lad. But she could appreciate that—and work with it. "Please, sit down."

He glanced pointedly at Lexi, standing at her elbow; at Buck, standing at his; at TJ, beside the door. "I prefer to remain standing, sir."

"And *I* am getting a stiff neck."

Tyeewapi's jaw tightened. His stance widened, fractionally more solid.

"Sit—down!"

The kid sat.

"Thank you," Cantrell said, returning to her deliberately polite tone. "Now, —remembering I already have Lt. Buchanan's account of what happened this morning, would you care to give me your recollection of the incident?"

Back to silence. Cantrell let her smile drift into a troubled frown, informing young Tyeewapi he was being an ass while she remained the soul of patience.

"You know, Mr. Tyeewapi, I'd looked forward to this meeting—although I'd planned it for planetside and including the rest of your family—when my official business was finished here. I have some background in terraformation genetics—had one of the best for a roomie once—and your livestock program is—"

"If you don't mind, admiral," Tyeewapi interrupted, "let's skip the flattery. We do nothing more than every other IndiCorps settlement does as a matter of course. We plant our crops, breed our animals and take care of our ThinkTankers. That's our job." Dark eyes flashed in TJ's direction as the prisoner glanced over his shoulder, then added softly, ". . . And therein, admiral, sir, 'lies the rub.' "

"Do I detect a hint of bitterness, Mr. Tyeewapi?"

No answer.

"What is it you want from us, young sir?"

No answer.

Cantrell studied the kid, frustrated. She placed her hand flat on Buchanan's report. "It says here that Lt. Buchanan was inquiring into the whereabouts of two Researchers when you attacked him."

Not a twitch.

"The 'Tank hardly comes under your father's jurisdiction, but it does seem, if SciCorps personnel are missing from the 'Tank compound, the IndiCorps personnel just might have pertinent information on—"

"IndiCorps personnel. And did *Lt. Buchanan's* report state *who* he was interrogating?" The cool facade slipped ever so slightly. She anticipated TJ's response, calmed him with a glance.

"Why don't you tell me?"

Tyeewapi rose and looked down his nose at her. "It was a child. A *seven-year-old child!* You tell me by what right *Lt. Buchanan* involved her!"

She tapped the report with one fingertip. "It says here that she was one of many people, IndiCorps and SciCorps, adults and children. A group of which *you* were a part. As far as I can tell, there was no coercion, no pressure on the child for information, no previous objection on your part. Now I must ask myself, why did you wait until the child spoke to attack him? —Was there something special about her?"

The indigene's lips tightened.

"Or was it—*what* she was saying?"

The indigene's control broke for an instant: his hand twitched as Cantrell laid the knife to one side and picked up the transcript of Buchanan's quiet-room interview tapes.

*Don't even think it, boy.* And without looking up, "Don't be foolish, Mr. Tyeewapi. Your elegant toy is fine right where it is. I assure you, it wouldn't help you at all." Tyeewapi grunted and she glanced up. "If your attack was warranted, even mistaken but understandable, you've nothing to worry about. —And it *was* warranted, you say?"

Again, the noncommittal grunt. But he *was* tracking.

"This matter of the missing researchers: your people claim

they never knew the two scientists in question. Doesn't that seem rather odd, Mr. Tyeewapi? I realize dealings between SciCorps and IndiCorps often tend toward minimal, but for the IndiCorps to be totally unaware of the existence of two FirstIn scientists . . . doesn't that strike you as odd? Even if you *weren't* socializing with researchers? Or odd that a child not yet born when those scientists supposedly entered the HuteNamid 'Tank should have sensitive information regarding their whereabouts?''

Cantrell paused, but Hononomii had gone unfocussed again. She returned to the report. '' 'I know her, Mr. Buchanan, sir.' —She seems to be speaking of Dr. Liu. She goes on: 'She's gone to live with the . . .' '' She cultivated amusement, lifted her eyes to the indigene again. ''. . . *'Chalupas'*?''

Tyeewapi's attention centered squarely on her now. He wasn't laughing.

Neither was she.

''It says here,'' Cantrell said, holding his eyes, ''that 3.2 seconds later, you attacked my security officer, screaming obscenities, if I understand them correctly—the computer seems to have had some trouble with the literal translation of no few of them—and advising him to leave HuteNamid and never come back. To take the—ahem—'Net and all its—well, at any rate, it would appear you would like to keep us away from information about missing Alliance personnel. That's serious, Mr. Tyeewapi. That, and the attempted murder of an investigating officer by the governor's son, raise very serious questions. Shouldn't we be concerned? Shouldn't we be curious? Shouldn't we widen this investigation beyond the 'Tank compound?''

Tyeewapi turned half about, faced the spacescape on the wall, hand clenching and relaxing several times. Cantrell signalled TJ *No* as young Tyeewapi glanced at her and said through his teeth, ''Damn you all, get out. *Go away and leave us alone!*''

And slammed his fist into the picture. Cantrell curbed her own instincts, signalled her guards to do likewise.

The QR's acoustics muted the crackling sound as the fragile-seeming surface split along fibrous interfaces, small flecks floating free, sparkling motes caught in currents swirling up again. Tyeewapi stood there, shoulders slumped, head bent, arms hanging limply at his side.

Damn. She'd loved that painting.

''Quite a demonstration, Mr. Tyeewapi,'' Cantrell said. ''Do you represent your father's opinions? Or do you personally know something about Drs. Liu and Bennett?"

Tyeewapi cradled his injured hand, rubbing the knuckles, no longer inscrutable, only a very nervous, very young man. Blood oozed from a myriad of tiny cuts on his knuckles and dropped on the slate blue carpet at his feet. Wicked stuff, crystillic diffraction filament.

"I'm going to call the doctor—"

The rug whispered beneath Tyeewapi's feet as he swung around, dark braids swinging free, eyes narrowed.

"—for your hand, son. I could add destruction of property to the charges. I won't. And if you're hoping to confuse the readings, it won't. It's just one more incident in a pattern, and a ruined work of art is nothing to the level of trouble you're making for yourself. Maybe for others. You have a very short time to provide me a reasonable explanation of your intentions and your actions against Alliance personnel—to decide how, not if, we get the full story fr—"

Without a flicker of warning, Tyeewapi dived for the knife on her desk—and Lexi dived headlong past her. She hit the floor and flattened, as bodies shook the desk and thudded onto the carpet.

"Drop it!" TJ said a heartbeat later, over the sounds of struggle.

Cantrell pulled herself up against the desk and knelt there a moment, fighting for the breath Lexi had knocked out of her. Lexi had the knife; TJ and Buchanan had the boy.

"Gently, young sir," Buchanan murmured into his prisoner's ear. "I don't want to hurt you."

The indigene twisted wildly, forcing Buck to widen his stance, but otherwise achieving nothing.

Cantrell grasped Lexi's outstretched hand, used that leverage to get to her feet. Shaking her head in bewilderment, she moved around to stand in front of Tyeewapi. Eyes squeezed shut: pain, evasion, —or both—breath coming hard past the arm held across his throat: they'd get no further this way.

She leaned on the desk, punched in the com. "Mo?" she said shortly.

*"We're ready, admiral."*

From across the room, the prisoner's eyes opened and fastened on her, and they were filled with some unspecified, irrational terror.

What was he afraid of? She shook her head again and asked softly, "Why, boy?" But she didn't really expect an answer.

And to the com: "So are we, Mo. So are we."

# iii

. . . and in the case of Nexus Space, these sub-divi\*\*\*\*\*\*\*
> **FILE VANREC\VNDJWS13.BDI ANNEXED TO ACS3\INSTDOA5932.FIN.**
> **LEVEL TWO SECURITY RESTRICTIONS APPLY.**
> **CLEARANCE CODES AVAILABLE: SEE C:CLRCD.HLP**

"What—" Stephen glared helplessly as the half-screen of invaluable text blinked away, leaving only the annex message on the monitor.

"Dammit!" What idiot would annex a Vandereaux Board file to the Department of Agriculture's financial files?
> *QUERY: VANREC—VNDJWS13.BDI ANNEX ISSUED BY?*
> *VANREC—VNDJWS13.BDI ISSUED BY VAN1984—VA-NAC04.*

He didn't even need to look up the number. VAN1984: Mike Vogel. He'd been a screw-up in class, and now he was out in the system being a screw-up for the Vandereaux Biology Department.

Someone in that department was going to be very upset to learn the file they thought was safely private—wasn't.

Idiot Vogel, anyway. He *still* hadn't learned to check his files before implementing. How he'd ever gotten certified in InterLinks was one of the mysteries of the universe. *Had* to have connections: the DataDiddler shouldn't be turned loose on a minicalc, let alone the 'Net. Now, some poor sod was going to have to take the time to release the Smith file and addendize the annex order on the 'Net records: the order to annex came through the 'Net; therefore, as far as the 'Net was concerned, that was where you'd find it.

No wonder the 'NetDB was a godawful mess when certifiables like Vogel never learned that the ProgImp key was a no-return situation. Idiot played Accesses the way he played Galactic Gargoyles.

He'd watched that performance once in the RecHall. Had let himself be talked into a challenge. He'd never played the game before.

He beat the pants off the . . .

*Just think, Ridenour. Screw up here and that 'poor sod' could be you! Screw up here, and you get to spend the rest of your life cleaning up after Mike Vogel.*

He pushed away from the terminal, kicked the chair back under the desk and paced the room. Now what? He needed that file—badly. He'd had no idea it even existed, squirrelled away as it was amidst General Inquiries rather than Hearing Transcripts, without a single flag of any sort raised.

Damned shoddy piece of InterLinks *that* was. It was no GI; it was one of Smith's pre-expulsion hearings. A most important hearing. Smith's first recorded mention of the revolutionary material discussed in *Harmonies of the 'Net.*

And he'd just lost it to the Department of Agriculture's Sec-Two—well beyond his clearance, for all Adm. Cantrell's concerns.

Beyond his clearance, but not beyond his reach.

It was maddening. He *could* get at it—could go in right now and pop the file out—if he dared.

Hell, the tiniest loop inserted into Cantrell's next 'Net-Trans—one little direct code worm to make an innocent data-stream read like a program and Mike's accesses were history. Probably wouldn't even get caught trying—if he cared to risk having *his* accesses denied forever.

He stopped beside the terminal, reread that maddening message.

Fact was, he was no gambler. The one real risk he'd taken in his life had been piggybacking into Dr. Phillips' access, and the payoff for that had been his own sanity. The only risk in accepting this job was time, not career. And the payoff—

The monitor blinked off, and in that darkened square not his own reflection, but green eyes, dark hair—a face no one could forget, having seen it once . . .

*("We've met, boy.")*

Not a question. He hadn't answered, had kept his back straight, his eyes focussed on the far wall.

*("You're the gymnast."*

*(Still not a question.*

*("Well?" Sharp enough to make him jump.*

*("Yes, sir." Clear as he can manage, which isn't very.*

*("Mialla's boy taught you well."*

*(The second secretary walking slowly behind him. His eyes involuntarily flickering to the left, anxiously awaiting his reappearance.*

*("Would you expect to include that in your curriculum here?"*

*("N—No, sir."*

*("Would you want to continue—practicing?"*

*("Please, sir." His voice no more than a whisper. "No, sir."*

*(Green eyes meeting his solidly. "Good! Good luck on your tests tomorrow. You can leave now.")*

Relief had made his knees weak; Dev's voice in his head had held him upright. At the door to Beaubien's office:

*("Sir, —Have I any real chance?"*

*("Pass those tests and it's better. You argued your case well.")*

He'd never told Danislav about that meeting.

He traced the outlines of the monitor with a fingertip, let that touch run slowly over the rounded lumps of the keys, relishing the smooth texture, the vibration they said only a 'Tech could feel, a vibration which might or might not be real.

The screen came back to life. The image fractured, cleared with a blink.

Design Programmer. To work RealTime with the 'Net and the 'NetAT's MasterProgs, who kept so much in their heads and behind the curtain of the 'NetAT security files. Minds inaccessible to a mere 'Link-in-training. Files which, as a DProg-in-training he'd have access to. Files he could absorb in privacy, and at his own rate, however slowly, once he was in.

The vibration reached his head first, then his heart, his gut —he wondered if that happened to others. If it happened to Smith.

*Smith* had been DProg track once and from the look of *Harmonies*, his interests still lay in that area. He wondered if Smith would have some of his answers, wondered if he dared discuss the *real* meat behind *Harmonies*, or if even that infinitesimal nonregulation discussion would undermine his chances. But if he got those answers—if he was right—could he stand by and let someone else test those theories? Could he stand by and not be a part of it? He wanted—*dammitall, no he didn't!*

He sighed and dropped back into the chair, spun it to face the keyboard.

> *FLAG: VICTOR LYNDSEY DANISLAV, VAN201.*
> *FROM: S. RIDENOUR, VAN2049.PEN.*
> *RE: VANREC\VNDJWS13.BDI ANNEX TO ACS3\INST-DOA5932.FIN.*
> *SIR: PLEASE NOTE: ABOVE ANNEX INVALID. HAS PLACED FILE VITAL TO ASSIGNMENT HERE UNDER SECURITY FLAG.*
> *IF CORRECTION DELAY POSSIBLE, PLEASE SEND CLEARANCE CODE IN NEXT TRANS.*
> *THANK YOU.*
> *SR, VAN2049.PEN.*

He read and reread the message, glowering at the .PEN suffix on his ID. If it weren't for that *pending*, he wouldn't be needing to send the damned message.

A twinge in the pit of his stomach, a pain behind his eyes warned him this was *not* a concern to dwell on. He entered the message to be included in the next 'Net transmission, and switched the terminal to standby.

All he could do now was wait.

His body informed him he'd been ignoring it too long. He gathered up his annotated copy of his report and headed for the bathroom.

One never knew when—or where—insight would strike.

A low moan escaped the huddle of medical personnel and Cantrell's nerves jumped; for all she knew it meant nothing. The early moments of Deprivil induced biological—artifacts. Hononomii Tyeewapi was perfectly fine.

Would she could say the same for her stomach.

TJ's hand touched her shoulder, rested there. Silent, steady presence behind her—he knew exactly how much she didn't enjoy this part of her job. Routine verifications on willing, known subjects like Buck was one thing. Trying to extract information out of a stubborn young fool was—something else.

Margo McKenna, *Cetacean's* chief medical officer, moved toward their corner. "We're almost ready, admiral."

"How's he doing, Mo?"

"Fine, now. His pulse *was* going crazy. What did you do to him?"

"I wish I knew. You're sure he's all right?"

Margo leaned against the wall, arms akimbo. "Just take it easy with him. He was a bit shaken, is all. He's perfectly healthy—a lovely specimen. We've taken twice as many tests as should've been necessary, but his specs simply weren't in the 'Net. As if he'd never been through a checkup in his life . . . or properly born, for that matter: postnatal scans are zip. Highly unusual, admiral."

"It certainly is. And one of the things I intend to find out."

The monitors clicked, beeped and flashed their carefully regulated patterns: the typical chaos of the EEG levelled to the easy rhythms of a brain on Deprivil, the Life Support Unit supplementing and regulating the body chemistry that artificially flattened activity could no longer reliably sustain.

Innocuous nonstress questions for a start: What's your name? Your favorite color? What's your favorite sport? What food do you like? He answered easily, the monitors pulsing smoothly, normally, and Margo indicated she could proceed at will.

Cantrell breathed deeply, steadied her own pulse-rate, reminded herself she and Mo had run hundreds of these probes, never mind the fact she was still playing God with a chemically altered, totally defenseless human mind.

She never had liked being God.

Still—better her than some she could name.

"Hononomii, I'd like to talk about the researchers in the 'Tank. Is that all right with you?"

"Yes."

"Do you know many of them?"

"Yes."

"Who?"

The indigene named names she knew. A long list of names, many of which were interesting, four of which were significant. Bennett and Liu being what had set him off in the first place, those could wait until they reached a deeper level of trust. Paul Corlaney was, for now, irrelevant. Smith . . .

Out of careful questioning emerged a rather odd picture of a bizarre personality: no surprise; with whom Hononomii appeared to work on a regular basis, which was a surprise. A researcher and an indigene given to attacking Alliance Security. Odd association.

"Hononomii, are you aware of a communication I had with Dr. Smith yesterday?"

"Yes."

"Because he told you about it?"

"No."

"Because you were with Dr. Smith at the time?"

"With—Wesley . . . yes."

"And *Wesley* agreed to talk with Dr. Ridenour regarding his work and the working conditions on HuteNamid; do you remember that?"

"Yes."

"After that conversation, did *Wesley* say anything that would lead you to believe he'd changed his mind regarding that meeting?"

"Yes."

She sighed. Getting a subject around to a specific point could be dreadfully tedious, and if you followed a bad lead, you ended up out of sight of the original question with no way back. Finally:

"Suspicious."

"Suspicious of whom, Hononomii?"

"R–rid—nour."

*Stephen?* "Why was he suspicious of Ridenour?"

"Security files. Tracks."

Cantrell met TJ's eyes, saw awareness to match her own. By all rights, no one on HuteNamid should know the *secured* files on Stephen even existed. By rights, they shouldn't know *Stephen* existed, other than on the very general mention they'd made of his presence here as their technical help and a potential transferee. Stephen's citizen file would not transfer into the 'Net until he was legally independent.

Unless some fool back at Vandereaux, thinking that because the boy had graduated he *was* legally independent, had prematurely transferred those records into the 'Net and into Smith's reach.

But *Can't access* was all Hononomii would say—or all he could say. Any attempt at further clarification could result in a loop from which the only escape would be to let him come out from under the Dep.

Neither would he say where Smith was or why he was missing. She tried more specific questions: Is Smith frightened? Is he angry?—the answers to which led absolutely nowhere.

Finally, Hononomii said in seeming irrelevance: "Not his job."

"Not . . . Hononomii, *what* isn't Dr. Smith's job?"

A momentary pause in breathing, a sudden increase in heart rate: dangerous question, that. Too many possibilities. *Damn stupid, Cantrell.*

"Hononomii, forget that last question. You don't have to answer it. It's not important. Just relax. Breathe slowly, with my count . . . one . . . two . . . one . . . that's fine, Hononomii."

She waited for the momentary spikes in his readings to settle.

"Hononomii, did Dr. Smith look up Dr. Ridenour's records on the 'Net?"

"Yes."

So. They *were* on the 'Net.

"Where did he get Ridenour's keycode?"

"Transfer order."

Or maybe *not*. Another glance toward TJ: nothing on *Smith's* temporary transfer order up to *Cetacean* would give *Ridenour's* key.

"Hononomii, whose transfer order?"

"Rid—nour's."

"Hononomii, how did he see Dr. Ridenour's transfer?"

The monitors blinked alarmingly. Damn. She cancelled the question. Calmed his heart rate, then put him on hold and, leaving him in Mo's care, signalled TJ to join her outside. Before she could say anything, he asked:

"When did you decide to include Ridenour's records in the Secured Transmit?"

"I didn't. I told you I edited that downlink."

"Shit."

"Are you thinking Smith may have tapped *Cetacean's* files directly?"

"Where else would Smith get at Stephen's records?"

"God, we *are* travelling in VirtualSpace tonight, aren't we? No, Vandereaux must've accidentally released Ridenour's Civ-Files to the 'NetDB. Either that, or Tyeewapi was mistaken and it wasn't Ridenour's files Smith was pulling up at all."

TJ put on his best *Who're you trying to kid?* face, and she laughed reluctantly.

"Okay," she said. "But he couldn't have accessed *Cetacean's* files. Not without setting alarms off all over the ship.

If Chet let that happen without telling us, he's fired. Unless—''

"Unless?"

"*Theoretically*, he'd set alarms off all over the ship. On the other hand, 'effective Security clearance of God,' remember? And this is the guy who wrote the infamous paper and crashed Vandereaux's system. What's *he* care about rules and accesses? —Wake Chet up. Have him run a complete check of the *Cetacean* system and see if—hell, *I* don't know, maybe he took his shoes off and left nothing but a heat trail. But I want that trail found, if it exists."

She left him heading toward the lift and resumed her seat at Tyeewapi's side. He remained quiet and cooperative, and Mo indicated it was safe to continue.

"Hononomii, when was the last time you saw Dr. Smith?"

"M–Morning."

"Where did you see him?"

"Office."

"Do you recall what he said?"

Hononomii's voice shifted, steadied into a slightly higher, more lively tone: "Damned if I go back into space again for any reason. I'm paid to create ideas, not justify where they came from, 'specially not to convince some CodeHead from Vandereaux that he wants to move in and fuck up my computer! Let him go elsewhere! *I'm* not about to waste my time! Call me when they lea . . .''

She made a note for the record that Hononomii voluntarily cut off the quotation and that the break was not a tape error.

"Hononomii, let's go from this morning in Wesley's office to the library plaza this afternoon. Do you remember Lt. Buchanan talking with you and a group of your friends there?"

"Yes."

"For a long time?"

"Yes."

"Hononomii, did you attack Lt. Buchanan?"

"Yes."

"Why did you wait so long to attack him?"

"Didn't."

"But you said you were in the crowd a long time."

"Didn't . . . wait. Didn't want . . . fight . . . Halona said . . . she . . . Co—Cocheta . . . *Halona, no!*''

His pulse began to race erratically. He tossed wildly, fighting the safety restraints, an autonomous control he shouldn't have.

Cantrell dodged out of the way. McKenna and her aides closed in and held the young man steady as the LSU fought to regulate his systems: instantly analyzing, instantly compensating, sending electrochemical signals flowing into his bloodstream and nervous system—signals which calmed the heart—which kept the lungs from hypering—which fought to save a young man's life.

When the furor died down, the monitors, except for the steadily beating heart, were virtually flat.

Stephen set his annotated copy of Smith's *Harmonies of the 'Net* on the bedside table, and propped on one elbow, staring at the black cover, praying for divine intervention—from any divinity willing to listen. He'd ceased being choosy days ago.

But when no divine downlink appeared imminent, he turned the lights down and lay back, dulling his neural activity by replaying the admiral's cryptic message against his eyelids' inner surface. No indication what was behind Smith's delay, but there'd been something elusively familiar behind the admiral, something in the muted colors of the room . . .

He opened his eyes to the blackened room. His initial tour of the ship. The ship's QR. Briggs' tongue-in-cheek warning to behave. Hamilton's message—a P2 call from the 'Escort team.'

Escort team? Who were they questioning? What the hell was going on? He sat up, swinging his feet to the carpeted floor, the lights coming up automatically at that touch.

What if Smith's absence *wasn't* Smith's choice? There were tales about planetary peculiarities, about colonies of Reconstructionist indigenes resurrecting old Earth hostilities against helpless researchers. Tales the students at the academy used to tell one another after lights out, tales to terrify anyone who considered committing to a planetary ThinkTank. Tales that—

But more likely, he told his stomach, Smith had cancelled the meeting because that tongue-tied performance over the com yesterday had convinced the man he was a total bit-brain and a waste of time.

Heaven knew it wouldn't be the first screw-up he'd created. But it might be the biggest and the last.

He was shivering. Cold feet. He pulled them up under the

robe and hunched over, pressing his legs against the churning in his gut.

Unless . . . unless Cantrell had lied and Dr. Smith *was* on-board and down in detention. What if *Smith* had done something illegal? Given his escapades while at Vandereaux . . . but those were just jokes . . . (Though if Beaubien ever heard him say so, his 'NetAT prospects were down the tube for sure.)

Why oh *why* had he been so stupid? He should have known from the way *Harmonies* was written, Smith didn't want attention. What if they were doing God knew what to him down in that small room because of something in that paper—something no one ever noticed until *he* brought it to the 'NetAT's attention? Dammit, he should have known, should have thought to look—

But he hadn't thought, had been too damned busy going *around* his advisor's blind spot to think to check *legalities* before citing Smith's paper to the 'NetAT, and too damned smug at the 'NetAT's request for further analysis to realize they were interested in something *other* than *Harmonies* and *his* cleverness.

And too damned focussed on his own theory to be suspicious when they gave him a special Key to wonder *why* certain files on Smith would be under such locks in the first place.

He'd found out, soon enough.

Academy legend maintained that a student had once created a worm which, if it hadn't crashed his academy's entire system first, might just have made it into the supposedly tamper-proof 'Net. Needless to say, the details of this incident were not public knowledge. Also needless to say, the Phantom Wormer had been expelled with his accesses fried—a warning every NetScience student received loud and clear, though never officially—and his identity was one of Vandereaux's best-kept secrets.

Until a certain bit-brained Recon would-be DProgger—with the help of those 'NetAT-assigned access-codes—turned over his securitied rock.

At J. Wesley Smith's final conduct hearing, he'd flatly stated his disgust with the Academic system, claimed his so-called joke had been a legitimate test of 'Net safeguards, and maintained that, instead of expelling him, they should be awarding him an immediate doctorate based on that test.

The Board, underwhelmed by this logic, had not only expelled Smith permanently from Vandereaux, but blacklisted him with every other major academy as well. The 'NetAT, equally unimpressed, had refused him certification even for 'Links, and relegated him to 'Tracking, where he'd remained quietly unobtrusive until Stephen had brought *Harmonies of the 'Net* to the 'NetAT's attention.

*If* he had. If it wasn't just one more damned setup.

God. It was enough—*more* than enough—to drive a man insane.

It was quite possible, considering Cantrell's seemingly casual conversation at dinner, that everything he'd been told was a lie and that this was some elaborate final test of character. Cantrell could easily be a 'NetAT agent—Chet Hamilton, head of *Cetacean's* Security Communications, almost certainly was—and while he'd been monitored constantly for years (all 'NetSci students were) the 'NetAT might still suspect him of going in where he had no right. Was that the idea? Throw temptation in the 'buster's path and see how he jumped?

Cantrell terrified him, plain and simple. SpecOps Admiral, ruler of this whole damned star-hopping station . . . what the hell did she care about a slimy Del d'Bugger? She certainly had no *social* obligation to fulfill, and yet, dinner every night, insisting he be included in ship social functions, even . . . he glanced at the picture set into the wall . . .

(*"It's wonderful. I've never seen one up close before. How could anyone be so precise? The strokes have to go down exactly right the first time, don't they?"*

(*"I've been waiting ten years to hear someone say that. Kid, you've just inherited a painting."*)

He shuddered and wrapped the robe (another gift from Cantrell, this time in response to another casual observation on *Cetacean's* constant chill) tighter.

He'd stifled all subsequent observations. But the painting was—he snuck another glance over his shoulder—beautiful. He wouldn't keep it, would leave it here after this job was done, but he'd gladly share his room with it in the meantime.

He'd thought he had it figured: good-looking, healthy female whose only prospects were her own crew—and maybe she considered them off-limits. He was used to that. Could deal with it well enough. But she'd never made the expected move.

Another shudder. What if she expected *him* to? Unusual in a woman of her type, but what if—

Oh, God.

A familiar spasm twisted his gut . . .

*Oh, God!*

. . . sent him staggering light-headedly into the small bathroom. He fumbled blindly in the medicine cabinet until his fingers recognized the Reglamytrin bottle, and leaned a hand on the counter, dismally balancing three tablets in the palm of the other. Ship's Pharmacy had warned him on his last refill: no more without Dr. McKenna's personal clearance.

*They* should have to live with his stomach for a day or two without.

A quick cup of water followed two of the three pills. Collapsing onto the toilet seat, he leaned his arm on the counter-top, rested his head against the cool surface, and slowly sipped a second cup.

Surely Loren Cantrell would never bring Dr. Smith aboard and not tell him. She knew what this opportunity meant to him. To his whole future. But if Smith *had* done—something—with the 'Net—

He stopped that speculation cold, disgusted with his own foolishness. Smith was a grown man now: thirty-two years old. He lived here, he belonged to the HuteNamid 'Tank on the tolerance of the Council. He wouldn't dare do anything to jeopardize that standing—

—Would he?

He couldn't have turned the department on its ear, gotten a SecOne StarShip diverted out here for some damned elaborate tail-chasing joke, and sunk his chances with the 'NetAT by failing to see it—

—Could he?

His hand clenched, fracturing plastic and spewing water over the sink and mirror. He flung the pieces into the recycler, plucked a sliver out of his palm and thrust his hand under the faucet. Two damned drops of blood and he'd have to account for them tomorrow. He sprayed plaskin on the hand and held it under the air jet to dry.

*Danislav's* comment on Smith (Stephen had asked) was that no other place would have him and HuteNamid, as a new colony, would take what they could get.

Danislav should know. *Smith* had been his protégé, and Wesley Smith had failed to meet Danislav's personal expectations.

Stephen knew all about failing Danislav's expectations. Pursuing Smith's paper meant walking away from Danislav's advice and his degree program just to be 'a pawn in an old 'NetAT grudge-settlement' after Victor Danislav had 'put his own professional credibility on the line so that his nephew could have a chance at a spacer education.'

He groaned and dragged himself back to bed, shedding the rest of his clothes along the way—*To hell with it. For once, I'll get them tomorrow*—wrapped the robe tighter, and crawled under the covers, curling on his side, clenching his fists in a pillow pressed against his aching gut.

Damn right, the 'NetAT had an old, old grudge against Smith —a grudge nearly as bitter, he imagined, as the one Smith must have against the 'NetAT.

## iv

"Mind if I sit, Ridenour?"

Someone slipped into the empty chair across the messhall table. Who . . . ? Vaguely panicked confusion eased as he saw her name patch: Tanner. *Gillian* Tanner: *Security* communications. A connection formed, he could recall the name from a screen reference. It was remembering faces that always proved difficult.

He glanced around at the otherwise empty room, and shrugged. "Sure, go ahead. Sit anywhere you like." And returned to his notes.

If he had to lose that file, why couldn't it have happened *before* the daily 'NetTrans? Now he'd have to wait for today's transmission, then another day before the file could possibly be cleared. What if it was *the* file that made the difference? What if there was no time to go over it before—

A cough from across the table, a clatter of utensils. He looked up, met Tanner's not-very-apologetic smile, and frowned. He pushed his untouched and now-cold breakfast out of the way, picked up his coffee cup and, remembering etiquette, asked, "—Get you a cup?"

"No. Thanks."

He picked up his notes and went to refill his cup, all the while conscious of her gaze following him to the counter.

What did she want?

"You know, Stephen, you *could* leave that pile on the table."

He jumped, spilling coffee over his hand rather than the Wytner in his cup. Hands appeared to save the cup and blot the dispenser as he grabbed for the papers slipping from under his arm.

"Dammit, Lexi!" he spluttered, registering who belonged to those hands. "Warn me, will you?" He started straightening the pages of notes, realized suddenly how that must have sounded and glanced up at her, certain he'd alienated this one friendly resource.

But Lexi only grinned and gestured at the papers. "I doubt anyone would get very far with them." She tossed his cup into the recycler, dispensed two more, one with Wytner, one without, and picking up a full plate in one hand, her coffee cup in the other, nodded toward his table. "Private party?"

Tanner was watching them: a look he couldn't read. "I—don't know. She just came over and sat down." And before he could give in to temptation, he said, "I'd best get back over there. Find out what she wants. I—see you later?"

The request was out before he knew he was thinking it. He muttered Never mind; and headed back for his table—but Lexi fell in beside him, saying, "If Gillian wanted you all for herself, she should have put her claim in earlier, eh?"

Lexi exchanged a private look with Gillian, got the come-ahead and slipped into the chair beside her.

Stephen sipped his coffee, set it down with a faint chatter of plastic on tabletop. "Lt. Tanner, is—"

"Just Tanner, Ridenour. Or Gillian, if you prefer. —Are you sure you don't want your breakfast? You're looking a bit green around the gills."

He blinked, opened his mouth, closed it without saying anything, then, with a confused shake of his head, tried again. "I'm sorry, what—?"

"You could use some food."

Confusion turned to an irritated scowl. "Thanks, but no thanks. —What do you really want, Tanner?"

Lexi sensed Gillian's tension, set warning fingers on her wrist. Stephen's eyes followed that signal, and the hand that reached to pick up his coffee trembled visibly now. He steadied the cup with his other hand and cradled it a moment, the scowl becoming a look of concentration as he stared silently into the cup. When he finally looked up, those pretty eyes of his wide and earnest, the wrist beneath her hand relaxed: hard-nosed Gillian was no more immune to that Look than anyone else.

Gillian said, "Look, Ridenour, I'd no right to crash your breakfast. Fact is, we've been working on a problem down in SecCom for the past six hours and it occurred to me you might be able to help us with it, if you've got some free time—if you wouldn't mind?"

His eyes dropped, his hands crept to his notes. But he said steadily enough: "Certainly. I thought that was why I was here."

"When you're through here, or as soon as you're free, if you could give us a buzz, we'll send someone to bring you down."

Stephen gathered his notes and rose to his feet. "Anything wrong with right now?"

The call from Margo McKenna came much later than Cantrell had anticipated. Outside Tyeewapi's room, she raised a questioning eyebrow toward the door.

The doctor shrugged. "Not real well, but he's awake."

"How do his readings look?"

"Normal, at first glance, but the damn things repeat. That's why it took me so long to call. Thought at first it was a fluke or a mistake in comp."

"Repeats. How closely?"

"Except basic bodily functions, exactly. Maybe those, too, given long enough to cycle. For all the work it's doing, the brain could be a tape on continuous loop. If you ask him something, he responds, but afterward, the pattern picks up exactly where it left off."

"Good lord." She felt TJ's presence in her ear a moment before he and Lexi appeared from a side corridor.

Lexi said breathlessly, "Sorry, sir. I was down in SecCom with Dr. Ridenour. They asked him to help check out those Vandereaux files."

She wasn't sure she liked the sound of that.

"Everything all right down there?"

"Should be. Chet's there."

"Good enough."

"How's Tyeewapi, Margo?" TJ asked.

"See for yourself." McKenna opened the door and stepped back, allowing them to precede her into the room.

Hononomii Tyeewapi sat in front of the viewscreen, feet flat, hands folded in his lap. The screen was blank. The doctor murmured something about the video being over and, going to the com, cut the library connection.

Damp sink in the bath, night clothes, obviously once folded neatly over the foot of the bed, in a pile on the floor now, a half-finished glass of water on the bed table . . . sheets rumpled . . . her sweeping gaze came to rest on McKenna. "His doing?"

"That's the good news."

"And the bad?"

"That's all he does. He acts independently to physical needs, period."

"Does he speak at all?"

"Only in response to questions. No real interaction seems to be taking place—no real thinking as far as I can tell, although what's happening below the surface . . ." A deceptively casual shrug. "It's as though he short-circuited and only part of the system came back."

"Any sign of drugs?"

"I'd never have let you at him if there had been."

She eyed the youth suspiciously. "For real? Or is this some sort of scam?"

"Who can say for certain? My training can't explain it, but in my gut-level opinion, the higher brain can't act on what he hears or sees. Habit seems to be working like an autopilot. The higher circuits are—busy."

Cantrell walked over to the seated figure and swivelled his chair away from the desk and the screen to face her. Tyeewapi offered no resistance. Ship fatigues had replaced the leathers he'd worn last night, and except for the sleek, long hair, he might have been one of her own men.

"Hononomii?" Dark eyes lifted to hers. They focussed, they even blinked. But they never wavered, not for an instant. A far cry from the impassioned, crusader eyes she recalled from last night.

But at least they were open.

"Hononomii? Can you hear me?"

A long pause.

Then, tonelessly: "Yes."

"Hononomii, do you want to go home?"

Another long pause.

Nothing.

He was indigene. For all his apparent confidence when he came aboard, he'd undoubtedly been frightened. Likely it was his first time in space and that under less than optimum circumstances. If she could somehow make him feel less threatened . . . more at ease . . .

"Admiral?"

"Yes, Lexi?" she murmured, not taking her eyes from the vacant face.

"If he can see and hear—what about showing him the planet? Perhaps *seeing* home could rouse him . . ."

She smiled faintly. Occasionally Lexi read her thoughts as efficiently as TJ. There'd been times she'd wondered whether she'd done the right thing, accepting Lexi's application: Lexi's temper had been a bit of a liability in the early days. Not anymore. She'd wondered—but not for a long time.

She called up an outside view display. HuteNamid filled the screen, and she turned Hononomii about again so that the light of the planet illuminated his face. He saw it—he couldn't avoid it. "Home, Hononomii?"

No reaction. But then, a second-generation indigene wouldn't necessarily associate a space view with 'home.' Reaccessing the video library, she called up the survey files of the valley where the Recon capital city lay.

The sights, sounds and smells of the planet filled the room, but Hononomii remained indifferent. The image shifted to the surrounding mountains, zoomed in from aerial overview to examination of geological and biological specificities. Towering waterfalls cut deep into ancient granite, forming dark swirling pools; a rugged cliff-face; sunlight creating a confusion of shadows and caves.

A muffled exclamation. Of a sudden, Hononomii's face was alive, searching the screen and the surrounding walls.

"Nayati?" She could barely hear the hoarse whisper. Abruptly, the view changed, shifted to another section of the continent altogether where tall grasses covered flat-topped mesas. Hononomii cried out, reaching toward the screen.

With a gasping sob, he collapsed back into the chair, hands covering his face. "Nayati, *shan'doo'aal . . . shan'doo'aal. . . .*"

The mutters faded, the hands settled carefully back to the armrests and Hononomii's face returned to the blank mask with mechanical eyes. She called up continuous replay on the cliff shots, carefully noting the planetary coordinates as they appeared on the bottom display. Then she killed the readout line, leaving only the images.

The shifting shadows on the screen reflected in Hononomii's wide dark eyes, eyes that shifted now, watching those shadows. Eyes with awareness behind them, that blinked themselves free of tears forming in their corners.

*Nayati.* A name? Person? Or place?

After a moment, she said softly, "Hononomii?" He blinked.

"What is that place, Hononomii Tyeewapi?" His mouth worked, but no sound came out.

"*Where* is it?" She felt McKenna's hands on her shoulders, urging caution, but she shrugged them off: far too much depended on this young man's knowledge, and whatever held him hostage was wavering.

His breath caught, and he whispered, "*Cocheta . . . Dena Cocheta . . .*"

"Loren . . ."

She raised a hand to silence McKenna. "Who's that, Hononomii? Who's Dena?"

A frown line appeared between his brows. After a long silence he shook his head slowly. "Not . . . who."

"Dena . . . Dena . . . Co—cheta. Why does that—mean anything to any of you?" She glanced around at Lexi who shook her head, at TJ, who did not. He had on his instant-replay look.

"TJ?"

He said, still concentrating, "Last night—just before he freaked out—he said: Halona said—pause—she—pause —Co—Cocheta." He refocussed on the room, shrugged and said, "There is, at least, an apparent link."

"Hononomii, —would you like to go to Dena Cocheta?"

"Can't."

"Hononomii, —can you *call* Dena Cocheta?"

A breath of a whisper, "Yes. . . ."

She signed to TJ: *Link up! Trace it!* Then: "Hononomii, would you *like* to call Dena Cocheta?"

His eyes misted. ". . . yesss . . ." And looking around him in confusion, ". . . keyboard . . . ?"

Keyboard? Why—

"Admiral?" Lexi's voice, anxious. She looked a question. "Stephen—he's down in—"

TJ set a hand on Lexi's arm. "It's all right, kid. Chet's already got him clear of the loop. Line's clear, admiral—ready to trace."

"Hononomii, can you tell us how to call Dena Cocheta?"

Greater confusion: *"Key—?"*

Whatever worked. Must be a computer link rather than a com. She turned Hononomii's chair toward the desk. "Here, Hononomii, here's the keyboard. Your access is cleared—"

His fingertips settled on the board, his eyes closed. He swayed back and forth several times, then began typing. Rapidly. Without opening his eyes. Whatever inhibitions he had against speaking certainly didn't extend to his manual dexterity. She concentrated on his face, watching for any break in the control, any evidence his condition was feigned.

At a choked sound from TJ, she looked up—followed his eyes to the screen where by rights the coded keystrokes should be echoing. Except for a simultaneous depression of seven keys—it was blank. Her eyes met TJ's—met confusion to match hers, but she dared not interrupt their strange patient now. She just hoped to hell for an echo *somewhere* in the system—that those keystrokes were indeed being recorded in Chet's lab.

Abruptly, a deep, young voice came over the speakers: *"Dena Cocheta. De'ninaah."*

Hononomii searched frantically about him, finally called out to the room in general: *"Nayati! Nayati Hatawa?"*

From the system: *"Hono?"* then softly: *"Damn. Where . . ."* and again clearly: *"Hono? Where the hell are you?"*

And Hononomii, his voice near breaking: "Nayati? Nayati Hatawa, tsinaa'o'oot 'a' shil son anit'o'oot 'a'! Shin'niilhi! Hodeeshtal . . . *Hodeeshtal!*"

And the system: *"Oh dear God, Hono, forgive—"*

Silence.

Cantrell hit the com connect: "Dammit, Chet! Get them back!"

*"Admiral? Get who back? I've been trying to get through. The boards show your frequency clear but not in use. What's going on? Did you want a transmission traced? Please verify."*

"You mean you *didn't?*"

*"Didn't what? Admiral, nothing . . . no transmission has left the ship in the last two hours!"*

"God!"

*"Sir?"*

"Never mind, Chet. Cancel the order. Cantrell out."

She got up, never taking her eyes off the prisoner, who'd lapsed back into his catalepsy. "If there was no transmission, nothing received, then what the hell were we just listening to?"

"Shit, Ridenour. Why'd you do that?"

Years of experience and many a lost program had trained Stephen's reflexes to clear his hands of the keyboard before he reacted to startling outside input. This time, however, the interruption seemed innocent enough, and his heartrate stabilized as he scanned the wall of faces surrounding him.

What had been Tanner and two other SecOps had grown to a veritable crowd, including—he felt the heat rise in his face—the admiral herself, who said, "Well, Dr. Ridenour, you going to answer the man?"

He swallowed hard. "I—I don't quite know how to explain. When you pull 'Net files to ref to a non–'Net store, a virtual link is created that's as unchangeable as anything that passes through NSpace. If you create a routine that traces . . ."

They weren't laughing. They were listening. He wasn't certain which was more disturbing: being laughed at, or being taken seriously. What if what he was saying was wrong?

"But how did you think to check this flag in the first place?" Chet Hamilton leaned over the monitor to point at a keyLink command upside-down. "It hasn't a damned thing to do with medicine, let alone laser-bonding of micros to tendons."

He didn't at all want to answer this man's questions. A mistake in front of this man would undoubtedly make it back to the 'NetAT, and he honestly didn't *know* how to explain why he'd checked under deep-core mining ops: it had simply seemed the thing to do at the time.

But SecOneDProg Chet Hamilton expected an answer, so . . .

"You—you need to look at all the possibilities. You need to think of all the people who m—might be interested in the subject and run a scan using *their* t–terminology rather than in-the-field keywords. It—it's like using Corlaney Gestaltion in reverse, using that mindset to pull out all the users at once. I—'' Hamilton's probing look disrupted his thought and he floundered into silence.

To cover his unease, he rose to his feet, saying, "I'm afraid that's all I can come up with, sir. Unless there's something else—?''

Hamilton's eyes left him and focussed beyond his shoulder. Then:

"You can do something for me, Stephen.'' Adm. Cantrell's voice. His heart skipped another beat: he'd totally forgotten her presence. He twisted around to face her, hit his hamstring against the chair, throwing himself off balance and abruptly back into the cushioned seat.

Cantrell, politely overlooking his GnC, said, "We've just had another incident in the system. That data glitch we're here to investigate manifested itself again. Take a look, will you? Check the system out. See if you can find anything—unusual.''

"You mean the 'Net Records problem is real?''

"Absolutely real.''

"What was the exact nature of the incident, admiral?''

"I'd rather not bias your thinking. Just do a general systems check; can you do that?''

"Of course.'' Odd, but he'd been given odder assignments over the years. You never knew what exec-types would want. And exec was, ultimately, what Loren Cantrell was.

He swung back to the terminal and narrowed his focus to the welcoming screen.

The datastream flowrate steadily increased and Stephen looked less puzzled and more intense as his long fingers danced over the keyboard, darted to the finger-key and back.

A stifled exclamation from Chet. Cantrell looked a question, but his eyes were fixed on the screen. Without lifting that gaze, he signalled those who hadn't discreetly deserted the little corner station already to leave the vicinity.

Some time later, the tapping of keys slowed, stopped altogether, and Stephen sat back, staring at the screen.

"Well?'' she asked.

That dazed look floated up to her and blinked at last. "I'm sorry, admiral. I did find a few things that seemed a bit abnormal in Local Systems—made a list of them there—'' He pointed to the screen and Chet said Send them to his terminal. Stephen did so while saying: "—but *Cetacean's* look fine. Nothing I could see that should disrupt dataflow or diddle—excuse me—affect in-transit files. Those are all I know to look for. If you could tell me . . ."

She looked to Chet for his opinion. He shook his head.

"That's all right, Stephen. We'll handle it from here. Don't worry about it. I just wanted to see if you'd spot anything Chet's crew happened to miss. —Maybe it's in that list you sent to his terminal."

Stephen had followed that exchange; his fingers left the keyboard and gripped the arms of his chair until the knuckles showed white. The look he flashed at them held a hint of desperation, but he said steadily enough, "If that's all, admiral?" And to Chet: "Sir?"

Chet, elbow resting on the monitor, chin supported in his hand, nodded toward the exit. "Take off, kid. You've got your own work to do."

Stephen stood up and excused himself diffidently. He paused in front of her, but she waved him on. "I'll see you later, Stephen. Thanks."

The worried look didn't fade. He started to say something, then nodded and headed quietly for the door.

"Stephen?" Chet called, and signalled two of his people to accompany him out of the restricted area. Stephen glanced back at them, his expression completely under control this time. "You did good, kid. Thanks."

The cool look thawed a degree. His color rose a shade. Other than that, he might not have heard. He turned silently and left with the two crewmen.

As the door whished shut behind them, Chet said: "Why the hell's that kid being wasted as a lousy 'LinkMan?"

"You tell me." She pointed toward his office door with her chin. And as the door closed behind them: "Where do *you* think he belongs?"

She settled into a chair inside the udirec walls of his office, watching personnel scatter on their various businesses, relaxing now the boss was out of sight and the Ridenour Diversion had ended. Chet pushed papers aside, perched on the corner of his desk—his *chair* was piled high with printout—and answered her at last and emphatically:

"Design, no question. He could probably show the 'NetAT's MasterProgs a trick or two."

"You serious?"

"Hell, they're so damned hide-bound—you tell them I said that, and I'll deny it, absolutely—they can't see their way out of the bathroom. What he just pulled was illegal for him to do—absolutely."

"What *did* he do?"

"Accessed the 'Net. —Went right in at system level. Something this ship allows that his academy system didn't—I'd wager he had no idea what he was doing was wrong—while he was doing it."

No wonder she hadn't recognized the infostream. "And after?"

"You saw him: he knew."

"Why'd he do it?"

"You'd given him a problem. He was trying to solve it."

"Nothing more?"

He nodded.

"Does he realize what you are?"

"I've made no secret of it. And he's been real cautious since he came aboard—kept his nose spotless. This time, he simply got so involved, he accessed without thinking and right under my nose. *Warn* me next time, will you?"

"Problem?"

"Not really. I didn't want to break his train of thought in case it led somewhere. I followed what he did—would've stopped him else—but this kid does things I'll guarantee he never learned in a classroom. I've seen it before—so have you—though never quite like him. Kids too bright to know what they can and can't do within the rules, caught between one level and another and having to make a decision— Only a mistake in judgment in this field can get you DSpaced for good."

"Maybe deep space is where he belongs. Dangerous?"

He shook his head. "Innocent as a babe. It's just—you saw him jump when Bill asked that question. Concentration. He was *thinking* 'Net. I suspect he's doing things on instincts and assimilating so rapidly he's not aware how *much* he's doing until too late. Could land him in a hell of a lot of trouble one of these days."

"*Is* it something to worry about?"

"I doubt it. He wants what we can give him too badly to

screw it up. I *am* going to have a serious sit-down with him before we get back into 'NetAT territory, however.''

''Where was he when that call of Tyeewapi's went through? Could he have been involved?''

''Nowhere near a terminal. From what I heard, Gillian was trying to talk him into the theater tonight. —Which is not to say he couldn't figure out what happened, if you want to come straight with him. I tell you, this kid's good.''

''You keep saying that and then telling me not to worry. Dammit, Chet, I might have to send that boy downworld. We *need* a contact in the 'Tank and he's the only one with a legitimate excuse. Is there danger in interface with Smith?''

''The boy's very cautious in some respects. But you saw him just now: he's desperate to make a good impression. I think the greatest danger is if Smith impresses *him*.''

''Any chance of that?''

''From what I've seen of Smith's work, it's been all downhill since the Vandereaux incident. This kid's got him way outclassed.''

''You've got that right. Stephen's ratings came in today.''

''That Priority Trans?''

She nodded. ''Fourth-Echelon.'' She was expecting amazement. At least surprise. What she got was coolth. ''Well, say *something*.''

''In InterLinks?''

She nodded.

''He was robbed.''

''He's *that* good?''

''In InterLinks? He could write his own ticket once he's certified—if he stays in that field. I've been vetting all his 'NetReqs personally and if the 'NetAT had any sense, they'd plug him direct into the 'Net and have him write Links for the next hundred years. He'd create a CAT a three-year-old could use. But my bet is he won't be in 'Links any longer than it takes the 'NetAT to yank him into DProg. Seems a shame he wasn't in years ago. —All the more reason to keep the kid from any long-term association with Smith. If the situation goes bad, he could be involved before he knows it, and that'll fry his chances with the 'NetAT for sure.''

''Wish we could send you down instead.''

"So do I, admiral. Next time, tell Eckersley to mind his own business, will you?"

"And if the 'NetAT engineered the whole thing? If Kurt's just fronting for them?"

"The 'NetAT doesn't work that way, admiral. If they want that kid, they've got him. My guess is, his talent's been covered up. I got a *Keep your eyes open* from Sect. Beaubien, but nothing that indicated *this*."

"Maybe they just don't want a Recon in their program."

"You think the 'NetAT gives a shit where the kid's genes came from?"

"I think Shapoorian does."

"She doesn't control the 'NetAT. Besides, there's one other factor you maybe haven't thought of."

"What's that?"

"No matter what Shapoorian, or anyone else for that matter, wants, that kid's going to end up with the 'NetAT, one way or the other."

"What do you mean?"

"No way I can completely ignore what I just witnessed, admiral. I've got to report it—I can bias that report in the kid's favor, but I don't want a space cadet on the 'Net any more than the 'NetAT does. If he's stable, if he's good enough, he'll get the proper training. If he's not, the MasterProgs'll keep him under their thumb just to know where he is. They can't afford to have a wildcard like him floating loose."

"You make it sound as though I should put him under lock right now."

"Not at all. At the moment, he's innocent as can be. *Don't* let him get fouled up with what's happening down there. If you must send him down, I'd suggest you use that naiveté to get Smith out in the open and up here real quietly where I can have a go at him."

"I could just have Smith arrested and hauled up for a session under Dep."

"Not and get out of him what you need. You need him awake and cooperative."

"You believe there *is* a problem then?"

"Absolutely. The kid checked everything and then some. Nothing wrong with *Cetacean's* system, and yet that Recon managed to talk with someone somewhere—I assume down-world. Only loose 'NetTech there is Smith.''

"Wonderful. —Did you figure out where Smith got that code of Stephen's?''

"If Smith got into *Cetacean's* files, nobody saw him. The bridge lock's secure, nobody but you has been in your personal files—he *can't* access those from planetside hardware anyway. Physical impossibility, aside from the BioScan locks.''

" 'Impossible.' They said that about FTL.''

"Don't remind me.''

"So, what are you saying, Chet? He just *dreamed up* Ridenour's code?''

"I'd believe that sooner than that he got it from this ship's 'Banks. However, Smith was a Vandereaux man—possibly retains some contacts through the 'Net. I'd guess Tyeewapi just mistook what file they were looking at.''

"Right. And the untraceable transmission? Hononomii's little stunt goes well beyond what Smith might have done with access numbers. We know damn good and well what equipment *he* used.''

"I imagine Tyeewapi set up some sort of odd frequency bypass loop with an onworld power source. I can think of several ways it might be done—now—and I'll set up a tracker just in case.''

"So you're saying it's all nothing? Smith's paper, your precious wiz-kid, data dropouts and untraceable transmissions are nothing?''

A tight smile. "Nope. Said there are other explanations. I'll cover for what *I* can imagine. The rest is up to you and the wiz-kid. I'd suggest *you* operate on the assumption that I don't know what the hell I'm talking about.''

"Why?''

"Because I don't.''


# V


It was the weights this time: good old-fashioned wear-me-out-til-I-can't-move weights. Full G. Maybe *that* would take his mind off—what it was he was trying to forget.

Stephen let the bar drop with a satisfying, eardrum-bursting *clang!* and ignored the enraged outcry from the pocket of *Cetacean* personnel huddled in the corner, ostensibly checking their collective pulse. He knew it was hard on the equipment—you were supposed to let pneumatics down easily, reset them politely.

But sometimes—you just had to do it. You had to let it go and to hell with the consequences.

He stood on the bench, gave a little hop to the pull bar, did a few front and back, then curled his knees up and over, hooking his ankles on the padded roll on the far side, and just let himself hang upside down for a while. Let the blood pound in his ears, let his back stretch out, let his—

—let his brain start functioning. Curl-ups. If those didn't run the SecCom specters out of his mind, nothing would.

He increased the pace, sweat running into his eyes now, his blood pounding wildly. Hamilton was going to report him. He was never going to talk with Smith. He was going to be banned from the 'Net forever—

*Goddammitalltohell!*

He pulled up and over, perched sidewise on the bar and wiped a hand across his sweaty face, not altogether certain some of the salty liquid was not sweat at all.

It just wasn't fair. He'd been so careful. He'd avoided getting into theoreticals with any of the *Cetacean* 'NetTechs; he'd hardly opened his mouth to Hamilton, much as he needed to ask what he should and shouldn't discuss with Smith; and the first time they'd asked anything of him, the first request Cantrell had made of him in the whole trip . . . *Damn—damn—damn—damn* —damn!

He flipped over the bar and down to the floor, grabbed his towel off the bench and stalked toward the door.

The gossip group hadn't moved. He had to pass through them on his way out. He muttered an apology, secretly wishing the lot would go to hell—wishing humanity in general there, at the moment—

—and tried to ignore the fact that he heard his name three times as he passed by. Not to him, of course not *to* him. Just about him. Always *about* him.

God. What must people talk about when he wasn't available?

> **Literal: (Proper Name: Nayati Hatawa)**

**Would that you might give me back permission to speak.**

Cantrell hit *Pause* and leaned forward, resting her elbows on her desk, studying the frozen image, striving to read the tormented face. The translator handled the words, not the meaning inside them.

*What is it, Hononomii? Has this Nayati conditioned you so completely, you go comatose rather than reveal his secrets? And who is he? There is no Nayati on the 'Net or the EtuSystem Records.*

"Continue. Rate: 0.1 RT."

As the image slowly changed, Cantrell never took her eyes from the indigene's hands—or what she could see of them. His hands were never visible, from any vantage, when he struck a key, and when he shifted to the finger-key, there was no way to tell what he was doing without the echo—

—which hadn't happened. Not even down in Chet's information BlackHole.

No sound at this speed, however the translation display continued. A brief explanation where he was and how he got here, but his last exclamation, just before 'Nayati' cut him off—

> **Literal: It is beginning to kill me. (Multiple meanings) I will sing. I will kick him.**

> **Suggested: Stet. He will tell what he knows. (Or: possible double entendre) He will attack to avoid telling.**

If that translation could be trusted—and with any Recon language, translation was marginal at best until a cooperative native speaker hooked into an Interactive—somehow Hononomii had shut down rather than betray this Nayati Hatawa's secrets.

A shutdown that was killing him—not even the computer had attempted to qualify that translation. But not dead yet. He retained sufficient awareness to make contact with this Nayati.

A call announcement lit in the corner of the screen. She hit the pause and windowed 'Com ID.

Stephen Ridenour.

She rubbed scratchy eyes. Damn. She promised she'd call. Now it was too late—well past what had become, during the trip, their normal dinner hour. She should have sent him an update—saved an overanxious young man a distressed afternoon and herself an uncomfortably incomplete explanation.

*Can it wait, Dr. Ridenour?*

She typed the query rather than establish audio contact. That, and the use of his title, should cue him that her refusal was not personal.

He answered, likewise via keyboard:

> I was just . . .

The readout reversed itself, and she chuckled at the contrast of his second attempt.

> Certainly, admiral. Please call back at your convenience. *Did you get your dinner?*

> Taken care of, thank you.

—Ridenour out.

*Ciao, Stephen.*

She made her sign-off deliberately casual to take the sting out of it, his unforeseen hyper-sensitivity adding yet another concern to the increasing pile surrounding her.

But if the Certification Board's judgment didn't raise his spirits—and his confidence—nothing would, and she looked forward to passing that bit of information along to him in person: her reward for getting this—*report*—finished.

The report she'd planned prior to her visit to Hononomii had been exactingly clinical: the boy's health being given top priority, her conclusion for the interrogation a dismissive *Isolated attack*, suggesting the boy's act had been personally motivated, possibly even a mental problem. *Not* indicative of local attitude.

Now?

A signal in her ear announced TJ's arrival. She released the door and waved Briggs and Lexi toward the couch.

Briggs ignored her, motioned Lexi toward the cabinet in the wall, and ensconced himself behind her on the desk. Without a word, he began massaging her neck and shoulders.

Muscles relaxed, her head sagged forward. She sighed. "You never need to worry about employment, TJ. When you get bored with CentralSec, you can make a fortune with those hands."

He squeezed her shoulders affectionately. "Not a chance. The councillor would can you within a week without my running interference."

Lexi returned with three glasses of wine. TJ paused long enough to take a mouthful, then set the glass down, and returned to his self-appointed task.

She waved Lexi away. "I can't, Lexi. I have a report to write, and tired as I am now, I'll fall on my nose."

Lexi looked a question at Briggs and he said, taking the glass from her and setting it close to hand, "That's the idea, Boss-lady; reports can wait."

She chuckled and pressed his hand. "Not this one." She grasped his wrist firmly, pulled him off the desk and shoved him toward the couch. "Sit."

She stretched to hand him his glass and stayed there, elbows on her knees, straightening sounding too much like Effort.

A sip. "My friends, I have me a Problem." Another: *not* a sip. "Using supposedly fool-proof methods, I have apparently turned a healthy young man into a vegetable, and I need to come up with a means of explaining that not only to his father, but to the Council and to the 'Net in such a way that I *won't* cause an uproar throughout the entire Alliance. . . ."

"Whoa, Boss-lady, ease off," Briggs said. "First of all, *you* didn't do anything that should have caused that reaction, and secondly, you don't *know* he's a vegetable. He'll come out of it. It's not an unprecedented reaction."

"No? All right, TJ, give me an example. Out of a healthy, drug-free individual, now. Dopers with less than half a mind to work with don't count."

"But—"

"There is no 'but' involved here, TJ. I've asked Chet to check Central's files, but I know already what he'll find. Nothing. Nada. And we don't know Tyeewapi will come out of it. By rights, I should have an emergency transmit already on the 'Net. By tomorrow morning, Mo should be accessing the best medical minds in the Alliance. What else did we create the damn thing for?" She fell back in her chair, wine splashing from her cup. She paused, momentarily fascinated with a drip's course along the side of the glass and down her fingers. She changed hands and licked the fingers, then said, disgusted, "Yes, and then *everyone* in the whole damned Alliance will know Dep had turned a subject into a mental potato. Panic in the Judiciary is the least of our concerns. Have you *any* idea how wide-spread the use of that drug is? Remedial ed . . . mental hospitals . . . VRTS, for God's sake. I should get Chet to pull the numbers on *that* out of the 'Net for me: if I'm going to develop an ulcer, I might as well make it a good one."

Briggs said, "Sure, this is unusual, admiral, but the boy's in no apparent danger at this time—his body has resumed normal functioning, even if his conscious brain hasn't—and Mo isn't pressing for an EmTrans. *She's* not that worried.''

"You want me to wait until the rest of his brain shuts down and he's on total life-support? Thank you, no, TJ.''

"I *want* you to wait until morning, when we're all thinking a little clearer. Then make your decision what to do about the report. There's nothing the Alliance at large can do for that boy that Mo isn't doing right now.''

"Shit.'' She glowered at her glass again. "I wish they'd figure out how to send ships wherever it is the 'Net goes. I'd love to walk through that door and tell the damned Council the situation and throw it all back in their laps. See how *they* like telling a father his son's got to be sacrificed to the mental stability of an already paranoid society.''

Lexi stirred uneasily. Briggs glanced at where he knew recorders were. They were worried about her indiscretion, here where every breath was recorded. Well, let them hear.

"Maybe,'' Lexi said cautiously, "Hononomii's father already knows.''

"Why do you say that?''

"Sakiimagan Tyeewapi's motivations bother me. Could he have staged this? Anticipated his son's reactions?''

"That boy's reaction is not staged.''

"But chemically? A—programmed time-bomb? Maybe even old-fashioned hypnosis?''

"Why?''

"Sacrificial lamb. Create an incident. Julius would have.''

"No evidence of that level of unrest here, Lex.''

" 'Get out and leave us alone'? Familiar words to me, admiral.''

"I suppose it's theoretically possible. I've heard of subjects so thoroughly indoctrinated against speaking, they went catatonic when questioned on certain highly specific topics. But once that line of questioning stops, they always come out of whatever box they crawled into, and of course, the response itself is incriminating. Tyeewapi's response, in contrast, was highly *non*specific.''

"So maybe Hononomii's been conditioned,'' TJ said, "and maybe his father did the conditioning. We're here on an investigation. Maybe there *is* something in this missing researcher business.''

The call announcement flared on the screen again: from the outside this time.

"Who is it, 'Com?"

*"George M. Downey, HuteNa—"*

"Dammit!" she interrupted the AutoCom. "Tell him to put it up his—"

TJ coughed. She stopped herself in time.

*"Admiral, I did not register the message. Put it up his what?"*

"Heaven save me from literal computers. —Never mind, 'Com. Tell him to put it in his report. Cantrell out."

*"Yes, admiral."*

TJ and Lexi exchanged glances, then looked at their toes, the walls, anywhere but at her. For this, she'd joined the service.

"All right," she said sourly, "what have we got?" She ticked off the list she had jotted down. "A) We know the 'NetDB is not exactly the source of Ultimate Truth. But considering what we've found here, a random glitch isn't a particularly satisfying explanation. B) A wildcard researcher with—according to our pet expert—a 'whole new concept in 'Net theory' that some experts back in Central *assume* spurious. C) Researchers disappearing off the 'Net (obviously unconnected to the spurious concept), and D) an indigene prisoner using *Cetacean* equipment for a long-distance chat, leaving no evidence of the system it was talking to, or the means of transmission. That about cover it?"

"—And E)," TJ added, "—an equally nontraceable access of *Cetacean's* internal files by the aforesaid spurious researcher—in the presence of the aforesaid uncommonly skilled indigene."

She jotted down TJ's *E*. "Isolated issues?"

"Like hell."

"I agree. But it indicates an uncommonly close working relationship between Recon and researcher."

Lexi said: "Unless Dr. Smith is *not* missing of his own accord."

"No overt interCorps problems downworld. The crew's mingling freely with SciCorps and IndiCorps alike."

Lexi shrugged.

"Meaning appearances are easy?"

Another shrug.

Wonderful. F) A possible kidnapping. And her crew already down there was urging their onboard mates to join them planetside. However, if Smith was being held against his will, they were being damned quiet about it.

If the fallouts were deliberate, who was behind them? With what motivations? The Tyeewapi kid appeared to be demanding independence from the Alliance altogether, but on whose behalf? and how could independence benefit the HuteNamid colony, who seemed to have none of the *normal* Recon complaints? It would put a decided cramp in their ThinkTank operations—or did Hononomii Tyeewapi want the researchers out as well?

She said: "If Smith's the *cause* of that missing information, he won't be anxious to take another expert in 'Net design into his confidence."

TJ said: "And if he *can* access *Cetacean's* SecFiles, he's going to check out any potential transfer more thoroughly than one might wish."

Lexi looked from one to the other of them, obviously just realizing who they were talking about and also obviously *not* happy. "Sounds to me like 'another expert' could be in a whole lot of trouble down on that planet and should *damnwell* stay at—"

The call light blinked red: Communications bypassing the AutoCom.

"Dammit!" Cantrell hit the audio button. "Who is it, Mat?"

*"A call from planetside, admiral. A Dr. P. J. Carlson. He refused the AutoCom, admiral. Used a Priority override."*

P.J. Carlson AKA Dr. Paul Corlaney. She exchanged a look with TJ and said to Mat, "Tell him I'm busy."

*"Yessirr."* And a moment later: *"—Sir?"*

"I'm here."

*"He says he heard you're coming downworld and he'd like to meet with you."*

Paul Corlaney: GenTech extraordinaire. *(Just ask him.)*

Paul Corlaney: The man who had perfected the DeLeon (if you could afford the price of the tests and production of the serum) Virus.

Paul Corlaney: Onetime friend, sometime lover, whose presence here had once—before life got complicated—been her chief incentive for coming to HuteNamid . . . after twenty goddam years: Let's do lunch. *(Only if your head's the entree, Corlaney!)*

"Tell him to go to . . ."

*"Sir?"*

"Sorry, Mat. Give him my—regrets. Tell him I'll be far too busy to socialize." *Tell him after twenty-odd years of silence, he can damn well do some waiting of his own.*

For the next hundred years.

"Cantrell out."

She slammed her fist on the *Emergency Only* button and looked up—

—to find two highly expectant faces.

TJ knew.

Lexi didn't.

Lexi looked from one to the other of them, the obvious question eating her up inside. A question Cantrell decided, reluctantly, was a Need-to-know.

"I don't need to tell you to keep this to yourself, Lexi, but I'm going to anyway. Dr. Paul Corlaney—" And seeing Lexi's look: "Yes, *the* Paul Corlaney—transferred here eighteen years ago—a security move—and has been publishing under the pseudonym P. J. Carlson ever since."

"But—"

"This is need-to-know, Lexi, and *personal*. And so help me, if you screw up on it, I'll *personally* throttle you. Paul and I are . . . old friends, and for all he's on this world under an alias, he's been trying to contact me since we arrived insystem. He and I are going to have a little get-together RSN."

Lexi opened her mouth as if to say something, then bit her lip.

"What is it?"

"I—admiral, does Stephen know?"

"Know what?"

"That Dr. Corlaney's here?"

"Of course not. I told you, the move was made under Security wraps. What difference does it make?"

Lexi shook her head. "Perhaps none. Perhaps a great deal. I listened to Stephen a lot on the way here, talking with some of the 'NetTechs about his paper—"

"*Our* 'NetTechs?"

Lexi nodded.

Certain 'NetTechs she knew were going to be filling out forms. Lots of forms. In triplicate. "What did he tell them?"

"Nothing really, admiral. They ask and he avoids saying much about his work. But Stephen . . . idolizes . . . Paul Corlaney."

"*Paul?* They're not even in the same field! Paul's lucky if he can manage to turn his terminal on."

"Something about research methodology? Some major publication on—"

"Shit." She slid off the chair and paced the office. That stupid *Holistic Research vs. Modern Scientific Method* crap Paul had been spouting years ago. *Sure* he had a point—but did he *have* to make it with Stephen Ridenour?

"Admiral, I'm sorry. I didn't know it was significant. —I—"

She shook her head. "Not your fault, Lexi. In fact, *I* should have thought—I've heard the boy mention him, but it was never an Issue, just the usual *I wonder what ever happened to him?* and *Such a shame to lose his input* . . . Hell, I've been ignoring Paul's groupies for years. *Stephen's* references to him were conservative."

"For Stephen? Or just in comparison with others?"

"True. I'd better try to get hold of Paul ASAP. —I'd meant to put it off a while longer, but if that's not practical . . ." She laughed: short and humorless. "It's going to be damned interesting if P. J. Carlson doesn't have the basic common sense to keep away from uncommitted researchers. Paul Corlaney isn't supposed to be on this planet, and *any* visitor, let alone a researcher who thinks he wrote the book on research methodology, is going to recognize him. That face of his is not Alliance's best kept secret."

"He might have changed significantly, Loren," TJ said. "He's been out of circulation for twenty years. If he hasn't, he might figure people have long since forgotten him and mingle quite freely."

She laughed again, this time with real humor. "Have you forgotten who we're dealing with, TJ? This is Paul Corlaney. But I *will* call him, soon as we're done here. He's got to keep away from Stephen. Stephen cites him as a source in his thesis, never mind they're not in the same field? Stephen *mentions* him more than once on the voyage—and I just happened not to suggest to Stephen he *might* be on HuteNamid? And happened not to mention *our* defunct relationship?"

"Defunct, admiral?" Lexi asked.

"Extremely defunct." She hit the call button. "Mat?"

*"Yes, admiral?"*

"Is Dr. Carlson still online?"

*"No, admiral."*

"Send him a message. Tell him we'll work out something. I'll be in touch." She put the *Emergency Only* back on and waved toward the door. "Thanks, you two. Now out of here. Time for me to put this thing to bed."

"Admiral?" TJ paused at the door. "What about the 'Net? If they really can diddle the data . . ."

"My worry, TJ. But thanks."

She kept the smile plastered until the door slid closed. Not because it would fool TJ, but because the fact the entire ComNet Alliance DataBase had been compromised *was* her worry, and hers alone. Until this issue was settled, until she determined the precise changes somebody had made in the DataBase, the 'Net—at least the EtuSystem Access—had to be shut down.

She had the authority. She *could* shut down the entire 'Net, if necessary. The codes for such a move were long since established—had even been utilized once before on a localized basis, though not by her. But the ramifications of such a move . . .

Cutting off the 'Net outside the Etu system meant far more than eliminating access to a possibly faulty database—that was mostly convenience anyway. Most systems had *some* RealSpace datadump. But disruption of RealTime infoflow would bring interstellar commerce to a virtual halt: the stock market would stop in mid-tick, starships would be stranded . . .

. . . though she had little patience with *that* ramification. She'd learned nav from one of the old-timers, one of those who'd calculated every hyperspace crossover to a fare-thee-well—and then prayed the ship didn't materialize some place embarrassing . . . or fatal—and made damn sure every one of her people were up to that challenge. But nowadays, most 'navigators' accessed Traffic Control through the 'Net, received an automatic heading directly before crossover and rode the signal through. And if the 'Net had to go down today, those ships in transit had damn sure better have followed proper procedure and *recorded* their exit coordinates, or they'd be awfully big fish in a very small pond for a long, long time.

A *very* small pond . . . Ships used an NSpace—not the infinitely small Nexus the 'Net accessed, but similar. But the 'Net transmitted the NCO-signal on which ships navigated. Did it transmit *through* ship's NSpace? Were the detectors for that signal the same as for the 'Net? How many folds upon dimensional folds could there be? How different could the accesses be? Could a system built to access one, access another?

Only 'NetTechs really knew what 'NetTechs could and couldn't do with a keyboard with 'Net Access. That was the spookiness of working with any of them, the spookiness of wondering how far she dare push young Ridenour right now, the spookiness of trying to second-guess a potential renegade 'Tech like Smith.

Shutting down the 'Net would paralyze Smith; would, in effect, put her in total control over the situation. It would also cut her off entirely from the Council's legal shield. In which case, she'd damn well better be right—especially if she determined it had to be a more than local shutdown.

But there was no reason—yet—to shut down the whole 'Net—only the local moon-based access to it. Once the transceiver on Winema was switched off, even if (heretical thought) Smith was using the 'Net system to somehow access another NSpace, he couldn't further contaminate the 'Net at large—one hoped.

Of course, should Smith's not-yet-proven System exist and prove capable of accessing the 'Net-link on Winema independent of existing hardware and accesses—perhaps even reactivate the link—only destruction of the Winema dish would stop him.

And if one were *truly* paranoid, one could imagine Smith able to access the 'Net without using the Winema-link at all.

But one did try *not* to be paranoid.

One also listened to one's paranoia when that paranoia suggested caution. Finding Smith and finding that outlaw system meant infiltrating the HuteNamid ThinkTank. She might use Paul Corlaney as an access—if he was still of a mind to trust her; but Paul was Genetics—worse than useless in getting to the bottom of this little 'Net-linked mess, because he'd *think* he could handle it. Only Chet and Stephen Ridenour had both the expertise and legitimate access to the people most likely to have the answers—namely Smith. And if guilty, Smith would *never* talk to Chet.

She pulled a battered notebook out of a side drawer, opened it randomly—

Or perhaps not so randomly:

**In algebra today, I asked a Very Stupid Question. I asked Dr. Wallinsford if any of the apples in the barrel were rotten, because rotten apples squash and take up less room.**

Dr. Wallinsford got Very Mad and said I was too smart to ask such stupid questions. Then he gave me a whole bunch more problems to do. Nobody else ever has to do so many. I think maybe he was lying and I'm not very smart.

Everybody else lies, so why shouldn't teachers?

Papa lied. He told Zivon to call him Papa, but he wasn't Zivon's papa. Zivon heard Mama say so. Then Zivon was Very Bad because he didn't tell Papa what he knew, and went on calling him Papa anyway. But if he's not Zivon's papa, then Zivon doesn't have a papa.

Mama lied, too. Mama lied when she sent Zivon away. She told him it was so he would be happy. But she really sent him away because he was Bad and she ordered a Replacement. She even made Zivon put his hand on her tummy so his Replacement could kick him, and then she made him tell his Replacement he loved it. She made Zivon lie. Zivon did *not* love his Replacement. Mama made Zivon be Bad and then she smiled and kissed him and sent him away because he was Bad.

Granther lied. Zivon doesn't see the Stars all the time. He can't go to the windows and touch the Stars. He has to wait for Special days to go to the Observation Deck, and then they only let him stay for five minutes. Then he has to go back to the Academy halls that look alike so he gets lost, and then his toes freeze because it's too cold and someday his toes will break off and then They'll all be . . .

I think maybe teachers lie, too.

The boy-Stephen had tried so hard to make his entries conform to his own understanding of Security. Danislav had told him never to reveal he was Recon—so he'd become a nonperson even in his own diary.

At least she could give the adult-Stephen good news with the bad. She searched the stacks on her desk for the diploma the 'Net had delivered only hours ago. Small wonder they'd taken so long to come through with that fourth-echelon rating: probably the reason for that retesting Danislav harped about.

She grinned tightly. That rating must have stuck in Councillor Shapoorian's craw when it crossed her desk. No convenient way she could veto his graduation after that.

But unless he'd changed greatly from the boy responsible for that diary, Stephen Ridenour wouldn't believe it—would perceive yet one more deception in his world—would perhaps even perceive this as a bribe to make the planetdrop, and add her name to that list of betrayers.

She wrote on the bottom of the transmission report:
*End trans.*
And her sign-off:
*—Armageddon: 60—*


The message alarm's low buzz wakened Stephen from the first real sleep he'd had in days. He groaned and rolled away from the wall and up onto his elbow to where he could see the monitor, focussed first on the time display: 3017.

So the 'NetTrans must have finished. Danislav already? But *Cetacean's* trans had just gone out. Even if he used his dispensation . . .

He squinted the screen into focus:

**Due to temporary conditions in EtuSystem, Winema 'Net-Link has been shut down. Estimated duration: two days. Adm. Cantrell regrets any inconvenience this may cause and assures you that all incoming notices and messages will be properly routed upon the 'Link's reinstatement. Thank you for your cooperation.**

He fell back onto the pillows. So much for that file. By the time the problem was rectified and the 'Net back up, his business with Smith would be completed. One way or the other.

Which meant he had to forget that brief glimpse at the file, or risk everything by accessing it on his own.

He felt the shakes start: sheer terror, no doubt. That, and exhaustion.

Terrific.

He thought of the pills in the medicine cabinet. Wondered if he should break down after all these years and take one of the sleepers. His stomach heaved at the mere thought and he assured it they'd do without.

The chills reached his bones and he asked the room monitor to start the shower—*high*. He waited until steam filled the room, then crawled out from under the covers and dashed for the open bathroom door, shedding clothes along the route.

Maybe if he could just get the shakes to stop he'd be able to sleep.

And maybe lightning would strike him here in his quarters, on a starship floating in space.

## vi

*"I don't understand, admiral. You say there are discrepancies in our 'Net records, and for that you have cut off our ability to access the 'Net?"*

"It's only temporary, governor, I assure you. There are questions regarding two of your researchers which we'd hoped your insystem records transmission would clarify. Since the irregularity remains, I've simply shut your 'NetLink down as a precaution until we can rectify the situation. We can't allow bad data to proliferate. I hope that those hardcopies I've asked to see will help us to track down and repair the glitch."

*"I'm a bit confused, admiral. How can our system records in any way affect the 'Net records? We're Recon. Those records are private—"*

"Unless questions are raised, governor. And questions have been raised. Your internal network and the ComNet are direct-linked, and current theory wonders if perhaps some echo between them is causing the problem."

*"How long is it to last, admiral? Our researchers are, you must realize, quite upset at this disruption of their work."*

Damn right she realized, thinking of jammed AutoCom circuits, all of them receiving the same recorded message:

*We regret to tell you the 'Net shutdown cannot be lifted for any reason. We are sorry for the inconvenience; however, we assure you this is vital to the integrity of your files as well as those of the 'Net itself.*

"We anticipate no more than the two days," she said. "Long enough for us to review those records and determine the scope of the problem."

That was going to make Lexi happy. Lexi had been worried about being dead weight since this mission began. Lexi had been doing the grunt work of three ordinary people, digging up all the 'Net files on HuteNamid's inhabitants and the Old Earth Amerinds they tried to emulate. Lexi had practically put herself into SickBay trying *not* to be dead weight.

Well, Lexi would pay her way now.

"There's another matter I wish to discuss with you, governor. When I come down tomorrow, I'll have a Dr. Ridenour with me. He's our advisor on the problem. He's hoping to meet with your resident 'NetSpec team and observe your Research facility in operation for a few days."

*"We've been expecting him since your first transmission explained Dr. Ridenour's situation. We had hoped Wesley's chat with him would salve his concerns and entice him down. It seems these hopes have been answered."*

'Wesley?' As in Smith? 'We' had hoped?

"Yes, well, I believe you'll understand my concern in sending Dr. Ridenour out on his own. He's young, never made a world-drop before and he's nervous enough. The last thing he needs is to get caught in the middle of an altercation such as your son's action yesterday."

*"Admiral, I have already assured you that was an isolated incident. Provided Dr. Ridenour starts nothing, he is perfectly safe here."*

Give the man an opening and he still didn't ask about his son. If Sakiimagan Tyeewapi had anticipated his son's reactions to interrogation, he was one cold-blooded bastard.

"I'm afraid that's not good enough. Your son is with us already. I would hate to be forced to bring up any more of your people because someone—misinterpreted Dr. Ridenour's presence. I want more concrete assurances, if you don't mind. Under the circumstances, I feel one of my security guards might cause unnecessary friction for him onworld. Perhaps one of your own people? A responsible person directly accountable to you . . . ?"

A long silence. Then:

*"Would my daughter as Dr. Ridenour's escort ease your mind, admiral?"*

Ease her mind? Put young Ridenour in the charge of the knife-wielder's *sister?* A girl younger than he was?

She said carefully, "You are aware, sir, that if *anything* should happen to Dr. Ridenour, your daughter will be held *personally* responsible?"

*"The honor of my household is at stake, admiral, and Anevai's*

*personal honor. I assure you, nothing will happen to the doctor while he remains with her. She will act as my personal representative wherever they go. —Does that satisfy you?''*

About have to, wouldn't it? ''Admirably, governor. Admirably.''

''1809.'' TJ checked his watch and rested his back against the wall. ''One minute to go.''

''Sorry, Teej,'' Lexi said from her monitor station behind the security desk. ''Here he comes.''

Ridenour stormed up the rimway from the 'mover, black thunder in his face, stopped at the desk—

''She in there?''

He didn't reprimand the kid: let Cantrell reap the rewards of this one—he just nodded and asked, curiously, ''Got any bombs on you?''

The kid glared his way through the scanner.

He lifted a brow at Lexi's screen, saw the All Clear. ''Shit. Guess not.''

At the push of a button, *1810* appeared in the lefthand corner of her office viewscreen, bright amber against the blue-black shadow of HuteNamid's night side.

Any second now . . .

As though on cue, a red security alert blinked above the time. Cantrell chuckled and touched another button on the console.

''Yes, Lexi.''

*''He just passed us, sir.''*

''Thank you.''

The alert disappeared and with a final glance at HuteNamid, she flipped the viewscreen off. No sense aggravating the situation further.

A blinking entrance request *and* (she was amused) a pounding on the office door announced the Arrival.

Another button released the door, and before the entryway cleared, Stephen was through it and across the room, and a printout was on her desk, obscuring half her monitor. Holding the sheet flat with the palm of his hand, he leaned across the wide surface and demanded, ''Are you going to explain this?''

She lifted his hand, set it down again. ''Looks like a transfer order to me.''

"You have no right . . ."

"Haven't I? Check again, lad. Civilian you may be, but when you signed on for this trip, you put yourself under my command right along with everyone else aboard."

"Blast it, no! This wasn't part of the deal!" Stephen slammed her desk top, then jerked around so that all she could see was his slender, tensely rigid back. Not an unpleasant view—hell, the boy *hadn't* a bad one—but not the one she cared to look at just now, either.

"What 'deal'? There's no *deal* involved here, Stephen, just a job: an important job which at the moment you're the only one qualified to do."

The hand hanging at his side clenched spasmodically before he half-turned to gaze at her out of the corner of one eye, his face little more than a deeply shadowed profile.

"And once down there? People don't come *back* from Planetary 'Tank assignments, admiral, and I didn't spend the better part of my life studying my tail off with the toughest bastards in the Galaxy to waste it on some back-system world trying to get some half-rate fool to explain a computer system he probably just *happened* to fall into in the *first* place! You're not putting me down there!"

He broke off, shoulders heaving, and even the profile disappeared.

She leaned back in her chair and tried to catch a glimpse of his reflection in the darkened viewscreen. "I'm not stranding you. This transfer's not permanent, though it may read that way. It's cover, lad, that's all. To get you close to Smith."

The stiff shoulders relaxed a degree.

"Smith's balking. What else am I going to do to get you to him—arrest him and haul him up here? Fine atmosphere for academic discussion that would be."

No answer.

"What's really eating you, Stephen?"

A further yielding of the silent back.

"ThinkTank this may be, boy." She heard his breath hiss: that *boy* was guaranteed to raise any twenty-year-old's blood pressure. "But remember what that means—what sort of person gets assigned to such institutions. Wesley Smith's no fool, and neither is anyone else in the HuteNamid 'Tank. If you approach them with that at-ti-tude of yours, they'll bounce you out on your

ass, no questions asked. —And that . . .'' she added thoughtful-
ly, eyeing the portion of his anatomy in jeopardy, ''. . . would
be such a waste.''

Stephen turned full about. *''Dammit, admiral, don't . . .''*
But his anger collapsed in the face of her indifference. He sighed
and dropped into a chair, thrusting his legs out and leaning his
head on one hand.

''I just can't do it, admiral,'' he said tonelessly. ''I've—never
been planetside before.''

*Who do you think you're lying to, boy—me? or yourself?*
Aloud, she said, ''High time, then, isn't it?''

*''No!''* Another slip of the self-restraint. ''I mean, I never
expected to. People just don't—'' She raised an eyebrow, and
he at least had the sensitivity to blush. ''Well, not unless they're
GravityWell SciCorps or planet-busters or—''

''Watch that term. Most indigenes don't take kindly to it, and
many of those we're dealing with here are second-, even third-
generation. Tunica's a capital city of a thriving nation now. Call
them indigenes, even colonials, but not—''

''Don't you understand? It doesn't matter! I'm not going down
there! I'm not going near those people! I'm not here to—''

*''Also . . .''* She tapped the thick report on her desk next to
his transfer order. ''. . . this indigene group's different from any
other IndiCorps I've worked with. I assure you—''

''You don't understand—''

*''—I assure you—''* She knew what he was trying to pull, and
she'd have none of it. ''—I intend to explore those differences. Ethnic Recon groups can be touchy, particularly where it
regards their customs, but these Amerinds . . .''

''Dammit, I don't care! *I don't care!''* He leaned forward
and gripped the edge of her desk. ''Amerind, Reconstructionist,
planet-buster—it's all the same. And it's *not my field!''* His
voice broke. He struggled to continue, tongue-tied, then slapped
the desktop in frustration and threw himself back into the chair
to stare sullenly at the floor. ''The less I know about them, the
happier I'll be.''

It appeared Danislav had done his job well: that Ridenour was
nothing more than a Recon academy-clone with a *special* problem with Recons. She couldn't conceive of a more useless combi-
nation. But she still had a job to do. *He* did.

''Never mind. I'll give you the brief on them and you can

read it or not. Let's say their unusual reactions to our presence disturb me enough that *I'm* going down with you and check out the situation personally. You may stay down there a few days and you may not.''

He shrugged, scowling. ''And I may not go at all.''

''I'm pretending I didn't hear that, boy.''

His fist slammed down on the chair arm. ''Dammit, I'm not a boy! For years, I've aimed at a 'Tech position—*in space*. I'm not a—a sociologist, not a diplomat. I'm not *good* at misleading people. *That*—'' he waved his hand toward the transfer, ''—isn't my job, and they told me—*promised*, dammit—that Smith would be brought up here. That I wouldn't *have* to go planetside.''

In the damn-fool department . . . *Who* promised him that? But she didn't ask. It didn't matter. What mattered was the fist spasmodically clenching and relaxing on the chair arm.

Finally, he asked, in an undertone, ''Tell me, admiral, are you doing this because of what happened in SecCom?'' His silver eyes rose to meet hers, steady, but intensely anxious. ''Is this my punishment for Accessing? Without a trial?''

Of a sudden, she remembered that look as he'd left SecCom. He'd been awaiting the repercussions ever since. Maybe his resistance had its basis in sheer terror.

''No, Stephen. Not at all. This—'' She held up the transfer order, ''—was always a contingency. Whoever promised otherwise, *lied*. I'd hoped not to have to use it, but—''

''You don't understand . . .'' The ancient cry of youth coming from a no-longer-sullen boy. She pressed her advantage.

''It's *you* who doesn't understand. Smith categorically refuses to deal with us. According to this response he transmitted up—'' *Finally*, damn him! ''—we've no business here. His job is to, quote: . . . *publish ideas, not recruit new researchers. Let him*—meaning you, son,—*come down and check the place out for himself. If he can't manage that, he certainly can't manage to live here, and he can go to hell or back to Vandereaux, whichever he prefers.*''

Stephen winced, and again she found herself doubting the academy clone image. Damn Smith for a stubborn fool anyway.

''Smith says, personally, *he'd* prefer hell,'' she said, softening her voice, trying for a smile. He just winced again. ''Stephen, short of my placing him under arrest and hauling him up, the only way you're going to do your job is for you to go to him. —And that means going planetside.''

"But . . ." A small sound, a bit plaintive, but it *was* a response.

"Look, Stephen, I've a bit more of a problem here than originally anticipated. Besides the data dropout I've got an Indi-Corps diplomatic crisis brewing, I've had to order a local 'Net shutdown . . . I don't have *time* for school-boy histrionics.''

"But . . ." Louder this time, stronger: her barb finding its target.

"I must be able to trust you to handle Smith. His research is still *your* primary purpose here, but the whole business with the indigenes is out of hand, —and of the two, diplomatic stability has far more call on *my* time and energy. The 'Net is your problem. It's broken and *you're* going to fix it.''

He tried again. "But I've never had the immune-shots or even been tested for—''

"Dr. McKenna's waiting for my call right now." He stared sullenly at her from under his brows. She proffered the transfer order. "So shut up, go see the Doc, and be ready to leave with me at 0900 hours.''

The sullen glare was far easier to handle than what he'd been radiating moments ago. She quirked the eyebrow at him and he relented. His lips twitched into a lifeless smile as he leaned forward to accept the paper. "All right, admiral. I suppose I can avoid the 'busters and do the social thing at the 'Tank for a few days. Only don't expect any—''

She grasped his wrist before he could lean back, forcing him to look at her. "What's that supposed to mean?''

A puzzled frown. "What does *what* mean?''

" 'Avoid the 'busters.' ''

"Just what I said. I'll go down with you, talk with Smith, check out the system, his notes . . . admiral, please let go of me . . . everything you and Councillor Eckersley want. And I'll stay out of the way of your ignorant indigenes. There's no need . . .''

"Ignorant indigenes?'' She challenged him scathingly. "Smith's assistant happens to be indigene. So is Lexi.''

His voice rising: "Lexi's civilized.''

She clenched her teeth, biting back sarcasm, remembering what he was. "I certainly didn't expect to hear—that—from *you*, of all people,'' she said, challenging that facade openly.

A challenge he refused—or didn't hear. He pulled against her hold. "Please let go, admiral."

"When I'm ready. I don't want you to run off without the other part of your assignment."

"What *'other part'*? —Dammit, let go of me!" His hand jerked this time—hard.

She tightened her grip. "Certainly . . . when you're ready to listen to reason. I need someone on the inside. Someone with a legitimate reason to be there. Someone to get to know these people—SciCorps and IndiCorps alike—to listen to them. To find out *why* some of them are agitating for independence. To find out who—"

"No." Flat and final. "I'm no spy."

"We all do what we must. For God's sake, Ridenour, don't make me pull rank on you. I'd prefer your willing participation, but that isn't necessary—not in the least."

"Let—me—go!" His fist clenched, tendons creating iron-hard ridges beneath her fingers.

"You'll be given a guest liaison for the first few days, Anevai Tyeewapi, the governor's own daughter—"

"I don't wan—*need* any liaison. Just get me to Smith!" His hand jerked again—strong little bastard—but she wouldn't allow him to turn away again. She didn't know what his problem was, but he'd damn well better solve it now.

"Stephen, *just talk to her.* Get to know her. Get her to talk about her people. We're not playing games here. They suspect my staff. They suspect me. You'll be in a unique position down there. If you hear anything I ought to know—make sure I *do* know."

He was no longer listening to her. His belligerence had disappeared, the pulling ended, though the wrist beneath her fingers remained rock hard. His already pale skin had turned deathly white.

The boy was terrified. Downright panicked. Of what? *Her?*

"—Admiral, please don't ask me to—to . . ." His whispered plea faded on a shaking breath, "P-please. . . let. . . g-go. . . ."

*What the hell's the matter, boy?* she thought. Rising slowly to her feet, she leaned across her desk, easing him back into the chair before releasing his wrist. He buried his face in shaking hands, then raked long fingers back through his hair, struggling to regain obviously shattered composure.

She studied him a moment in silence, then crossed to the wall bar under the viewscreen and poured him a Scotch. With water: he had blood tests coming up.

One large gulp. A second.

She asked quietly, "Well?"

Give him credit, he didn't ask *Well, what?* He said, "I—I have a—problem—with 'busters."

"Obviously."

A fingertip pushed an ice cube through amber liquid. He licked the finger, then sipped the drink. She didn't rush him. Sometimes, a body just had to think.

Eventually, he murmured, without moving, "There's really no other way?"

"None."

Steady, expressionless eyes met hers. "What clothes should I pack?"

"Shit. You win, Lex." TJ Briggs yawned and turned away from the office monitors. He twisted around, braced his back against the wall and crossed his legs comfortably on the Security Station counter-top. "I was sure we'd be scraping him off the walls by now."

Lexi grinned at him without taking her eyes from the security boards. Ridenour was leaving now, but one never knew what those last minute readouts might give.

Cantrell's door hissed open and Stephen stepped out, turning for a final word with the admiral. The boy was calmer, but still far from content as he walked through the scanner. He paused to sign out—never mind he hadn't signed in—smiled mechanically in their general direction, and headed up the rimway toward the 'mover.

Lexi stood up as Cantrell joined them. Cantrell leaned against the SecStat counter beside TJ's feet, and stared down the rimway at Stephen's retreating figure, and for several moments after he had disappeared.

"Kids," she muttered, shaking her head and turning half about to rest both elbows on the counter. "I did *not* handle that well. I must be getting old—and I *still* forgot to tell him."

" 'Bout what, Boss-lady?'' TJ asked.

"His ratings—they came through this morning—damn good ones, too.'' Propping her chin in one hand, she looked up at him. "I don't like it, Briggs. Not one bit.''

"What don't you like now, Boss-lady?''

Her eyebrow twitched. "Meaning discontent is a normal state of mind for me?''

"No comment.''

She snorted. "Maybe you're right. But Something New has been added.''

"The kid's distaste for indigenes?''

"You were monitoring?''

Briggs assumed his best offended-pride look. Cantrell smiled grimly and jerked her head toward her office. "Good. Saves me explaining. Come on in. —Lexi, you too. The boards'll watch themselves for a few minutes.''

Lexi killed the screens on the SecBoard and hurried after the admiral and TJ. By the time she arrived in the office, Cantrell had the VD of the interview running, the biofunction analysis displayed on the side.

After a few minutes in silence, TJ grunted and said, "It's all right there. The monitor readouts won't tell you anything you didn't already know.''

"Mm-hmm. And that lack of control could prove a major problem.'' Cantrell cut the sound but left the video running. Over the speakers a faint bang followed by a curse—quite an eloquent curse, Lexi thought: Stephen was full of surprises today.

Cantrell shook her head. "Fool kid left his transmit on.'' She turned the volume down but not off. "We'll see how long it takes him to figure it out. Teach him to pay attention. It's forgetting the damn details that'll get him killed if he isn't careful. After this—'' She jerked her head toward the screen. "—I've no profound confidence in his discretion.''

"Maybe, admiral,'' Lexi said. "But you caught him off guard on a very sensitive topic. You could do that because he's gotten very relaxed with you. Down there, knowing what's expected of him and in front of strangers, he should do fine.''

"I hope you're right. All this time, I assumed he avoided the subject because he could never *return* to Rostov-on-Don. A case of making do with the hand life had dealt him. I thought he'd jump at the chance to—''

"Thought, Loren?" TJ's tone made the simple question a distinct challenge. "Or hoped?" Cantrell scowled at him. It was the closest Lexi had seen her come to real anger with TJ, and he continued as though he didn't notice—or didn't care: "Don't try to make him into something he's not, admiral."

*"I'm not, dammit!"* She seemed to catch herself then. "God, Teej, I'm sorry." Which she didn't have to say.

"I honestly think he'll be all right, admiral," Lexi said. "I've been watching him on this trip. Everything—social situations, the crew, the ship itself—was new to him, but he's an excellent mimic: catches on fast when he's done wrong and adjusts. And remember, he's managed to survive for years with some of the richest inner-system intellectual bigots in the Alliance. I suspect he closed himself off from the past, tried to pretend he was one of them. But once that lot found out—"

"You're *sure* those kids were referring to him? His family history's classified; his name was changed. How could they have found out, unless he told them himself?"

"I don't think he was ever *that* naïve, admiral. But—" She flashed on that half-heard argument in the bubblecar. "—they knew. And I suspect they knew quite well from the beginning. I'm convinced everyone in Vandereaux System has Recon-radar installed at birth. The child responsible for that diary could never have hidden his differences. Not from that crowd."

"What was he when they moved him into Vandereaux?" Briggs asked. "Nine? Ten?"

"Not even that, Teej," Lexi said. "His mother listed him as nine. She was dealing with *planetary* years on Stephen's application. Rostov's are short."

"No wonder he was 'undersized,' " Cantrell said.

"He's hardly undersized now, Loren," TJ said. "Hasn't been for a long time, considering he was varsity the minute his *legal* age allowed him on the team. And if the kid was hassled, wouldn't his psych records say? Why blame the kid and tack the A-social on *his* records?"

"When did spacer-psychs ever understand indigene profiles, Teej?" Lexi sensed bitterness in herself and curbed it. "I doubt they ever even supposed he *could* be unhappy. Probably figured 'his kind' would be grateful simply to be included with inner-system children. He was a bright kid, used to figuring things out. He probably gave those psychs exactly what they signalled they wanted. He might have figured hassling was a social cue he wasn't understanding. He couldn't possibly win a fight—I imagine he simply held on as best he could and tried to become a better spacer than they were."

"And ultimately more bigoted," Cantrell said. "Wonderful: brainwashing by administrative apathy. —Still, I wonder . . ."

The admiral scanned the tape forward, and they watched in silence as Stephen leaned forward to accept his transfer order, saw resignation turn to panic as he discovered it wasn't just a transfer to interview Wesley Smith.

But her own proposal notwithstanding, it seemed to her that the panic was *not* aimed solely at this change in his instructions. This was something different. It was as though . . .

She looked over at the admiral, who was staring at her, not the screen. "Well?"

"There's not much choice, is there?" she said, carefully. "I mean, he's got to go down, doesn't he?"

Cantrell nodded.

She said, with a cold feeling in her gut she couldn't explain away, "I think maybe there's a great deal that's not in those academy records of his. I think maybe Danislav had good—very specific—reasons to fear a blow-up. Reasons Danislav *didn't* bother to tell you. Reasons *not* in that diary."

"Why?" Cantrell asked.

She had to shake her head. "Something wrong in that reaction. I don't *know* what I'm picking up there. Violence. Panic. I just don't know."

"Slow down, you two," TJ said. "Let's not overreact. The kid was feeling trapped, personally and professionally. Loren trapped him physically as well. Maybe that was the only trap he *could* react to—the only one he *could* do something about."

The admiral smiled—still grim, but less so. "You're right, TJ. Sometimes, you just go with the cards you're dealt. As long as the Tyeewapi girl is with him, we should be all right, but Ridenour doesn't wander the streets alone at night, and any sign he's cracking, he gets busted right back up here—with or without Smith."

Stephen nursed his third cup of very hot, very white tea, and finally admitted to himself the justice behind Cantrell's orders.

Raising the mug to the blank viewscreen at the foot of his bed, he said, "To you, my lady admiral, check—and—mate."

A deep-throated chuckle answered from the speaker.

*"Damn!"* he muttered, and slammed his hand down on the transmit cutoff.

Fool! Stupid, stupid fool! The blasted thing must have been wide open all this time. Now *that* piece of brilliancy was recorded for posterity as well.

As well as that scene in Cantrell's office. He set the mug down and slumped forward, resting his elbows on his knees and rubbing his eyes. *That'll look wonderful on her recommendation to the Councillor, now won't it, Ridenour? Lose your head the first time you don't like the terms. But dammitall—*

" 'No deal.' —Hell, what *else* would you call it?" he glumly asked the four walls, and when they failed to answer, reached a toe to pull a drawer open, sighed and began pulling out shirts and slacks in neat stacks, wondering what and how much to pack. 'Several days' worth, temperate, mid-latitude spring.' *Thank you, admiral; that's so helpful. . . .*

He straightened a shoulder seam, smoothed wrinkles from soft indigo silk. At least he could look the part of a Vandereaux graduate. Academy training sometimes paid off in odd ways: one of the few things he'd never had to worry about on this spit and polish vessel had been wrinkles in his clothes.

A few on his face, on the other hand, might have been welcome.

And that bothered him. Not so much the unavoidable fact of his youth, but because he'd let that government man, Benson, *use* that fact to entice him into this venture in the first place.

At the time it had seemed odd that a Council rep should extend the 'Source Verification' job offer, but when Benson had mentioned *Cetacean's* involvement, it had all seemed to make sense. Council assigned *Cetacean*; therefore, Council handled the mission reps. But when he'd mentioned Sect. Beaubien—

*("You know, son,")* the Council rep had said—at which presumption Stephen *still* bristled. He was many things, but he was *not* that . . . *person's* son. *("Science Councillor Eckersley has a staff opening you might be interested in. Of course, he would prefer a much older, more experienced individual—but a good report from a seasoned veteran such as Admiral Cantrell on a mission such as this, and a little word from, say, the second-secretary of the 'NetAT?—")*

And he'd reacted to that keyword like a biochip to a photon.

God help him, he'd thought that meant the 'NetAT *was* interested—had set up that . . . *interview* with Beaubien. Could he really have been *that* desperate?

Then yesterday had happened.

He kicked the final drawer shut, glared at the inoffensive (and unmarked) silkrylic surface, then began pacing the small space between the bed and the door. Had there ever even been a glitch? That whole incident in the Security offices could have been designed to make him betray himself in full view of a 'NetAT rep and throw the whole investigation over to one of their own.

Could it—could it possibly mean the 'NetAT *was* interested, at least in Smith's ideas, if not in Stephen Ridenour, so they sent a nonentity 'LinkMan as a cover for a *real* 'NetMan like Chet Hamilton? What was one degree, more or less? Small enough price for a cover story, especially if Cantrell happened to leave him stranded here in the HuteNamid 'Tank where no one need ever find out . . . and that unlawful 'Net access was more than enough excuse. They wouldn't *need* a trial.

Dammit! He fought down panic and concentrated on putting a travel kit together. He had to go down, one way or the other; best if he were packed and ready to leave before the medical tests. Who knew what shape he'd be in afterwards?

*You'll be allowed one security safe-case*, Adm. Cantrell had told him, a case which Briggs alone would check, and that in his presence. It was impervious to outside scans of all sorts, and the locks would require either his or Briggs' ID. It was intended for his notes and records on the Smith case, but there would certainly be room in the corners for his prescriptions, explanations for which were invariably embarrassing, and Briggs already knew more about him than he knew about himself.

He set the empty Reglamytrin bottle on the counter as a reminder; Cantrell said Dr. McKenna would be supervising his immunology tests, and he certainly wasn't going downworld without *that* protection.

He balanced the shoulder brace in his hand, debating:

(*The next time*, the academy surgeon had warned, *the damage will be irreparable. At least for what you'd want. Prosthetics are good, boy, but they aren't the real thing. As it is, competition's out of the question.*)

That, after he had taken up gymnastics to avoid surgery in the first place. Typical.

He should have followed Dr. McKenna's suggestion and gotten the joint replaced during the flight—any one of their leisurely in-system coasts would have allowed ample recuperation time and competition was no longer an issue—but he couldn't afford the surgery now any better than he could two years ago, and he wasn't about to accept anyone's charity, no matter McKenna insisted the practice would do her good.

He tossed the brace toward the bed. Better not to go without *that* protection either. He'd rarely needed it outside the gym, but if he *should* require it, there sure as hell wouldn't be anyone *down there* that could make one for him.

He set the safe-case by the door, then pulled a suitcase out of the wall storage.

Though no one had ever said a word to him about his baggage, he knew it had provided the crew no small source of amusement: he'd seen the look on Briggs' face that first day. Given his choice, he'd have left most of it at Vandereaux, but . . .

*(One way or another, you're through here. We need the room . . . You bought it—you take care of it.)*

He chose and packed each article of clothing with meticulous consideration, smoothing the fine fabrics as much for the pleasant sensation as to avoid wrinkling.

The admiral had stressed the need for formal clothing: that sounded ominously like State Dinners. If there was anything he disliked more than eating alone, it was eating *en masse*. But how formal could a backworld 'Tank be?

He settled on a conservative black, caught a glimpse of color as he eased it from the locker, and on a whim pulled that color out as well. Pale blue iridesced beneath his fingers. The suit was a favorite, the rare fabric a gift from a Vandereaux tailor he'd never met face to face, the buttons a special commission.

The design was his.

Hell, if Danislav was right and he blew his job here, maybe he'd go work for the tailor.

*If* the admiral didn't strand him here.

He slammed the lid down, dropped the suitcase beside the safe-case and flung himself onto the bed to await Dr. McKenna's call.

*Could* this be an attempt to strand him here? Smith's paper—whatever its origins, whether Smith's alone or from a committee of thousands—reinforced all his own most basic problems with the so-called postulates of 'Net theory, and if he was in any part right, he should be back at the academy right now pursuing that thread. If he were truly paranoid, he would believe the people who had sent him to deal with Smith actually wanted him out of the way while other, more *distinguished* minds, in the 'NetAT and elsewhere, investigated the possibilities suggested in Smith's paper and *his* analysis.

And if Smith *was* a wildcard, a researcher outside the dataflow, without co-researchers, his paper a—leap without precedent, without related sources in the 'Net, without attributable contemporaries . . .

—*Except, perhaps*, he thought with a barely controlled shudder, *another wildcard*. Except, perhaps—driven by the same perception of a 'Net DataBase veering disturbingly close to chaos—one graduate student at Vandereaux? A graduate student who had never quite shaken the belief that *he* was right and his instructors and those damned VRTs were wrong?

Either Wesley Smith was brilliant (a definite possibility), or they were both mad (equally possible). He had to discover which, terrified as he was of proving the latter. He could handle *facts*. It was the half-truths, the qualified maybes and the downright *lies* that frustrated and angered him.

And how could he concentrate on these *important* issues with Cantrell's damned extraneous *diplomatic mission* preying on his mind? An extraneous mission with this Recon guide . . . He felt the chill start in his gut, fought it back desperately.

*Oh dear God, make them leave me alone. Let me get this over with and back into space. I want to go back to Vandereaux. I'm not one of Them . . .*

The intercom buzzed and Dr. McKenna's voice summoned him impatiently, asking Where he'd been and Why the hell hadn't he answered his calls? Stephen tapped the button which acknowledged the call and headed for the door.

*. . . not anymore.*

# III

## i

The *Cetacean* drifted slowly out of view as the shuttle eased free of the core docking bay, its gentle thrust giving the passengers at least an illusion of direction if not real weight. Here and there on the vast bulk of the cruiser, patches of outside lights, like stars shining on the outer edge of some dense nebula, marked active repair stations.

As they rose slowly from the core, the blue and white crescent which marked their destination appeared beyond the outer rimway's dark curve: sharp contrast which hurt his tired eyes. Stephen felt a momentary twinge, a nervous tick in his stomach, but fought it back and concentrated on the friendly stars beyond that planet.

"Here you are."

He turned from the viewport and gratefully accepted the covered mug Adm. Cantrell handed him. She slipped her own into the magslot in the armrest before sinking gently into her seat. Such slow motion belonged in a training gym; it didn't conform with cramped cabins and contour seats.

"You okay?" she asked.

"Fine," he lied, forcing a smile past frozen lips. "Thanks."

Cupping both hands about the mug, he sipped the hot tea and wondered whether the insulated mug was really that efficient or if his fingers were nerve-dead. His hands started shaking, and despite his efforts to control it, the shiver spread rapidly to the rest of his body. *Good thing the mug is covered*, he thought absently, *or we'd be chasing tea all over the cabin*.

He felt the seat shift as the admiral pushed off again, heard the door slide open behind him. More than likely she was seeing to some other business in the main passenger section of the shuttle. He'd never been around her during normal working hours and she was constantly being called on for one thing or another.

It was all very confusing to his present state of mind. —But then, solving a two-dimensional differential equation would be confusing to his present state of mind.

He sighed and sipped the tea.

Differentials, hell. He couldn't add two and two. Just as well he was tucked away in this small, private cabin; wouldn't do to have Cantrell's crew know she was delivering a brain-dead researcher to the 'Tank below.

Soft, prewarmed folds drifted down around him; competent hands tucked the blanket in against free-fall and the drop into the atmosphere. He didn't even twitch. Not in surprise, not at the unexpected touch. If he weren't so tired, he'd bother to be amazed. Maybe Dr. McKenna's witch's brew had killed every nerve in his body. If only it had been as efficient elsewhere—

—Like his head.

The tremors gradually diminished, and he turned his head carefully to face Cantrell, his stomach not being equal to abrupt changes in focus this morning.

"Thanks again, admiral. Sorry."

She examined him closely. "Are you sure you don't want some breakfast?"

"God! Don't even mention it!" He closed his eyes, pressed a knuckle to his mouth as his abused stomach heaved. He gulped tea, burning his tongue but startling his stomach into more civilized behavior.

If only Dr. McKenna hadn't insisted on those scans before she'd renew his Reglamytrin prescription . . . and *then* given him a short bottle and threatened to go to the admiral with the results of those tests if he didn't promise to report back to her as soon as he returned to the ship . . .

No way those tests proved anything. That poison she'd made him drink was enough to make anyone's insides object.

Maybe by the time he returned, McKenna would have forgotten the whole thing. Blasted rule-following prig. Why should she care? The academy doctors had simply put him on a refill-as-required at the pharmacy. It was an old problem and none of her damned business.

And certainly none of the admiral's.

But at least they talked about him coming back.

He sipped the tea, thinking of those last few moments before boarding, of Chet Hamilton waiting for them at the lift that would take them to the core-docking. Of himself, stumbling off the 'mover behind the admiral and Dr. McKenna . . .

*("Well, kid, you ready to face our favorite Wormer?"*

*(A flash of resentment. That and his terror at the upcoming flight momentarily overcoming his awe of this man. A steady, "Sir, if I might have a word with you in private?"*

*(A glance passing between Cantrell and Hamilton. A shrug, a motion with the head drew him away from the others.*

*(Himself, tongue-tied, trying to keep his tea and dry toast in his stomach where it belonged. Hamilton growing impatient and turning away.In desperation: "Sir! Please, can you tell me— What should I— Is there—" Hamilton faced about expectantly. "P—please, sir, is there anything I shouldn't say to S—Smith? Any subjects—a—any questions I sh–shouldn't—")*

. . . and Hamilton smiling—laughing at him, but for manners: "Say anything you like, kid. Won't make any difference one way or the other. Go down and have a good time."

What had he meant by that? That a 'LinkMan couldn't know enough to do any damage or comprehend anything of consequence? Or possibly that his chances with the 'NetAT were already so screwed, nothing he did now would affect them? Or did Hamilton mean he should find out everything he could, no matter what?

*But does that mean he believes I'll be able to explain it afterwards?*

He shivered again—a chill that started deep in his gut and reached up to paralyze his throat.

"Really did it up properly last night, did you?" the admiral said, a smile in her voice. "Funny. I've never known you to get even slightly—"

"It's not my f–fault! It's the d–damned *cocktails* Dr. McKenna—gave m–m–m— Oh, —*shit!*"

The mug spun off wildly, scattering tea droplets everywhere, as he reached frantically for his pocket buried beneath the blanket. Tangling his hand in blanket, seatbelt and jacket, he searched for the bottle McKenna had handed him not twenty minutes before.

He didn't quite make it, but Adm. Cantrell was there, one hand on his shoulder steadying him—

—the other holding the vacbag.

* * *

*HuteEtu drifted through the trees to lie, mottled and golden, in the arms of his lover, Yoluta, who . . .*

"Oh dear," Anevai Tyeewapi sighed as a toski-bug lighted on the flower in front of her nose. "I'm afraid what we have here is a lover's triangle."

A second sigh. She rose to her knees, tucking her notebook away in a back pocket. "I'll never get it right, now."

Ruthlessly plucking the perfect flower from its patch of sunlight, she added it to the pile already in the basket, then watched the blue-spotted insect flit away on the spring breeze. "Mmmm. Fickle, fickle lover, Lady Yoluta. You must settle for old Etu after all."

A screaming boom shattered the morning quiet. Atmospheric entry.

*Oh, shee-it.* Anevai glanced skyward, then at her watch. It was later than she thought. Dad would have her hide if she missed the landing.

Because this time Adm. Cantrell *herself* was coming down. Adm. Cantrell was personally shepherding a new researcher. A new researcher who was so fragile he had to have a personal escort to keep the big bad Recons away from him.

Shee-it. Such an *honor! —Such a delight!—*

—Such a hassle.

She grabbed the basket, flipped the lid and headed toward home at the ground-eating pace she could hold for hours, trusting moccasined feet to instinctively adjust to the irregularities of rocks and winding roots in the path.

She had at least an hour before she *had* to be at the spaceport. She could leave the flowers for Benah—she'd know what to do with them. That would leave her time for a shower and a quick—

The basket went tumbling as a flying body tackled her from the side. The next instant, she found herself flat on her back with a very sharp knife at her throat and a very large, very heavy, shadow between her and the sun.

"Better work on those reflexes, *olathe.* Your next attacker might not be quite so friendly." At which the shadow began getting friendly indeed.

Never one to ignore sensible instructions, she brought her knees up in a move not as *un*friendly as might have been and rolled the shadow over her shoulder, coming to her feet and taking possession of his knife in one swift movement—a movement *he'd* taught her.

"You've got a lot of nerve, *friend*. If just one flower's bruised, you're going to replace it! Cantrell's shuttle's coming in and I've got exactly forty-five minutes to get to the airport."

Nayati Hatawa, still sprawled in the dirt, grinned up at her, raised a finger and sneered, "Who cares? Let the spacers fend for themselves for once."

"Pro-to-col."

The grin changed to a scowl as Nayati gathered himself up off the ground. "Protocol be hanged," he growled, brushing at his backside. "Tell them to go—"

"Drop it, Nayati. We've more than enough trouble without adding your brand of insult to the fire. Besides . . ." She flipped him the knife; he caught and sheathed it without taking his eyes from her. "I'm liaison for the new researcher."

Nayati snorted. "If he's a researcher, I'm from Alpha—"

"Yeah, right. He's a spy. Nayati, why don't you give it up? Why should they bother? We're new, we're quiet. Let's keep it that way."

"I still don't like it. What did Smith say about him? Checked his stats, didn't he?"

"I don't know exactly. Hono was there when Wes looked up the records, but he was arrested before I could talk with him. I haven't talked with Wes—haven't seen hide nor hair of him for the last couple of days, actually."

"Maybe you should have found out before you volunteered to be the spy's escort."

"I *didn't volunteer!* And quit calling him a spy when you don't know anything about him."

"I know SecOne cruisers don't shuttle researchers to and fro for the hell of it."

"And *how* would you know? Besides, it's not just delivering this Ridenour. They're doing some records checks and I—"

"What sort of records?"

"*I* don't know! Something's screwed up on the 'Net, and this Adm. Cantrell asked to look over some originals. It happens, Nayati."

Nayati looked decidedly ill at ease. She hadn't paid much attention to her father last night.

Maybe she should have.

"I've got to get a move on. Calling a Warrior meeting?"

"Yes."

"When?"

"Tonight. In the barn."

"Fine. See you." Rescuing the basket, she turned to go.

"Annie!"

She froze and glared back at him. "Don't call me that. You know I hate it."

He shrugged. "I heard from Hononomii this morning."

"*You* heard from him? Why didn't you say something sooner? Is he all right? Why did he call you? *How?*"

"Via the WinTap." Nayati's voice was grim. Justifiably so: the 'Tap was for emergency only use. Especially with the Alliance ship in-system. "Tell your father he's . . . gone. You'll hear the rest tonight along with the others."

"Gone? Gone how? Nayati, what's happened?"

"I said I'd tell you the rest tonight. Just tell your father not to trust this Adm. Cantrell any farther than he can throw her."

The wicker handle bent in her fist. "You can't expect me to leave it at that. He's my brother. *What's happened?*"

"Settle down, woman. He'll be all right. We've just got to get him back."

*"Gone how, dammit?"* But Nayati remained stubbornly silent. She pressed her lips together and turned to go. Sounded more like another of Nayati's numbers. Just like him to drop an implication like that and not explain it—and lately he'd say anything to get the Warriors' Society fired up against the Alliance. How bad could Hononomii be if he'd managed to get at—and use—a base to contact Nayati? And of course he'd use the 'Tap if he didn't want everyone aboard the ship to know he was calling.

"And, Ah-nehv-'ai."

She stopped and scowled at him over her shoulder.

"Make sure the new guy sees you leave tonight."

"Whatever for?"

"Just do it!"

She opened her mouth to protest, then flung her hands up in disgust. "I've got to go."

"Scuze me." The admiral reached past Stephen to flip the cover up on the window, and light flooded into the cabin. He winced away, squinting. "First time down, you don't want to miss."

"Don't I?"

She grinned broadly at him: "Trust me."

He shuddered—not entirely in jest—glanced back at the window only to wince again at the brightness. He fumbled in his carry-on kit for the dark glasses the admiral had handed him before they left *Cetacean—What are these for? Trust me, Stationer-lad, you'll need them!*—and with a deep breath, he took his first look.

A single glance, at which his stomach heaved in protest. He closed his eyes—fought nausea while his brain registered what he'd seen. It was no different from vids. He could think of it that way, framed as the view was by the port.

Cautiously, he opened his eyes again—

—on a lush, green and blue surface white-stippled with clouds, on textures and colors no holo could reproduce.

But those textures and colors weren't right. *They weren't right!*

Stephen gasped as reds and golds overlaid greens and blues in a dizzying, fractured mosaic. He removed the glasses and rubbed at his eyes, startled when his hand came away damp.

Adm. Cantrell said something to him, but he couldn't hear through the roaring in his ears. Her hand on his arm shocked him back to the present and he said quickly: "I was dizzy for a moment. It was the height . . ."

She smiled, said something about 'getting used to it' and 'over soon.' He muttered a noncommittal answer, and turned back to the window, forcing the disturbing image into out-of-focus blur. . . .

Final approach, a few hundred meters above the highest snow-covered peaks and dropping rapidly. Their flight-path headed them over rugged foothills to the lush, green valley where the landing field was located.

Stephen grasped the armrests until his fingers ached. What had been harmless-looking wrinkles and folds of velvety green and brown were growing with each passing moment into larger and sharper rocks and crevices.

Studying and believing the theory of flight was one thing. Trusting that theory to keep you from falling into very solid-looking mountains, which until now had also been highly theoretical planetary geology, was quite another matter.

A hand patted his. He glanced around and encountered an understanding look on a face which, for a moment, he couldn't recognize. . . .

*(His notebook and bag cutting into trembling hands. Himself pressing into the corner of seat and wall, certain he would get in someone's way the instant he moved. The crew rushing about the cabin, checking systems, stowing unidentified packets in the overheads, pulling equally strange things out.*

*(Tears gathering in his eyes, blurring the images but not allowed to fall. Mama had left him at the Spaceport and told him to do as he was told. To be good and use the brain the good Lord gave him, because she and Papa were going somewhere he couldn't. And now he was in Space—he knew that because he'd watched his home shrink outside his window and turn into a strange round thing—where Mama and Papa couldn't come.*

*(I'm trying, Mama. I'm trying to be good, but they haven't told me anything. Maybe no one remembers I'm here. Maybe no one can see me anymore. Mama, am I an Invisible and you didn't want me to know?*

*(Is that why you sent me away?)*

White against blue against white. Iridescent gleam of heat-shielding.

The shuttle drifted elegantly through broken clouds, sleek, sweeping lines different from ordinary jets or their own station's clunky cargo shuttles. Moments before touchdown, the stabilizers glided forward into landing config, making her outline less alien but no less beautiful.

If it weren't for the presence of the Alliance Security designation on the shuttle's side, Anevai would have welcomed this opportunity to stand by her distinguished father and greet the visitors. As it was, all she felt was bitterness and resentment.

The craft eased to a precise, on the marks—military—stop. The Alliance Security force might *claim* to be a 'police agency' rather than military, but she'd sure like to know where they made the distinction. Their own Tribal police would never bring a ship in like that. No Tunican police officer would stand at attention while waiting for the hatch to open and the gangway to extend.

Police officers were loose. Relaxed. Friendly. People you could go to when it was late and the tubes were down, to get a lift home so the parents wouldn't skin you alive.

They didn't arrest VOSsy dreamers like Hononomii and drag them into space and leave them there.

These men of Cantrell's made her nervous. They were fighters—like Nayati was a fighter. Quiet movers. Friendly. And always *on*. Just because formally declared war in space hadn't existed for centuries didn't mean there was no army. And while the ship floating somewhere above them might not be called a 'warship,' it carried more firepower than any planet could boast. Not an army—?

It made her teeth ache.

And because of this non-military peace-loving admiral's arrival, the whole place felt like a mausoleum. To 'avoid further incidents,' her father had ordered the east terminal closed for the duration of *Cetacean's* presence insystem. For the admiral's convenience he'd shunted all regular traffic to the other side of the city—never mind the convenience of a quarter of a million *Dineh*.

"*Nituna*, have you the schedules and the lists of equipment and personnel the admiral requested?" Sakiimagan Tyeewapi's voice resonated through her thoughts, shattering them into a thousand brittle pieces and pulling her back to the business at hand. *Nituna*: 'eldest daughter.' (Never mind she was his *only* daughter.) So, formal-mode had begun.

"Yes, father, it's all here," she said, patting the briefcase in her hand and echoing his formal Voice as best she could. Not an easy skill, but a valuable one to learn.

"Is Dr. Ridenour's suite ready?"

"Yes, father."

He said, without taking his eyes off the parked shuttle, "It would be best if his check-in happened to be delayed. His specialty, if the 'Net is to be believed, is the ComNet itself—"

She glanced at her father in surprise. "A 'NetTech?" Why, if she was supposed to watchdog him, hadn't anybody bothered to tell her that? Or was that *why* her father had flung this task her way? "Did you want me to—"

He frowned, the slightest tension between his straight black brows. "Your job is to guide him, Anevai, to keep him out of trouble, not to question his veracity."

So much for parental confidence. "So you want Wes to check him out before he turns him loose on the system?"

The frown line eased. "Precisely. And since Dr. Smith is discussing the current situation with the department heads this morning, he won't be available until later."

And they all knew what *current situation* he was talking about. She asked, formality slipping, "Dad, can't we do something to get Hono back? He didn't do anything. And he's *your* son. Doesn't that count for anything?"

"He did indeed 'do something,' Anevai. He did a very stupid something." Sakiimagan's tone, his impassive face, belied the criticism: in some ways, she suspected, he was proud of his son's actions. *If*, on the other hand, it had been his *daughter* who had willfully attacked a security officer, she'd have been on bread and water for a week. "But he didn't hurt anyone, and I have every confidence we will get him back—*if* we do nothing to antagonize this Cantrell, and *if* we raise no further suspicions."

"But Nayati says—"

"I fail to see how Nayati can know anything for certain, but he said himself that Hononomii will—and I quote what you told me—'be all right.' If that's the case, we would do best to work within this Cantrell's realm and not encourage her to investigate *ours* more deeply. The best way for us to get Hononomii back is to be cooperative and get the admiral's authority working with us, not against us. According to Paul, she could be a powerful ally if we don't alienate her. Do I make myself clear, *nituna?*"

*Dr. Paul's been here twenty years*, she thought. *How well can he really know her after all that time?* But she closed her mouth firmly on another protest. "Perfectly, father. —Will you come to the meeting tonight?"

"I'm certain my presence will be required with our guests." He smiled down at her. "You will be my surrogate in your brother's absence. Nayati may be over-reacting to Hononomii's incarceration, but he's nothing you can't handle." His near eye narrowed: a half-wink. "I doubt I shall be disappointed."

"I'll do my best, father," she said, Dutiful Daughter. Blast it, she was nineteen 'NetStan—*twenty* planetary—and any way you looked at it—legally, physically, or emotionally—an adult. Her father had a hard time seeing that, especially with mum gone . . . . but as soon as the *Cetacean* people left, mum'd be back and things could get back to normal.

She shifted her weight to ease an itch in one foot. As soon as *Cetacean* left: that couldn't happen too soon for her.

Adm. Cantrell had disappeared into the rear section the instant the shuttle touched down and he was feeling ridiculously low— abandoned: silly remnant of that long-forgotten nightmare.

*Don't be an idiot, Ridenour*, he chided himself. *You're no kid, and Loren Cantrell sure as hell isn't your mama.*

He cast another glance out the window, thought between one blink and the next that he saw a blond-haired man running toward them, but there were only the two indigenes waiting on the tarmac: according to Adm. Cantrell, the governor and his daughter.

He searched the terminal for a glimpse of Someone Else. Another, far more recent memory whispered in his mind's ear: *You know, 'Buster-boy, you're writing your own death sentence. Those 'busters will know exactly what you are. Like recognizes like. Once that secret's out, no way Smith will even talk to you.*

A wave of sheer terror blackened his vision. When it cleared, he thrust that memory back into the pit where it belonged. Whatever else he might or might not be, he wasn't *like* those two standing calmly in that blinding sunlight.

*Grow up, fool! Pull yourself together, and quit sitting here like a useless lump!*

He folded and stored the blanket, set Adm. Cantrell's personal kit as well as his own on the seat beside him, and by the time the admiral returned from the main cabin, had completely restored his composure.

She nodded approval and held out a steadying hand as he stood up in the cramped quarters and circulation began returning to his legs.

"Sorry to desert you, Stephen. Good old George-in-the-station. Remind me to tell you all about it later. You'll be— Scuze me."

She brushed against him as Briggs and Lexi squeezed past her to pull their own personal packs from the overhead. He staggered, catching himself on the seat. The admiral's hand on his arm kept him from falling, a jerk which shook the sunglasses down on his nose.

He grunted softly. "—Heavy."

"You will be. I told you to work out in GPlus. Gravity here's a bit over Standard and you've lived most of your life at nine-tenths at Vandereaux Academy. I tried to warn you.''

"You might have said *why*."

She grinned and patted his back. "Then? —Don't worry. You'll be fine. I've been watching you work out: you'll acclimate. All right now?''

He swallowed hard, nodded reluctantly, feeling those extra kilos stressing at every joint with every move. He jammed the glasses back onto his nose and gripped the handle of his safe-case firmly as he followed her through the door.

He certainly *would* be fine—

—and back on the shuttle within the week.

## ii

The security guard at the doorway stiffened as a tall, erect figure emerged from the shuttle. *Finally!* Anevai thought, and wiggled her toes. Real soon now she'd get to move and the pesky itch would go away.

The admiral, it could be no one else, negotiated the steps with the easy grace of someone who had made the transition to planetary gravity many times before. Tunica Air & Space had perfectly good covered gangways, but her father preferred not to use them for incoming spacers. He was proud of the view their mountains afforded and particularly delighted in sharing it.

The admiral better appreciate it or she could bloody well turn about and go back to her cold empty space.

And the same went for the man following her down the steps. Anevai took note of that anything-but-cavalier grip on the railing, the way the two security guards closed in on either side of him as he stumbled across the tarmac, and looked hopefully back to the shuttle's door. But no one else appeared.

—Which meant the admiral's skinny, awkward shadow had to be Ridenour.

*On the other hand*, she thought, working hard to be charitable, *maybe he isn't clumsy. Maybe he's just been sick*—

—*And maybe*, (as he came to a swaying halt in front of them, a step behind the admiral) *he's drunk.*

"Adm. Cantrell, we are honored," Sakiimagan said, State-occasion formal. "Though we regret the circumstances which precipitated your coming, let us hope their resolution will require a minimum expenditure of your time, and give us ample opportunity to share our world with you."

"A pleasure, Governor Tyeewapi." The Recon name rolled smoothly off Cantrell's tongue.

*That's one for you, admiral*, she thought.

"And this—" With a sweeping, all-inclusive gesture. "—is even more impressive than the vids. Thank you—" Cantrell turned back to them with a wide, friendly smile. "—for arranging the weather. The flight down was spectacular."

*That's two*. She found herself grinning back and quickly straightened her expression—*not* before the admiral caught it and gave a half-wink in her direction.

Cantrell said to her father: "For the most part, my time is at HuteNamid's disposal. I am here to clear up some discrepancies in the records, but I'd like to take the opportunity to discuss with you any needs you might have—to open a dialogue, if you will, between the Alliance Council and HuteNamid."

Anevai's foot began to itch again. Formality upon formality. Everyone saying the proper thing, everyone meaning something else. She wanted to get past all this and on to the business of Hononomii's arrest and release. Not, as her father had pointed out, that the tode didn't deserve to be arrested. But he'd better be all right.

Cantrell stepped to one side, drawing her stumbling shadow up beside her. "May I present Dr. Stephen Ridenour?"

The spacer stood rigidly, hands clasped behind his back, a frozen smile on his lips. Extremely dark glasses obscured much of his pale-skinned face, making it difficult to judge his age and impossible to guess his thoughts.

Anevai hated sunglasses.

"Dr. Ridenour's a recent graduate of Vandereaux Academy—"

*Recent graduate? Fairly young, then—and Vandereaux? Not bad, not bad at all. Wonder if Wesley knows. High amusement potential there.*

"—Echelon-four."

*A fourth? Maybe not so young after all. Probably a return engagement for an academic upgrade.*

"Top of the top ten." Cantrell finished, obviously expecting to impress them, but no TT10 'NetTech was ever released to a

'Tank—they were all snatched up by the 'NetAT. And TT10 would indicate he *had* just graduated—to fourth. But that was impossible. So what was he really? And what sort of fools did Cantrell think she was dealing with.

But a spy? Spies had *believable* credentials. Spies had to blend in. Spies had to be able to protect themselves. This Ridenour couldn't stand upright, let alone protect himself, and no self-respecting spy would blush bright red at his introduction. But if Cantrell was telling the truth, why didn't the 'NetAT want him?

Her father extended his hand. "Welcome to HuteNamid, Dr. Ridenour. Your presence brings us honor, and your care will be our duty and our pleasure."

Perhaps some people wouldn't have noticed that slight hesitation before the spacer accepted her father's greeting, or the jerk with which Ridenour pulled away from the handshake, but she did. Her father undoubtedly did.

Recon Contamination. She'd heard of spacer prejudices before, but never thought anything of it, certainly never run up against it before: their researchers were here because they wanted to be here. Ridenour patently did not. So why was he? What was wrong with him?

*And why're we stuck with him?*

Her father, of course, said nothing. Did nothing except courteously extend the introduction to his daughter. And she, with superb control, determined she would *not* break this Dr. Ridenour's hand should he try the same with her.

To her vast disappointment, he gave magnanimity no opportunity: she sensed no hesitation this time in his cool nod of acknowledgment, but no warmth, either. *Too fine to touch us, are you? Well,* that *will get cured in a hurry.*

*And those sunglasses have got to go!*

Cantrell exhibited all the affability her tight-assed recruit lacked. "Anevai, is it?" she repeated the name carefully, as though imprinting it on her memory, and then she smiled. A nice smile. Warm. Friendly. Like dad's. "I read about your *ko'sii* breeding program in the reports. How's it progressing? Has the baby arrived yet?"

Anevai wondered if that similarity should appease or concern. "I'm honored, admiral. It certainly has: a healthy little boy."

"Congratulations! I look forward to seeing it. —But first, governor, we've some business to discuss. I don't like to rush things, but we've got a hold on the 'Net we'd like to get off as soon as possible. If the technical people turn up any problem, I might need to return to the ship tomorrow morning, and I'd like to make a good beginning on our work here. Were you able to gather those records I requested?''

Anevai handed her father the briefcase, and he said, "Thank you, *nituna*. I will take Adm. Cantrell to the office we've set aside, where she can review these in comfort. Why don't you help Dr. Ridenour get checked in and settled.'' He paused ever so briefly, and added, "Should there be time, introduce him around. If there is not, this afternoon—or even tonight, should he care to rest—will be soon enough. I trust he will be with us for a long time to come.'' And to Cantrell: "If you will come with me?''

Stephen drew a breath as they entered the low terminal building, and pressed Lexi's arm gratefully. She winked, then deserted him to join Briggs behind Cantrell.

They took the lift down to the Transport Terminal as a group, but drifted apart on the waiting ramp: the admiral's party was headed for the governmental offices in the city, while he and this—young woman—were headed in the opposite direction to the Science Research Complex: the 'Tank itself. To where Smith was—or should be.

The terminal was strangely silent. They'd seen only a few service individuals in the corridor, and this waiting area was completely vacant. He tried not to stare, tried not to show his unease, but it wasn't easy. Was it always like this? Where were the people?

He shuddered and turned his gaze toward the indigene girl who was looking him up and down, openly contemptuous now the others had left them. He fought embarrassment with righteous anger. Dammitall, he'd *tried*, and not done too badly until he'd been fool enough to look up—and seen mountains rising behind the terminal buildings.

Walking along that flat, no-curvature expanse of concrete had been the hardest thing he'd ever done—harder than any move in the gym. Instincts screamed he was walking down an increasingly steep ramp, but the gravity lied and lied until, finally, he simply shut his eyes and allowed Lexi to steer him the final few steps.

But Lexi was gone now, or would be as soon as the transport bubbles arrived. From here on out, *fourth-echelon Dr. Ridenour* would have to make do with his own two feet.

Fourth-echelon: God! Where had that come from? And *TT10?* He *couldn't* be. Surely she couldn't lie about something so easily verified. But if the Council had awarded him that rank to impress the locals, could they as quickly rescind it afterwards? Even with it already on the 'Net?

*Of course they could*, he thought glumly. *And give me the task of tracking down all references to that standing, everywhere it might have infiltrated, and addendizing each and every one.*

The girl was speaking to him. He shook the progwuzzles and said, "I'm sorry. I—"

"Wasn't listening," she interrupted him abruptly. "I've met your kind before." The words, the tone were rude, but she was half-smiling, as though amused, which left him thoroughly confused. The bubblecar floated to a silent stop in front of them, its door rising automatically, and her follow-up, as she stepped into the gently-bobbing car, only confounded him further: "Not a person in the whole damn SciCorps ever hears a practical question. You'll fit right in, Ridenour!"

With no advance warning, the bubblecar burst into sunlight. Erosion-etched rock strung with sparkling rivulets—run-off from last night's big storm—spring greens popping up in every pocket: the three-kilometer-wide Great Rift stretched out before and around them in all its rugged glory. Down in the valley, far beyond the landing field, orchards glowed pink, yellow, and white.

Gods, she loved this land! She'd visited cities all over HuteNamid, seen deserts and the oceans of water and tall grasses, but *none* of them compared with her mountains.

She'd chosen the scenic, above-ground route purposely. Slower, it fit in with her father's request to delay the new man, but more importantly, it gave her a chance to show off the beauty of her home. —And from the gasp at her side, her tactics were succeeding admirably.

She glanced eagerly over at Ridenour—she didn't really *want* to dislike him: she spent too much of her time at SciComp for that—but he faced straight forward, tight-lipped and clench-jawed. The dark glasses prevented her from seeing his eyes, but she'd lay odds they were focussed on the panel in front of them—not the view.

Phlegmatic tode. So much for special effects.

So she tried the hard way: pointing out man-made landmarks, things which should impress even spacer aesthetics. Below them, Tunica: the capital city, with its elegant interlacing of condominiums and kivas built on the valley floor by the river and butting up against the north wall; the twin towers: governmental offices where her father and the admiral had gone, rising above the central amphitheater; the Amphitheater itself, its clear dome, like those of the smaller kivas, invisible at this distance; ahead and above, the Researcher Condos and Science Complex, built onto and over the edge of the cliff-face. But the spacer seemed singularly unimpressed. Didn't even turn his head to look.

Definitely a tode.

She tried pointing out the best views, nature-created landmarks, some of her favorite spots: the Eagle's Beak, her personal haven on the cliff, though she didn't tell him that; the Zaltana Mountain Range to the west, source of the river which cut the rift itself; the Bridge to the Sun, spanning the rift's narrowest point.

Wasted effort. Ridenour sat statue still, his bony hands gripping his silly briefcase as though he expected her to snatch it away from him. Under the glasses, his spacer-white face remained blank, the irregular rise and fall of the Adam's apple in his skinny neck all that moved. And if not for that patently insincere apology at the station she'd swear he was mute.

So she quit trying and sat filing her nails and grinding her teeth until they glided into the SciComp terminal, where she announced like some adVid tour guide: "Here we are. Tunica Science Complex Administration, end of the tour. Everybody out."

Still he didn't move. She shrugged apologetically in the direction of the people waiting in the terminal.

"Well, c'mon, Ridenour, there're folks needing the bubble. Tube's been shut down for the last half-hour—all for you." She gripped his arm, gave it a shake. "C'mon, man, move it."

He jerked violently away, muttering, "Keep your hands off me!"

*So you* do *have a voice, CodeHead*, she thought, thinking also where she'd like to grab him and what she'd like to do with him once she had him. Instead, with admirable restraint and a plastered-on smile, she crooned, ''Anything you say, Ridenour. Just kindly get your butt out of this car before I kick it out.''

He muttered something she couldn't hear, but he stood up, staggering as the car bobbed, then climbed stiffly out onto the platform.

She followed on his heels, ready to perform introductions, but Ridenour brushed past the waiting group without even a Sorry for the delay. or Hi, how are you? and strode toward the inner hallway.

''*Ridenour!*'' she called sharply after his retreating backside, but he didn't even pause. Raising her hands in frustration, she turned to the group, one of whom—dammit—was Dr. Paul, his meeting with Wesley evidently over.

The tall, silver-haired researcher gazed after the tode, then asked mildly, ''That the new one?''

''Yeah. Sorry 'bout his manners.''

He grinned down at her. ''What can you expect? He's A-ca-de-my. You'll straighten him out. I have confidence in you.''

''Yeah, well, if I don't, someone else sure as hell will.'' And thinking of who that someone would likely be: ''Is the Wesser in his office?''

''No. He's off sulking. Good thing for Ridenour: the mood Wesley was in, that at-ti-tude would probably get him royally wessed at the moment.''

''Sulking? What's *his* problem?''

''He's pissed as hell at the entire situation; particularly at the 'Net being taken down. Everybody's on his case for information location and he's screaming for time to do his own work.''

''Can't really blame him.'' She looked reluctantly toward the corridor. ''I'd better go before the CodeHead gets lost. See you later.''

She headed after her irritating charge. He'd better have a good excuse or by God, she'd give him one.

With a stifled sob of relief, Stephen located the restrooms. He pushed through the swinging doors, barely made it to a stall in time. He couldn't believe there was anything left to come up. Maybe he was turning inside out.

He certainly felt like it.

The water swirled away in a dizzying rush that was easier on his senses than the trip here. The terrifying flight down couldn't begin to compare with the horror of dodging at breakneck speed through rocks and trees in a tiny, crystal clear compartment. Even narrowing his focus to the bubble's control panel, the peripheral chaos had come close to overwhelming his inner ear.

Several minutes later, his face tingling from cold water, his stomach settled by McKenna's little pills, he exited the restroom to:

"Couldn't hold it long enough for a polite Excuse me? We use better manners here, Spacer-man, and you damn well better remember it."

He clenched his fist on the precious safe-case, and breathed deeply, cultivating serenity. "Shall we get on with the check-in?"

She snorted and headed down the corridor. "Keep it up. You're making points real fast, Spacer-man. C'mon, then. Move your tail."

Only in the remotest sense did this so-called Reconstructionist city resemble any Amerind records Lexi had pulled off the 'Net. The subtle earth tones that lent a warmth to strictly geometric designs; the tapestries on the walls and rugs underfoot—so exquisite one wanted to walk around rather than across them—echoed without duplicating the styles and motifs in those records.

Most recognizable were the hand-thrown pots in which native plants flourished. Lexi's own parents had been potters of no small skill; she herself had tended the kilns many a long hot afternoon. She knew quality when she saw it, and hoped she could somehow afford a small sample to send home—if the indigenes were willing to sell. No matter it might take years, 'NetStandard, to reach her parents: it would be worth it—particularly if she could also talk these Tunican potters out of the secrets of their glazes, maybe send some local samples of that as well.

But she wondered at the lack of information on the tapes. Why weren't the Tunicans exporting? It was a well developed style. The plants—if she recognized them correctly from the survey tapes—were years old, so it wasn't a recently discovered art. HuteNamid's colonies could be rich beyond imagining if there was more than one individual or group producing these, considering what *HomoSpatialis* were willing to spend for the most *mediocre* Recon products.

Lexi shook her head and joined the admiral and TJ as they followed Governor Tyeewapi up an open, curving staircase. Twenty minutes ago, this routing might have surprised her, but not now. If Tunica had one single-level building, she hadn't seen it, and while this office building had a perfectly adequate lift system, it must be mainly for service. The stairwells were full of people headed in both directions quickly, courteously and with frequent, friendly exchanges.

Architects had worked hard to make this open stairway a showpiece: intricately carved banisters to either side, knot-work hangings on the interior walls, and sculptures on every landing brought the shapes and colors of the outside in. Large windows looking out across the multi-unit dwellings, office buildings, shops, and restaurants that were Tunica completed the illusion.

Like all those in view, this building, for all its clean lines and state-of-the-art man-made materials, unquestionably *belonged* here, on this one planet, in this one valley. It *felt* as though the very fabric of HuteNamid itself had risen from the ground to form the city.

And for all its beauty, it was wrong. Significantly wrong.

At the administration tower receptionist's desk the governor's secretary, Winona Wichado, greeted them with what seemed unfeigned pleasure. The receptionist checked them in with that same friendly ease, and registered their Bios and IDs in the building system so, Wichado said, they could come and go at their leisure.

That attitude seemed the norm here, Anevai Tyeewapi's behavior with Stephen aside. Everyone they had chance-met—a mixed group the transport had picked up partway to Tunica, individuals waiting in the terminal below—had seemed genuinely at ease in the admiral's presence.

The governor led them through a minimal security door, (which rated a disapproving look from TJ) and up the lift several floors to a spacious office with large picture windows overlooking the city. *Not* a place for a person with acrophobia: these Tunicans liked their views.

"Is that the Science Complex, governor?" Cantrell asked, pointing to buildings rising out and over the rift's edge.

"Yes, it is, admiral. The view from there is quite spectacular."

"I can imagine . . ."

So could Lexi. She hoped Stephen's Equilib prescription lasted the week.

Stephen gulped and turned away from the wall of windows to the comparative comfort of the SciCorps Admin offices waiting room. All his academy life he'd longed to be surrounded by windows—now he had them, and instead of the stars he'd been promised, he had rocks. —*Lots* of rocks. Lots of very sharp, very hard, very far-down-a-cliff rocks.

He paced the waiting room, carefully avoiding that wall of windows facing out over the rift. Could he have grown up around such cliffs? Perhaps been able to stare at such perspectives with impunity once? He shuddered to even think of it. He remembered so very little of his world of origin: that was part of the *before* Dr. Danislav had told him to forget.

*Spacer-man*, indeed. His classmates at the academy would be amused at that. *On the other hand*, he thought dourly, *perhaps amused isn't quite the correct term.*

So much for Bijan's dire predictions of his early exposure. He felt *no* sense of recognition; not to the environment, *certainly* not to that—female he'd been encumbered with.

He glanced toward the office into which the planet-buster had disappeared at least ten minutes ago. What could be taking so long? The admiral had assured him she'd completed the necessary paperwork. So his 'temporary transfer' was official, and he was stuck here—for all his admittedly unrealistic hopes of walking into Smith's office, completing his inquiry in a few brilliant, inspired moments, and being back on the return shuttle tomorrow morning.

But unrealistic or not, meeting Smith soon now would be—nice.

He glanced around for a clock, caught the windows before he remembered, gulped and closed his eyes. Very soon. Please, God, very *very* soon.

"I trust you will be comfortable in here, admiral. If there is anything else we can get for you . . ."

Cantrell glanced around the large, conveniently-appointed office, then turned back to Sakiimagan Tyeewapi lingering at the door.

"Coffee?" And remembering TJ's addiction: "—with plenty of sugar, and then we should do nicely, governor, thank you."

Tyeewapi dipped his head. "My offices are down the hall, second left. This entire floor is administrative. Should you require anything else, Winona is at your disposal. If you will excuse me I'll order your coffee and attend to my own duties."

As the door closed behind him, Cantrell laid the briefcase on the desk, gave it an absentminded pat as she moved around to stand beside Lexi before the vast window.

"Dammit, it's not right." she said abruptly, to no one in particular.

"What's not right, Boss-lady?" TJ asked from the desk. He had the briefcase open and was already leafing through files.

Lexi said quietly, "It's the architecture, isn't it, admiral?"

"Yes." One hated to appear an overimaginative fool. Even with one's closest associates.

"Looks okay to me," TJ said, hard at work with the portable, comparing something in those printouts with secured 'NetAT records from the ship's 'Bank. "At least it's not going to fall down around our ears like that *thing* we slept in on Albion last time."

"Nothing wrong, just not right. Not utilitarian colonial, but not Recon either. It seems more an integral part of HuteNamid itself. As if it were native to *this* world—not to old Earth. And yet these people claim to be Recon."

"Admiral," Lexi said, "Tunica didn't appear anywhere in the 'Tank recruiting advertisements. The only visual references of HuteNamid anywhere in the 'Net are those original survey tapes. If they were to advertise even minimally, Recons—and possibly even researchers, much as I hate to reinforce Shapoorian's notions—would flock here. It's an architectural showplace *and* an environmental paradise. Far different than I expected. But aside from a few—I can only call them token—similarities, I'm not sure it corresponds to any Amerind file I pulled."

It was as though Tunica didn't care whether they attracted researchers or not: a self-defeating attitude, since their Alliance standing—and their funding—depended on the researchers' output.

Another reflection of young Hononomii's secessionist thinking? Don't advertise? Don't draw interest? Was it that simple?

Did they just want to keep the natural bounty for themselves? If so, how did the 'Tank feel about that attitude?

"I agree, Lexi," she said. "I don't know what I expected from those old RecVids you found: tepees and feathered headdresses, perhaps. It certainly wasn't this."

"Good lord. Now I've seen it all." TJ, propped on the edge of the desk now, had a datalog on his lap, a page of hardcopy in his hand.

"Well?" she demanded.

TJ looked up, a very strange expression on his face, and asked, "Any way you know of that someone can have two biological mothers?"

The sculpture that nearly filled this foyer was without question the most beautiful statue Stephen had ever seen—but then, it was the *only* statue he'd ever seen outside of ancient 'Net records, and he was damned sick of this one.

He threw himself down in a plush-cushioned chair, tossing the briefcase into a neighboring seat. With no one around to notice, he rubbed his shoulder, striving to ease stiffness. *You'd think*, he thought vaguely, daring to close his eyes on the empty room, *if I had to ruin a shoulder, I'd have had the sense to make it the right one.* A moment later he caught his head with a jerk as it fell backward toward the cushion. Shaking his head to clear it, he pulled himself from the chair: last thing he needed was to fall asleep *now*, with Smith so close.

Set out on a small reception table, coffee, tea, a variety of juices and foodstuffs. The Recon had waved a hand at them with a Help yourself. before disappearing through that door. His stomach made rude noises, but he ignored it and went for what he knew was safe.

But even the coffee tasted odd—good, but strange—so he swallowed a sudsie just in case. That would keep his stomach under control and keep *him* awake long enough.

Long enough to meet Smith.

God. The last thing he'd ever expected to be was a 'NetAT Del d'Bugger.

He remembered once asking an instructor *why* it was necessary to establish that solid, theoretical link to the past—was it necessary for the viability of the concept? or was it a political reason? The bored instructor had responded with: It's the Law.

Eventually, he'd figured out it was only fair that the person who had an idea should get credit for it and that the person who put a bunch of ideas together should get credit for putting them together, but not for thinking them up in the first place.

And he'd learned that money was involved. Lots of money. And that people got the money according to their contribution into the final product. The percentage they received was proportional to their input on the 'Net and, once a patent was involved, on the profits of the end product.

And at a somewhat wiser twenty-almost-one, he knew it was far bigger than economics and fair play—

—because the 'Net's NSpace DataBase was a mess; and false or erroneous data cost billions each year to index and addendize. The government employed 'NetTechs throughout the system full-time for that purpose alone, and the linkages grew more convoluted with each passing second. In one notorious instance, a fraudulent piece of research had proliferated so egregiously through the scientific community, it took one 'NetTech's entire career to track down the linkages. Someone caught *purposely* dumping fraudulent data onto the 'Net immediately graced the Alliance's Most Wanted list, and since you could no longer delete the programming or the data, you deleted the individuals responsible for them.

And that was what he was supposed to do to J. Wesley Smith.

Coffee spilled over his hand. He dropped the cup in the waste and blotted up the spill, trying to ignore his shaking hands. The napkins followed the cup and he grabbed up the briefcase.

Long enough. He headed for the office door, resolved on a straightforward assault—

—and stopped, baffled. No buttons, no monitors: how were you *supposed* to announce your presence?

He raised his hand to knock—

—and the door swung out, sending him staggering back into a solid carved-wood chair.

He'd forgotten: doors here didn't slide.

Anevai Tyeewapi's head appeared around the door, all wide-eyed innocence. "I thought I told you to wait over there."

Stephen glared at her, wondering if she'd known he was standing there. Wondering if in fact she'd been waiting for him to tire of waiting. Entrapments had been too common in his life for him to believe in coincidence now.

The girl shrugged and beckoned to him. "C'mon in, Spacerman."

### iii

*No one*, Anevai thought, hauling her annoying charge down to Admin's back exits, *no one, researcher or indigene, is worth putting up with this*.

Who needed the bit-brained prig, anyway? And if she was to make certain nobody else did to Stephen Ridenour what *she* wanted to do herself, who was going to protect him from her?

She supposed it hadn't been the nicest thing she'd ever done, leaving him cooling his heels for half an hour in the waiting room, but her father *had* said delay him. And she hadn't *meant* to hit him with the door; she'd just meant to open it before he got there so that he couldn't substantiate a complaint.

But then just because Lehni had . . . slowed . . . his processing a bit, feigning ignorance on certain procedures, the Code-Head had brushed Lehni away from the terminal, brought up the appropriate files in seconds, (hardly even checked a directory) then stepped oh-so-courteously aside to let Lehni fill in the blanks.

Now, like it or not, he was *going* to see his apartment over in the Researcher Condos. She and Nigan had worked hard getting Scot's stuff moved out and into his new house so that this Code-Head could have one of the big suites.

He'd better like it.

Ridenour was lagging behind. Again. She opened the back exit, sniffed fresh breeze, and waited for him to catch up.

And waited.

*Gods!* What if he'd decided to go find Wesley on his own?

She rushed back into the hall—

—and found him leaning against the wall, rubbing his eyes with one shaking hand, the glasses pushed askew, the briefcase on the floor by his feet.

His head came up and she caught a glimpse of pale, tired eyes before he pulled away from the wall and settled the glasses on his nose again. He rubbed his shoulder (not surprising: that briefcase thudded every time he set it down), picked up the briefcase and hurried toward her.

"I—I'm sorry," he said, panting, though he tried to hide it. "I—was admiring—the painting."

"Huh?" She scanned the wall where he'd stopped. A very mediocre ad poster with a torn corner? She looked back at Ridenour. His chin rose a degree as though he dared her to challenge his taste in art.

"Yeah, right," she said, and crossed her fingers behind her back like a kid. "Glad you like it."

But, remembering that shaking hand, she led him more slowly this time, past the exit and down the ramp to the tube terminal. "I don't know, Ridenour, seems like it might rain." She tried not to think of that cloudless sky outside the door. "I think maybe we should take the tube rather than walk. That all right with you?"

Funny thing: he didn't argue.

Consequently, they missed the rainbow foyer where bevelled glass refracted sunlight all day long: Ridenour could catch that later—if he cared to. But in a last ditch effort to spark some evidence of appreciation from him, she stopped the lift on the main floor of the Researcher Condos and hauled him along the huge atrium's twisting paths, past conversation nooks where deep philosophical discussions—or whatever—were in progress, to the wide staircase leading to the upper-level suites.

Sunlight poured in through the clear dome overhead, sparkled all around them: off water falling over rocks, or swirling and eddying in pools; off greedy fishy mouths kissing and popping at the pool's edge as they passed. The sweet smell of plants and good rich earth permeated the room, and occasionally a bird's courting song broke through the watery murmur.

But the tode didn't notice—didn't even slow up—had the *nerve* to urge her to hurry up. So she hurried him up all right. Ran him up the stairway and along the balcony toward his corridor till he was wheezing like a two-hundred-year-old man. Here he was, in the most beautiful living complex on HuteNamid—probably in the galaxy—and he retreated to the wall, as far from the balustrade as he could get.

Probably allergic to green.

"Here we are, Ridenour," the girl said in that determinedly cheerful voice. "You ought to feel right at home."

She stopped in front of one door in a hallway of doors that all looked alike. In that sense, it was very like 'home.' But at least the academy had the decency to number rooms.

Stephen frowned, looked up and down the hallway, at geometric designs of mirrors and tiles, and wondered how he was ever to tell his room from all the others.

The girl sighed and said, "The *doors*, Ridenour. ThinkTank barracks re-gu-la-shun."

What *was* she babbling about?

She shook her head, plucked the keycard from his fingers and punched it into the slot and he finally understood: the door *slid* open.

There was a window in his room.

A very *large* window looking out over that same God-awful gash into hell. Even through the darkened lenses the sunlight stung his eyes.

The room was . . . big. Airy, private—and it gave him chills. For as long as he could remember, living space had been at a premium, dorm rooms scarcely big enough to get a drawer open, the nearest neighbor a scant breath away. Here he couldn't be certain he *had* neighbors.

Even the furnishings were oversized. A bed with more surface area than four academy bunks combined dominated the room; and everything he'd brought down with him would fit into one drawer of the massive, real wood dresser. Along one wall, clear-fronted bookshelves a lifetime of profligate spending could never fill. A large desk, a remote keyboard and a monitor adjustable for viewing anywhere in the room—what would he need an office for?

He stood in the doorway, reluctant to enter that light-filled vastness. Finally the indigene girl, Ann-Nevvy? Annev-Eye?— blast it, he had a difficult enough time remembering *normal* names—stifled a sigh and asked:

"Well? How do you like it?"

Controlling his nausea, he managed to smile in her direction without really looking at her. "It's—fine."

Someone had delivered his baggage and set it just inside the door. He really ought to go in and put his things away, but he couldn't. Not right now. Later, maybe, after the sun went down and it resembled, as much as it could, the other rooms he'd been assigned over the years.

But that bed . . . dare he request a smaller one? He needed a clear head and he'd never get any rest flopping about in that vast emptiness.

Unless—

*(Rough texture against his cheek. Another body forcing him against the wall on a bed designed for a grown man and nearly wide enough for two boys.*

*(Rougher hands holding him and more. Inescapable whisper in his ear: Watch it, 'Buster-boy, want me to fall out?)*

"H—how many others are as—s—signed to this r—room?" *Damn! Stop stammering, fool!*

She gaped at him. "Only you, of course. What do you think we are here?"

There was no polite answer to that. He shuddered and turned to the relative comfort of the interior hallway.

"*Mr.* Ridenour!"

He hesitated, several steps down the corridor, and asked without turning, "What is it?"

"Don't you want to see the rest of the suite?"

*There's more?* With a casual confidence he in no wise felt: "Didn't you say I would love it? I—trust your judgement in that. Now, *if* you don't mind, Ms. Tye . . . ee . . . ah, I'd like to get on to the Complex. I'd *like* to meet my associates."

"You will," she said. And a slow breath later: "Soon enough."

He was back at the door in three long strides. The 'buster was leaning against the window's edge, a silhouette in the glare, knee propped in casual ease on a thick-cushioned built-in seat. Outside air blowing in through the open window carried strange scents and stirred her long hair with invisible hands.

"What's wrong with right now?" he demanded.

The silhouette shrugged. "No one'll be there right now. Lunch. They're scattered all over the complex—half of them probably clear to Tunica. The few workaholics who *won't* leave wouldn't thank us for interrupting whatever it is they're missing lunch for. So, you wait." She stood away from the window. "Of course, if you'd rather take it easy—maybe lie down and rest awhile, since you seem kinda tired—there's always tonight."

"What's happening tonight?" For some ridiculous reason he was shaking. He wanted out of this room, away from the window and too-large bed. He wanted Smith and a terminal and two quiet hours, not endless, meaningless introductions and mysterious 'tonights.'

"We're having a dress dinner in honor of Admiral—your arrival. Everybody will be there: that would be the best time for introductions. Certainly better than fouling up their work schedules."

The dreaded State Dinner. He could think of no *worse* environment for meeting Smith. "I—" He tried to think of a polite way out. "Could I possibly excuse—"

"Shee-it," she muttered, "Wesley's warned me about you academy-types." Then louder, "Don't worry, Ridenour, I'm sure we can scrounge up *something* that will fit you."

He frowned but held his tongue. She shrugged and turned to stare out the window. "Just trying to be hospitable, Ridenour."

'*Wesley's warned me about you academy-types.*' He could guess which Wesley. Wonderful. If Smith *started out* hating him—what chance did he possibly have of winning the man's trust?

He leaned against the wall, pulled the dark glasses off, and rubbed his aching eyes, shutting out the disturbingly alien view. His eyes hurt from too bright light; his head hurt from lack of food the very thought of which made his abused stomach scream; and every joint in his body was angrily protesting his weight increase. If only it were over and done with, he could close those lovely *heavy* drapes on the light, fall on that bed, huge as it was, and—

A few hours'—hell, two minutes'—rest was all he needed.

But it wasn't done. There was so much—so very much—he had to accomplish, in so little time: the whole morning wasted with the governor's feckless daughter and her tours. Precious time: he wanted Wesley Smith and his notes and he wanted them now.

But Cantrell had said (and meant) *Don't do anything that might raise suspicions, whatever you do. And be friendly.*

Well, he was trying—God knew he was trying—for all the good it was doing.

The indigene stirred restlessly. "This is ridiculous. You stay here and sleep, or—whatever. I've got responsibilities. I'll be back in a bit; then we can go grab some lunch and see if Wes is back."

Relieved at this chance to be rid of her, he said, "You go

ahead. Attend to your responsibilities.'' And since he *could not* handle the thought of exotic food right now: "Have lunch without me: I'm not really hungry. I'll stay here and—''

Something warm pressed against his ankles. He swallowed a startled cry and staggered backward into the door frame, heart thumping wildly.

It was a cat—at least it looked something like the pictures of cats he'd seen. Almost, but not quite. A long-haired, blue almost-cat that stared up at him with indignant gold eyes. Stephen felt a twinge of embarrassment as the 'buster chuckled, a twinge that grew into anger as she laughed outright.

"What's the matter, Spacer-man?" she mocked him. "Our wild animals too much for you?" She leaned over. "C'mere, fuzzybutt.''

The creature flicked a tufted ear in her direction, then as though it had actually understood her, turned that disdainful stare away from him and padded across the room to her.

Anger gave way to a tiny prickle of envy as she picked it up and stroked the long fur. He'd never felt real fur. At least not fur like that. Not with the warm body still inside it. At least . . .

*(Long blond hair, falling free about her shoulders and over the tiny creature she held to her breast. Himself, reaching eagerly for the kitten, jerking back as she frowned at him. Mustn't touch. Never touch the babies. He might hurt them and make the Mama mad. Mama, don't be mad . . .)*

He blinked, caught a ragged breath as the girl held the creature out to him.

"Here, Ridenour, tell him you're sorry.''

He pulled back as far as the wall would allow. "I don't . . .''

She tipped her head to one side and studied his face while she stroked the almost-cat. Her expression softened, became almost-friendly.

He didn't trust friendly looks.

"Sit down,'' she said quietly, still stroking the blue fur.

"Why?''

"Just *sit*, Ridenour. Stop asking so many silly questions.''

Well, she wasn't the only one tired of arguing. He found a chair and complied willingly enough, stifling a groan as sore joints settled. She squatted down beside his feet, the animal cradled in her arms.

"Hold still. And don't—" As he opened his mouth to protest. "—ask why." She grinned and said softly, "*Trust* me."

She set the furry lump down on his lap. He tensed and the creature attempted to escape, a move countered by the Recon's lightning-quick reflexes. "I said hold still, Ridenour."

Easier said than done, as sharp claws dug into his leg, but the girl showed him how and where to hold it, and before long the creature lay draped across his lap, vibrating softly and kneading those claws contentedly on his pant leg while he gingerly stroked that soft fur.

It relaxed; so did he; and he found his hands easily locating what Anevai called the *special spots* to scratch.

Or was it the almost-cat who turned so his fingers reached where it desired?

Curious about this apparent intelligence, he placed his hand over the round head and waited to see how long it would take for the creature to stretch up and rub against his fingers. The response was immediate: a cushioned paw, quite human-like with its curiously opposable digits, reached up to curl around his fingers, bringing his hand back down to cat-head height. Evidently even its small brain was capable of learning, possibly even of elementary reasoning, an analog ability—

A soft giggle roused him out of his preoccupation. He glanced up at the girl, found her watching him with that head-cocked deliberation.

"Quick study," she said.

"It certainly is," he said, his fascination momentarily overriding his caution. "Can it be trained for . . ."

The girl's grin widened. "I meant you, Ridenour."

He flushed and bent his head over the creature once again.

"Hey—I meant that as a compliment, Ridenour."

*Sure you did*, he thought. But it didn't really matter. He resumed his rhythmic stroke. The soft rumbling sound grew louder and the small body vibrated against his legs. He found himself drifting on that sound; found it increasingly difficult to keep his eyes open and his head from nodding. He smiled to himself. He should get McKenna to prescribe a cat instead of pills.

The 'buster shifted, and he blinked himself awake. She settled onto her knees, leaned an elbow on the chair's armrest, and began rubbing the creature's wedge-shaped face between the eyes and down the hairy nose. The nose stretched up, eyes closed, and whiskers pulled forward: total, hedonistic ecstasy.

"He's very f—friendly," he ventured, thinking he should say something. "I—I didn't know cats came in blue."

"It's not a cat! We can't have cats here. They'd disrupt the ecosystem. It's native: we call it a *pii'chum*."

"Oh." Having completed his image of ignorant fool, he looked away—

—but the persistent girl leaned forward, craning her neck to catch his eye. "It used to be striped: brown and black. The blue is Dr. Paul's sense of humor."

"Whose?" He leapt on the unfamiliar, sensing a diversion.

"You'll meet him later." The creature reached out that hand-paw and patted the girl's hand. "All right, pest," she giggled and scratched its throat. —And went right back to her former thought: "Why'd you think it was a cat? Don't you have *real* cats where you come from? All the other researchers have had them—or at least have seen them—at one time or another."

So much for diversions. "No. The academy didn't let us have pets."

"What about at home? Didn't you or any of your friends have them?"

He wanted to tell her to mind her own damn business, but somehow, the truth came out instead. "I don't have any home other than Vandereaux. I've been there since I was a child— nine—ten—something like that anyway. I—don't remember much before that."

"That's awful!"

He flinched, and the pii'chum growled, jumped down, and was out the door in three bounding leaps. Stephen stared at the 'buster, rubbing his knee where sharp-clawed feet had found purchase.

"I—I mean," Anevai stammered, making a vaguely apologetic gesture, "it just doesn't seem fair . . ."

He half-smiled. "Which, no family? or no cat?"

"That's not funny, Ridenour."

As though it might be to him. "Isn't it?" he said caustically. "I'm so terribly sorry."

Dark eyes widened. She jerked to her feet, and stood there,

hands clenched at her sides. He glared up at her, challenging her to strike, the tension between them resurrected with a vengeance. But she didn't, and a long, uncomfortable silence later, he gestured toward the terminal and said, "Look, you said you had things you needed to do. Why don't you go on. I'll stay here and get acquainted with the system."

"But you can't . . ." She broke off, biting her lip.

"I can't what?"

"Well, I—it's not hooked up. We just moved Scotty out, and he never used it, and we thought you'd like a day or so to rest up. Get to know people, get acclimated and such. —Besides, we figured you'd use the one in your office and . . ."

What did she think he was? He hadn't needed help to get a system onLine for ten years.

"I think I can handle it. Go on. I'm not hungry. Enjoy your lunch and I'll see you at—when did you say Smith will be back?"

"It's really hard to say; time schedules are pretty relaxed around here." She laid a hand on his arm. "—C'mon, Stephen." *Stephen?* He held himself rigid, not trusting this return of cordiality at all. "It's my job to see you get around, but the colt's my personal project, and I really should check on him, since I've been busy all morning. I don't have time to go down to the barn and come back here for you; and you've got to eat: you're too skinny." His face burned, but she continued blithely, "You'd never find the dining hall on your own, and you don't want to eat there anyway. Besides, I'd, um." The color rose in *her* cheeks this time and she looked down at her hand on his sleeve, brushed nonexistent lint away. "I'd *like* to show him to you—please? If you think ol' fuzzybutt was something, wait until you see the *ko'sii*."

He slumped back in the chair. One more delay, one more long side trip wearing him out in this heavy gravity and making him that much less prepared to deal with Smith—always presupposing they ever caught up with Smith.

"We might even find some of the gang down there."

Gang? What *gang?* What business was it of her Recon crowd if a new 'Tank member arrived? It was all very confusing. On the other hand, could this be part of what the admiral wanted to know? If so, it was one answer he couldn't possibly find in the computer's familiar accesses.

And he was awfully tired of fighting. He turned his head toward the persistent 'buster. "*Ko'sii?* What's that?"

"Truth, admiral? That, like beauty, is rather well in the eye of the beholder, is it not?"

They'd been at this verbal fencing for a long time. —Too long.

Cantrell made an impatient sweep of her hand. "I'm not interested in poetry, governor. Getting back to the point and away from philosophy: of those two thousand twenty-seven individuals unaccounted for, only a handful are registered as deceased. Another very troublesome handful—twenty-three, TJ?—twenty-three fail to appear on the 'Net at all." She swung around to face him, and caught a glimpse of shock on his stolid face, gone the following instant. "Where *are* those people, governor?"

"What difference does it make? These are indigenes, not researchers." A fast cover, but not quite fast enough. The governor either did not know about those missing individuals, or he didn't think she'd find out. "This is a large planet. We've spread out. We've no terminals in the outback—and babies are born. If we choose not to keep exacting records on our own people, isn't that our business?"

"*Exacting records?* One of those exceptions is your *wife*, governor. Are you aware that if the existing records are to be believed, your children have two biological mothers? Each? That the woman registered as your wife and the biological mother of your children on the 'Net is not the same person listed in those records you brought us? That your wife according to the 'Net, one Ayunli Tyeewapi, has been dead for five years; but according to those records . . ." She pointed to the stacks on the desk. ". . . your children's other mother, Cholena, is still alive and well: except for the fact no one has heard from her in three months? What happened to her? Where is she now? And babies may be born in the outback, but they're still citizens of the Alliance as well as Tunica. The 'Net records are vital for them to receive the full benefit of that citizenship."

She'd hoped to throw him off-balance. It didn't work. Tyeewapi propped his elbows on the chair arms and rested his chin on his steepled fingers. After a moment, he said evenly, "I might argue with you what those advantages are, but it's really quite simple, Adm. Cantrell. We have no mystery here. Babies are born. And sometimes people just leave.''

"People . . . just . . . leave." Cantrell drew a long breath. "And go where?"

"Out," the governor said easily, apparently unaware of, or choosing to ignore, the rising temperature in the room. "To become one with this land. It's a beautiful world: more like our ancestors' earth home than any other mankind has yet found. Is it so surprising that some of my people, whose souls are traditionally one with the land, should choose such a path?"

"It's a bit late to turn esoteric Recon on me, governor. If you Tunicans were that sort, you'd be wearing feathers in your hair."

A smile touched the corner of Tyeewapi's mouth. "Some of us do, admiral."

"Dammit, stop avoiding the issue! Where are these people going, governor, and why?" But Tyeewapi only gestured vaguely toward the mountains outside the window. Another deep breath. TJ shifted uneasily over by the door, and she signaled *All's-well*. "And your wife, governor? Or should I say *wives?*"

He shrugged. "I understood you were here to correct a problem in the 'Net. I know very little about such technicalities, of course, but it does seem to me, perhaps that is what has happened here? That we have—I have no real idea—can 'Net glitches combine records? I certainly knew a woman called Ayunli who is no longer living, but my 'Lena is quite well, thank you. At the moment, she is deep in the mountains. I have no idea when she plans to return. She is a very free woman."

"What about the other names that fail to appear on the 'Net. While the IndiCorps is allowed to keep personal records intact and separate, every birth and death is supposed to be 'Net registered—not simply system-recorded. For God's sake, man, it's the only way their citizenship can be protected—your census is all that determines HuteNamid's representation in Congress."

"It's their decision."

"Is it? At birth? Precocious babies you have here. Who chooses which children will be registered and which won't? How are you governing those who've—left? It's not only irregular, it's potentially detrimental—even dangerous—to the 'Net Alliance itself, not to mention the individuals. For God's sake, man, how many unregistered births have there been? How many defections have there been? What's happening to your population here?''

''We know these *defections* are somewhat unusual. Rather than spark an all out investigation—such as you appear set on undertaking—we have endeavored to keep our little—idiosyncrasy—to ourselves, while working toward a solution we *will* find, admiral.''

He looked straight at her, any former hint of humor or indulgence completely gone. ''A solution we will find by ourselves, thank you. We're IndiCorps, *not* researcher, and our laws are our own.''


Halfway down the path to the barn, Anevai realized Ridenour was still standing in the doorway, a shoulder propping the door open, looking across the meadow toward the barn.

''You got a problem with doors?''

The hand hanging at his side clenched, then gestured toward the telltale mounds running in every direction from this rear side of the researchers' quarters. ''I don't suppose the tube goes there?''

''It does. But it's only—'' She stopped her protest and headed reluctantly back up the hill. She was *tired* of taking the tube. The day was too nice to waste inside.

What could she do? If he was too tired . . . ''Sure. We can go back inside and call for the shuttle. It will take longer for it to pick us up than for us to hike down there, but if you really aren't up to it . . .''

Ridenour muttered something she probably didn't want to hear, and stepped out into the sun, his face fiery red even at this distance. He staggered the first step or two, but by the time he reached her, his color was normal, his step firm.

Still there was something . . . She studied him as he approached; and as he passed: ''You all right?''

''Fine.'' Without slowing, he strode on toward the barn. But that something in the way he moved: stiff-backed, set-focussed, the apparent drunkenness at the airport which wasn't . . . Suddenly she knew.

''Hey!'' She caught up and fell into step beside him. ''You ever been planetside before?''

He stared straight ahead and said nothing, but the flush returned.

*Shee-it. I should've realized* . . . Then out loud: ''Why didn't you say something? Don't you know some people go totally schitz their first time out?''

He clenched his jaw and shot her a warning glance. She ignored the warning—and the resultant stagger: served him right for being a stubborn bit-brain. She grabbed his elbow, forcing him to halt and face her. "Listen, Ridenour, we've got no time here for vanity. You got a *problem*, you say something. Don't put on with me. Last thing I need is a crazy on my hands to explain. You got me?''

He jerked his arm free and glared at her. "Dammitall, that's *Dr*. Ridenour, and I said I'm all right!" But his voice came near to breaking at the last.

She threw her hands up in the air. "Fine! Odds are you'll fall on your ass, but far be it from me to stand in your way.''

His jaw clenched under the dark glasses. He drew a ragged breath, then turned for the barn and began walking, stiff-backed and with a stagger or two, but he beat the odds. Anevai chuckled reluctantly, and followed.

Stubborn bit-brain he might be, but tougher than she'd given him credit for.

## iv

*(Laughing men and women funnelling through the lean-to, tossing equipment every which way, while he scurried about, picking and putting like Mama had told him . . .*

*(A slender man with broad shoulders, his pushed-up filter mask sending blond hair askew, picking him up and tossing him in the air, while he kicked and screamed with fear and excitement . . .*

*(That same man hugging him close and telling him to let the lazy grown-ups put their own junk away, then carrying him slung over that broad shoulder into the noisy warmth of the great hall . . .)*

". . . but most of the equipment's farming stuff and kept—oh, never mind.''

Stephen shook his head and blinked. "I'm sor—" he began, but the girl pushed past him, shoving him against a railing just inside the door.

He rubbed his hand across still-hazy eyes. The hand came

away damp. Where did that come from? He blinked his eyes dry and stuck that damp hand into his pocket, before following her across the barn.

Aboard the shuttle, in the room—now here.

God. He wanted out of here—away from these *places* that kept muddling his thinking. He wanted—

But he stopped that thought.

The light was subdued here, the sunlight filtered through unseen openings, rays of sparkling dust motes. It was the first truly restful spot he'd been in since leaving *Cetacean*. He removed the irritating dark glasses, tucked them into a pocket, then rubbed the sore spot they'd left on the side of his nose.

The indigene girl had crossed to the far side of the building and was standing beside a chest-high railing. She was speaking, but in so low a voice he wondered if her words were meant for him at all.

"I'm sorry, Ms. Tyeewapi, what was that . . . you . . ." He halted two strides short of the railing as he saw *what* she was talking *to*.

"You did that quite well." Her commendation came in that same gentle tone. He transferred his attention from the shadowy Thing inside the railing to the girl. She was smiling at him. He frowned. He wasn't used to people smiling at him. Didn't trust smiles. Just *what* had he done 'quite well'?

"The Name," she clarified, and ducked through the railing. She straightened on the far side of the fence and rested her elbows and chin on the top rail. "You said it right."

He felt the heat, hoped the dim light in here hid the blush. "Not a talent you should expect more from, I fear."

"No problem." Another smile. "You can start working on 'Anevai' now." He stared at her in dismay as she turned to face the Creature. "What do you think of him?" she asked in the same low tone.

"Is this the *k–ko' sii?*"

She nodded without looking at him as the creature tottered over on long, large-jointed legs.

Anevai squatted down to meet it eye-to-eye. Then putting one arm around its neck, she rose smoothly to place her other arm quietly around its rear, countering a quick leap forward with an easy shift of her weight, all the while speaking in that soft voice, mostly nonsense sounds to him, but not, from the mobile ears' back and forth flicking, nonsense to the creature. As the colt relaxed, the indigene girl eased her hand up and over the black, hairy neck, fondling and rubbing all the way to the flexible ears. Its large whiteless eyes closed in obvious delight, reminding him of the cat—the *pii' chum*. At least it appeared placated by similar stimuli.

The girl's senseless croon took on the cadence of a song or poem, and Stephen strained to catch the elusive words. But either they were nonsense, or, more likely, in some Recon language. He supposed he'd known another language once. He didn't recognize a word of this one. It was disconcerting to have someone clearly saying something you couldn't begin to understand. But he didn't need to understand. Her tone sufficed: it was reassurance she offered.

Anevai looked up at him, face aglow. For a startled moment he didn't respond. *Couldn't*. He didn't know how. Unfed, the glow faded. She turned back and buried her face in the fuzzy neck beside her.

He felt answering pain in his gut. He was losing his edge, that was what. He'd been on *Cetacean* just long enough to thoroughly disrupt his carefully cultivated self-sufficiency, then dropped into an environment where any moral support, even from a 'buster, would be welcome.

Besides, the admiral had said to cultivate 'friendships.'

But he didn't know where to start. Didn't know how to just *talk* to someone his own age. A female someone. Conversation was what one did at State Dinners where one was expected to occupy the visiting dignitaries' bored spouses and travelling companions.

He edged over to the wooden railing, ran his hand along the rare substance, marvelling at such careless extravagance, then bent to pass between the bars as she'd done. Suddenly, the corner shadows heaved up to tower over the girl. He recoiled and stared at the huge beast, afraid for an instant that the girl was in real danger and equally afraid to do or say anything which might provoke an attack.

But the creature remained calm, sniffed the girl and its smaller counterpart, nuzzling both indiscriminately. A giggle escaped from the tangle of girl and animals and a hand disengaged from the smaller creature, cavalierly pushing the huge head aside: "Get back, Mama, I'm on duty."

*Mama.* Evidently mother and baby. A half-remembered comment at the airport: this was the 'baby boy' Cantrell had asked about.

Anevai released the baby entirely, and returned to the railing. With an easy hop, she settled on the top rung, tucking her feet back and around the second. "Bet you don't have anything like that where you come from."

He moved back to lean gingerly against the rail next to her, keeping an anxious eye to 'Mama.' "What is it?"

"A *ko'sii.* That's one of the Old One's words for horses, but obviously they aren't really, any more than our 'cat' is a cat."

"What are horses?"

"Don't you know anything?"

Resentment flared. The 'conversation' was *not* going well. He forced lightness into his voice: "I'm a 'NetTech, remember? You're talking pre-space biology. Do *you* know what a three-base-ring-in-NSpace pilogarithm is?"

She frowned, looked suspicious. He didn't blame her: neither did he. But surprisingly, the frown turned to a grin and resentment faded.

"Touché, Ridenour. Horses were on old Earth—still are, for all I know—but Alliance sure doesn't have any now: never brought 'em into space: too big. Like these sweethearts. My people and most of their relatives had a long-standing relationship with horses on old Earth, and we hope to begin a similar acquaintance here."

Her eyes followed the two beasts as they moved restlessly around the stall until the baby, twisting its head around at a seemingly impossible angle under its mother's stomach, pushed insistently. The mother settled. Anevai's eyes crinkled at the corners as the baby's contented suckling found a steady rhythm.

(*"Mama! Mama! Meesha's having her baby! Hurry, hurry, hurry! Papa says come . . . Now, Mama!"*)

As a scientist, Stephen understood; as a civilized spacer, he supposed he should be embarrassed by the very earthy scene before him, but he wasn't. Probably Bijan was right after all, and there was something basically unrefined about him—something at the genetic level—but at this moment, he didn't care; didn't give a damn.

The Meesha of that fleeting memory might have been no taller than this baby, but she'd been fiercely protective of her new offspring . . . as Zivon Ryevanishov had discovered the hard way. Stephen Ridenour remembered the lesson if not the particulars and wondered if this huge creature would react in the same way. He'd hate to be run over. But the lure of the baby was the same, and he envied Anevai her ease with them.

A low melodic hum filtered into his memory. The ko'sii's ears flicked, and she tossed her head, throwing the longer hair around her ears into disarray, then relaxed, still standing, her eyes half-shut.

Stephen, drifting with that hum, leaned against the partition, crossing his arms comfortably on the top rail. "What . . ."

The indigene girl leaned her shoulder against the corner post which stretched from floor to ceiling, one foot propped on the top rail. Her eyes were closed, too, but she ceased humming to say: "Another question, Spacer-man?"

"Dammit! Don't call me that!" The protest escaped before he could stop it.

The eye nearest him half-opened. "My, my. Touchy, aren't we?"

His hands clenched painfully on his upper arms.

"What was it you wanted to ask, Dr. Ridenour?"

"Nothing worth mentioning."

"Ridenour, you're enough to drive a saint to homicide. And I give you fair warning: I'm no saint. What did you want to ask?"

"I wanted to know . . ." The whole conversation had grown ridiculous. "I was curious what the poem was—that one you were reciting to the baby."

Her eyes opened wide, staring at him. "Well, I'll be a—'Net-Head, you'll prove me wrong, yet."

He thrust himself away from the fence and headed for the door.

"—No, *wait*." He heard a thump behind him. He stopped. A hand touched his arm, a tentative touch. "Stephen, I'm sorry. I really am." He half-turned to look at her, and she tugged lightly on his sleeve, urging him back to the railing. "It's one I began this morning. It . . ." —For once, *she* looked confused. "It doesn't translate real well, but I'll do my best. Just—if you laugh, Ridenour, I'll smear your face into the ground, so help me I will."

*That* was a motivation he well understood. He replied earnestly, "I wouldn't even consider it."

"Gods." She looked down, kicked the railing with a foot. "Remember, I'm not spacer. I—we look at things a bit differently here. It—it goes something like:

*"Black jewel horse, on North sky wind,*

*"I sing for Be'yotcidi.*

*"Mane and tail of dark storm clouds,*

*"I sing for Be'yotcidi.*

*"Ears of lightning, stars for eyes,*

*"I sing for Be'yotcidi.*

*"With reins of rainbow, I ride the wind,*

*"I sing for Be'yotcidi.*

*"Child of . . .*

"—No, I don't like that. You're in luck, Ridenour, that's as far as I've gotten."

He said nothing, involved in studying his own reactions. She fidgeted, and he blinked over at her. "I—thank you, A–Anev–yah. It's a vivid image. In any language."

She grinned. "Okay, Dr. Stephen, you pass. You can stay. Anyone who can say that with a straight face is okay by me."

He smiled back hesitantly, and for the next few moments an unexpectedly companionable silence reigned. Then, thinking of Meesha and her tiny duplicate, he said, keeping his voice low, "Strange how different the baby is from its parent. It's difficult to believe he'll change that dramatically. Or are the differences sex-linked?"

She looked at him strangely. "Differences?"

"Well, the ears, for instance. Hers are distinctly round while his—" He reached over the fence to emphasize his point, and the mother's head rose, instantly alert. He jerked his hand back, tried not to take offense at the giggle from his side. "His are definitely pointed and set differently on his skull. And he seems very large in proportion to her, if I understood what you said at the airport to mean he only arrived recently. Doesn't that size make delivery difficult?"

That strange look still on her face, she said, "You're very observant for a spacer 'NetHead."

His heart skipped several beats thinking of Meesha and his parents' barn, then respiration reactivated as he realized: "Just because my specialty's 'Net InterLinks doesn't mean I didn't have *some* biology. Last time I looked, mammalian babies in general look like their mamas.''

Her strange look faded. She seemed—disappointed. ''Oh. Well, there's not much the native strain can do, as they were when we got here, so we've been experimenting in breeding a more useable type. The original stock was much . . .'' She paused, seemingly distracted, then continued: ''. . . much smaller, lighter-boned than . . .'' That intense look on her face was still there. She held a finger to her lips and whispered, ''Listen.''

He had no idea what to listen for, but a moment later, Anevai ducked through the fence again and headed silently for the far corner of the enclosure.

''And what of Liu and Bennett, governor?'' Cantrell asked. Trying to be reasonable. Trying to give the man a graceful way to answer. ''My men asked questions of your citizens and the only one who seems to have ever met them was a small child. Don't you think I should wonder about that?''

''I'm sorry, admiral, but that is SciCorps business. I know nothing about them.''

''And the indigenes who are likewise missing? Am I to assume they just—retroactively *removed* themselves from the 'Net?''

Deliberate bait—

—which Tyeewapi failed to bite. ''Removed from the 'Net? Ah, admiral, I believe you are being humorous. —I can hardly answer for the researchers, but for my own people. I shall be totally honest with you—''

''I would appreciate that.''

''—and tell you that this was the first indication I have had of this problem in our records. Have you a list of the names in question?''

She looked to TJ. He handed her the list he'd made. Tyeewapi perused it carefully, this time without a flicker in his features.

''I'm sorry, admiral,'' he said, handing her back the sheet, ''but I still have no idea why these people aren't on the 'Net. With your permission, I'll make a copy of this list and check into it. I'll get back with you as soon as I know enough to give an—official answer on the matter.''

''Within the next two days, if you please, governor. I'm not fond of wasting time.''

He acknowledged with a slight nod.

"—Another curiosity, governor. There are projects listed here with your people and the SciCorps working in conjunction. None of these projects appear on thé 'Net records. Would you mind telling me why?"

"Why, admiral, surely you realize that any IndiCorps project directly related to the homeworld is legally exempt information."

"When it involves SciCorps?"

"They're *our* projects, admiral. SciCorps is only assisting. They should be on the System records, but since we *are* the system for all practical intents and purposes, we may have gotten a bit—careless—about transferring some things into the Winema databank. For that, I apologize and will take steps to see it rectified."

"That's a very unusual procedure, governor. Most people consider input from systems outside their own an advantage. They consider publicizing their world an advantage. And on this technicality you've incidentally managed to disguise some of your SciCorps' better accomplishments, while undoubtedly depriving them and this world of revenue from users who might very well be interested in their work."

"We're not ready to apply for patent yet. On a patentable process—a company can withhold details."

"You're not incorporated."

"There is a precedent for a colony holding a patent. Vandereaux. The silkmoss detoxification process."

Which made a damn fine whiskey—like hell the man wasn't prepared for questions. "Are the researchers aware you are doing this editing?"

"Who said we were editing, admiral? They know there will be value in the work. Someday. Like us, they are in no hurry."

She glanced through the reports, looked up again. "I have to compliment you on an unusual achievement. How do you do it? How do you get these people to work together? It always seemed a sensible course to me—a pooling of ideas and viewpoints, so to speak—but the Alliance has, frankly, discouraged such—cooperation. Particularly in the last few years."

"Perhaps the Council fears divided loyalties," Tyeewapi said cautiously. "What more can we give you, admiral? Tell me—I shall endeavor to oblige you."

*How about one straight answer, Tyeewapi?* she thought wearily. To all appearances, the problems here should be soluble. The governor's affability seemed real enough, but she didn't trust it. For all his vaunted cooperation, she *knew* nothing more than she had an hour ago.

"I can't help but feel there's much I'm not being told," she said finally. "When vital information is bypassing the 'Net . . . when Alliance Security officers are being attacked without clear provocation or cause . . . what am I supposed to think, governor? What would *you* think?"

Tyeewapi leaned back in his chair. "Perhaps that you are dealing with a people who desire a modicum of privacy. Besides, I think we have been tolerably cooperative. I wouldn't presume to speak for Dr. Smith, his decision to stay or go is his own; however, we gave you the records you requested—"

The man was running her in circles! "*After* leaving the information off in the first place and *after* I brought up the discrepancies."

"As you say. But did we ever deny the existence of those records? Did we try to keep them from you? If we were truly some kind of—criminal organization,—would we not be far more clever in our machinations?" He gave his ghostly smile, "Admiral, we simply have a slight problem with members of our community reverting to nature. —Look around you. My people trace their lineage to one of the last of the human groups to embrace the technological culture of the 'White-man.' Is it any wonder that, faced with the riches you see here, they prefer to leave that technology behind them? To live as one with the land and, just perhaps, reach out to their own gods once again? All I have attempted to do is protect that decision from an interfering, over-zealous government."

"Turning esoteric on me again, governor," she said darkly.

Sakiimagan dropped the formal facade at last, and leaned forward intently. "All right, admiral, let's *be* honest. Had these records appeared in the 'Net over the last twenty years, you'd have been here, just as you are now, trying to *force* these people back to us. I know it, and you know it. As it is, I have finally begun to make strides toward reintegrating my people and, frankly, I don't care to have outsiders destroying my work!"

She said slowly, "I can understand that—and, as I said when I first arrived, I'm here to help, not interfere. *Make* me understand the rest, governor. I'd always believed the prevailing Recon policy to be—self-defeating—but I find a system here functioning on what I would have said a healthy level; yet in the twenty years since you began recruiting researchers, there's been nothing of significance out of your very heavily staffed 'Tank. In fact, as far as I can see, your semi-legal patent protection system may be your most significant accomplishment. Can you show me a reason *why* the Alliance shouldn't simply recall you all and start over with a more traditional group which might get better results? Where's the return on the taxpayer's investment?"

"Patience, admiral."

She leaned toward Tyeewapi. "*Give me a reason for patience.* I want to support you in your efforts here, but the Council won't wait indefinitely. You've already admitted editing some of your 'Net reports. If there are major developments, *any* developments, in the works you've kept off, let me take that information back to the Council with me. *Convince me* it doesn't belong on the 'Net—and I promise you, that won't be difficult to do: some investigations *should* be kept private until one knows what one is dealing with—and I'll make that exchange top security. Take it straight to the Council and no further."

Sakiimagan gazed beyond her at something she knew she wouldn't see if she turned. Finally he said, still gazing into that nowhere, "I think, perhaps, our goals are not altogether at odds, admiral. But I must have time. It's not only my decision to make." His eyes came back to her. "You return to the ship in the morning?"

She nodded. "Yes. I'll be back."

"Give me, if you will, until your return to HuteNamid to consider the issue and consult our own Tribal Council."

She considered a few issues herself, then nodded again.

"I think there are five . . ." Anevai said, straining to see into the darkness behind the hay bales.

"No—six," Ridenour whispered, his breath warm on her neck. He pointed over her shoulder. "See. There's one more tail . . . I thought you said they didn't come in blue."

She twisted around. He was kneeling in the straw beside her, oblivious to the dirt rapidly covering his fancy jumpsuit. She grinned. She'd make a Recon out of him yet.

"They're not supposed to," she said, keeping her voice low so as not to startle the new mama. His eyes, free of the dark glasses now, flickered from the mama *pii'chum* and her kits to meet hers, and she grinned at him. "Guess we know who at least one of the papas was, don't we?"

Strange, pale eyes which mirrored his thoughts—

He blushed and pulled away, to settle back on his heels. "I—I suppose so."

—No wonder he kept them covered.

Over his shoulder she could see Bego, full now and curious, meandering toward them. Keeping her face perfectly straight, she said, "We'll have to make sure Dr. Paul gets down here to see them. If we can determine the old blue-boy was the papa for all of them, he'll probably want to keep records."

Stephen relaxed a degree and said, "That's the second time you've mentioned this Dr. Paul." But she was barely following what he was saying. Bego had gotten within reach and was stretching his nose out toward Stephen's curly hair. "Is he one of the 'Tank researchers? Do you actually work—"

She bit her lip, tried not to smile as Bego's curiosity got the better of his common sense and he grabbed a lipful of dark curl.

Stephen felt a moist warmth on the back of his neck, a tug at his hair—

—and wrenched himself to his feet, lashing out blindly, hitting a hard, furry body.

A furry body that squealed and reared backward. God—it was only the baby! He tried to grab its neck as he'd seen Anevai do, but the angle was wrong. The creature's twisting topple continued, dragging him with it, his hand caught around the sinuous neck.

A deeper squeal, a flash of brown, a sharp blow to his temple and the world exploded around him. A second, glancing blow to his back and his shoulder cracked ominously.

Anevai yelled, but he couldn't understand through the roaring in his ears. Fearing the creature was attacking her, he rolled to his knees, swinging his right arm to distract what he couldn't see. Something seized that flailing arm and thrust him violently against the railing. He grabbed at that solidity and clung there while his vision cleared.

In pain-hazed confusion, he watched the girl kneel beside the fallen creature, urging it back to its feet while keeping her body between him and its mother. She got it to a wavering stand—unless that unsteadiness was an artifact of his hazed vision—then, interspersed with low coos to the baby and admonitions to the mother to stay back, she said without changing that soothing tone: "Get your spacer-ass out of this stall before I turn her loose on you. If you've harmed one hair on him, so help me, I'll kill you myself."

He stared at her in disbelief, as anger-induced adrenaline temporarily cleared his head. What had he done that was so terrible? The filthy creature had attacked him, and he'd tried to save it from falling. He clenched his jaw on a wave of nausea and struggled to his feet, leaned against the railing, clutching his injured arm to his side, and closed his eyes on a barn which tended to swirl madly around him.

The shoulder was bad this time. Very bad. The doctors had warned him. He'd known it was simply a matter of time. But that it should occur here, now, before he'd even *met* Smith and with no hope of anything like the *Cetacean's* facilities . . . if he were any clearer-headed, he'd be terrified.

The girl ordered him out again—at least, he thought that was what she was saying. Any hint of camaraderie was shattered. But he didn't care. He'd like nothing better than to grant her wish and leave this place forever. Only . . .

. . . Only leaning over at this particular moment might prove humiliatingly disastrous. God! He couldn't think straight. *Why* had he refused the admiral's breakfast offer? He nearly laughed aloud at that—and coughed as the bile rose in his throat.

The 'buster twisted around on one knee, one hand on the creature, the other a fist at her side. *"I said, get out!"* Then twisted back, burrowing her face into the furry neck.

One deep breath. And another. Then clamping his shoulder more tightly still, furiously ignoring the fresh wave of nausea the grip produced, he lifted one leg over the lower rung. But when he bent to follow with the rest of his body, the barn went grey and liquid, and he fell rather than stepped to the other side.

"G'n'C, Spacer-man. Grace 'n' charm. Get on your feet and get out of here. Go back to your room or wherever else you please! No place you can go that I can't find you. Don't worry. I'll see you get to supper on time! Until then, you can damn well entertain yourself!"

His room: excellent idea. From there, he could call the *Cetacean* for help—*discreet* help. He looked around, searching for the 'Tube terminal. He had a much better chance of making it back to his room in a bubblecar than on foot. A much better chance.

But then, twice nothing was still nothing.

## V

Anevai rested her cheek against the trembling body, pointedly ignoring the clumsy spacer, giving him no opportunity to get around her good sense again. If she hadn't gone soft in his room in the first place and read something into that fascination he seemed to have for old BlueBoy that wasn't really there . . .

Shit. Try to be nice to the CodeHead, and he turns around and—

A low moan from the other side of the fence. A thump. Double shit. Maybe the mare got him worse than she thought. Reluctantly, she turned an eye in the spacer's direction.

He was still on the ground, hunched over on his knees.

"Hey, Spacer-man," she said, "you all right?"

"Where . . ." He coughed. His back heaved. She heard him gasp for breath, and when he continued, she could barely catch the question. "You said . . . shuttle came . . . where's . . . terminal?"

"Over there." Perversely, she pointed, forcing him to look at her.

The dark head twisted slowly around until she could just spot one pale eye, then followed the direction of her arm to the darkened corridor where a dim light marked the stairway to the underground terminal.

She heard a gasp, more a smothered sob, and felt a twinge of conscience. Could he really be hurt? She felt herself weakening, and turned the weakness into a taunt. "What's the matter, Spacer-man? Can't even get that far?"

"Damn you!" he muttered furiously, and she ceased to worry.

A spidery-fingered hand flew up, grasped the fence rail and, with an oddly fluid twist, he was on his feet and heading for the stairwell, stubbornly ignoring her.

Then he staggered, his left arm swinging in what was all too obviously *not* a normal manner.

Shit. Dad was going to kill her. *"Dammit, Ridenour, are you hurt?"*

He staggered again—this time unable to recover. He fell to his knees and thudded up against the stacked hay. He grasped weakly for a handhold and slipped bonelessly to the floor.

"Shit!" She scrambled through the fence and ran to his side. "Ridenour? I *said*—"

"I heard you . . . the first time." His voice was little more than a hoarse whisper. "I'm *fine*. Just . . . tired. Not . . . used to . . . gravity . . . Leave. Go. *Get out*."

"And get myself arrested by your precious Adm. Cantrell? Thank you, no. Now, what did you do?"

His head fell back against the hay, his face no longer spacer-white but sickly gray. "I said . . ."

"I heard you the first time." She echoed him, and knelt beside him, setting a hand on his shoulder.

"Dammit! Leave . . . me . . . 'lo . . ."

His voice faded. His head fell forward, his breath coming in short, shallow gasps. Sweat beaded his face.

Fainted. Wonderful.

Straightening him out proved more difficult than she'd expected: not quite the lightweight he appeared. But she managed, then concentrated on that left arm.

Not for the first time, she thanked the gods her MedTech grandparents had taken the time to teach her a thing or two. Not a break, but the shoulder had been messily dislocated. Very messily.

Her sure touch raised one small, quickly smothered groan. Not unconscious, then: ignoring her. Waiting, possibly, for her to go away. Well, she wasn't about to accommodate him. She took a firm hold on the arm—

—and paused as his right hand curled weakly around her wrist.

"Please, Ms. T–Tyee—"

She took pity on him, saying clearly, " 'Sokay, Spacer-man. The name's Anevai, and I know what I'm doing."

"Thank . . . you, but, no . . . please, Anneh . . . Ann . . . N–" His voice caught. "Nevyah, please . . . c–call . . . admiral . . . Get M–McKen . . ."

"Listen, Spacer-man," she said, holding his sweating face securely between her hands, *willing* him to shut up and hear her, "I know what I'm doing, Stephen. Trust me. Your arm can't stay like this."

Without giving him time to answer, she braced her foot in his armpit and gave the arm a quick pull and twist. It slipped back into the socket with ominous ease and her unwilling patient gasped and fainted—for real this time. *Just as well.*

She placed his hand carefully on his chest and raked loose hay up under and around the arm for support, then dropped back to her knees. She loosened the front of his jumpsuit and closing her eyes, probed the joint, laying her hand flat on the bare skin of the shoulder and clavicle, visualizing the underlying structure the way Grandfather had taught her, manipulating the soft tissues into alignment with gentle massage.

*Skinny, maybe, and spacer—but not soft, Ridenour,* she thought, massaging hard, contoured muscle with both hands, wondering idly what a 'NetHead did to make it that way. Taking his hand onto her lap, she freed his arm of its fitted sleeve, running her pocketknife carefully up the seam to expose the elbow.

A second gentle twist, more massage, then: *You'll do.*

She left him lying and went on a search for the good, *strong* liniment—the other would likely do as well, but arrogant, patronizing spacers should get what they deserved.

*He was late for the third time in as many days, and the corridor ahead seemed endless. Had he taken the wrong turn again? Please, God, let this be the way.*

*The professor wasn't going to let it go this time. He'd tried and tried, but he simply couldn't adapt to the time changes in this place. The light in the dorm room was too soft and didn't wake him up the way the sunlight at home used to. And he kept falling asleep too early, then waking up in the middle of the night, or sleeping too late. And the others were always careful not to disturb him when they left.*

*Once—a long time ago—he'd thought they meant it as a kindness.*

*From a side corridor several meters ahead, a yellow light blinked. Speakers announced History of Alliance 1103 would begin in three minutes, and he sighed with relief. He was nearly there. He hadn't taken the wrong hallway after all.*

*Disregarding all the rules, he sprinted for the lighted hallway. He was two strides short of the light when seemingly from nowhere, several of his fellow 1103 students stepped out to block the hall in front of him.*

*He skidded to a stop, dropping his portable and his old-fashioned notebook. As he knelt to pick them up, a large foot planted itself squarely on the diary. Other feet surrounded him; he stared at those feet until his eyes were stinging, too frightened to blink.*

*His heartbeat pounding in his ears, he fought, as he'd learned he must here, to control his face before allowing his gaze to travel up the perfectly tailored and creased uniform to the equally perfect face grinning down at him.*

*"Look what we have here, gentlepersons. I do believe it's a 'buster-boy all down on his hands and knees like a good boy. Looking for some dirt, 'Buster-boy? How sad. Won't find any here. Spit'n'polish, 'Buster-boy, Spit'n'polish."*

*A frightened glance at the classroom door.*

*"Don't worry about being late, 'Buster-boy, no class today. We've got us three whole hours free. So my friends here and I, we thought we'd do a little . . . cultural Anthropology for extra credit. Study us a little . . . Recon History. Know who's going to teach us?"*

*A tiny shake of his head: all the answer he dared make.*

*They knew. Somehow they knew. He'd done like Dr. Danislav had told him—he hadn't said—but somehow, they'd found out anyway.*

*"You, 'Buster-boy. But since you're Dr. D's pet and too good to talk to us, we thought you might just let us see that big fat book of yours. Good as a TextFile—probably a whole lot better—TextFiles leave out all the—good stuff. But you don't, 'Buster-boy, do you?"*

*He clasped his hands tightly on his diary, confused, as Bijan's insinuation set the others to laughing.*

*"I'll bet you want to know how we know what's in there." He refused to respond, but the older boy grinned and continued, "Joe, here, he heard you talking in your sleep—"*

*He shivered and Bijan's grin widened. "That's right, 'Buster-boy. You talk in your sleep. Well, Joey, industrious fellow that he is, took a look at that diary of yours: it—fell—out of your bunk. . . . Knows all about you now, he does. Know what he says?"*

*Again, the headshake.*

*"Seems you're too smart to waste digging dirt, and your mummy didn't want you. So they brought you here to play in*

*the big leagues. Well, we don't like dirt-diggers, 'Buster-boy, 'specially smart-ass ones like you that ask too many questions and waste our time. Might just be spies. But Joey, here, didn't have time to finish that book of yours. We thought today would be a good time to do that. What do you think?''*

Teeth clamped painfully on his lower lip, he searched desperately for a break in the tightening circle of feet. There: that was Tony. He wasn't that *much bigger*—

A quick yank on the notebook sent Bijan sprawling and scattered the circle as he leapt to his feet and darted down the corridor. He was fast . . . almost fast enough.

Hands closed on his shirt, yanking it from its carefully smoothed tuck and jerking him from his feet. He twisted around and tried to bite the hand pressing him down, but another hand struck him across the face, snapping his head back. That same hand reached down and grabbed his notebook as Bijan's voice pierced through the ringing in his ears: *"Probably keeps his spy notes in here."*

But he wouldn't let go—*couldn't*. Home was in there. They would laugh—even worse than they did already. Better they should laugh at him than at Mama and Papa and Granther and Petros and Nevyah. So he held on until finally someone grabbed his left wrist, yanking it behind him while he curled his other arm and body around the notebook trying desperately to keep it from them.

They pulled his arm, jerked it back and up and up until he felt more than heard a sickening crunch and pain exploded through his body. He screamed and collapsed, unable, now, to prevent the theft.

The strange buzzing in his ears wasn't sufficient to drown the awful laughter. Page after page drifted down around him as Bijan read one passage after another: aloud and in terrible, mocking tones.

However, someone wasn't laughing. He heard a tiny whimper—realized it was his when one of the others, Don, his dazed mind thought, heard him and pointed out to the others that he hadn't moved.

Bijan shut up. A fist grabbed his hair and lifted his face to the lights. "Shit," Bijan said, spraying his face, spit mingling with the tears he couldn't hold back. "Let's get out of here."

Feet pounding—followed by utter silence.

*When he was certain they were gone, he twisted his head around, saw in disbelief his mutilated book lying just beyond his head.*

*He reached for it and the attempted movement sent waves of pain screaming through his body, echoing again and again and again from his mouth, try as he would to close it.*

*Again, and again, and again . . . until finally someone heard.*

A high-pitched scream echoed through the barn. Anevai dropped the bottle of liniment. A quick millimeter-above-the-floor save, a dodge under a cross-tie, and she was out the door and at the spacer's side. Still far from conscious, he screamed again: a scream of sheer agony which this time didn't stop. But—why? There was nothing. Unless—

Could that *shoulder* cause all this? Maybe she hadn't been as clever as she thought.

"Stephen?" She slapped his cheeks with gentle pops. "*Stephen?*"

He shut up as though a switch had been thrown and she sat back on her heels, a bit weak in the knees herself, and waiting for her heart to slow.

He didn't look very arrogant anymore, lying there on the hay, tears mingling now with the sweat on his face. He didn't appear old enough to be a graduate, let alone a fourth. Perhaps she *was* being unfair. Perhaps what she took for arrogance was . . . well . . . something else.

She was rubbing the liniment gently into his shoulder when the spacer's eyelids flickered—and immediately clamped back down, tearing: this time from the fumes.

After a long moment, they raised again slowly, carefully, and she watched, fascinated at the swirling colors, as the pupils slowly adjusted and the eyes focussed.

"What's that God-awful smell?" he croaked.

She grinned down at him. "You."

Stephen rubbed a gritty hand across his face, recalling, dimly, their last heated exchange—an exchange which didn't match her easy grin. He remembered being ordered out of this place in no uncertain terms.

Letting his hand drop, he touched hers lightly. "I'm truly

s—sorry, Ms. T—Tyeewapi. I—I didn't mean to hurt him. Is he . . ."

"Better than you, Ridenour," she said, still smiling. "I'm the one should be doing the apologizing. It wasn't your fault. I should have remembered you were a greenie. Handling critturs takes practice. —*Lots* of practice."

He raised his head gingerly, then groped with his right hand for leverage. A solid arm behind his shoulders helped him sit up, steadied him as the barn danced in circles around him.

Passively, he waited for the dizziness to end and the pain to begin. Except: there was no pain—at least, none compared to what he'd expected. Remembering rumors about indigene medical practices, he looked at the girl in no small fear.

"What did you do to me?"

"Nothing much. Your shoulder was dislocated—"

*"I know that."*

"—so I put it back in."

*God.* He closed his eyes, swallowed hard.

"I've done it before. It'd just slipped out, there were no real complications and it wasn't frozen-up yet so I just—popped it back in, that's all. Also, it's a lot worse than it feels right now. That stuff I put on it is pretty potent, a real topical anesthetic. Be careful till the Meds can get a proper look at it." She rose to her feet. "You all right?"

He nodded and she held out her hand. He drew a deep breath and grasped it with his right. She pulled easily and slowly, drawing him up on uncertain legs. He was even grateful for the arm she placed around him, steadying him until the world settled properly into up and down.

"Stephen," the girl said quietly, carefully, "I know I'm butting in where I don't belong, but that shoulder of yours . . . it's bad. Happened before, has it?"

He hesitated, but seeing no way to avoid the issue gracefully, nodded briefly.

"When?"

"When I was—a long time ago."

"Why haven't you had it taken care of? Bad as it is now, it's going to need a total restruct."

"It's always *been* bad, and there was never the time."

"Surgery and recovery would take what, five days, a week maybe?"

"Let it be, will you?" He turned away from her, brushing the dirt and straw from his clothing. His left sleeve fell away from his arm and he fingered a tear in the knee ruefully. That *might* be mended, but he doubted the stains would ever come out. The smell almost certainly wouldn't. "At first the Meds said to wait till I was fully grown, and by then—where I've been five *hours* off would have left me so far behind I'd never have caught up."

"Shee-it."

Sensing, from her tone, some small return of friendly relations, he glanced over his shoulder, smiled tentatively and held up a filthy hand.

"You might say that. Do we possibly have time for me to clean up?"

The door closed behind Tyeewapi, and Cantrell said, disgusted, "Well, that got us not much of anywhere fast."

"What did you expect?" TJ asked. "That he would up and confess everything?"

"One can always hope."

"Perhaps we learned more than it at first appears," Lexi said. And elaborated at her questioning look: "Governor Tyeewapi was *surprised* at the missing IndiCorps personnel. Not the researchers, but I'm certain the other caught him unaware."

"And he knows now—" TJ said, "or should—that you're willing to work with him. Your remark about how some things should remain off the 'Net did not go unnoticed."

"Let's hope he doesn't realize I haven't the authority to back it up: that's a 'NetAT decision. Brilliant idea, however—using the indigene involvement in projects to keep them off the 'Net. I wonder what their *real* reason is for doing it." She thought of Paul. Thought of Paul's ego among other possible egos of the other researchers in that pile of resumes. Not to mention Smith. Non-conformists, all. Could the Council and the SciCorps transfer committee really be so blind to the talent Tyeewapi had amassed here and their blatant lack of production? Or possibly they were glad to have a sinkhole for all their problem children.

Nonconformist researchers. Researchers who never left here. *Perhaps they fear divided loyalties*, Tyeewapi had said. Did the *researchers* have reason to fear divided loyalties? Was this, in fact, all a 'Tank problem and not an IndiCorps coverup at all?

"TJ, get into the researcher records. Check into the reasons for transfer here, check contacts before and after, see if any pattern begins to show up. I want to know how and why people opted here. Let's find out what sort of researcher they're used to here. —Lexi, you help him, I don't care the Security Level involved.''

Tandem nods as she reached for the phone. ''*I'm* calling Corlaney. He's got some explaining to do.''

The soft clicks and taps behind the bathroom door stopped. The shower hissed.

'*Bout time, Ridenour*, Anevai thought, and crossed her ankles on the window seat. BlueBoy, who seemed to have chosen Stephen's room as the current Spot, oozed out from under the bed and up into her lap. She petted him idly, striving to ignore her belly's rude noises. She told it flatly to shut up: lunch was coming.

And Ridenour would get something more than pills on his stomach. He'd taken a fistful the minute he got to his room—and that after he'd had dry heaves twice on the way back from the barn. Not smart, for all he'd *looked* the better for those pills.

She had to admit she was finding it increasingly difficult to condemn the 'NetHeaded spacer, even more difficult to give any credence to Nayati's theories for his presence here. Stuffed shirt that he'd seemed at the airport, once you got past that, he turned quite nice, and anything but spyish.

For one thing, spies didn't stutter. She grinned down at old Blue, who squinted myopically at her. The *pii'chum* had turned Stephen as squishy as that stutter of his had turned her. Considering he'd never been around animals, his concern for Bego was really kind of sweet, especially since (she was willing to admit now) what happened hadn't been Stephen's fault at all.

*And* the Alliance could damn well afford spies whose parts weren't falling off. Living with that shoulder took guts, too. Guts or stupidity.

Her stomach grumbled again. She glanced at her watch. Past two. She wanted her lunch and she wanted it now, never mind where Wesley was. Odds were the minute they found him, he'd buzz off somewhere else, anyway.

She yelled at the bathroom door, ''Get the lead out, Ridenour! We're late.''

The sound of the shower stopped. A moment and muffled

curse later, the door opened and he stuck his head out, water dripping from crazily curling hair and off the end of his nose.

He sniffed and rubbed the back of his hand across his nose. "Would you please hand me the brace? —There—" He gestured toward the bed. "—that thing on the bed. I forgot it."

She examined it curiously before handing it to him. "For the shoulder?"

He nodded and reached around the door to take it from her, giving her a good look in the mirror as he did so. She raised her eyebrows and grinned appreciatively. "Not bad, Ridenour. You're not as skinny as I thought."

He cocked his head to the side, puzzled-looking, like some kind of spook-eyed bird. Suddenly, those weird eyes opened wide, and he jerked his head and arm back, pushing the door firmly closed.

She stifled a laugh and said, "I'm sorry, Stephen. I didn't mean to embarrass you. People are pretty relaxed here."

No answer.

"C'mon, Ridenour. Forgive me?"

Her only answer was the buzz of the blowdryer. And when he emerged from the bathroom, he seemed perfectly composed, immaculate in slacks and sweater—

—and *very* easy on the eyes, now he'd shed those glasses so you could see his face.

Still, she hoped . . . "Stephen, I really am sorry. Are you sure that shoulder will be all right? Don't you want to have the EMTs take a look—"

*"No!"* Then far more quietly: "I'm fine, A–Anevyah. R–really."

That silly stutter—how could she possibly take offense? She calmly changed the subject with an appreciative sniff. "What *is* that smell?"

His mouth quirked and his rare, *real* smile appeared. "Don't ask. Suffice it to say, it's the *strongest* one I've got."

She put on a puzzled face. "I can't imagine why you think you needed *that*."

He looked worried. "Too much?"

She was amazed how easily she could read him now. It might be the elimination of those stupid glasses, or it might just be the elimination of reserve—on both sides. "It's terrific. C'mon, Doc. We're *late*." She giggled, grabbed his sound arm, and headed for the door, taking no offense when the arm jerked: still didn't like Recon contamination. To do him credit, he tried to control it and she patted his arm encouragingly before releasing it.

Anyway, if he stuck around, Wesley would cure him in short order. She was beginning to look forward to that meeting. Hoped they *would* locate Wesley at the *Hole*. Somehow, she suspected Wesley's mad would evaporate at his first good look at the new recruit. Somehow, she suspected Wesley would be trying very hard to *make* Stephen Ridenour put that transfer through permanently.

And if his brain was as good as the rest of him, she wouldn't put it past the Wesser to do a little Ridenour-napping if Stephen tried to return to *Cetacean*.

She waited while Stephen locked his door. The tiny green LED acknowledged his departure, and he slipped the keycard into a pocket as they headed down the hall.

A feather-light touch on her arm brought her to a halt.

"Ms. Tyeewapi, will you explain something to me?"

"Can't answer that till you tell me what you want to know, can I, Dr. Ridenour?"

His eyes dropped from hers. "You said in the barn . . . at least I thought you did. I . . . wasn't exactly copasetic . . ."

She shifted her weight impatiently. "C'mon, Stephen, out with it. I'm hungry."

"You said, you didn't want to get arrested by the admiral. Why . . . why should she arrest you because *I* did something stupid?"

"I'm your appointed watchdog, didn't you know that?" Apparently he didn't know, from his outraged look. She grinned. "Never mind, Ridenour. *I* don't. Not anymore. Let's go eat." As she hurried him down the hall, she asked hopefully, "Forgive me?"

No hesitation this time, though the ready color rose in his cheeks. He smiled that shy, hesitant smile, and said softly, "Sure."

*"I'm sorry, Adm. Cantrell, but Dr. Carlson has not yet returned to his office. May I take a message?"*

Cantrell exchanged a worried look with TJ.

"Just tell him I called and that I'd like to speak with him ASAP."

She gave the secretary the extension number and hung up. Without a word, she rang Smith's office. Same secretary, same response. No. No message at this time.

She called the Condo operator, got Stephen's room extension, and tried it. Nothing. She left her name, and See you tonight on the message machine, and hung up.

A final call: this time to their onworld Security base.

*"Yes, admiral?"*

"Call Chet. Tell him I want to know where P. J. Carlson is, and I want to know now."

*"Yessir! Anything else, sir?"*

"That'll be all. Cantrell out."

They heard the music and the laughter, smelled the food, long before they turned down the hall leading to *The Watering Hole*. Wes still hadn't returned to his office—no surprise: Wesley had sworn to avoid Ridenour as long as possible—and since this was the best food and drink to be had on all HuteNamid, Anevai was willing to bet he'd be here.

She paused in the doorway, giving her eyes time to adjust to the low light. Beside her, Stephen asked, his voice low and unsteady, "Are you sure it's safe in here?"

"Huh?" *Elegant, Tyeewapi, real elegant.* "Ridenour, it's only a pub!" But his worried look remained.

What did he think would happen here? The researchers told tales of places on stations, places along the docking bays which harbored all sorts of rough individuals: free traders, drug dealers, merchanters and such; dark bars where weapons (such as could be detected) were appropriated at the door; but how much resemblance could they possibly bear to *The Watering Hole?*

"Hey, relax, okay?" she said. Standing on tiptoe, she scanned the crowded room, waving to one person and another. Finally:

"Looks like you beat the odds, Ridenour. There he is. —*Hey, Wesley!*" she yelled out, waving one arm above her head and jumping up and down. She felt Stephen start, then draw back into the shadows as the whole room seemed to turn toward the door.

Everyone except (the tode) Wesley, who was standing over by the bar, nose buried in his beer, and his backside stubbornly to the door. He either hadn't heard: unlikely; was too busy flapping his mouth: distinct possibility; and/or was flat ignoring her: almost undoubtedly.

And Stephen received the message, loud and clear. He ducked his head and turned away from the restaurant door, mumbling, "Let's go. I'll talk—"

"Forget it, Stevie-lad. He's just approximating an ass. C'mon." Anevai darted through the packed room, dodging waiters and tables with practiced ease.

"Look out, Ridenour!" She swayed away from an overloaded tray floating through the air on one upthrust hand. She glanced back to ensure Stephen's safety—and he wasn't there.

The spacer was still standing back at the entrance, making a major production of the removal and storage of his sunglasses. A surreptitious survey of a room gone private again, and his shoulders visibly relaxed.

Suddenly, his actions made a bizarre kind of sense: Stephen didn't like being the center of attention—for whatever reason. But that wouldn't work in this roomful of egos and curiosity. If he wouldn't go to Wes, the Wesser would simply have to go to him. Easy done: all she had to do was get the Wesser to look up.

She worked her way the last few steps to the bar and grabbing Wes by the shoulder, shouted in his ear, "Wake up, Doc! Time to go to work."

He yelped and jumped away from her, tripping over the stool next to him and managing to lay his hands all over its shapely occupant in his resultant fight for balance. Tracy, long since immune to him, just grabbed his elbow with one steadying hand, and sipped foam from her mug with the other.

"Wesley, knock it off, will you?" She wanted her lunch and she sensed potential trouble brewing in Wesley's hyperactive RAM.

Wesley scowled at her and turned to Tracy, pulling her around to kiss her soundly. She indulged him until she'd swallowed her mouthful of beer, then pulled away, patting him on the cheek. "Go to work, dear. You have to earn your keep somehow."

The scowl deepened and he muttered, "I earn my keep just fine. Don't need no stinking grad-u-ates from Vandy-roo screwing my computer."

If she didn't know him better, she might believe he was serious.

"Hey, Wes, he's okay. And he's a nice boy—shy. Take it easy on him, will you?"

She followed his glance to the deep shadows beside the doorway into which Stephen had melted. But—dammit—Stephen was A-ca-de-my again.

"Right," Wesley said sourly. "A Vandy-roo pretty-boy: vaporware for brains and virtualware for—"

*"Wesley."*

He shrugged and turned back to the bar. "Just what we don't need. Well, —screw him."

She grabbed his arm and hissed in his ear, "Dammit, Wes, you're not being fair! C'mon."

He glanced at her over his shoulder. "No? Let's find out, shall we?" And turned back to his beer.

"Wes, what're you—"

"Trust me."

"The hell I will!" She tightened her grip on his arm, started to pull.

Suddenly, he yelled, *"Help! Rape!"* And leaning across the bar, grabbed the far side.

"Wesley, what—" He winked at her. *Oh, shee-it. Jonathan Wesley Smith, what are you up to?* Whatever it was, he wasn't getting away with it—"Nigan! Grab his other arm!"

And Nigan Wakiza, bless his homely heart, helped her drag Wes away from the bar, quite literally kicking and screaming, while the crowd cheered them on—them or Wes. Pretty soon they'd be laying bets.

*"Dammit!"* their victim gasped, pulling hard. "Lemme go! Them's m'workin' arms!"

Someone shouted over the answering roar, "Don't you fret, Wes, old man. You can always type with your toes, like any good anthropoid!"

She spotted Stephen over Nigan's shoulder. For a split instant, his face mirrored dismay, and she couldn't blame him for wondering: Wesley certainly wasn't acting much like the brilliant researcher he claimed he was.

Wesley's backside was aimed straight at Sarah Metcalf, who was eyeing the view with open appreciation. With a meaningful glance at Nigan, Anevai released her hold. Nigan, following her cue, did the same, and Wesley staggered backward onto Metzky's lap. Metzky obligingly wrapped her arms about him and kissed his open mouth soundly before he had a chance to escape.

Not that an escape attempt was likely.

When it became obvious *Wesley* wasn't about to break the clinch, Anevai shrugged and headed back toward Stephen yelling at the top of her lungs, "Guess we better leave, Ridenour. Looks like he's down fer th' count."

Wesley yelped and jumped up, rubbing his posterior and glaring with injured pride at his assaultress, who had already resumed her lunch. His shoulders heaved. He placed a hand on his heart and declared himself wounded for life—that a hermit's life was the only choice left for him—and staggered, hangdog, for the door—

—straight into a startled Stephen, who caught at his arms, jarring him to a halt. It was truly one of the Wesser's better performances, albeit undermined by rude remarks and ribald laughter from his audience.

The shuffling walk continued for several more steps, going nowhere, pressing Stephen's elbows to the wall behind him. Finally, the shuffling stopped. Sun-bleached hair in front of Stephen's nose tipped back and Wes (the wretch) said breathily, "Hi, there. New in town?"

Stephen stared back, spook eyes a bit crossed at the close focus, his mouth slightly open. *C'mon, Ridenour, call his bluff. Don't just stand there.*

Wesley's hands crept to 'new in town's' sides and up under the loose sweater. Stephen, his back against the wall, seemed to freeze.

"Oo-oo, leather," Wesley crooned, and hid an over-the-shoulder wink to the crowd under a *pii'chum*-like rub of his head against Stephen's chest. "*Kin*—ky."

The brace: Anevai was not amused.

Stephen quite obviously was not.

Panic. Mindless, irrational panic: she'd seen it too often in animals not to recognize it. But Stephen was no animal. And—dammit—he'd been making such an issue of meeting Wes—well, here he was. *Call his bluff, ya damnfool!*

Finally, Stephen licked his lips and swallowed visibly. Closing his eyes for a split instant, he whispered in a constricted tone, "Dr. Smith, I . . ."

She exchanged a disgusted look with Nigan, moved up behind Wes, grabbed his elbows and pulled back. "—Knock it off, hotshot! This is a nice boy. —A *nice* boy, hear?" She grew less and less amused as Wesley, his hands held out of action, began to press bodily up against Stephen, whose face was no longer red but deathly white.

She hissed in Wesley's ear, "Dammit, Smith, that's enough! You're not funny anymore!"

Wesley sighed heavily enough to make Stephen blink and stir his curls, and straightened up. He accepted the napkin someone handed him and delicately wiped the lipstick from his face, ran a hand casually through his mop, miraculously transforming it into hair, and extended his hand as though nothing had happened.

"How do you do, Dr. Ridenour. I'm Wesley Smith."

Stephen eyed the hand, the calm, professional demeanor, then looked desperately at her. She shrugged and turned to Nigan standing next to her. *You're on you're own now, Ridenour.*

But she kept an eye on him, all the same.

He stepped away from the wall, got the open door at his back, then wiping his palm covertly on his slacks, smiled hesitantly at Smith, and took the proffered hand, saying in his soft voice, "I've been waiting a long time to meet you, Dr. Smith, —ever since I read your paper."

Wesley looked an I-told-you-so at her, then asked Stephen, "Which was that? *The Consumer Dynamics of Infopropagation? Econometric Systems as Pertains to 'Netly Intercourse*—"

"N—no, sir. Although I d—*did* read the *D—Dynamics* as well." He was blushing again—she could hear it in his voice, though she couldn't see it in the pub's low light. "I was s—speaking of *H—Harmonies of the 'Net.*"

*Well, I'll be . . .*

Stephen winced as Wesley's hand closed convulsively on his, and Wesley, marginally sane at last, relaxed his grip but continued to hold on, studying Stephen through narrowed eyes. Stephen blinked, but otherwise held steady. After a long moment, Wesley grinned, clapped him on the shoulder, and drew him toward the bar, the crowd dividing to let them through.

As they passed her, Wesley called somewhat wistfully, "You *sure* he's a 'nice boy'? "

# IV

## i

The receiving line was breaking up, the visitors free now to mingle with the locals. Loren Cantrell left her spot in the reception line, casually scanned the crowded foyer one last time, then signalled TJ. He nodded, an imperceptible dip of his head, and wended his way—a quiet word here, a handshake there—through the waiting guests to her side.

The old fellow did have class when he cared to show it.

She met him at the lounge set aside for the offworlders' use. The instant TJ closed the door behind them, she said darkly, "He'd better have a good excuse for this delinquency. His absence has become an Issue. Find him."

"Have I your permission to knock some sense into him when I do, admiral?"

She snorted. "You get him here and I'll help. —And, Briggs—" as he headed for the privacy exit at the far side of the room, "if Corlaney's with him, I want to know—immediately."

He nodded and disappeared into the corridor. One part of her hoped the kid was all right, another part was ready to kill him if he was. Why hadn't he at least reported in? Where the hell was he?

She took a deep breath, regained her composure and returned to the reception area where the party was well underway. Pure spring water—a greater treat to a spacer's palate than fine wine —glittered in the late afternoon sunlight, cascading down marbled terraces to fill the glasses of indigenes and researchers as well as *Cetacean* crew members.

Rather more of the latter than she'd envisioned. Extra Security (her orders) and some forty-odd off-duty personnel whose presence required even *more* security guards. These enterprising individuals had chanced to talk with Buchanan and the rest of his team and realized the trade potential of the local *objets d'art*—objects ranging from statuary to silver jewelry to intricately beaded clothing, priceless examples of which graced every Recon and researcher present.

Dammit, this dinner was Official, it was Important, and the guest of honor was missing.

"—but, Wesley, if your NSpace viewpoint's already been compromised—"

"*C'mon*, Ridenour. *Dinner* engagement, remember? *We've got to go!*" In desperation, Anevai grasped Stephen's right arm, urging him away from the bar.

And Stephen Ridenour, for whom she had taken half a dozen elbows to the ribs, at least one bash on the head, not to mention various and sundry blows to other parts of her anatomy; this—*person*—she'd protected all afternoon from the casual jostling one received perforce in a crowded public bar; this—so-called human being upon whom she'd avoided laying violent hands for the past hour to avoid embarrassing him again in front of the gang—was so deeply involved in his conversation with Wesley that he simply patted her hand and said, "In a minute. Just let us finish—"

Well—screw embarrassment! "That's what you said an hour ago!" she growled, and set her feet and pulled.

His stool toppled and Stephen grabbed for the bar as the stool skidded away. She staggered back, crowd pressure behind keeping her from falling as Stephen's hold slipped and he fell on top of her.

She pushed against Stephen's chest, saw hands close around his upper arms: "*Wesley, look out for his shoulder!*" Together they managed to get him back on his feet, only to have an injudicious shift of crowded bodies send him staggering into her once more.

She steadied him, his arms closed around her, and he clung there gasping.

"Stephen?" she said, on her own gasping breath. "Are you all right?"

He didn't answer, only leaned more heavily as his gasping breaths achieved an odd choking sound. Gods, she'd warned Wesley about that arm—had been forced to explain to them all, once Wes'd made such an issue about the 'leather'—alarmed, she pushed Stephen away—

—and found spook eyes turned to sparkling crystal: Stephen Ridenour was laughing.

Anevai watched dumbfounded as her sober charge, who'd barely cracked a smile all day, leaned on the bar, breathless with laughter.

Laughter out of all proportion with the incident: a fact he seemed finally to realize. He caught a breath, bit his mouth shut. His eyes, flicking from one face to another, settling on hers.

Definitely red-faced. Embarrassment or laughter—or the two and a half beers he'd had on a still-empty-except-for-a-few-chips stomach—it was hard to tell. He hiccuped, eyes tearing. He hiccuped again, and everyone broke up.

"That's okay, Annie-love," Wesley said, gasping. "*We'll* get him ready for dinner!" Grabbing the laughing fool around the shoulders he headed for the exit.

"Not on your life, Smith!" she yelled, and chased after them. She seized Wesley's arm and dug in her heels. He stopped obligingly enough, but didn't release his prisoner. "I let you take him to his room and he'll never get his dinner!"

Wesley grinned and winked. "You're probably right. You'd better take him up."

Stephen looked from one to the other, and slowly the sparkle faded. He disengaged himself from Wesley's hold, and backed away, one hesitant step. "That's—all right, W–Wesley—Anev–yah. I'll manage by myself." Another step.

"Stephen?" Wesley asked with a puzzled frown.

"I—" Of a sudden, Stephen's Academy-face was back. He smiled—the cool, Clone-smile, not his real one—and said, "Shall I see all of you at dinner?"

TJ's alert beeped in Cantrell's ear as Governor Tyeewapi approached.

*"The kid's fine. He's been in one of the local bars all afternoon with a group from the Complex, —including Smith but not, according to the bartender, Corlaney. Can you talk?"*

"Adm. Cantrell," the governor said, "may I present Yokhi and Dhichali Dohosami, senior members of our Council of Elders? They'll be joining us for dinner tonight."

She smiled graciously and tapped a negative as she exchanged a few words with the elegant indigene couple and accompanied them into the dining hall.

*"They're all off changing for dinner now. Do you want me to light a fire under him?"*

She considered the matter: negative. Let Stephen handle the situation himself. If he'd been with Smith all afternoon, hopefully that meant he was making headway with the elusive scientist and knew what he was doing.

He'd damnwell better know.

He'd laughed. Hard and in company.

He couldn't remember the last time that had happened to him. He thought perhaps he'd made a fool of himself—he'd been more than a little drunk, he feared—but none of the others had seemed to care. Not then. No, the fool was the idiot who had overreacted to Wesley's banter. He'd ruined the whole mood, over something no more serious than Smith's initial craziness.

Stephen sighed, ran the comb through his hair one last time, then turned away from the mirror, pulling down his sleeves and buttoning tight, ruffled cuffs.

It was just their way here. Anevai had said they were—relaxed. If he was going to function here, if he was to fit in here, he'd simply have to learn to—relax as well. And he did—need—to fit in here.

At least long enough to do his job.

He could handle it—wouldn't be the first time. Part of the undergrads' duties at state dinners had been entertainment of bored spouses. At least, for all the jokes, the governor's *daughter* didn't appear so inclined.

He slipped on his jacket—the blue, not the conservative black—hoping the brace wouldn't show. Color rippled over the surface as he twisted in front of the huge mirror, getting his first *real* look at the coat. He'd ordered it in blue. When the package arrived he hadn't had the heart to send it back, no matter the fabric would have taken his entire savings.

But the only charge that had appeared on his records was for the insured delivery. Under *itemization*, the tailor had entered *Happy Birthday*. Of course—the mirror image smiled wryly, smoothed an iridescent blue sleeve—in a way, he *had* paid for it, several times over.

Mirror-imaged eyes, but the face was younger, the hair longer, the clothes (he shuddered) grey shirt and slacks. Grey. A 'color' he hadn't even known existed before Vandereaux. Year after year of grey: academy-issue grey clothes, keeping to grey shadows of grey-painted corridors, slowly learning the rules of dress and behavior by observation, making fewer and smaller mistakes overall, until finally he'd decided he was through playing the game by their rules and that it was time to come out of the shadows.

He had credit; he'd received the same personal-use stipend as every other student—Admin's attempt to smooth the economic discrepancies between students—but he'd never had any hobbies, and between his studies and the gym he hadn't had much time for socializing: so after a particularly unpleasant fifteenth birthday left him in need of a new wardrobe . . .

The sartorial results were—unusual. Not in the quality: most of the students were from Families who made certain they were dressed in the height of their Family's fashion; but because he dared to compete with those Family Images with an Image of his own.

Not that he had intended a conscious challenge to them—initially. Initially, he'd simply chosen fabrics which felt good to him and styles which gave him confidence—which generally meant styles designed for his own peculiar body type.

But while it hadn't begun as a conscious challenge, he did admit to a certain satisfaction this last year in seeing Bijan and his multitudinous cousins walking around in Family variations on designs *he* had suggested to Vandereaux's most exclusive tailor.

He'd never said a word—not to Bijan. To the tailor who had sold his designs, he'd sent a thank-you note and an *official* release.

If his confidence needed a boost, nothing he owned would do it better than this jacket. He'd worn it only once, at his first dinner with Adm. Cantrell, and she'd talked about it for a week afterward. But what he really wanted was to look his best for Anevai's 'gang.'

He knew their acceptance wouldn't last. Soon, he'd have to

separate Smith from the others. Soon, he'd have to explain to Smith why he was here. After that, the warmth would be gone. The laughter would be gone. Until then it might be a cheat, *he* might be a lie, but he'd be one of them, the best he knew how.

*A nice boy*, Anevai had said of him. He'd certainly never been called that before. Had it been another private joke? Or was that *really* the way she saw him? Could it—

—Could it possibly even be true? Somehow, he doubted it. But it was—nice—*someone* thought so.

*Damned security nightmare.*

Briggs worked his way down terraces and steps, through a veritable maze of natural rock formations, plants and waterfalls toward the admiral's table, taking mental notes at each level and alcove he passed of who was where.

First the airport, without even a police escort provided—no real protection whatsoever. Then those government buildings vulnerable to the oldest, cheapest snoops on the market. Now this.

The *Miakoda Moon* was a large restaurant, and it was filled to capacity for this special occasion. Yet it was designed with a variety of visual and sound barriers to give the illusion of eating outside and to allow the patrons to be as private or as social as they liked.

It was natural. It was beautiful.

It made his skin crawl.

Overhead the silkrylic dome (which had been semi-opaque this afternoon when his security team had checked the hall out) had been set (without notifying him of the change) for crystal clarity. Unscreened late afternoon sun sparkled everywhere: on running and falling water, on beads and jewelry, on bevel-edged glass and mirrors. In another hour or so, the sunset would be quite spectacular from in here.

And a sniper would be impossible to spot in the glare.

*You've done dumber things, Loren Cantrell, but don't ask me when. Just because everything appears civilized at the moment . . .*

As far as they'd been able to determine, the dining hall was free of all surveillance equipment, even their own: admiral's orders, blast her hide. *She* wanted no *incidents*—

This, after she had as much as thrown down the gauntlet to Sakiimagan Tyeewapi this afternoon.

—*He* would have felt infinitely more at ease if they'd found a professional Recon video crew hiding in every corner.

Damned security nightmare.


"Admiral, forgive us for missing your reception. We were—unavoidably detained."

*So*, Cantrell thought, *this is the elusive Wesley Smith.* "That's quite all right, Dr. Smith." Smoothly: she knew the game he played. Possibly even better than he. "I quite understand. It's a pleasure to make your acquaintance—finally."

An easy laugh, a slight bow: the man had all the moves plus a few of his own. He'd been brought up in political circles (not to mention Vandereaux) and it showed: good-looking, though nothing outstanding, he could be attractive as hell—

"Ah, caught in the act, admiral. But you see, there was method to my madness. I was quite taken with Dr. Ridenour during our first brief exchange, and meant for him to get the full impact of our lovely planet firsthand. Can you think of a more potent argument for transferral?"

—to someone gullible enough to swallow his act.

Smooth. So smooth. And challenging her to doubt him. On the other hand, he didn't get that build sitting behind a computer all day, nor the tan, she suspected, from a booth. As with all the others she'd met here, the mountains evidently *were* a very real lure to the inhabitants of HuteNamid.

"You do have a point there, Dr. Smith. And now that you've met Dr. Ridenour, do you still feel your action justified?"

"More than ever, admiral. More than ever. Not only is he personally charming, he boasts an intellect which, given proper encouragement, might actually challenge my own brilliance. Such a—gem—is not easily cast aside."

He smiled at her as though they shared some secret knowledge. She didn't return the favor. She no longer wondered about Danislav's reservations about Smith—

—but she doubted the problem lay in Smith's writing.

His smile broadened. "It is, after all, so very difficult to find a challenge—or even a second opinion—when one is . . ." He tipped his head modestly. ". . . the very best in one's field."

"Your academy records do you an injustice, Smith. Your modesty is only equalled by your sheer gall."

"I'm flattered you bothered to check them, admiral."

"Oh, *I* didn't. Others—saw fit to warn me."

He laughed delightedly. Was joined by the other guests at the governor's table who had been following their exchange. Smith rose to his feet and bowed gracefully. "I see I have no chance here. My wit must go where it has no match in order to be properly appreciated."

She raised her glass to him. He bowed again, and started down the stairs to the large, nearly full table a level below.

*Using the planet as a lure, were you? What kind of fool do you take me for, Smith?*

Suddenly, he glanced up one last time, and she had her answer. He knew precisely what kind of fool she was not. That had been a deliberate provocation by a man no stranger to diplomats or politics—a dangerous encounter, especially to someone like Stephen Ridenour. More dangerous, possibly, than a meeting with Paul Corlaney could ever be.

With that smooth affability, Smith could blow a number of very careful, very delicately balanced plans straight to hell.

That eye-liner was still too harsh. Rush home. Rush to get dressed. Rush back to Stephen's apartment in the Condos. How was she supposed to get her makeup right under such pressure?

Anevai wrinkled her nose at her reflection in the mirror strip that ran the length of the hallway wall, softened the offending line with a fingertip and flicked the fringe of her tunic before rapping sharply on the door.

"Hey, Ridenour, I'm—" She broke off, stared speechlessly as her charge stepped out, resplendent in a pale blue evening jacket and skin-tight indigo slacks. The entire outfit had an elusive, iridescent sheen which traced—interesting—patterns as he moved.

"Shee-it, Ridenour. Your clothes . . ."

His brow knit and he glanced at his reflection. "Won't it do? I wasn't certain . . . and after your offer this morning . . ."

She eyed him narrowly, suspecting mockery not altogether undeserved, for all she thought they'd passed beyond that this afternoon. But a second look assured her he really was worried:

if so elegant a personage could chew his lip, Stephen Ridenour was definitely chewing his lip.

"It would only take a minute to change."

"Don't even suggest it, Dr. Stephen. The other women would *never* forgive me for depriving them of such a vision." He blushed violently, and she laughed outright.

She tucked her hand through his arm and led him toward the lift. Shaking her head in amazement, she said, "You're priceless, Ridenour. How you've survived this long, I can't imagine, but I wish you luck tonight. Just do me a favor?"

A little smile. "What?"

"Make my 'job' easier, and keep that jacket buttoned. Light-fingers Smith hasn't seen any—thing—that irresistible in years!"

## ii

Most of the diners were well into the second course by now, but one large central table had yet to begin because *someone* was still missing. Cantrell sipped her wine and did the social bit with her fellow diners while keeping an eye to that increasingly jovial hodge-podge group below.

Hard heads that lot must have, to be drinking steadily for the better part of an hour and not show the effects any more than they did. Or perhaps, not so hard as they appeared. She saw far more water being refilled than alcohol, and she hoped Stephen would be equally sensible—when he finally deigned to join them. For all their apparent rowdiness, this crowd was in control, definite diplomatic mode. It was no time for Ridenour to get loose-tongued.

A wave of silence rolled across the room from the direction of the foyer. Cantrell, along with everyone else at the table, looked up in time to see Stephen Ridenour and the governor's daughter appear from behind a rocky pillar.

About bloody time.

They made a striking couple as they moved along the mezzanine, stopping for a moment at each table they passed. She was relieved to see Stephen's Vandereaux training assert itself at last as he responded with grace and composure to Anevai's introductions. If his alma mater managed nothing else, it turned out proper little party-pups.

The governor, seated beside her, was watching the youngsters along with everyone else. His face remained impassive, but somehow she didn't think he was at all pleased with the vision now descending the terraced stairs to the lower-level dining areas.

And that pleased her. She felt a slow, appreciative smile spread across her face: the kid sure knew how to make an entrance.

From somewhere in the restaurant, a piercing wolf-whistle broke the silence. Stephen's heart skipped a beat. He paused, missed a step, and scanned the room, looking for the source. Anevai laughed and pulled him on. He kept his face carefully controlled, smiling and nodding to the multitudinous parties as Anevai introduced him.

Highly integrated multitudinous parties: another of Bijan's dire predictions shot down. Not only were these researchers mixing freely with the Recons, if what he'd witnessed in the bar this afternoon was any real indication of prevailing attitudes—it was a totally voluntary integration, not something contrived to impress the Council's rep.

He wondered if he should mention that observation to Cantrell. How unusual was it? If only he *had* pursued the truth behind the Vandereaux students' anti-Recon rumors: such knowledge would serve him better right now than all the state dinners he'd ever attended.

Because state dinners at Vandereaux had never been anything like this.

At an academy dinner, he would have passed unnoticed. Here, he was unique. Not, as he'd feared from Anevai's reactions, over-dressed, just—different. Non-local. New.

No one was rude: quite the contrary. The dignified men and women, the perfectly behaved children, would have graced any formal function he'd ever attended. (So much for Bijan's assessment of Recon social behavior.) They simply radiated open, justifiable curiosity at his obvious foreignness—curiosity which happened to make his stomach churn and his skin crawl. Thank God for Anevai: long enough at a table for politeness, moving him on before the hard questions got started.

As they passed Lexi and TJ's table, Lexi winked imperceptibly, and Stephen, feeling his stomach settle a notch, smiled back gratefully. Maybe he wasn't doing so badly after all. He even found himself able to greet Adm. Cantrell and Governor Tyeewapi on the next level with appropriate G'n'C.

The governor invited them to join his table, but Anevai said, "I don't think that would be wise, Dad. The pack is growing restless. They haven't been fed in at least an hour, and if they discover they waited for Stephen and Stephen doesn't show . . . well, things could get pretty ugly."

He looked from Anevai to her father. They seemed perfectly serious. He said quietly, "Perhaps if I went and explained to them, Anevai—"

Anevai stared at him a moment open-mouthed, then laughter gurgled in her throat and she squeezed his arm. "That's okay, Ridenour, I can stand them if you can."

Laughter surrounded him. Laughter from all these distinguished people. Even the admiral joined in. He clenched his jaw and smiled tightly. Nice to know he could still provide a cheap source of amusement. Evidently, Anevai had been too slow getting him away this time.

Anevai's hand patted his arm. "C'mon, Ridenour. Let's go eat."

A bow of precise deference. A smooth: "It was a pleasure. . . . If you will excuse us?" And a turn toward the stairs without a stumble—

—Thank God for Vandereaux.

"Stephen, I'm sorry . . ." He winced at Anevai's murmured apology, her assumption of a guilt that was his. ". . . I really am, Stephen. I didn't mean . . ."

He stopped, drew a breath, and faced her worried gaze. "Look, I . . ." He took her hand, tucked it back into his elbow. "Old war-wounds, Tyeewapi, that's all. Not your fault."

*"C'mon, you two—we're dying!"*

Wesley Smith: waiting for them at the foot of the stairs. He waved vigorously with one hand as he held the other to his stomach.

Anevai grinned and squeezed his elbow. "What say we go rescue the Wesser from starvation?"

"The—who?" Mood swings and topic changes were making him dizzier than the pills and alcohol.

"Come, now, Stevie-lad." Anevai glanced down at Wesley and back to him. "Do you *really* need to ask?"

* * *

Laughter rippled around the table as 'the Wesser' bowed deeply to Anevai and seated her in a manner reminiscent of Vandereaux State Dinners. Reminiscent of, but definitely *not* Vandereaux. Stephen didn't think the Board of Conduct would be amused.

However, everyone at *this* board was most definitely amused. A surreptitious glance around the table revealed most were familiar faces from the bar and the prevailing mood more friendly than formal. It felt odd, but pleasantly so. Meals for him had been solitary affairs, other than his spousal escort duties at state dinners, and the thought of conversing on thoughtful matters throughout the meal was certainly more conducive to digestion than convincing some Significant Other that his attentions did not extend beyond the dinner table.

Anevai seated, Dr. Smith—*Wesley*—turned to him. Wesley gave him no cue. Wesley placed an arm around his shoulders and turned him toward the table, swept his arm in an all-encompassing flourish, and said:

"Stephen, meet the Gang. Say *Hello*, Gang."

A chorused *Hello, Gang* cut off at a second wave of Wesley's hand.

"Now, Dr. Ridenour, be it understood, names will be learned by association. I refuse to be responsible for exposing you to some of the—lower elements which somehow got invited to this table. —And since those are the only ones I know, you're on your own." Under cover of the general laughter and out of the corner of his mouth: "Don't worry, kid, you'll figure 'em out soon enough."

He flashed Wesley a grateful look. *The Watering Hole* hadn't been exactly conducive to sorting names and faces, and Wesley seemed to be assuring him mistakes would be understood. He smiled generically at the table and moved toward the empty seat beside Anevai.

A firm grasp on his elbow stopped him.

"And this, troops—" In dismay, Stephen realized his own introduction wasn't to be so easy. "—is Dr. Stephen Ridenour, fresh from—" Wesley struck his chest dramatically with the flat of his hand. "—my own beloved Vandereaux."

From somewhere down the table: "Yeah, Wes, but *he* graduated."

A puzzled look, a shake of his head. "That's right, he did. Oh well, there's no accounting for taste—'specially not that of Vandy-o's BoD. —Speaking of taste . . ."

Wesley turned to face him, looked him up and down, and began fingering the lapels of his jacket. He drew back from that touch, confused. Over Wesley's shoulder, he saw Anevai watching them, her dark eyes twinkling, and of a sudden, he remembered: *'Do me a favor—keep that jacket buttoned.'*

He wondered, then, if he'd been set up. Was sure of it when 'Light-fingers Smith' smoothed his lapels and said, "Is this what they're handing out for unies now at Vandy-o? Sure was different in my day."

Their audience hooted and Wesley's fingers tightened again on his lapels. He froze, profoundly disappointed at the familiar turn events were now taking. So he was wrong: the *faux pas* in the bar wasn't forgiven; he'd *hoped* things would be different here; he should have *known* better.

"Doesn't seem quite fair to me, nice coat like this on a grad-u-ate when I'm stuck with three-year-old sweaters."

And from some table above: "Only because you're so cheap, Smith!"

The subsequent hoots and jeers were aimed at Smith, not him. But Wesley, for all he acknowledged them, might as well not have heard them. Was he simply used to it? Was he *their* resident fool?

Or was the practical joker who'd been thrown out of Vander-eaux alive and well and living on HuteNamid? Smith's tone, as he continued, did not suggest the fool, but rather the unregenerate joker who berated the Board for denying him an early doctorate.

"*Moi*, . . . the gem of—where did I graduate from, again? oh, well, wherever—and ten years—nine you say? oh well, again—*nine* years in the trenches. And *never* had a coat like this. Look at it! Look at the cut—the style—the line! And this *fabric* . . . I mean, well, it's simply out of this world!"

Smith's audience laughed appreciatively as he pulled Stephen around, making certain everyone saw the details as he pointed them out. But outrageous as Wesley's actions were, his touch was gentle, the laughter friendly, not derisive. Perhaps it was not, after all, chastisement for this afternoon. Perhaps, Wesley even meant to offer him a chance at revenge.

He felt his mouth twitch. Perhaps he'd even accept.

* * *

Anevai kept outwardly relaxed and as appreciative of Wesley's little performance as all the others, but ready to step in the instant the Wesser wessed too far; after all this *was* a public—very—place.

So far, Stephen was managing pretty well. He'd phased out for a heartbeat or two at first, and Wesley, which she'd *never* seen the Wesser do, eased off, only turning it on again when Stephen openly relaxed.

Wesley's encomium had reached the crystal buttons—each of which was worth the price of Wesley's sweater (a fact made clear in said performance)—and he was methodically unfastening those buttons, working his way, with suggestive winks and comments, to the wide-belted waist.

Spook-eyes widened: an instant of fear. She edged her chair back from the table. But those eyes began to sparkle as they had at the *Hole* and she relaxed again. Stephen was going to be okay.

As the belt fell free, Stephen slipped smoothly away, leaving the object of Wesley's lust hanging like a swag of liquid rainbow—

—and leaving the Wesser speechless. Where were the vidCams when you needed them?

Lifting the jacket from the for-the-first-time-in-recorded-history speechless Wesser's hands, Stephen shook it out, folded it, and proffered it with a flourish the equal of Wesley's own, and meeting Wesley's open-mouthed gaze with one of bland innocence.

"Homage, Dr. Smith, to a master."

Master of what? Anevai wondered—along with everyone else within earshot.

For a timeless instant the only sound in their little pocket was the ripple of water over rocks: everyone at the table waiting for the Wesser's next move. He was going to break, he had to. Certainly his eyes were brimming, but:

"*Touché, child,*" Wesley murmured. Down-but-far-from-out, he looked from the coat to Stephen, down at his own sweater-clad belly, and finally focussed on Stephen's waist. His expression turned wistful, and he sighed—quite audibly—as laughter rippled from every table within view.

Underneath that sweater was a damned good body—she'd seen it on several occasions. She'd *also* seen Ridenour's—but then, so could everyone within eyesight of the table: those pants and the sleek silk shirt blousing above them, left no doubt as to who could squeeze into that jacket.

And who couldn't.

Undaunted, Wesley accepted the offering and began carefully checking the width of all the seams. From somewhere along the table, (Nigan, she'd wager, though it was impossible to tell through the laughter) ''Give it up, Smith. You'd have to starve for the next hundred years!''

With a second, even heavier sigh, Wesley mournfully held the coat out for Stephen to slip back into, buttoning it up with far less ceremony and far more regret than he'd removed it. A tug set the jacket straight, then Wesley placed his hands on Stephen's shoulders, and looked him in the eyes. No telling what Wes thought he saw when he did that, but he drove people crazy with it.

Not this time. All Stephen struggled to suppress was laughter, and from where she sat, she could just hear Wes say, *You're okay, kid*, quietly, soberly, before he said aloud, ''Let's eat! I'm starving.''

Maybe, just maybe, the Wesser had finally met his match.

As Stephen slid into the chair next to hers, Anevai caught his eye, grinned, and was relieved to see an answering smile through his heightened color. He'd beaten the odds again. His Vandereaux finals were nothing compared to the test he'd just passed with Wesley. She hoped he realized it and had the guts to follow through. The Wesser needed to be—out-wessed occasionally.

### iii

For such a reluctant recruit, Stephen Ridenour had certainly settled in rapidly. Cantrell glanced up at Lexi, who met that glance, the unspoken question it contained, and shrugged, evidently as perplexed as she was. Could be they were both guilty of misreading him all along. A potentially disastrous mistake in judgment, considering: he'd apparently charmed them all, indigenes and researchers alike, and managed it with something other than the studied grace he'd used on her during the voyage. Between the two of them, he and Smith had an entire section of the room laughing like school-kids on holiday.

Between the two of them . . . Was it *Smith's* influence they were witnessing? Danislav had taught both young men. Danislav didn't approve of Smith, that was obvious, but could he have been bright enough to realize what *meeting* Smith might do to Stephen?

Between the two of them . . . Was this the result Danislav had feared: *'Going into a Reconstructionist camp at this point in his life might or might not be a good thing . . . I'm not nearly as concerned for what's on his head as what's in it . . .'*

Stephen admired Paul, he admired Smith, he was down here with a crowd of their friends—

*If he defected to HuteNamid it'd really blow your experiment, wouldn't it, Danislav? Was it the Recons you feared? Or the researchers? Perhaps one researcher in particular? But if you're a Shapoorianite, you slippery turncoat, it would support your most cherished arguments, wouldn't it? Either way, you win.*

On the other hand, —*Sometimes, people just leave*—as though it were the most natural thing in the world.

Perhaps it was, —on this world.

"Dr. Ridenour seems to be adjusting nicely, admiral." So Tyeewapi had noticed, too. "I hope that means he plans to stay with us. Dr. Smith would welcome a colleague in his own field."

"I'm not surprised," she said, "I begin to understand why my services have never been needed on HuteNamid."

Yet another burst of laughter from the big table. Tyeewapi smiled indulgently until the uproar faded, then: "And why would that be, admiral?"

"Modesty is unnecessary, governor." She made a sweeping gesture toward the room in general. "Over the last thirty years, I've dealt directly or indirectly with every other Planetary 'Tank in the Alliance patching Recon/Researcher disputes, and there's not another 'Tank in the Alliance where indigenes and research teams voluntarily mix the way they seem to here."

"HuteNamid is a young world, admiral, our researchers young, without bias."

She laughed. "Really, governor, you know better than that. Age has nothing to do with it. The majority of the problems I have to troubleshoot stem from an outdated system which brings all the research team members in from the Outside."

"There's really little choice, is there," Yokhi Dohosami,

seated across the table, broke in, "when the academies refuse even to consider applications from colonials?"

"There are those who're trying to change that. I realize you haven't the population or seniority yet to have voting Representatives at Central, but if your resident Senate observers were to—"

General laughter from around the table interrupted her. She looked to Tyeewapi for enlightenment.

He said, "Forgive our levity, admiral. Our Senate observers are—how can I put this—not quite of this universe, let alone our beloved HuteNamid." A bitter edge crept past his cool control. "We sent eager activists once, but they chose to return. For those of us who love the planet, exile in space comes hard."

"Not to mention," she said carefully, "the frustration when cries for simple justice are ignored."

"Your words, admiral, not mine."

"My words, indeed, Governor Tyeewapi—but words I'm not alone in saying. You're very isolated here, and virtually autonomous. There seems to be little the Alliance can offer that you've really needed thus far, except, possibly, an academy education. But that's only a part of the larger problem. Most planets aren't as rich as HuteNamid, yet the opportunities for their indigenes to leave are virtually nonexistent, and the development of technology to make their lives more pleasant receives the lowest priorities."

"And what's to stop these indigenes from developing their own technologies—those appropriate to their worlds—as we have done here?" Wynono Wichado, another of the tribal Council of Elders, asked from his seat halfway down the table, the interests of the company evidently shifting to Tyeewapi's end. "We've *made* our prosperity."

"Time. Funding. Education. The colonials were promised certain benefits, but somehow, year after year, the funding goes elsewhere. And there are worlds incredibly harsh in climate and in resources. They demand a great deal of the Alliance even after the initial terraforming stages."

"This isn't my people's problem, admiral," Tyeewapi said.

"It will be, governor. The social movements that keep your people out of academies are the same social movements that vote down Recon funding and Recon citizenship. Whether or not you ignore their existence, eventually Shapoorian's Separatist movement will affect you. You're here on the Alliance's credit. Sooner or later, your bill comes due, and if you have no representation in the Council or Congress, you won't have a chance in hell if they decide to give your world new residents—''

"Your scare tactics don't impress us, Adm. Cantrell,'' Wichado said. "No world's ever been—repossessed—''

"No world's ever been this rich. You might find yourselves with a most unusual problem for colonists. While it's increasingly difficult to find people willing to take on the challenges of real terraforming, here the problem might be keeping people away. Give the Council *reason* to—repossess, as you so aptly put it—your world, and they might just do that. Or even more likely, bring in *other* colonials who might not favor your colonial style, bringing direct controversy right to your doorstep. Are you prepared for that?''

Tyeewapi said calmly, "Our people were one of the first Recon groups to apply for IndiCorps status, yet even with that high priority we had to wait many years for HuteNamid. Would you like to know why?''

"I'm interested in anything which will aid my understanding of you and your people, governor.''

He studied her face. "Politically correct words, admiral; yet I believe you sincerely mean them. —We were given HuteNamid because no one else wanted it. It was—inconvenient. Too far from the major trade routes, too remote from Capital Station for strong representation in Council and Senate—''

"And your people didn't object to that remoteness?''

"My people had only one stipulation on their contract with the Corps. It was what kept us from attaining a planet earlier and what gave us HuteNamid. We refused to terraform: we didn't care how harsh the world, only that we could live on it as the universal spirit designed it to be, not as humanity wished it to be. Evidently, the Corps Assignment office didn't have a world we could live in without modification until HuteNamid came available. My people accepted it sight unseen. —As you can see, we were richly rewarded for our faith.''

"And do all your people feel equally blessed?''

"Absolutely. No one is welcome here who seeks to harm the planet, admiral. Not researcher. Not Recon. To live as one with the planet is *the* universal law here.''

"And if Council disagrees? If Council requires more of you

and the planet? If Council says they are sending in people who *will* act as instructed? And you must admit that, if *Council* were to advertise HuteNamid, they would have no few takers for the IndiCorps position.''

''I sincerely doubt, admiral, that any human coming to this world from space would find it easy to destroy what we have discovered. I think—even were Council to replace us—that eventually, other colonials would join our cause, not dispute it.''

''If you were replaced, governor, what *cause* would you have?''

Leyland Sanchez, head of geology, broke in. ''The Council would receive no support from us in any move to disrupt this government. Neither would we researchers ever put *in* a request for change. We know a good thing when we have it. And Sakiima and his people are what *we* want.

''Personally, I'd hate to see HuteNamid become a test case— but that could happen. Do you keep up with what's going on in the capital? Do you read the news reports? That very preference the SciCorps shows for a *specific* group of Recons could act against you all—should the Council decide to move in another, more . . . cooperative . . . group. I've spent most of my career patching up relationships between groups of blind fools. Fools on both sides of the atmosphere: indigenes can be as pig-headed as spacers. That's why we have wars on planets. You challenge that ignorance by your very existence.''

Wynono Wichado laughed. ''They'd have to *catch* us before they could replace us, admiral. Unlike other colonials, we're not tied to machines which give us life. Our planet is our machine.''

''Still, if you wished to influence new colonials, you'd have to come out of hiding.''

''Our influence isn't necessary, admiral,'' Tyeewapi said quietly. ''It is HuteNamid's law, not ours. One does not live on HuteNamid without converting.''

''Don't worry, you get used to it after the first month or so.'' Wesley grinned across the table at Stephen, who was picking suspiciously at a very small portion of the least curious concoction.

The cooking staff had outdone themselves tonight. Perhaps they'd felt a challenge in Adm. Cantrell's experience on other colonial planets. But while the table overflowed with dishes of every color, shape and texture, there wasn't enough food on Stephen's plate to keep a rodent functioning.

Anevai sighed. *She* was going to have to run ten miles to burn off this meal. Uphill.

"Lordy, Ridenour," she said, disgusted, "no wonder you're so skinny."

"Not, skinny, Anevai," Dr. Metcalf said, giving Stephen the eye. "Definitely *not* skinny."

Everyone laughed except Stephen, who gazed studiously at the food on his plate, his too-ready flush rising.

She frowned at Metcalf. *Dammit, Metzky. Can't you keep your hyperactive hormones under control for five minutes?*

Just because you could see Ridenour's pulse through those pants . . . She shook off that thought. Stephen had no concept of what he did to female blood pressure. He didn't at *all* understand.

The laughter faded into uncomfortable silence, as the others realized Stephen was not sharing the joke. She caught Nigan Wakiza's eye. He could always be counted on for distraction.

Nigan winked, and looked around him for possibilities. A wicked grin spread across his face and he snatched one of the hard rolls out of the warming basket.

"Hey, Ridenour! Try this!" He called and pitched the roll, low and hard.

Stephen's head flew up, and with reflexes she wouldn't have attributed to him, he ducked toward her. She laughed, snagged the roll one-handed out of the air above his head and whipped it back at Nigan. Nigan's neighbors, already admonishing his manners, saw it coming, and grabbed his arms so that the roll hit him dead center.

Freed, he collapsed to the floor, moaning in agony. She was impressed. First Wes, now Nigan: everyone was in top form tonight.

"Nigan?" Beside her, Stephen leapt up, and Anevai groaned as his chair tipped over and crashed to the floor behind him.

*C'mon, Ridenour, wake up! I can't keep covering for you.*

Stephen froze, looked around him at faces which didn't share his obvious concern, at faces waiting expectantly for the next move to be made.

Slowly, in rigid dignity, he straightened his chair, sat down, and picked up his fork again.

*Good lad. Now what?*

As the moans faded, someone said sadly, "Looks like Cooky's rolls did in another one. Wonder what he puts in 'em?"

Stephen reached for one of the contested rolls, bounced it in one hand, then let it fall to the plate.

It clanged: exactly the way a good, hard crust should.

He stirred the pellet peas on his plate, and stabbed at one. His aim was off—or perhaps perfect—and the pea shot across the table, straight at Wes. Stephen's whole head followed the pea's trajectory, until his eyes, wide and innocent as a baby's, met Wesley's crinkled-at-the-corners, definitely *not* innocent stare.

Innocence turned tragic. "Two months of this, Wes? By then, I fear I shall be dead of starvation."

This time Anevai laughed as hard as the others.

As the group below settled into serious eating, Cantrell leaned back in her chair, shaking her head in bemusement. "Amazing." She shifted her gaze from Ridenour to the man seated beside her. "I've been wondering, governor, why your people choose to apply the term 'Reconstructionist' to yourselves at all. I find little of the—one hates to say typical when speaking of Recons, but in this case it *has* been typical—elitist attitude anywhere here. Walking the streets of most other Recon cities is like walking through a history book designed by idealists. People speak Standard only with great reluctance. They make an issue of their individuality. It's little wonder their researchers can't deal with them: a trip from their science complexes to the indigene colonies is a trip through time. They're tourists there. Nothing more. Often far less."

"In what way do you find us different?" Wynono asked.

"Other than your freely socializing population? For one, your architecture," she made a sweeping gesture with her hand, taking in the room around them, "is—unique. There's a continuity of style which makes moving from one complex to the other a change of venue, but not a shocking change. It's not Reconstruction. It's not Spacer. It's something else. What?"

Sakiimagan rubbed a hand along his chin, then answered slowly, as though examining each phrase before speaking. "When the People first came to this world, they were also determined to re-create the ancestors' visions. But when the descendants of the Natives of the Ancient Americas gathered and began assembling archival records—and more importantly, exchanging family histories—they realized how many different —*worlds*—that term pertained to. Some were desert dwellers, some from rich coastal forests, some agriculturalists, some foragers. *Which* of those lifestyles were we to choose? *Which* language were we to speak—especially when not one of those languages was ever thoroughly and properly recorded?''

''But that's the problem all Recons face,'' she said, ''in varying degrees.''

''Allow me to finish. Unlike those other Recons, my people—*all* my people, for they are all my philosophical ancestors—*depended* on a verbal history. That history and the understanding of what we are was—interrupted. When the European invaders came into our country with their superior destructive power, a generation died—more than one generation. Connections were lost. Not a genetic genocide, but a cultural one.''

''Most so-called cultures are amalgams—most have seen conquests.''

''I can't speak for those other people. Only my own—and that, as we now perceive ourselves. Those of our ancestors who did survive saw their children forced to the cultural standards of the interlopers. Perhaps some felt the best interests of those children would be served by training them in the spirit of the conquerors; perhaps they felt the rituals and beliefs would be contaminated if passed on to offspring incapable of understanding them.''

Noisy laughter from the table below broke the peace. Sakiimagan paused, waited patiently for it to die down, then continued:

''Whatever the reason, a generation passed without the holders of the deep secrets passing those secrets down. By the time the grandchildren became aware of the—theft—it was too late. Many of the Elders were dead, taking with them the knowledge. All of our wishes cannot resurrect the knowledge . . . or the faith. What *was* ultimately written down was itself selected information—selected by those who saw beyond the absolutes of the dead elders and saw value in those beliefs for all time and all people. So when we came here, when my father and the other Elders came here, they had already inherited a tradition which respected our ancestors too much to create caricatures of their beliefs. Instead, they sought the truth underlying those beliefs and based our society on those universal truths—not surface manifestations: the essence of those beliefs.''

Elsewhere laughter had no power this time to disturb Tyee-wapi's spell.

''What was our Universal Truth? What did our ancestors leave us, that made this difference? A sense of unity with the world. It makes no difference in what way you say the words; it makes no difference what exact shape you make the house: what makes the difference is the respect with which you regard the thing and how it harmonizes with its environment. Therefore, we accept no world whose—soul, if you will—must be destroyed that we might live. Therefore, we honor our beloved rift and mountains with this room, while protecting our own nature from its harsher aspect with the use of our technology. Our technology, serving us, is part of our understanding of the whole.''

He sought and held her eyes. ''Do you understand what I am trying to say, admiral? Have you *any* inkling?''

*Not* a light question. Not really a challenge, either. She responded carefully, ''Evidently your founding fathers placed the *essence*—the *spirit*—of your ancestors above the trappings. That spirit seeks harmony with—Nature herself. In essence, with this planet. In that, you, your people and evidently your researchers as well, have no schisms.

''But you Amerinds weren't the only ones to recognize your—Universal Truths. Unfortunately, while other Recons have come to similar conclusions philosophically, culturally they remain linked to the quantifiable: the *things* of the past. They concentrate so profoundly on how they're unique, they've lost sight of the value of the whole. They break out in schisms and feuds over what those identifying quanta are, and when they pick and choose only those aspects of the parent culture they wish to emulate, they undermine their own desire to be taken as serious historians by their spacer contemporaries.''

Sakiimagan said, ''As to that—we care nothing how our *spacer contemporaries* view us. We know something of the colorful ceremonies of our ancestors and we strive to reconstruct the art of them. But you don't create belief. What use are stories of Raven and Buffalo when you've never seen these creatures? But we *can* understand the philosophies they represented and pass those standards on to our children and grandchildren.

"Our Peoples' names once had significance. Today we name our children out of books, choosing their names for the delight of the sound, and occasionally—" with a glance down at his daughter, "—in hope of what they might be.

"We chose an ancient language with the most complete references for the basis of our world-language, but we pick and choose from many of our ancestors' terms. Athabascan might have been the start, but if we can't find an appropriate term in the 'Net from the Navaho, we won't begrudge a suggestion from our Nez Perce, Choctaw, or Wyandot ancestors. And we are actively adjusting our language to make it reflect *our* world."

"And where do the researchers fit in?"

"Let me answer that, Sakiima." Joanna Carpenter, head of Psych, interrupted. "The community you see here, *admiral*, is because Sakiima's people have never isolated themselves from us and have encouraged us to do likewise. Their work is as vital as ours, and mutually beneficial. We know that. More importantly, the People know it. We encourage interaction."

"For most of us," Sanchez added, "it's much simpler: we are as much a part of HuteNamid as the People. We've as much right to be here and as much right to love it."

Sakiimagan said, "The kivas may no longer have the religious connotation they held for our forebears, but the spiritual connotation is very strong. When we enter there, whether as an individual or as a gathering of all the People and Researchers, it is with the intention of becoming unified in spirit and in goals. Between meetings, the kivas serve as constant visual reminders of that philosophy."

"But it does seem to me," she said softly, "that there must be some flaw in your system. The researcher unit ought to be more productive than the *'Net* records indicate. Shapoorian's Separatists—you do know Shapoorian, of Vandereaux?—claim world and family ties undermine a researcher's focus and inhibit his judgment. They oppose indigenes getting into the academies—to keep them out of the 'Tanks. —Are they right?"

She paused . . . took another sip of wine. Tyeewapi had woven a spell which she tried now to break. Golden tongues could not protect against greed and corruption.

"It seems to me that the true concern is that onworld family ties would create a bond between the world, the IndiCorps and the SciCorps, which someone, in their infinite wisdom, deemed a Bad Idea. We came into space from many nations. In space, we live in one society. *Our* predecessors feared redivision. They feared wars—they were reluctant to allow Reconstructionist so-cieties to have planetary settlements, but it happened—because they had no choice: there was no one else with the necessary drive to colonize. Now after more than two hundred years of peace, shooting wars happen again—on planets. Between Recon factions. Is Shapoorian right?''

No answer.

''What you have here is very interesting. It threatens some people. That what you have seems to work—threatens ideas. That your 'Tank devotes so much time to Recon projects—would disturb some people profoundly. I can see reasons for your secre-cy. I'm in sympathy with those reasons. My commission, specifi-cally to deal with Recon worlds, wasn't granted me because I oppose Recons. I oppose wars. I also oppose oppressive, outdat-ed systems—wherever they exist. Don't view me as a threat. What's going on here could stir powerful debate. It could also frighten some people, and reason might go by the board. Do you understand those fears?''

''Perhaps,'' Sakiimagan said, ''they fear divided loyalties.''

''You seem fond of that expression, governor.''

''It's a potent fear.''

''How would you answer that fear?''

''Our peace. Our harmony with this world. Our researchers who find their harmony with us.''

''And your—divided loyalties here on HuteNamid?''

An almost-smile and then Sakiimagan said, ''I don't believe in them.''

*And then they disappear* . . .

*I don't believe in them* . . .

''And what,'' she asked softly, ''if that very peace is what certain interests find most threatening?''

Another moment of silence. Then Sakiimagan pushed his emp-ty dessert plate aside. ''We should let our young people carry our philosophy to the fireside: they must be restless in our formal-ities. Admiral?''

# iv

They were on their way to 'The Pit.' If he hadn't spent all afternoon in a place called 'The Hole,' this fact might have worried him. Now, on a stomach full of fresh berries and ('Of course, it's real, Ridenour.') cream, and fortified with four glasses of excellent wine, Stephen let the human wave carry him into the heart of this rock maze without protest.

Up one long twisting flight of carved rock, and down several steps, two strides through a carved tunnel, then down again. He finally began giggling stupidly, protesting they were trying to confuse him.

Wesley turned on him, glaring. "Close your mouth, brat."

The giggle-bubble popped.

Then Wesley shoved his face so close his eyes crossed and the bubble formed again. But he obediently kept his mouth closed and the bubbles popped out his ears.

"Now the eyes."

That was harder, but Anevai's hand slipped into his and guided him forward. Hands on his shoulders turned him a few degrees and Wesley's voice in his ear said, "Open wide, kid." And a moment later, "Your *eyes*, bit-brain."

No giggle this time, but honest laughter. Laughter that disappeared along with the intoxicated bubble when he opened his eyes on the descent into the Pit.

He no longer cared their route had been circuitous. To have come upon this too abruptly from the ambiance of the dining area would have failed its creator.

All around him was space-black stone—sometimes shot with sparkling silver, sometimes solid black—honed into sensuous, freeform shapes which created pockets and eddies of stars, rose in delicate galactic arms overhead and swirled back into the floor. Each surface was polished to a mirror sheen, glistening in the flickering light from the fire pit.

Before this world, he didn't remember ever having seen free-running water. Here, it was everywhere, inside and out—carved statuary fountains, waterfalls . . . in the Pit it was thin streams between stones and in a moat around the fire: a moat smooth and round on one bank, an irregular overhang of star-stone on the other: poetic interphase of traditional geometric and fractal mathematics.

It was like nothing and no place he'd ever seen before—

He touched the black polished stone at his side, trailed his hand in sensual fascination along its slick surface as he slowly descended the stairs. No one rushed him. No one said a word. Partway down, he paused, touched a petal on a single flowering vine trailing over the stone wall: intruder from the Outside seeking the stream below—

—and he felt as though he had been searching for it all his life. He reached out—explored a single, large crystal, a silver-dust halo, with the tip of one finger. *Granther, you didn't lie. I can touch the stars.*

The child-Stephen had never found that promised place. The adolescent-Stephen almost had—once. That Stephen had been so close. He'd heard of the restaurant in Vandereaux Station—had even dared the strange environment to find it; but he'd never made it to those crystal walls. Now, adult-Stephen had found the place at last.

—And he'd had to come back downworld to do it.

At the pit's edge, he turned slowly, watching the flickering play of fire-cast shadows; the sparkling stars in the stone around him fragmenting and multiplying as he blinked his eyes dry.

*"Well?"* A free neuron identified the voice: Wesley, growing impatient.

"I . . ." He spread his hands in tongue-tied dismay. "It's . . ." —*beautiful* was what he nearly said, but that was empty.

"Tell us, Stephen; tell us what you're feeling."

He bit his lip and turned toward the fire. Once, a long time ago, he'd tried to share such thoughts as he was having now. He'd learned not to try. Sometimes, not even to have the thoughts. But Wesley persisted and finally, defiantly:

"You'll laugh, but it feels like a piece of home." He gestured toward a graceful, starry curve overhead. "The stars that surround us: even when you can't see them, you know they're there." Then to the perfect circle of the fire-pit itself. "The one Sun: Sol, Etu, Albion, or—" His voice caught on a word he didn't even remember knowing: "—Solntze: whatever you call it, it's the one Star that gives light and life." Of a sudden, he was shivering and he clasped cold hands behind his back lest they betray him. "Here, in the heart of the room . . . it's almost like . . . almost like a shrine . . ." He paused, confused by his own impression. "No, that's still not right. Not a shrine. More of a . . . more of a reminder of our . . . our interdependence, or . . ."

A glance toward Wesley: hope for reassurance—this place was obviously special to them—but Wesley's face gave no clue. He focussed once more on the fire. ". . . Or a warning. A warning against . . . forgetting."

Movement at his peripheral vision: Wesley, sitting on the hearth-side, somberly searching his face—again. Wesley Smith should terrify him. One moment crazed, the next intensely serious, he was the personification of the uncertainty principle he'd fought all his life. Certainly, he wasn't the source of all knowledge he'd thought he'd come here for: though they'd discussed *Harmonies* and 'Net theory all afternoon. He should be eager to reveal his true purpose here, get the job done and escape from Smith's vicinity—the man was Disaster awaiting opportunity, and proud of it. But instead of prudently pressing the issue, he found himself hoping for excuses to avoid that revelation.

Wesley got up and put an arm around his shoulders. "C'mere, kid. There's someone we'd like you to meet."

"Who?"

And Anevai said, "Always with the questions, Ridenour. Dr. Paul."

The mysterious Dr. Paul, creator of the blue pii'chum. Suddenly, the ceremony—the mystery surrounding this Dr. Paul was disturbingly ominous. He resisted Wesley's urging, moving out from under his arm. "I don't think—"

Wesley grinned and said softly, "Oh, yes you do think. Occasionally quite profoundly. As to Dr. Paul: do the name Corlaney mean anything to you, Stevie-m'lad?"

The Elders had, many of them, gone home. Sakiimagan had excused himself to his office to look further into the matter of those missing Recon files. In the corner pockets, private debates still flourished—on mutagenetics, chemistry, and the condition of a warehouse.

Cantrell slowly sipped the very excellent wine, allowing herself time to think—or more accurately to stop thinking. The die had been cast. It remained now to see what it read.

She drained her glass, signalled TJ and Lexi and started for the pathway up which the young people had disappeared some time before. This wasn't the time to lose track of young Ridenour. Something had happened to him today, and she wanted a report out of him before it got fantasized out of all proportion.

She rounded the final turn into the pit, heard laughter below, and saw Stephen, in the center of the crowd, jerk his hand back from the fire and shake it wildly. One of the women, botanist Sarah Metcalf, if she remembered the picture-files correctly, caught the hand in mid-shake and began blowing on it. Then, to the delight of the observers, she kissed the fingers one by one.

A raised eyebrow from Lexi, a frown from TJ. Changes, indeed. She shrugged, called up a friendly smile, plastered it on her face, and eased down the steps.

Stephen looked up, eyes bright in the firelight, reclaimed his hand and held it out in ingenuous welcome. "Look, Loren, it's *real!* Isn't it wonderful?"

*Loren?* Teeth clenched behind friendly smile. Changes upon changes. Ignoring his proffered hand, she clasped his shoulder—signalling caution with a squeeze. He flinched from that minor pressure as his hand fell, but responded to her questioning look with a barely perceptible shrug and turned away from her.

*Later, kid.* For the home crowd's benefit, she smiled and asked cheerfully, "Certainly nothing like it back home, is there?"

More laughter as Dr. Metcalf said, "Just ask Dr. Ridenour. Only a tried and true Ree-sur-chur would *test* to see if a fire was real or not."

"He *didn't*."

"He certainly did."

Stephen protested, but she ignored his indignation, saying pensively, "Sad, but what more could you expect from a poor spacer-lad whose only contact with Reality has been computer-generated facsimiles . . ."

"Don't you mean *fract*-similes, admiral?" That from Wesley Smith, perched on a rock near the fire, all friendship and charm.

She waited for the universal groan to fade, then said, "You're going to love it here, Ridenour; they all talk like you."

"Puns? I never—" Stephen began, and Smith interrupted:

"—Not intentionally."

Stephen chuckled softly in the general mirth. She couldn't recall ever hearing him laugh quite that way before. She couldn't say she enjoyed hearing it now.

*'Perhaps they fear divided loyalties'* —*Do you know something I don't, Sakiimagan Tyeewapi?*

"I have a story . . ."

Anevai Tyeewapi's barely audible announcement, drifting out of a shadowy nook, commanded instant attention.

"I was saving it for the summer solstice blowout, but since Adm. Cantrell is here for such a short time, and in honor of Stephen's arrival, I thought now might be a good time . . ." Her voice trailed off expectantly, and her implied question met universal approval.

"Admiral?"

God. Social duties. "By all means, Ms. Tyeewapi. I'd be delighted."

"Stephen?"

But Stephen was gone—lost in a private exchange with Smith. He looked up, confused, while Smith murmured, "Say yes, Stephen."

"But—"

A group chorus: *"Say yes, Stephen."*

"I . . ." His lost gaze moved from one to the other, and she prepared to bail him out, but he shrugged and said, ". . . yes?"

Worse and worse.

Anevai emerged from the shadows and settled cross-legged on the stone ledge by the fire. Her audience arranged themselves in a rough semicircle around the girl's chosen spot, perching on every artistic curve of stone which could possibly serve as a seat. Smith pulled Stephen down beside him, settled an arm possessively around the boy's shoulders—

—an action apparently not the least objectionable to 'the boy.'

Anevai said, "This version of the Bridge of the Gods is brought to us courtesy of Wesser, Inc.'s efforts in the Lit files—"

Smith stood up and bowed right and left, throwing kisses. The crowd booed, and hands, Stephen's among them, grabbed and pulled him out of their way.

Anevai paused, allowing the sound of fire and water to drift her audience to a place far from the *Miakoda Moon*.

*"Long ago, when the world was young, the People were very*

*happy. No one was hungry and no one was cold, because the Great Spirit provided all their needs . . ."*

Cantrell, prepared for an endurance test, was pleasantly surprised. It was a common enough story of feuding brothers and gods spiriting them away from their homeland to give them a second chance at behaving themselves, but the girl was a gifted storyteller, evoking her fantasy realm with gesture, tone of voice, and even sound effects, drawing her audience into a land of mountains and valleys: a land divided by a single great river. The land to the north was given to one brother, the land to the south to the other.

*". . . and across that river, the Great Spirit built a bridge, a wonderful bridge, wide enough for fifteen men on horseback to cross at once. And the Great Spirit told the brothers, "As long as you and your people remain at peace, the great bridge will stand as a symbol for you."*

Stephen squirmed uncomfortably and turned to Smith, who forestalled his question with a smile and a finger held to Stephen's lips.

*". . . For many seasons, the People lived in peace, crossing back and forth at will, but eventually, they began to forget, as people will do. They forgot the Great Spirit's promise—and warning—and they began doing small things: telling small lies, cheating small amounts, stealing small things. But small evils beget larger ones, and eventually small arguments became very large indeed.*

*"The People began doing truly wicked things. They became selfish and greedy and the Great Spirit grew angry . . ."*

Stephen leaned forward, revealing Wesley Smith propped against a rock and watching Ridenour. He looked up and in the instant before Stephen shifted back between them, she read a distinct challenge. Curious. Smith certainly didn't act as if Stephen had already explained his mission here; and even if he had, why should Smith take offense at her presence? What had Stephen told them about *Cetacean's* reason for being here?

*". . . The Great Spirit loved the People and believed in them, in their ability to change and grow. So he did not destroy the bridge, but instead ordered Father-sun to stop shining on the People.*

*"When the rains and snow descended upon them, the People had no fire. They were cold and afraid and they prayed to the*

*Great Spirit to take pity on them. They swore they were sorry for what they had done and promised to be good . . ."*

Anevai paused, reached down and pulled a glowing brand from the pit, flourishing it out and around until it flared anew.

*"The Great Spirit's heart was softened by their prayers and again he took pity on the People, believing they had learned their lesson. He went to Loo-Wit, an old woman who lived all alone and had kept herself from the quarrels and wrongdoing of the People. Loo-Wit had fire in her lodge and the Great Spirit said to her, 'You may have anything in this world you wish if you will share your fire with the two Tribes . . .' "*

"Anev-yah?"

Hostility rippled through the listeners and Stephen glanced around, obviously distressed. But Anevai, unruffled, lifted a hand to silence the muttering. "Yes, Stephen?"

"If—if the P–People didn't have f–fire, where did L–Loo-Wit get it?"

The flickering branch in Anevai's hand sparked off her beads and cast strange shadows across her face, but she could swear the girl smiled: a mere hint of a dimple at the corner of her mouth.

"The old text doesn't really say. Perhaps Loo-Wit wasn't what she appeared. Nowhere does it say she's of the People, only that she'd kept herself from their wrongdoing. Perhaps she, herself, is of the supernatural. Perhaps that's for the listener to determine."

Stephen sat back, silent, his brow puckered in thought, and Anevai, shifting her voice to that of the Great Spirit, deftly re-established the mood:

*" 'Is there anything you want, Loo-Wit?' To which Loo-Wit promptly replied, 'To be young and beautiful again.' And the Great Spirit said to her, 'Take your fire to the Bridge and give it freely to the People of both Tribes. Keep it burning always as a reminder of the goodness and kindness of the Great Spirit.' "*

Anevai lowered the brand. Its flames, died to glowing cinder, created eerie under-lighting for her face.

*"The following morning, the sun rose on a young and beautiful maiden sitting by her fire in the precise center of the Bridge. The People of the Tribes saw her, and rejoiced for the warmth which had returned to their homes.*

*"Once again, peace lay between the two Tribes, and prosperi-*

*ty came to their lands. For many seasons, the People came and visited the maiden often, but none so often as the young men of the Two Tribes: they had seen the beautiful maiden and their desire for her was strong. Loo-Wit's heart was stirred by two of them, each the handsomest and bravest of his Tribe, and she could not choose between the two, fearing that, in choosing, she might rekindle jealousy and hatred between the Tribes.*

*"Despite her wishes for peace, the young men grew jealous and began to quarrel and at last to fight. Their anger spread to their People and fighting began on both sides of the river. Many of the People were killed."*

Raising the brand, she thrust it into the stream of water at her feet. With a hiss, steam rose and curled around her. Her voice, when she continued, was very soft, though without doubt it reached each and every listener.

*"The Great Spirit was very angry and no longer listened to the cries of the People. They no longer deserved his kindness. He struck down the Bridge and let its mighty stones fall into the Great River: what was once a strong and mighty link was now and forever more an impassable rapids, and the brothers and their people forever—separate. Forever—alone. Forever less than they might have been—together."*

Her head dropped, her hands folded in her lap, and she whispered, "Da neho."

Silence reigned for several heartbeats after the final whisper faded. It was as though everyone was waiting for someone else to say something, someone else to break the spell. Bewitchment must run in the Tyeewapi genes. Curious choice of story. She wondered at whom the indigene girl had aimed.

Eventually, all eyes came to rest on Stephen. Slowly, very slowly, he got to his feet. Anevai's head came up, revealed eyes brimming with unshed tears.

Stephen held out both hands, Anevai placed her fingers in his and rose fluidly to her feet. With that odd, archaic grace which could seem so natural in him—and was the subtle antithesis of his academy airs—he bowed his head. "I now know the meaning of the word enchantment. Thank you, Ms. Tyeewapi, for a truly memorable experience."

Where the hell did it come from? Academy-clone or Recon gentleman—he should be one or the other—but amalgam he was and able to slip from one cloak to the next with disturbing ease. She'd give a great deal to know if it was a controlled metamorphosis or an instinctive response to the friendly environment.

"Thank *you*, Stephen," Anevai said. "I rarely have an opportunity to share our stories with a new audience, let alone one appreciative enough to ask what's important to understand." Thus quelling any residual resentments. Thus placing Stephen *above* those who objected. The girl was destined to be a diplomat: slippery as her father.

And Ridenour . . . Assessing a situation and adjusting his actions accordingly, Lexi said. But he wasn't 'fitting in,' he'd made a spectacle of himself and was either oblivious to that fact or—worse—revelling in it.

Whichever, bringing him down here was a mistake. A major mistake.

In the ensuing chaos of casual exchanges, Cantrell sensed a growing excitement in Stephen, saw him catch Smith's attention and look a question. Smith smiled and nodded indulgently; Stephen moved purposefully toward her.

"Adm. Cantrell." His voice was alive with controlled excitement. "There's someone here I'd like you to meet."

The bad feeling in the pit of her stomach grew, the apparent bonding between Stephen and Smith no longer the cause. Stephen took a light hold on her arm, and urged her toward Anevai's one-time shadowy alcove—an alcove which she now saw contained several more bodies draped comfortably on and around each other.

A moment of relief: firelight glinted off unfamiliar silver hair. But that same firelight limned a hand draped over another's shadowy shoulder. A long-fingered hand she *well* remembered.

"Admiral." Stephen's eyes glittered. Such a treat he believed he was giving her. "*This* is Dr. Paul Corlaney."

She might have known it would happen like this: somehow reunions never occurred the way one so fondly imagined. Dammit, she should have dealt with him the minute they came in-system. She should have had a team out after him this afternoon when he didn't return her calls. She should have known better than to expect him to play by sensible rules. She'd been a fool to think he'd keep out of *anything*.

"H'lo, Loro." The silver hair was new. The liquid voice —like the hand—was unchanged. " 'Bout time you got here."

## V

God, he'd missed her. He hadn't realized just how much until she'd glided down those stairs into the Pit. Ordinarily, the tone of young Dr. Ridenour's introduction would have irritated him—he abhorred youthful idolatry—but now it was simply a means to an end.

Carefully extricating himself from the pile of bodies, Paul Corlaney stood up and reached for Loren, longing, in the after-glow of Anevai's story, to sweep the woman into his arms in the best romantic tradition and carry her off to—wherever he could convince her to go.

But the lady wasn't biting. She held out her hand and said flatly, "A pleasure to meet you **aga**in, Dr. Corlaney. It's been a long time."

This was *not* going the way he'd planned. Not at all.

"A damn sight too long," he muttered, and brushing her warn-off aside along with her hand, he wrapped his arms around her, letting his hands rove, revelling in the feel of her as he whispered into her ear, "Loosen up, Loro. We're all friends here." And pressed his mouth down on hers.

When he came up for air she murmured against his lips, "If you don't want to sing soprano for the rest of your life, Corlaney, you'll modify your behavior immediately."

Puzzled, he tipped his head back to study her face. She was *serious*. He gave one of his (as she had dubbed them) 'damned irresistible lopsided grins,' and released his grip, holding his hands up in the old-as-mankind gesture of defeat.

Perversely, the woman slipped one arm around his waist and said, loudly enough for all the onlookers to hear:

"Bit of an audience, don't you think? Meet me later?" And released him with a pat on his backside. Paul grinned and raised his hand once more: this time, in a fencer's acknowledgement of a hit.

This was much more like *his* Loro.

Under cover of the kids' laughter, he murmured, "Try to keep me away, admiral, sir."

She shook her head at him, her face hard. The hell! A warn-off? After that come-ahead? But before he could figure, her gaze slipped away, searching the crowd. He knew, without seeing that search end, what she was looking for.

Ridenour: withdrawn to the fire's far side, sulking, *up*set at losing the center of attention.

He'd seen the type before. Cloistered students accustomed to the extravagant praise of their instructors, so convinced of all the great things they would achieve. —And the minute Life hit them, they folded. This Stephen Ridenour, leaning against the stonework and staring into the fire's depths, was classic: from his coiffed curls to the mirror polish on his shoes; from his smooth voice to his Byronic posturing.

Know them? Hell, he'd *been* them!

*("Don't* ever *call me that again! Not in public, not in private."* Angry voice ringing through the ringing in his ears. *"I've been too lenient with you, boy. You call me Dr. Danislav or Sir. Nothing else! Do you understand me? I'm not your Uncle Victor. I never was!"*

*(Himself, desperately, "But—but Mama said—"*

*(Another blow. A taste of blood. "I don't care what she said! You'd damn well better hope none of the others heard you!")*

Stephen's gut twisted, and for a moment sparkling stone blurred and whirled around him. He leaned heavily on the stonework waiting for the dizziness to pass.

Adm. Cantrell was angry—justifiably so. What in hell had induced him to such familiarity with her? He was here on business, dammit, and he was losing sight of that reality.

He knew better: another conditioned response these too-friendly people had destroyed. (*"Dammit, Stevie-lad, the name's* Wesley! *W-E-S-L—E?—E-Y!"*)

Still, it hurt. Her anger—their ridicule—hurt in a way no one and nothing had been able to hurt him in years.

She'd known. She'd known all along—*he*—was here, and made no attempt to warn him. *Corlaney* had been too polite to throw his ignorance in his face, had feigned ignorance of his own until he'd forced the introduction. An introduction he'd begged Wes to allow him to make. Wes knew Paul well. Surely Corlaney must have mentioned his—friendship with the admiral. Why hadn't *Wesley* told him they already knew each other?

Stephen stretched his cold hand to the warmth of the fire,

studying the play of light and shadow on flesh and bone. Had he just been the brunt of another joke? Or was it more complicated than that? Were they trying to use him somehow? Giving him this knowledge in order to trap him into doing what they wanted?

Paul Corlaney's presence here must be one of the best-guarded secrets in Alliance. So why was *he* being allowed in on the secret? What was he supposed to do with it now he had it?

Chet Hamilton had said *Ask Smith anything*.

Why? Because whatever he learned here, he'd not be remembering it after his report? Was he programmed to forget—as he'd forgotten other things? Or would they put him under Dep and *make* him forget? What *else* would they take from him?

The hand silhouetted against the fire started to shake violently. He tucked it against his side, felt the chill through the jacket.

It was terrifying, considering the stakes these people played for. Far greater stakes than Bijan could imagine. And it hurt far more than anything Bijan could have done, because Bijan had never pretended to be his friend.

Most painful of all was the knowledge that he was stupid for hurting. What these people thought of him changed nothing in his life—ultimately. What they did to him changed nothing. Whatever rules *they* were playing by, *his* actions remained the same. *He* had to operate as though the offer from Councillor Eckersley, the thesis proposal lying in some 'NetAT office, were worth something.

Because that *something* was all he had, ultimately, and all that mattered was that these people, Recons and researchers, believe his story for a few days—long enough for him to clear Smith's paper and get out.

Still, she might have warned him, before—

—before he'd made a damned fool of himself.

The boy's pale eyes flickered at them, then back to the fire. A hand clenched, marring the studied grace of his pose.

"Excuse me, Paul," Loren said, and Paul watched in silent disgust as she worked her way quietly through the crowd toward the boy's chosen stage. But there was something almost convincing about the pose now, in the pale-eyed despair; Paul felt a response deep in his gut—

—and shied furiously away from that feeling: *God, Loro!*

*Take him back with you. We don't need his kind here, and he undoubtedly functions better in your bed than he will in Wesley's computer.*

"Paul? *Paul!*"

He turned, raised his brows at Wesley's imperative tone, at Wesley's rather painful grip on his elbow.

"Yes, Dr. Smith?"

Wes scowled. "Don't give me that face, Corlaney. Put your eyebrows where they belong."

He grinned. Wesley didn't. Wesley was *serious*. He wasn't at all certain his heart could stand the shock.

"Listen, Paul, go easy on him, okay?"

"Easy! He's a damn—"

"No, Paul, he's not. You're wrong this time—and so was I, at first. I'm not sure what he is, but I'm sure he's more, not less, than he claims, and if you hurt him . . . do *anything* to drive him away I'll . . ."

The ever-loquacious Wesley Smith—Wes, who was notoriously rough in hazing the new researcher recruits—actually floundered searching for the words to tell *him* to mind his manners.

"You'll what, Smith?"

Wesley's mouth tightened and he said, ". . . If you hurt him, Paul, you'll have to deal with me, and I'll—I'll—" His lower lip protruded in a pugnacious scowl. "Well, —it won't be pretty."

He'd occasionally wondered if he'd missed his calling. Now he was certain of it. He was a good GenTech, a *damned* good geneticist, but what he might have accomplished on the stage . . .

Without so much as an eyelid's twitch he said, "I promise you, Wesley, your pretty brain-child is safe from me."

And he turned abruptly away—before the strain became too great even for *his* thespian talents. He followed Loren around the fire-pit, grinning broadly now—

—now that Wes couldn't see his face.

"You're damned lucky you're dealing with such a forgiving crowd." Cantrell's voice said at his back: hard, low, and audible only to him. "I want a word with you."

Without looking up Stephen answered, "When?"

"*Loro?*"

He jumped, caught himself from falling into the fire with a hand to carved stone.

Dr. Corlaney's voice: "Loro, my dear, forgive my—interruption—"

And hers, as low and hard as it had been to him, "Dammit, Corlaney, get out of here!"

Stephen leaned against the sculptured curve, keeping his face in shadow, trying to slow his racing heart, trying not to hear the argument going on a short stride away. Trying, God knew, not to hear the intensity in Corlaney's whisper.

"For God's sake, Loro, it's the *Miakoda*, the event this place is named for. I've waited for years to share it with you and in half an hour, it'll be over and done with until fall. Come outside. —Please?"

"Corlaney, your sense of timing is—"

"*Please*, Loro."

"*All right!*" And in a gentler tone: "You're right, Paul, once-in-a-lifetimes should have some precedence."

People were leaving. Perhaps this would be a good time to—

"I'm not through with you yet, Ridenour." The gentler tone did *not* extend to him. "Come with us. You'll enjoy this."

*Not* an invitation.

"Admiral, what are you talking about?" he whispered, his heart racing again. He was travelling in accesses he did *not* understand. People were acting in ways which confused him. This *Miakoda* was something Paul Corlaney wanted to share with his old friend, not with *him*.

"Never mind, Ridenour, just follow us." With that, she let Dr. Corlaney lead her toward the stairs.

"C'mon, Stevie-lad, move your butt or we'll miss it!" Wesley came up behind him and grasped his arm.

Whatever *it* was, others were going as well—even Briggs and Lexi were following Cantrell up the stairs. Reluctantly, he allowed himself to be pulled along.

"Miss what?" he asked as they hurried up a different, surprisingly short staircase to a large glass door.

"Again with the questions!" Anevai closed in on his other side. "You'll see, Ridenour."

And Wesley: "Trust me."

# vi

The only light out here was that of the stars. The building at their backs, adjusted now to allow light in but not out, kept the lights inside from dimming their view of the stars. And it was the sky everyone was watching: the eastern sky which already showed a faint silvery glow.

The spring night was warm enough, if one could avoid the wind funnelling down the rift. But that wasn't difficult: the rock maze theme inside continued out here, extending along the length of the rift, descending into a terraced honeycomb of observation balconies and alcoves, each offering its own unique view and degree of privacy, a honeycomb which also served to break that constant flow of air into gentler eddying swirls.

Halting in one of the top-most, least private alcoves, Cantrell watched in detached amusement as the group dissipated down the pathways: more than architectural ingenuity would keep hands warm tonight.

Paul stationed himself beside the pathway, exchanging pleasantries with each and every passerby. Obviously, the man was as popular here as he'd been at Ptolemy. More so. At Ptolemy 'TankStat, half of admin had been out for his hide half the time. —The rest of the time, everyone else had wanted it.

She caught Stephen's eye as he passed, signalled him to stay where she could see him. He nodded and stepped to one side, Smith and Anevai moving with him.

Their conversation carried to her stoney corner—with a little boost from her implant.

Smith: "Did some personal editing on my story, didn't you?"

Anevai: "Storyteller's prerogative, friend."

Stephen: "Why did you change it, Ms. Tyeewapi?"

Anevai: "Lord, Ridenour, you *trying* to make me crazy? Try again."

Stephen: "S–sorry, Ms.—"

Anevai: *"Stephen!"*

Stephen, reluctantly: "A–An–nevyah."

Anevai, chuckling: "Close enough. Ask me again tomorrow; right now, I'm done. Forgive me if I give out on you early?"

Smith, indignant: "Forgive you? You must be kidding. Go!

Git! The kid here and I have *things* to discuss. *Universes* to save. Answers to—''

Anevai: ''—*Speaking of answers*, I've got a question for you, Professor-Wessor. What's a three-base-ring-in-NSpace pilogarithm?''

A choked cough from Stephen.

A suspicious: ''Is this another of your sick riddles, 'Nevyah'?''

An airy: ''Oh no, I just heard it somewhere and wondered if I *should* know what it was.''

More laughter from the girl. A muttered: ''Ms. Tyeewapi, I'm—''

The laughter ceased, and before Stephen could finish whatever he was going to say, Anevai gave him a quick hug. ''Stuff it, Ridenour. Breakfast. Tomorrow. Be there! Both of you!'' And sailed away amidst noisy goodbyes. An exit just a bit too obvious, just a bit too clearly intended to be heard for her peace of mind. She signalled Lexi, who nodded and slipped after the indigene girl.

A rocky step below, TJ, talking animatedly with Dr. Metcalf, appeared not to notice Lexi's departure, but she knew better. When a young indigene put his arm around Metcalf and headed her down the pathways, TJ shrugged eloquently, blew the researcher a kiss, and melted into the shadows.

Smith and Stephen wandered in her direction, chattering away in fluent ComNet-ese, totally oblivious to their surroundings, heads so close dark hair mingled with light. Good old Wesley Smith: she might have known, anyone that hard to find in the first place would be equally difficult to get rid of.

And, God help them, there was a look of sheer, unadulterated joy on Smith's face. She'd be willing to wager young Ridenour had never seen that look turned on him before. *She'd* be willing, but doubted she'd find any takers. God. What was this going to do to the kid?

She felt a presence behind her—*not* TJ. There was only one person present TJ would allow in that position unchallenged: her own damn fault for not instructing to the contrary. She felt hands on her shoulders, a long-fingered touch she remembered very well indeed.

''Loro?'' Time was, he wouldn't have bothered asking. But

then, neither would she. Paul Corlaney was a question mark
right now—a very large question mark—but with Stephen's
effectiveness here in question and the growing complexity of the
situation, Paul's potential value trebled. *If* he could be relied on.
There were ways of testing that reliability, and if this was the
way he chose to play the game—

She leaned her head back, finding his shoulder there. His
hands slid down her arms and slowly circled her waist. She didn't
object. He moved closer, fitting his body to hers as easily as he
had all those years ago.

—she could cope.

She relaxed against him. "Well, hello there."

She felt more than heard his throaty whisper, and chuckled
back, "Howdy, partner."

His embrace tightened and he said, so quietly she wondered
if he intended her to hear, "Don't I wish."

Somewhere down the rift, the mellow sound of a wooden flute
wove itself into the soughing of the wind down the rift. She
pressed Paul's forearms against her waist and swayed gently to
that distant song, feeling his chest rise and fall in concert with
his breath on her neck.

"Patience, old man," she murmured. "Your turn'll come
soon enough."

She felt his chin resting on her shoulder, his cheek pressing
against her hair, as he whispered into her ear, "I wish I could
count on that."

"The *Miakoda's* the time for wishes, isn't it? So I've read.
Can't hurt to try."

"The *Miakoda's* a bit past its prime, admiral. Late in the
season. But it still might work."

"Depends on how much it's changed, doesn't it, Corlaney?
Depends on how much this atmosphere's affected it."

"The atmosphere changes the light, the appearance; it doesn't
change the structure or the spirit. Can you say as much for the
cloak of Alliance Law?"

A soft-spoken alert echoed up the rift. She turned to the easter-
ly down-rift view where a touch of silver in the sky heralded the
moons' arrival, and murmured, "Catch me later, Corlaney."

"I've waited twenty years," Paul muttered hoarsely.
"Damned if I'll wait any longer."

The silver glow had deepened until now it silhouetted the far end of the Teyuwit valley, the Zaltana foothills to either side. She endeavored to ignore the interesting things Paul's mouth was doing to the back of her neck and murmured, "Paul, look. You can just see the small moon."

The mouth paused. "Yoluta. The large one . . . there." He pointed over her shoulder. "That's Winema-Yepa." The mouth returned to her earlobe. "—But you know that."

Of course she did. But somehow, the connection between the iridescent disk of atmospheric luminosity emerging from beyond the horizon and the 'NetLink-hosting GravityWell she'd sent a security team into last night—escaped her.

HuteNamid's primary companion was huge and highly reflective, its surface the condensed remains of a primitive atmosphere. But knowing the physics couldn't lessen the magic. Even Paul stopped his preoccupation with her earrings to watch the magnificent natural phenomenon.

Silver clouds coalesced into a glowing disk rising with stately elegance to spread its light over viewers and landscape . . .

". . . like some snowy winter queen—" She caught herself, blinked in self-disgust. "God! I'm getting poetic in my old age!"

His arms squeezed her hard. "That's okay. It's essentially what the name means anyway. Just pretend you knew all along—I'll never betray your dark secret."

"Promises, promises."

"I keep mine." Bitterness crept in at the edges of his voice.

"Meaning I don't?"

"That remains to be seen, doesn't it?"

"That's some statement coming from someone who disappeared without—"

"Later, Loro. Watch the moon. Don't spoil it."

As the optically flattened disk cleared the horizon, silver rays touched the mountains below, a peak at a time, and cumulus clouds above, so that, as the moon rose, the edges of earth and sky appeared to draw ever closer to the watchers on the cliff's edge, as peak after peak acquired the moonlight.

Of a sudden, it all made sense. Of a sudden, she knew why Paul had been so adamant she witness this. Of a sudden, she remembered a lecture hall filled with very different Recons on a very different planet, and a much younger Paul seated beside her.

She pressed closer and whispered, "Apollo's walking the dog a bit late tonight, isn't he?"

His chest vibrated against her ear, then his hand cupped her chin, turned her face to his. He brushed her lips with his own, then said, "Apollo's walk, HuteNamid-style, love. Just for you."

"Quite a show, my friend." She turned back to the moonrise. "But I still don't buy it. Apollo's been snoring for hours. Has to be Artemis."

A gasp from the other side of their viewpoint prioritized out Paul's answer. Stephen: gazing eastward, the silver light making his face as ethereal as Winema herself. Beyond him, Smith: watching Stephen with an odd intensity, a look which slipped past Stephen to her. As their eyes met, the remnants of the animosity he'd shown inside vanished, and in its stead, a slow smile stretched his mouth.

She heard Stephen's breath catch, heard him whisper, "Oh, God . . . I . . ." He turned to her, hand out-held, eyes glistening— "Admiral, I remem—"

—and looked past her to Paul standing there with his arms around her, his chin resting on her shoulder.

Stephen's hand dropped back to his side and his face went dead, more self-contained than it had been the day he came aboard the *Cetacean*. He said very, very quietly, "It's getting chilly, admiral; if you don't mind, I'll wait for you inside."

He was turning away when Paul—*Paul?*—murmured: "Stephen."

The boy stopped, carefully keeping the moon at his back: old habits rapidly reasserting themselves.

"Won't you join us, son?"

Taking ruthless advantage of Paul's lapse in character, she held out her hand. "Come, Stephen, a few more minutes, then we'll all go inside. We'll keep you warm."

The moon's reflection flickered in Stephen's eyes as he looked first to her hand, then to Paul, and back to her face. The flicker disappeared momentarily, then he shrugged and moved slowly into the offered circle of her arm.

"Did the admiral say *anything* about Hononomii, dad? Anything at all?" Anevai found it impossible to sit still. She wandered about her father's office, straightening pictures, picking up scattered papers, anything to keep her hands occupied and distract her thoughts.

Sakiimagan caught her hand as she passed his chair, pulled

her to face him, and took her other hand as well. "She said he had
a reaction to the Deprivil, but that he's doing fine. Personally, I
believe she is far more interested in keeping him aboard that ship
for other reasons."

"What other reasons?"

"Primarily my cooperation. There are some discrepancies in
the computer records. Discrepancies that puzzle me. That's what
I'm looking into now."

He let go her hands and turned back to the stack of reports on
his desk. Flipping through them randomly, he said, "I'm uneasy
about these missing files. Ask Nayati if there's any chance
his—cleanup—work affected other files. If he needs to contact
Wesley for an accurate assessment, tell him to do so. Also, I
expect a full explanation of his comments to you, not his emo-
tional interpretation of Hononomii's message. I want to know
precisely what your brother said to him."

"I'll ask him. For what good it'll do. He's been driving me
crazy ever since the *Cetacean* came and he headed for Acoma.
I never know when he's going to—fly out of the bushes. And
he hasn't given me a straight answer to anything in days."

"You know he feels more strongly than most about Alliance
Security's presence. Don't let it worry you. —What do you think
of Dr. Ridenour? Do you think there's anything to Nayati's
suspicions this time?"

"I don't know. Stephen *is* unusual. For someone who's thinking of a permanent transfer, he showed a remarkable lack of
interest in everything except Wesley until—" She smiled, remembering Stephen and old Blue.

"Until?" her father prompted.

"Until I took him down to the barn. He seemed to like the
animals. It's people he has problems with."

"What *problems?*"

"Nothing to worry about, dad. I think he's just real shy.
—Not, in my opinion, a particularly valuable spy-trait. Most of
the time, I think Nayati's full of it, but . . ."

"Guard what you say on that, Anevai."

She looked around at the room, realizing suddenly he meant
listening devices. Devices that need not even be *in* the room.
"How do people live that way all the time? Never knowing if
they're being listened to or not . . . Do you know she had me
followed here?"

"Take care, *nituna*."

"Don't worry. I'm going straight home from here." And from there she could go virtually anywhere on the planet undetected—as long as she stayed out of buildings. But she wasn't staying out of buildings. She was going to the condos to await Stephen's return and then lure him down to the barn.

She sat on the edge of her father's desk, playing idly with his desk knife, balancing it on the tip of the blade. Ostensibly, it was a letter opener, but with her new awareness, she wondered if it had other purposes. In her father's hands, the razor-sharp blade could be deadly. Her father dealt with spacers and Security all the time. Her father understood securities.

"It doesn't seem fair, somehow. Stephen's so . . ." The narrow blade slipped, leaving a scratch in the polished wood. She licked a fingertip and rubbed at the spot. "Sorry."

Sakiimagan leaned forward in his chair and placed his hand on her knee. "Never mind. Eminently repairable. Ridenour's so—what, Anevai?"

She shook her head. "I can't explain. But if he's for real . . . well, all I can say is tricking him's a lousy way to begin a relationship."

"And what does Wesley say?"

She chuckled. "Wesley's in love."

"Naturally, but what does he think about Dr. Ridenour's credentials?"

"I told you. Whatever else he may be, Stephen's credentials are for real. He and Wesley haven't stopped nattering about *Harmonies* since they met." She chuckled ruefully. "Or maybe I should say 'Nettering. Ugh. I'm starting to wes as bad as the Wesser himself."

"They've been discussing Wesley's paper?" her father asked sharply.

"Mm-hm." She nodded. "Personally, I think that's why Stephen's thinking about transferring here. He read it, understood it, and wants to work with the man who wrote it. It sure isn't because HuteNamid itself attracted him. If he ever got his hands dirty before this afternoon, I'd be exceedingly surprised."

He gave her knee a squeeze. "Then you've nothing to worry about, have you, my dear? If Dr. Ridenour's an honest man, he'll openly ask your business or ignore you altogether. Don't be afraid to test him. Most of all, *nituna*, don't listen to your heart."

"*Dad,* —"

"I saw you with him tonight, Anevai. Don't try to deny you have more than a casual interest in him. And I repeat: do not let your feelings cloud your judgment." His face hardened. "And *remember* what I said this morning."

She scowled. In other words: Don't say anything about the 'Net. Don't ask for news of Hononomii. Don't talk about the researchers' projects. In other words, continue to play the village idiot. She asked, resentful and a touch suspicious: "Should I pass the word on to Wes and Dr. Paul? What about Nayati? Or have you spoken to them already?"

"I'm sure they'll observe proper cautions."

She didn't trust herself to say anything for a moment. Then: "You feel compelled to *order* me, and yet you trust *them* to use their judgement? *Why?*"

"They aren't impressionable young girls."

"But—" She shook her head in frustration. It was a waste of energy: Sakiimagan had already made up his mind about her motives.

She wondered when he'd last checked out Wesley's.

Or Dr. Paul's.

He patted her knee lightly and stood up. "Now, hop down and get out of here. I have work to finish. Come and see me first thing in the morning."

The moonglow extended well past them now, the phenomenon virtually over. Ridenour remained stiff and unyielding despite the arm Loren placed around him, and Paul began to wonder if the ungrateful puppy had it in him to appreciate anything.

What in hell had prompted him to call the boy back to them tonight? —a *fait accompli* before he had known he was considering it. He certainly had no desire to attach an idolizing schoolboy to his bootstraps: he'd come to HuteNamid to get away from that kind of nonsense—a purpose the flamboyant egos in this 'Tank admirably satisfied.

On the other hand, Loren obviously thought a great deal of her young fashion plate, while Wesley, on a few hours' acquaintance . . .

'. . . *If you hurt him, Paul, you'll have to deal with me, and it won't be pretty.*'

Well, he'd promised Wes he wouldn't hurt the boy, and he'd abide by Wesley's judgment—until that judgment proved wrong. But not hurting the kid did not include adopting him. If Wes wanted his pretty Academy Clone protected, Wes, standing forlornly off to one side playing the neglected child, could damn well do it himself.

He flashed Wesley the high sign and Wes responded with rather appalling eagerness. But as he closed in on Ridenour's free side, the boy flinched, reflex consciously controlled—a control that didn't fit with the rest of the academy clone image. One of Cantrell's? Security in researcher clothing?

He didn't have the rest of the moves.

Wes noticed but didn't appear in the least put out: he hugged the Clone as warmly as Loren had. —Not such a bad turn of events, he told himself: get himself karma with both Loren and Wesley at the same time.

All of which after-the-fact circuitous reasoning did nothing to explain why he'd been moved to reach out in the first place. He shuddered to think that after all this time simple school-boy angst could drive him to utter stupidity.

It was too bad, really. The boy had made none of the typical attempts to impress him. Quietly voiced opinions had been well considered and only in response to questions: Ridenour'd listened more than he talked, and when he'd talked, he'd made sense. Under normal circumstances, he might even come to like the boy.

But while wounded puppies were hard to resist—wounded puppies with the keys to the henhouse were damned dangerous.

A sudden, violent shiver passed through him. He thought it was his own—perhaps part of it was—until Ridenour muttered an apology and tried to move apart from them, a move Loren prevented, murmuring: "It's all right, Stephen. What was it you started to tell me earlier? What was it you remembered?"

Another shudder, less quickly subdued, then suddenly the waves stopped, and the kid relaxed for the first time since joining them, leaned toward Loren—a move which required him to adjust *his* hold—and whispered to her.

"On Rostov . . . moons . . . red . . . gold . . ."

He felt Loren's tension as she whispered something into the boy's ear, something which set the kid to shivering all over again, which in turn caused Wesley to ask, "You okay, kid?"

What in hell had Loren brought to them? In Paul Corlaney's experience, there was only one way the words *remember, moon*, and *Rostov* in the same sentence added up, and what was that sum doing in this academy-brat's memory?

"—Anevai says it's *Yepa*, the snow maiden." Dr. Corlaney's deep, velvet voice floated above their heads, then settled around them like a blanket. Stephen envied that voice. People respected a voice like that—listened to it. "It does this twice each year, in the fall and spring. In a couple of weeks, there'll be an equally spectacular sunrise when HuteNamid's reflected light causes the new moon to shine gold before it disappears in the sunlight."

Behind him, Dr. Corlaney shifted toward the admiral, and when he spoke again, his voice was muffled. "Any chance you could stick around long enough?"

The admiral's arm tightened on Stephen's waist and she said, "Who knows? I'm here for as long as need be, Paul." But her silent warning hadn't been necessary. Somehow, the possibility of lingering on HuteNamid wasn't as repulsive to him as it would have been a few short hours ago.

From the Wesley-shadow on his left: "Anevai claims Yepa brings the snow with her in the fall and Etu, the sun, melts Yepa away in the spring, which brings the rains. The golden reflection is her ghost, checking to see that her rain has renewed the land. One year it was too cloudy to see the ghost-moon, and that summer saw the only flooding recorded since survey."

He shuddered, felt Wesley's arm tighten around his shoulders; heard another whispered *You okay?* which he couldn't quite bring himself to answer. Repeating a tale from a by-gone age was one thing: creating that imagery out of your own experiences and imagination . . . Forcing the words past a tightness in his throat, he said, "It's a very . . . poetic thought for such a practical individual."

He felt warm breath on the back of his neck as Dr. Corlaney murmured, as though to him alone: "Anevai Tyeewapi is an exceptional young woman. One should listen carefully to what she says."

The admiral stiffened and turned to stare at Paul. Angry: for reasons he didn't understand. Without thinking, he whispered, "Admiral, —please, don't—"

Her hard eyes glittered at him in that bright moonlight; but rather than take offense, she leaned close, brushed his cheek with her lips in absolution—

—Or so he thought until he saw her glance past him to Dr. Corlaney. Heard Corlaney's quick intake of breath behind him, leaving him feeling as though he was being used in some private war between these two powerful personalities.

But the sensation passed, powerless against the magic of the moonlight. Now and again a cloud pattern, a reflection of cascading water on the cliffs opposite them, would inspire comment; but otherwise, they were silent, listening to the wind, the strange rhythmic buzz and click of insects.

He recognized the sound out of the same half-memory—*Papa, who painted the moon tonight?*—and that elusive memory dissipated as quickly as it had formed. Faded against real images. Real people. Real friendship.

At least, he was free to think of it that way until the magic ended, and he held that moment off as long as he could. But the next time he shivered—truly the cold this time—the others, ignoring his protests, hurried him out of the night wind and into the restaurant's warmth.

The lights were muted now. Here and there the rock glowed: echoes of the fire pit. Sporadic murmurs from shadowed alcoves evidenced a few remaining occupants.

Wesley yawned widely and said, "Time for this working man to go to bed." He held out his arm. Raised questioning brows. "—Stephen?"

"I don't think . . ." He looked to the admiral for a cue.

"I've some details to clear up with Dr. Ridenour before he retires, Dr. Smith," she said, easily. "Forgive me if I—deprive you of his company tonight."

He blushed, wondering just how far she expected him to carry this—imposture. Or was she deliberately rescuing him from a potentially difficult situation? *Did* Wesley mean . . .

"You do me an injustice," Wesley protested, "I meant to see him safely to his rooms. No more, no less." His voice turned cool, suggestive—"Certainly, if you've other plans . . ."—and brightened: "But much as I sympathize, I suggest you get used to being without him. I promise you, Admiral Loro, you'll be going back alone. No doubt about it, he belongs here with us. —*Regardless* of what brought him here in the first place."

Cantrell laughed easily. "That's up to Dr. Ridenour, of course, but should he *choose* to stay, I might, in some ways, envy him that exile. —Good night, Dr. Smith."

Wesley winked at him, and sauntered down the corridor. As he disappeared around a corner, the admiral said quietly, "Paul, will you meet me in my rooms in, say, an hour, give or take?"

Stephen looked around and intercepted the researcher's narrow-eyed scrutiny, an impenetrable gaze that turned to Cantrell and softened. Corlaney reached out to stroke her cheek with the back of one finger and said, "I repeat, my dear, try to keep me away."

Stephen studied the slate under his feet, acutely embarrassed and out of place without the moonlit magic, wishing he dared postpone this meeting until tomorrow.

A touch on his arm jolted his lapidary preoccupation: Dr. Corlaney's hand, extended now to him. He grasped it shyly, and Corlaney said, "Welcome to HuteNamid, Dr. Ridenour. I look forward to working with you."

This time, Stephen dropped his eyes out of fear. Fear that he would give in to his sudden desire to say something—anything. Fear that Dr. Corlaney would somehow see through his imposture. He had an almost overwhelming urge to be honest with this man, if no one else here.

Almost, but not quite. *Don't tell anyone—don't* trust *anyone until we truly know what we're dealing with*: Adm. Cantrell's caution. And he owed her . . . for tonight if nothing else.

Now the magic was over, payment came due. So he met Dr. Corlaney's gaze firmly and said, "Thank you, sir. Good night."

## vii

Cantrell led the way slowly down the stairs into the fire-pit, and settled with her back to the light. Stephen sank to his knees on the flagstones near her feet and extended his hands to the fire: warming instincts as old as mankind. He was shivering quite visibly now, though she felt overwarm.

A plush rug carelessly flung over a nearby stone seat caught her eye. She drew his attention and gestured toward it. "Pull that over and sit on it, Stephen. Keep the cold out."

"But—" He looked at her uncertainly. "—it looks like *real* fur. Are you sure . . ."

The boy seemed determined to make everything a wonderment tonight. She said dryly, "As common as silk in space, Stephen: different worlds, different assets. That's what makes a universe. No one will mind. It's meant to be used."

He rose slowly, with none of his usual fluid grace and with a tiny intake of breath. Suddenly suspicious, she watched his hesitant few steps to pick up the rug, and when he held it out, silent invitation to share his find, a distinct shadow crossed his face.

She touched the softness to oblige him, but: "You're hurting. What happened?"

A stifled sigh. An evasive dip of his head. Stroking the rug draped over his arm, he said in an offhanded manner, "Bit of an accident this afternoon . . . My blasted shoulder acting up. It's an old injury. I'll be fine. I brought my brace down with me—have it on now—and it won't prevent me from doing my job."

"Was Ms. Tyeewapi with you?"

He nodded, but added quickly, "Not her fault, admiral. Not in the least. I was stupid. —Clumsy fool. Fell. It's this HeavyG."

She frowned. Dammitall, he was lying. She didn't like this evasiveness in him. Didn't like his too-quick defense of Anevai Tyeewapi. "Get Mo's staff to check it when you're back on board. —Better yet, get McKenna, herself. Tell her I said."

His lips tightened rebelliously.

"No arguments, lad. Only practical. —Now sit. We've a lot to cover and we're both too tired to waste time on nonsense, don't you think?"

Young pride assuaged, he knelt again and carefully arranged the fur before settling onto it, facing the fire which seemed to hold such fascination for him and so close his shoulder brushed her knee. He didn't seem to notice.

"Well, Dr. Ridenour," she said, "I don't need to ask how you and Dr. Smith are getting along."

A thoughtful gaze scanned the surrounding rocks. "Is it safe to talk here, admiral?"

*Very good, boy. You're learning.*

"TJ's crew cleared it this afternoon. And I have means to know. Where I am, you're in a safe zone." She touched her ear, where a very sophisticated bit of TJ's equipment remained silent. "My people are keeping it that way. They always are. —Which isn't to say we get careless as you did out there. That was a complete mental slip. Do I make myself clear?"

He put his hand on her arm and looked up at her, his unusual eyes gold in the firelight. "I know it, and I'm sorry about that. I'll be careful. —But you did know, didn't you? You knew all along?"

"That you're Recon?" And when he nodded, "Yes, Stephen, I knew."

His hand dropped and he stared into the fire, expressionless.

"Does it bother you?" she asked.

He said in a hushed voice, "No. It's just . . . Sometimes, I wonder. Sometimes, I wish I knew . . ."

The boy was clearly near Danislav's edge—a question now whether he could do his job. Damn. All she'd wanted was to shake him free of his academy attitudes about Recons, not this. Tonight Danislav's warnings made a disturbing lot of sense.

Stephen was an enigma to her in many ways. His sheer youth hampered her understanding of him. Her dealings were with adults.—

"Let it rest, Stephen. That's the past. Concentrate on job at hand."

—Adults like Smith. Smith she understood: smug, intellectual chameleon—she'd met him by the dozen. Stephen might or might not know what he was dealing with—might even take offense at a warning and fall right into Smith's orbit.

At the moment, the boy was the best means they had of getting Smith up to the ship, but once there, unless he could convince Chet of his harmlessness, Smith would face detention and trial with the 'NetAT—

"Tell me about Smith. What do you make of him?"

—And she couldn't help but wonder what that would do to Stephen.

He blinked, wiped a shaking hand across his eyes. A shaking hand which shone damply in the firelight before he hid it against his side. "He's incredible, admiral. The expansions he's made in the time since that paper was written, and virtually on his own

. . . Lord, if I understood *anything* of what he said this afternoon, he's just one step short of test implementation. They have one woman here—I *think* she's one of the *indigenes*, if you can believe that, who's a master at—What would you call it?—creative computer hardware? Anyway, she and Wesley have been working together for—''

"Who?'' she asked sharply. He shot her a puzzled look over his shoulder. She elaborated: "*Who's* he working with?''

"I—I don't know, admiral. I'm sorry.'' He grew distressed, "I sh–should have thought—I'll see if I can find out tomorrow— It's just—Wesley and I—''

"It's all right, Stephen. Tomorrow's *fine*.'' Shit. Unstable as hell. "Tell me about Smith, son. How did that go?''

He shifted his weight, grunted softly as he caught his balance with his left hand. He stretched his legs out toward the fire, and rubbed the shoulder absently. "Wes is . . . I don't really understand him, admiral. *Him*, not his theories. He's amazingly courteous to me—listens as though he hasn't already thought of it all long ago . . . and yet he's *lightyears* beyond anything I'd even considered.''

"Ever occur to you he might listen because you're saying something worth listening to? Because he's interested in what you might think? How many people throughout the 'Network even took him seriously, let alone understood what he wrote?''

A tiny shake of the averted head.

She shifted position to get that stubborn profile in sight. "I was watching him with you. He's obviously as impressed with you as you are with him.'' His brow tightened. "God's sake, Stephen, for once in your life, will you just accept the fact that you're special—take advantage of it. Take advantage of his friendship. Learn all that you can from him—''

*All, Stephen, not just about the theory—and not just from Smith.*

"—Then take that wisdom . . .''

*Wisdom, boy, not just knowledge.*

". . . back with you. *Use it* in ways Smith can't even contemplate here.''

His eyes squeezed closed, and he asked, his voice agonized, "My God, Loro—'' *Loro? Thanks, Corlaney!* "—Is it really that simple? I honestly don't know if I can do it—lie to him any more, I mean. When I accepted Council's commission—when you ordered me down here, I didn't even think—how could I have known . . . ?'' What the hell did he *think* he knew now? He turned away from the fire to sit cross-legged, crossed arms pressed to his stomach. ''I—I almost gave it all away just now with Dr. Corlaney.''

''But you didn't.''

''Only because you were standing there.''

''I doubt that. Trust me in this, Stephen.'' She put her hand on his shoulder and pressed lightly. He tried to shake her off. When she insisted, he twisted to face her. Not the wounded child she'd expected, but a young man rapidly calculating input. Not unlike that moment in a SecCom station; only *this* time, he was very much aware of his surroundings. Not one to *trust* anyone.

A quick revision. ''More importantly, trust yourself. There are degrees of deception—and nothing you're doing is capable of hurting these people.''

''Nothing?''

She lifted the hand from his shoulder, brushed the hair back from his eyes: attempt to reestablish that closeness they'd shared out on the rift, and said, ''Trust me, son.''

He stiffened. Drew back from her touch. Something—or someone—was lacking.

He had no idea how to cope: he dealt with computers, not people. Lexi said he mimicked behaviors: his reactions were *not* his own, they were what he thought others expected of him. Who really knew what he was thinking behind those haunting eyes?

And because she didn't know: ''You're going back to the ship with me in the morning.'' His mouth opened to protest and she pressed his arm. ''No argument, Dr. Ridenour. Some people are cut out for this line of work; others aren't.''

He jerked away.

''That hardly agrees with what you said yesterday! What happened to 'We all do what we must,' *admiral?* And what reason could you give them that wouldn't compromise the whole operation?'' He ran out of breath—and anger. Finished on an anguished whisper, ''My God, don't do this to me.''

''Don't worry, Stephen. This turn of events won't affect my recommendation to Councillor Eckersley. You have handled yourself very well, but—''

*''Dammit, do you think that's all I'm thinking of?''*

He lurched to his feet, stood with his back to her.

"Keep your voice down, *Dr*. Ridenour!"

His whole body jerked and he faced about, openly shocked, hurt.

She continued coldly, "You'd damn well *better* be thinking of it. It's your *future*, but it's my people's *necks*. I am *concerned* over your ability to function as the impartial advisor I need you to be if you stay. I am *concerned* about your saying something stupid to the wrong person at the wrong damned time! Can you assure me those concerns are unwarranted? Dammit, boy, I need the help of an adult, not some emotionally screwed-up child."

The stricken look on his face confirmed her worst fears. She softened her tone a degree. "Stephen, you're being seduced by these people." She raised her hand before he could protest. "I'm not implying malicious intent on their part, but what are you planning to do? Put that transfer through for real?"

His color rose, his eyes dropped. She pursued the point ruthlessly. "I thought so. And then what, friend? What happens when your fantasy explodes? And it is *when*, not *if*. You're no more suited to this life than I am. Yes, it's quite romantic and the people are charming, but you have a position waiting for you: a politically *important* position due to your unique abilities and background."

A bitter, choked laugh. "Unique, certainly, and my *uniqueness* will only be a detriment."

"Not if you have the vision to see beyond that, Stephen. You've accomplished something no one else has managed in generations, and the position Eckersley's creating—yes, *creating*—in anticipation of your success here could make you the one to break the political backbone of the Shapoorianites—"

The boy jumped. The color drained from his face. *No small nerve, that*, she thought—and pressed the point:

"But by the time you finally admit that possibility to yourself, it could be far, far too late. With Eckersley's backing, you have a good chance with that 'NetAT application you put in—" At his startled look: "*Yes*, I know about it. And they *are* interested, boy! Chet tells me you've got a damned *good* chance—*if you don't blow it now!*"

Pain showed in his eyes. *Severe* pain.

"You know as well as I there's no Councillor in the Alliance, and damned few academies, that will have you on staff after you once made a decision to commit to a Recon World. Politically *can't*, do you understand me?''

A muscle worked in his jaw and he said tonelessly, "How could I be any more *contaminated* than I already am?''

"Easily." And watching those eyes as a barometer of his emotions, she added, "Your leaving doesn't mean you won't have more time with Smith. We know where he is now. We'll get him up to the ship. Do the business the way it was supposed to be done at the beginning. Will that help?''

Very low: "Wesley doesn't *want* to go back into s–space. *Nothing* will get him there. You—you'd have to a–r–rest him.''

"I doubt that, Stephen. For a chance to work with you? I've seen him with you, son. He'll come. Quite willingly.''

"And th–th–th—'' A *deep* breath. "If W–Wesley does c–come, will y–you ar–r–r—'' Another deep breath through clenched teeth. "Will he have to s–stay?''

"I can't promise anything, Stephen, but not if I have any other choice.''

The hand hanging at his side twitched. His breathing grew ragged, the pale eyes closed.

She'd pushed him long enough. She patted the rug and said placatingly, "Come and sit, Stephen. Nobody's going to force you to do anything.''

He took a step closer, but remained standing. "Like nobody *forced* me to come down here in the first place?" *Not* as off-balance as he appeared.

"Touché. But I require an agent down here with his eyes open." She reached out, caught his hand. "I'm not asking you to make a decision tonight, son.''

"I'm *not* your son.''

"No, Stephen, you're not. But I'm advising you as I would my own son, as I would any *Cetacean* crew member. I'm *asking* that such an important decision be made with a clear head.''

—And *not* in the afterglow of moonlight or the presence of certain charismatic individuals.

His expression didn't change.

"Did you get *any* sleep last night?''

A dismissive jerk of his head.

"—I thought not. Nor likely to tonight, from the look of you. Sit with me a while more: just to slow down. We can talk or not, as you wish.''

His fingers tightened on hers and his thumb moved aimlessly over her knuckles. A strong grip: not surprising when one thought of what he did in the gym, but unsuspected in his slenderness—as other surprising strengths were hidden in him—

—A strength which could work for or against his people. She'd done her best to influence those answers. The rest was up to him.

She stroked his fingers gently with her thumb. With a murmured apology, he relaxed his hold, but she didn't let him go.

"What about . . . what about Dr. Corlaney? Won't he wonder where you are?"

She tapped a message against her ear.

"Paul can damn well wait."

# viii

StatSeven was on line when TJ's hand touched her shoulder.

"Gotta run an errand for the Boss-lady, Lex, back in half, 'less I beep differently."

She nodded, then held up a hand for him to wait. Richland's report ended and she sent acknowledgment, then pulled the mute from her head.

"You want me to listen in while you're gone, Teej?"

"Don't worry about it. Keeping tabs on external is more important. We've got three on visual in there. I'll follow through the beeper and if there's reason, I'll signal."

She nodded and put the mute back in place, settled deeper into her nook near the *Moon's* entrance, while TJ headed inside, a cheerful bounce in his stride. It was possible Cantrell's errand had injected that bounce. Equally possible he was just glad to be moving. So far tonight, *she'd* gotten the only break from the boredom of surveillance—

—as he hadn't stopped reminding her since she got back from seeing—from a discreet distance—Anevai Tyeewapi into her home before turning the task over to the team assigned to that region.

TJ's beeper signal, a red dot on her Security MC's schematic, danced down the hallway and into the 'Tube. She grinned and wished him a silent farewell.

Don't worry about it was TJ's way of saying the conversation in by the pit might well take a politically delicate direction. *Fine, Teej. But don't blame me if I forget something you forgot to tell me in the first place*.

*She* knew her partner's existential memory limitations, even if Old Man Morley didn't.

A blip on her MC: StatEight's check-in. She tapped the *proceed* and prepared to listen to the latest tale of freezing-toes-woes.

Briggs nodded to the guard outside the admiral's sitting room before closing the door, and facing the couch. On the coffee table, a huge bouquet of local flowers which hadn't been there before.

"Dr. Corlaney?"

Paul looked up from the paper he was reading and smiled, tossed the paper down beside the bouquet and rose to his feet, hand outstretched. "TJ! What's this *Dr. Corlaney* nonsense?"

It *had* been a long time.

"Dr. Corlaney, —Paul, —Adm. Cantrell requests your patience. She'll be a while yet. Perhaps as long as an hour. If you'd care to wait, feel free to make yourself comfortable here." He gestured to the bar, but Dr. Corlaney ignored the invitation.

"What is it, TJ? Is Loro all right? Can I—"

"She's fine. Her session with Dr. Ridenour is taking longer than she expected. They've become—good friends during the trip." Let the good doctor wonder.

Paul's expression hardened. He turned abruptly to the bar, muttering, "Damned academy puppy!" He jerked the cabinet open, set bottles on the counter with thoroughly unwarranted force. If he broke one of them, the Good Doctor would clean it up himself.

An empty glass raised: a silent query. He shook his head, keeping his face straight with some effort. The Good Doctor's current speculations must be . . . entertaining.

A quick Scotch—straight up—drained; another poured—at least a double. TJ frowned. That was no way to treat good whisky. And that *was* good. And local. He'd told Chet to find out what they'd aged the distillery barrels with.

Chet had told him Go to hell.

Paul threw himself back on the couch, gestured at the chair to his right and said, "Sit down, TJ. Relax. Talk with me awhile since your Boss-lady's seen fit to desert me."

He shrugged and sat down. "I suppose the admiral won't mind a few more minutes alone with Dr. Ridenour."

Paul scowled and swallowed another large mouthful. Too large. He began to choke. Briggs jumped to his feet, slapped him solicitously on the back: a blow that nearly sent Paul from the couch, but ended the coughing fit in a grunt.

"TJ, for God's sake! Take it easy!" Corlaney gasped, and straightened with a decided groan. He arched his back gingerly. "God, you broke it."

"Sorry." God's sake, indeed. He liked Paul, he truly did. But sometimes, the man had to be reminded he was a part of the human race.

Paul sat back, took another, more cautious, sip and said, "Who's your new partner?"

"Alexis Fonteccio. Sergeant."

"Good looking woman. Recon?" At his nod: "I thought so. Loro still on that kick, is she?"

"More than ever."

"She good? —But of course she is. You wouldn't have her otherwise. And Sylvia? Where's she?"

"Dead," he said shortly. "Recon sniper in the Albion outback, four—five years ago, 'NetStan."

"Damn. Sorry, Teej."

A shrug. "Shit happens."

"Yeah, right." Paul swirled the Scotch, his brow puckering. "TJ, we've known each other a long time—"

"Correction, Dr. Corlaney: we knew each other a long time ago."

Paul raised the glass in silent acknowledgement. "I stand corrected. I know better than to depend on that former friendship for my own sake, but I also know you would never willingly endanger Loren. And she *could* be in danger here, TJ."

"Is that a warning or a threat, Corlaney?"

"Neither. I'm just worried about her. What her real purpose is here. Who she might inadvertently push against a wall."

"And who might that be, Paul?"

"Any number of people. Every place has its secrets, for all some people prefer to think otherwise."

"Like people who disappear without a word?"

"Some of us have reasons, Teej. Some of us *can't* send secured messages."

"There *are* other ways; we both know that."

Paul lost some of his self-assurance. "Perhaps for some of us, forgetting is easier than the alternatives."

"And now that she's here you expect to pick up where you left off?"

"No." Quietly. Almost humbly, for Paul Corlaney. "Not really." His head came up, eyes hard. "Why *are* you here? I've *got* to know, man. What's her interest in that pretty puppy? She never inclined that way before. Has she changed that much? Or is the puppy unusually good?"

He didn't ask Good at what? but headed for the door. Corlaney was prodding in areas best left to Cantrell. "Save your questions for the admiral. I've been gone long enough. Particularly if she's pushing *someone* out of shape by talking with the kid. If . . . someone . . . has a problem with that, perhaps they'd best straighten out their own life first."

He didn't like the feeling he was getting from Paul Corlaney. The man he'd known had been an arrogant bastard, but he'd been stable. Whatever else Corlaney was now, highly stable wasn't part of the equation.

"What's the *kid's* purpose here, TJ?"

He stopped at the sitting room door and looked back at Paul. "What he says: a researcher looking for a home."

"I should have known better than to ask. What's he to Loren? Will you just answer me that?"

He frowned. "You know damn well you relinquished any right to ask that question when you chose to take yourself out of the equation in the manner you did, Corlaney. But don't worry. He's just a good kid with a job to do—"

"What kind of job, TJ?"

"Same as any 'Tank researcher, Paul. Same as all of us. If some have chosen to relinquish *that* responsibility as well, I'm sure it's not my place to criticize. Now, if you'll excuse me, I've my own . . . responsibilities."

As the door swung shut behind the security guard, it was all Paul could do to keep from flinging the glass in TJ's wake.

*Damned upstart. Who does he think he is? Relinquish my responsibilities—hell! It's my own damn business if I chose to—*

Suddenly, he realized the drink was shaking violently, splashing liquid over the rim to run down his hand and soak through his pant leg.

*What in hell . . . ?*

He stretched carefully to place the glass on the coffee table, then buried his face in still-shaking hands. God! What was wrong with him? TJ was his *friend*; the boy's only crime was being an Alliance flunky: what he and Loren chose to do in their spare time was their own business—

—and certainly couldn't compare with what *he* and Loro had.

*They'd* been a team, and a good one. A team he'd voluntarily dissolved to come incognito to HuteNamid. She didn't know spit about chemistry and he cared less about politics, but that had been the beauty of it—the intelligent but outside-the-field feedback. Feedback he'd been denied at the most critical moment in his career. A denial that left an angry, festering resentment in its wake.

But could that resentment against the system be why he felt the urge now to throw glasses through the window and throttle a harmless boy?

The hand he reached to pick up the glass again was still shaking, but he managed to finish the drink without further waste, and the strong bite of the alcohol brought a modicum of relaxation with it. He leaned on the counter exploring thoughts and emotions he barely recognized as his, then pushed himself away. He had to get out. He couldn't sit here, waiting patiently for Loren to finish . . . whatever she was doing with the youngster.

" *'Com!*" The anger in his voice startled him. He took a deep breath, connected into the HouseCom and made a civil request of current activity in the Condos, took notes, and headed out in search of distraction.

As he passed the bouquet he'd brought with him, he paused. On a second thought, he plucked the central blossom out and crossed instead to the bedroom door.

"How long have you known him?" Stephen's soft query startled Cantrell out of preoccupied half-sleep. She was sitting on Stephen's rug now, her back to the stone and the dwindling fire. Stephen had slid down to curl on his side. Asleep, or so she'd thought.

"Who 'him'?" As if she didn't know.

"P—Paul."

She touched the hand absently petting the fur between them. "A long time, Stephen. A very long time."

His hand shifted, and started stroking hers as he had the fur, weaving his fingers down and around the back and palm, down each finger's length. But it was with the fascination of a child . . .

"You were l—lovers?"

. . . not the sensuality of an adult.

What response could she give that he could understand? A long time ago, a child had been sacrificed in the name of bureaucratic red tape. Was that forgotten child surfacing now, at the worst possible time for the adult the child had become?

She answered cautiously, "I loved Paul in many senses of the word."

He released her hand and sat up, his back to her.

"How come . . . Why didn't you . . . why didn't you tell me he was here? That you knew him? Wh—why did you let me make myself a fool in front of him?"

So *that* was what had been bothering him. She almost laughed aloud.

"You didn't make a fool of yourself, Stephen, though I'm not certain I would claim the same for Paul. I knew he was here, but I haven't heard from him in years . . . since before he transferred to HuteNamid. It was a securitied move and I, frankly, didn't suppose any of us would see him at all. I certainly didn't expect to find him casually mingling with people from the ship. I *couldn't* say anything to you—he had to make that choice."

But now, Security be hanged: it was bring Stephen in on this case in its entirety, or lose him to an increasingly ruinous situation. A 'NetTech would understand what was at stake here. Best have the 'Tech understand before a lonely young man trusted Smith too much—and before Paul Corlaney became an irresistible distraction.

"Stephen, I've got something to tell you—"

* * *

The game was as one-sided as always. For a smart researcher, Corey Templeton played a lousy hand of poker. Anevai had been robbing him for an hour.

"Saved by the proverbial bell," Corey muttered as he leapt up to open the game room door.

Dr. Paul sauntered in, checked Corey's cards, muttered ominously, peeked over her shoulder then sat on a nearby sofa. "Who's been winning?"

Corey grunted. "Don't ask."

He shook his head. "Better concede, friend. You haven't a chance."

"Gladly," Corey said and tossed his cards face down again. "What's up?"

Dr. Paul grinned. "Waiting for my date."

"You devil." Corey whistled appreciatively. "Didn't take you long, did it?"

The smile faded. "Only twenty years. Not long, in the scheme of things."

She cocked her head at him, asked the question which had plagued her all day. "Did she mean a lot to you, Dr. Paul? Funny, I don't remember you ever mentioning her before."

He held out his arm and she moved to sit next to him, snuggled against his side: a position of safety and comfort she'd known all her life, more familiar than her own father's touch—

"More than anyone before or since, love. I met her the year she took off to have her son."

—and yet of all the secrets they'd shared as she was growing up, all the stories of his past he'd told her, he'd never mentioned this so-important woman.

"She has a kid?" Somehow, that was hard to imagine.

His hand stroked her arm absently. "Had, Anevai. He and his father turned up missing some ten years ago on the boy's first team mission. They were FirstIns. Went down and that was the last anyone heard from them."

"What ship?" Corey asked.

"*Cetacean.* One of Loren's first command assignments with her."

"Gods," she murmured. Then: "Didn't they have beepers?"

"One would think. But I heard about it through the 'Net and the details require a higher security rating than I've got. I should have contacted her, but by that time, I was here and not about to contact Loren Cantrell or anyone else that close to the Council.''

"Did she know?''

"That I was here? Possibly. Probably. If she wanted to know. Her clearance is right up there with Council now—possibly higher in some cases. When your job's running interference, you can't afford surprises—from either side.''

"What do you mean, 'run interference'?'' she asked.

"She's SpecOps: a special interests mediator between Recons and 'Tanks. Didn't Sakiima explain?''

She shook her head, feeling resentment kindling. First her father failed to tell her Stephen was a 'NetMan, now this—

"Maybe he thought you already knew,'' Paul said, reassuringly, making excuses for her father—like he'd been doing all her life. "Anyway, love, she's a good person to have on our side, so let's take care not to alienate her, okay?''

"So why didn't you tell her when you applied to come here?''

"Personal, Anevai, not professional. I hadn't seen her for some time and after I received your father's invitation, I wasn't about to entrust my reasons to anyone. —But what are you two about, playing cards this late at night?''

"Waiting for Stephen Ridenour.''

His brow tightened. "You, too? God, what is it with you women?'' His voice chilled. "He's with Loren at the moment. What do *you* want with him?''

She rolled her eyes. "Not what *I* want. Nayati's called a meeting and *Nayati* wants to—talk—to him, provided Ridenour's interested.''

"Your cousin's paranoid, Anevai. And he's bargaining for trouble. This isn't the time.''

"Tell me something I don't know. I've never seen him this bad.'' She picked up his hand, started playing with the large amber ring he always wore, watching the play of light bring the encased bug's eyes to life. Her father had dismissed her fears. But Paul at least *seemed* receptive—so far—and Sakiimagan did listen to Paul. She said cautiously, "I'm worried about him. Nayati, I mean. I really am. He—*feels* wrong. I don't know how else to describe it. First he said Hononomii's 'gone.' I thought, from the way he said it, he meant like—''

Dr. Paul interrupted her, "Gently, sweetheart, gently.''

She jerked on his hand. *Some* things had to be said. "*Listen* to me! Then he turns around and says Hono'll be all right—just that we have to get him back. Now—I don't know what to think. Dad says the admiral claims Hono had a 'reaction' to the Deprivil. Maybe that *is* all, but—Hono's had Dep all his life and never 'reacted' to it. And why was Nayati so damned *certain* he'd be all right?"

His arm tightened on her waist and he said, "Don't borrow trouble, love. One day at a time. We'll get him back, okay? Loren's one of the good guys. Trust me."

She didn't answer that—twenty years was a long time and people changed. "I really do *not* want to deal with this. Not with Nayati being weird."

"Be careful, child. There's more to that lad, Ridenour, than appears."

"Why's everyone keep saying that? He read *Harmonies*, and came here to work with Wesley. Isn't that how the SciCorps system is supposed to work? Isn't that *why* Wes wrote *Harmonies?*"

"If that's why Ridenour's here."

"Do *you* think Nayati's right, then?"

"I didn't say that. I am saying, don't underestimate Stephen Ridenour."

"Don't you like him, Dr. Paul?"

"Did I say not? He's a very likable young man, Ms. Tyee-wapi. But you wait until he's checked out and properly transferred before you take him to your shapely bosom."

She hit his arm—hard—with her fist and said to his startled face, "Don't *you* start! So help me, next time someone accuses me of being in lust with Stephen Ridenour, I'll smear them into the ground! And that includes *you!*"

Dr. Paul laughed, held a hand to intercept her fist and said, "All right, love!" Then he leaned over, murmured directly in her ear, "Just remember, if that boy *is* Cantrell's, he could be wired for sound—and a great deal more. If not him, Briggs or someone comparable could be backing him up. I *wish* you'd let this go."

She laughed and said aloud: "I think it's a lot of worry over nothing. Stephen's not going outside on his own. He's never been downworld before—won't admit to it, but I can tell. —You should have seen him with Bego."

"You took him to the *barn?* On his first day down?" Corey gasped. "Cruel and unusual, Annie-girl."

"Call me that again, Corelotto, and I'll belt you. —And yes, I did. Did all right, too, until Bego tried to bite his hair."

Dr. Paul wasn't laughing. "Did all right, how, Anevai?"

"Made it across all on his own—stubborn so-and-so, he is—and then crawling around in the stall like he'd done it all his life—once we spotted the kittens. —Oh, that's right. Dr. Paul, there's a blue—"

"Like he'd done what all his life, Anevai?"

His deep voice sounded—strange. She leaned forward to see his face better. "What's wrong? All I meant was he seemed more comfortable in the dirt than most of the researchers I've been around, once he discovered it wasn't deadly."

"And Bego? What happened? Is the colt all right?"

"Do you think I'd be sitting here otherwise? Dr. Paul, what's wrong?"

"It's this Ridenour. I wish you'd stay away from him."

She shook her head. "Can't. But don't worry. He's okay, I tell you. Wesley adores him. If he had his way, he'd kidnap Stephen right now and put him to work first thing in the morning. And from the way he talked in the *Hole* . . . He's for real, all right."

He still looked worried. "Just—don't make noise. The admiral's not uninterested in this young man. Questions have to be answered. But don't raise any."

Stephen stared at her in apparent disbelief. "They couldn't possibly . . ."

His voice trailed off and his stare slipped beyond her to the shadows of the fire-pit, his mouth moving imperceptibly, as though he were talking to invisible colleagues.

"Oh . . . my . . . God . . . of course," he breathed. "Using a direct tap . . . It could be done . . ."

Long moments passed. Very long moments as Cantrell awaited further explanation, trying not to interrupt the 'NetTech thought trail.

Finally, his eyes came back to her, wide with excitement. "If I understood half of what Wesley said today, it could be done. They could even be doing it right now. The test systems *I* was talking of were in lieu of the 'Net, but a tap . . ."

"Tap?" she ventured.

"Of NSpace itself. Of—of a space close to Nexus, utilizing

the same equipment—creating a new—NSpace directory if you will, direct access rather than memory cache. And once you begin that . . .''

"He told you that much already? Is the man crazy?"

Stephen shook his head. Of a sudden, he seemed less certain. "No. N—not really. We—we didn't t—talk s—specifics at all, but I *th—think*—'' His expression hardened. ''—no, dammit, I *know*—where it's all heading, and it could be done.''

He paused, brow puckered. Then, "Not even any laws or regs against, as far as I know. No one's ever thought of the possibility.'' He laughed shortly. "*Will* be illegal, soon as the 'NetAT hears of it.''

"You're certain?" Recalling Danislav's assessment: *He's too inclined to trust his beliefs . . .*

He hesitated, biting his lip, then nodded. Once. Emphatically.

"Well, my friend, you've just paid for your trip. I'm afraid Smith's system isn't *ready* to test: it *has* been tested. The Alliance needs to know how it's being done—how to detect it—and what has been done to the 'Net. We've got to get you *and Smith* safely aboard *Cetacean*.''

"Can't I just ask—"

"We don't *know* he's the one using it. He might be involved or he might not. If we can get him safely to the ship, away from whoever is using his system—he'll have his chance to prove himself, and he and Chet—and you—will have a chance to stop whatever game they're running down here.''

"Yes, but—" His voice caught. He sighed softly, and his chin came up. Although she could see his eyes glistening in the firelit profile, his face was dry. Unnaturally controlled, given the circumstances.

He murmured, "Nobody ever promised life would be fair, did they?"

"Quite the contrary, my dear," she said, keeping her voice gentle, the endearment out before she realized it. But he didn't seem to notice.

"I—I won't argue the matter, admiral. I doubt, really, I ever intended to. It was just a passing thought. A—pleasant passing thought, but certain options have been closed to me for a long, long time.'' He drew a deep breath. "But I don't think I should go back to the ship tomorrow. It would raise too many questions, possibly jeopardize your investigations here.'' His eyes closed a moment, then: "Give me two days—maybe three. I—I can find out what you need about the system and s–still make it clear to—to W–Wesley and to A–Anevai that I'm not the person for the job. That I d–don't fit in here. I—I can make it so they'll be g–glad to s–see the last of m–me."

"Stephen, that's not neces—"

"It is for me, Lo—admiral. And maybe, now I know what to—listen for, maybe I'll hear—something—"

"You won't find anything worth the risk, Stephen. And we'd *still* have to get Smith up on the ship. He *must* be protected while we're investigating here—as *you* must be."

His gaze dropped. She followed that look to his hands clenched on his knees. Watched those hands relax, and long fingers spread deliberately. "Perhaps you're right. But I've got to—cut off what's started today. I can do that. I'm actually quite ac–com —plished—" His breath caught. A ghost-smile touched his mouth. A smile with odd-under-the-circumstances real humor behind it. "One of my 'special talents.' —Please, admiral. One day. Maybe two. Then I'll come back to the ship with—with Smith in tow. . . . I promise. I won't . . . argue about staying. I'd be foolish to, wouldn't I, with my thesis to the 'NetAT rather well-proved?"

For several heartbeats, she waited for him to break, for his resolution to collapse, and the real reason for the request to emerge. But he didn't. It didn't. And perhaps that *was* the real reason.

"I'll think about it," she said slowly. "Let you know in the morning. I don't like it—I'll make no secret of that. You've become too valuable."

She rose to her feet, drawing the session to a close, and headed him toward the tube. "Either way, you *are* going up with me tomorrow morning. If I do decide to let you come back down here, Mo's going to put a beeper in your head first.—*And* take a look at that arm. We'll use that accident as an excuse to your friends in the morning."

"But—"

She stopped, made him face her. "Stephen, this is not negotiable. If you stay here, I'm *going* to know where to find you. You're too valuable to lose. Do you understand me?"

He stared back at the dying fire, the heart of the *Miakoda Moon*.

"Well, do you?"

His eyes met hers at last: dead tired, otherwise expressionless. "I suppose you're right . . ." And as the fire disappeared behind them: ". . . Now."

# V

## i

Poker had resumed, and Corey was going to fold: she knew the look.

Of a sudden, the HouseCom beeped discreetly and flashed a message: Admiral Cantrell and Stephen were in the 'TubeTerm.

Anevai gathered herself reluctantly to her feet. "Well, wish us luck, Dr. Paul."

"I'll do more than that."

"Oh?"

He grinned. "I consider it my bounden duty to assist you in every way I can. I shall take it upon myself to keep Adm. Cantrell as . . . occupied . . . as humanly possible."

"In your case, Dr. Paul—" As she headed for the door. "—That's a lot of possibles."

A second thought. She paused, returned to the table and flipped Corey's discarded hand. She gazed in disbelief, then laughed. Corey looked from one to the other in growing dismay.

She glanced up at Paul. His grin widened.

"You *are* a devil," she murmured and hauled a groaning Corey out the door.

From the door of her own suite, Loren Cantrell watched Stephen's retreat toward the atrium walkway, his straight, blue-clad shoulders and steady stride belying the tension he was under. Generally, when she set out to destroy someone's life, she was convinced the end justified that loss.

"Lexi," she said very quietly, "follow him. See he gets to his room. But don't let him see you. It would embarrass hell out of him."

Lexi nodded and slipped down the hall in Stephen's wake.

"Too bad for the kid."

She'd learned a long time ago how to keep her heart beating when TJ's voice—even the real thing—sounded unexpectedly in her ear, and almost as long ago not to be surprised when he read her mind.

"Yeah, right." She moved through the foyer into the sitting room. An empty glass on the bar, a carelessly flung magazine, and a huge bouquet of native flora greeted her, but no Paul Corlaney.

She glanced a question at TJ, who shrugged. "He was here when I left, rapidly drinking his woes away."

"Because I was with *Stephen?*" And at TJ's nod: "Lord help me, Paul Corlaney jealous of a twenty-year-old kid. Will wonders never cease."

"Groundless concerns, are they?"

*"Of course they are."* And to his skeptically raised eyebrow: "TJ, don't tell me you're as blind as he is. Of *course* I've more than a passing interest in the boy. With the Council's attention already focussed on him, damn right I'm interested. But he's hardly cut out for public life. If I had any real choice, I *might* even leave him here. But I haven't got that choice. He *must* go back."

A pause: loud in its silence. "For *his* sake, Adm. Cantrell? or *yours?*"

"You forgot a choice, TJ. For the Alliance."

"I didn't forget."

She rubbed her aching forehead. "Is this place tight, TJ?"

"It's not only tight, it's off-record at the moment."

She shot him a look, not certain she'd heard correctly. "You serious?"

"Absolutely. This is between you and me."

What the hell was he up to? *"You* heard us: he's done what we asked him to do. He's solved the disappearing data problem—at least he's on to it. With what's in his head, I can't leave him here, and once he's back in Vandereaux System, the 'NetAT's going to swallow him whole."

"He *says* he knows: big difference, Loren. He *might* know what he's talking about. But you get Smith up to the ship and spilling his brains to Chet and we don't *need* Stephen's of course. We don't *need* the kid anymore. He's done his job. He was onboard as an advisor and he figured enough to give you the legal opening to arrest Smith. That's all you need him for: either leave him here, or haul him back to the 'NetAT with Smith. Personally, I would suggest the latter, unless you enjoy being on the 'NetAT's Most Wanted.''

"Wait a minute, Briggs. That *system* isn't the only problem we've got going here. I've got Sakiimagan and his people ready to start talking. I'm *not* blowing that by hauling Smith and Stephen unwillingly up to the ship *if* there's another way. —And as far as Stephen is concerned, there's hell and away *more* he can accomplish if we don't blow this now. If he can get Smith onboard willingly, crack the system with Chet as witness, and go back with Smith eating out of *his* hand, the 'NetAT won't have a large enough *mouth* to swallow him up.''

"What fantasy land are you living in, Loren? The 'NetAT will hush anything they damn well please. Ridenour. Chet. Me. Even you. And Smith won't be eating out of your wonder-boy's hand. In case you haven't noticed, the kid's the one eating out of *Smith's* hand.''

"Smith's trying to *use* Stephen, anyone can see that, but for what purpose rather depends on what Smith is up to. It might be strictly personal: Stephen's damned good-looking, but somehow, I doubt that. Smith's got to suspect why Stephen's here. He's got to know we're checking records. If he suspects we're on to him, and arrest is imminent, he might try to pull strings with Stephen to avoid prosecution.''

"So?''

"So, Stephen doesn't *like* being pushed. Doesn't *like* being used. I nearly lost him more than once tonight. And remember, he went *around* Danislav to file that application with the 'NetAT. I *don't* think that was an accident. I think he knew full well Danislav would try to stop him. And he outmaneuvered him. He hates being lied to. If I'm reading Smith correctly, a few days in his company and Stephen is going to jump. If we play him carefully, it will be toward us and we get Smith. Play him wrong, and we haul back a time bomb: resentful, knowledgeable and proof behind the 'NetAT's closed doors that Shapoorian is altogether correct about Recon stability.''

TJ said slowly, "Safer and kinder to arrest Smith and leave Stephen here—before he knows too much.''

She keyed the personal lock on her room door, let it swing open before she turned back to him and leaned against the jamb.

"Two things wrong with that, TJ.''

"What's that?"

"He wouldn't be happy here without Smith. Out there, he's got a future with the 'NetAT, with, or without, Smith. Here—he's got nothing. That's one."

"And the other?"

She let her head fall back against the polished wood frame and looked at TJ under lowered lids. "He already knows too much."

Stephen let his hand slide along the polished wooden balustrade and wondered, in a detached way, who kept it that way. Who was it took the time to remove the streaks careless hands like his left in their wake? When did they do it? Would it spoil the magic to see them rubbing that gloss to life?

He stopped and leaned his elbows on the railing, looking out over the atrium.

He'd heard the other students talking of exotic restaurants and even parks with plants and small wildlife; but the closest equivalents AcStat boasted were the biology and botany labs.

He was mildly surprised when his earlier compulsion to hug the wall failed to manifest, but the height seemed friendly now, allowing him to view the harmony of rocks and plants, to see the design as a whole rather than close-range fragments. Maybe it was the Equilib, maybe it was exhaustion—

—and maybe it was just that now he knew how to look at it.

"I've had it, Teej," Cantrell said, "I'm for shower and bed."

"Speaking of which, do I let Corlaney in if he shows?"

She thought about it. She was tired—too tired. But she nodded anyway. "I've got to find out what he's up to, see if he knows anything."

"Be careful, Loren, the man's—irrational."

"I'll be careful. Who knows? Maybe he's been forced to live here. Maybe he's thrown in with Smith as the only free game in town. But I'll be all right. Paul doesn't intend to do much talking."

"For God's sake—"

She chuckled. "*Don't worry*. Besides, Paul talks in his sleep far more honestly than when he's awake."

"I warn you, I'll be listening anyway. At least until you signal an all's well. Maybe longer."

She reached a hand around his neck and leaned her forehead against his. "Only reason I dare, Teej."

His out-of-focus face grinned tightly. "Go get your shower, Boss-lady. I'll send the bastard in, soon as he gets his butt here."

She laughed outright, gave his neck a squeeze, and closed the door in his face.

The heavy drapes were pulled back, leaving only the billowing sheers to mute the moonlight streaming through the window into her bedroom. Cantrell enjoyed the effect for a moment before destroying it with the overheard lights. But as light flooded the room, an eerie glow from the bed caught her eye.

There, placed carefully on the center pillow, a single flower rested, identical to those in the outer room save for one small detail.

It glowed.

Silent, mirrorlike pools, bubbling springs, water falling down layer after layer of rocky shelves. One such spring bubbled and popped into a small pond on the balcony—so close he could sit down on its rocky edge if he thought he could get up afterwards. The overflow followed a narrow, curving aqueduct to the uppermost tier of pools where it joined with other streams from other bubbling springs to form the central waterfall.

Stephen closed his eyes, letting his body absorb that peace, letting the exhaustion he'd held at bay all evening creep into his limbs, feeling the tiny aches and pains come rushing in, now he had the leisure. Any moment—not this instant, but soon, *real* soon—he'd go back to his room, remove the tight jacket and the now exceedingly uncomfortable brace.

He'd been so careful at first, as he was with any new dish at the Academy, testing, waiting, trying to anticipate which adverse reaction he'd have and which pill he'd have to take to counteract it. But there'd been none—no reaction what-so-ever, unless you counted overeating to the point of pain as a reaction. Neither had there been any of the bitter aftertaste so common in station food. He'd had no gag reflex to inhibit, no acidic reaction to neutralize, and he'd found himself restocking his plate every time the servers passed their table without once accessing the pillbox in his belt pocket.

And if he didn't remove the jacket soon, even its well-stitched seams would be in jeopardy.

But at the moment, he was too tired to move.

He buried his face in his arms, shutting out the peaceful beauty before him. Because the admiral was correct: his choices were gone—if he'd ever really had any. He could never put that transfer request through now—not with the security of the 'Net itself at stake. He knew that, even while the prospect of leaving this place grew less attractive with each freshly scented breath.

For a few brief moments, out on that moonlit cliff, later by the fire, he'd been so tempted. Somehow, the appeal of 'NetAT isolation had weakened. For an instant, it had seemed thoroughly possible: the transfer had already been filed: all he'd have to do was remain here when *Cetacean* left.

Luckily, Adm. Cantrell had been there to remind him of priorities. Best simply to trust the admiral. The admiral knew the situation here. The admiral knew his history. The admiral knew his choices, knew of the 'NetAT's interest, knew Eckersley—trusted Eckersley. The admiral knew—

He lifted his head and stared blindly out across the waterfall.

—The admiral knew too damn much.

How much did she *really* know about how the 'Net worked? She didn't *need* the background to ask the questions. *Chet* was in charge of Security Communications. *He* could have been prompting her for the technicalities right through the beeper she wore. Would have heard every arrogant, *stupid* flight of fancy he'd made, imagining it safe to talk.

The admiral ordered him down here knowing his background, knowing what Recon contamination might do to him—*had* done. She'd *known* Paul Corlaney was here. She'd forced him into meeting Wesley Smith here, in this—place, *knowing* Wesley's system was operational—

—or so she said. She'd said that *after* he'd begun thinking about staying. *After* Wesley had shown such interest in his staying. Adm. Cantrell worked for the Council. Adm. Cantrell *worked* for *Eckersley*, dammit! And Eckersley wanted him for some damned post—to be shown off by the Council like some —*freak!* (Look at him: the Recon who made it all the way through Vandereaux Academy! Who could read a paper and think he knew more than all his professors. Who could—)

—God.

*You're certain?* she'd asked, in reference to the 'Net tap. And he'd emphatically endorsed a—*thing* he had *no* physical evidence whatsoever could be done at all, let alone with existing hardware. What if she'd lied to him and that transmission *hadn't* happened?

*What would you do? Put that transfer through for real?*

She'd known what he was thinking all along.

There was no way out. Nothing he could do to stay down here with Wesley. With Anevai. With the almost-cat. She'd get him on that ship—use him to lure Wesley up, then arrest him—maybe arrest them both, if Wesley's system proved real. The 'NetAT wanted Wesley, and now they were going to have him because one stupid Recon bit-brain hadn't seen through their plan.

How much power did the admiral really have? *Illegal . . . or will be once 'NetAT hears of it*—On the record, he was some sort of *expert advisor*. He had no idea what that *really* meant. Had his casual remark given her the legal endorsement required to arrest Smith without existing law? Could she condemn Wesley Smith to some living hell because of what *he* had told her? What if he was *wrong?*

He buried his head again: not wanting to see the water, not wanting to smell the flowers, not wanting to see, think—or feel—anything ever again. He'd allowed these people to touch him, and look where that trust had gotten him.

He could shut out the sight below, but the sound of the water rippled inexorably through his nervous system, easing tension to the point of enervation, making his concerns seem very far away.

Suddenly, through that mesmeric ripple, so low it seemed a part of the water: "It *is* beautiful, isn't it?"

The boy jerked around, startled. Lexi watched his reaction out of the corner of one eye as she scanned the tranquil atrium. She hadn't meant to startle him, but the water-sound must have drowned out her footsteps.

She let her gaze drift around to meet his and said, "Mind if I join you?"

"I thought—shouldn't you be back with Adm. Cantrell?"

She shrugged. "She and TJ are—"

"Oh," he said, turning back to the atrium, blushing furiously.

She chuckled and leaned on the railing next to him. "They're discussing matters outside my security range, so I had to leave."

"Oh." The blush grew more pronounced. She grinned at him

and looked back at the waterfall, giving him room to regroup: she'd dealt with fragile egos before: male, female and a few she'd never been quite sure of.

Eventually his soft voice said, "It truly is—beautiful, I mean. I—I hate the thought of leaving it forever. Of never seeing it again. To never see— How, Lexi? How could you leave your home? your family? your—f–friends. Didn't it—hurt?" And while she was wondering how best to answer: "Lexi, I'm *sorry*. You don't have to—"

She said very calmly, meeting his distress with a casual over-the-shoulder, "That's all right, Stephen. I don't mind. Who else've you got to ask? Sure it hurts. But nothing you can't live with, and eventually that hurt goes away. Venezia—that's *my* home planet—wasn't quite so welcoming as HuteNamid: special filter masks were—and still are—a necessity in most places. But it *was* beautiful in its own weird way, and my family is, well—Family."

He whispered, so low she nearly didn't hear, "Are you ever—sorry you left?"

She shook her head. "Never. Sure I miss them, sometimes, but right now I only really remember my brother—and that, I suspect, is because in some ways you remind me of him."

He blinked. "Is—is that why you always seem to know when I'm—"

"Not really. Mostly I remember the problems I had when I first left home. You're not *that* unique." She shifted her weight to one elbow and reached a cautious hand to touch his hair, careful not to startle him. But, she'd always loved . . . "Tony had hair like yours. That's what made me remember him first."

He made no attempt to draw away from her touch, even leaned his head into it for an instant. The sad, lost look on his face made her want to hold him the way she used to hold Tony when the world had grown too harsh for him. But there was nothing she could do to help Stephen with what he faced—as there had been nothing she could do for Tony at the end. They had their own battles to fight. She hoped Stephen's had a happier ending.

She let her hand fall to his shoulder, held it briefly. "He was about your age when I saw him last. And—" She chuckled. "—he had a penchant for getting lost, too."

Stephen blushed again, and she laughed outright, but gently, and turned back to the falls, relieved when she heard him laugh as well.

"That's what's so wonderful about the best things, Stephen, and especially the best people: no matter where you go, something will remind you of them—sometimes years down the line—something you wish you could share with them, something you'll appreciate in ways you might not have otherwise, because you'll try to see it as they would. In that way, they're always with you. The bad things fade, one doesn't want to be reminded of them; but the good ones—the special people—are a part of you forever."

He was quiet a goodly while—considering, she reckoned. Finally, he turned to go: distractedly, the way he would. A pause. Then over his shoulder, he said, very low, "Good night, Lexi. And—thank you."

She smiled. "Thank *you*, Stephen, —for making me remember."

## ii

Stephen slipped his keycard into the lock, and as the door slid silently into the wall, glanced back toward the atrium where Lexi lingered, apparently as entranced with the waterfall as he had been. He leaned against the doorjamb, still staring down the hallway, but thinking now about what she'd said, seeing not the railing or the atrium beyond, but a blond-haired man with laughing brown eyes.

For the first time in years, he welcomed that image, the man he'd called Papa. Lexi had given him that memory back; Lexi and Anevai and Wesley. Papa: as Zivon Stefanovich knew him, not as Victor Danislav had forced Stephen Ridenour to remember him. The Stefan Ryevanishov with big strong hands that held him close, the deep voice that called him *son* and taught him to watch the stars; not the stranger who'd left that world of red and gold to go Someplace Else and written to Victor Danislav never to tell Zivon where that place was.

Papa would have loved watching the moon rise over the valley. Papa would have loved the Pit, with its flickering light and magical stars. Papa would have—

And Mama would have called him a damnfool! What the hell was Lexi really doing here? Following him to make sure he went to bed like a good little boy?

Or maybe Lexi *could* sense things about him—like maybe he was thinking clearly for the first time in days, and *she* had to put a stop to it. Like maybe he was starting to resent people manipulating him, and *she* had better remind him of Obligations. Cantrell obviously didn't want him talking to Wesley before they had that *beeper* in him. Probably put an 'ear' in him while they were at it. Better yet, Cantrell wanted him *and* Wesley on that ship of hers where every breath they took would be on record.

Wesley might be crazy—might even be doing something illegal—but he deserved a chance to explain *before* microphones compromised that conversation. Once he went with Cantrell tomorrow, he'd be stuck with *her* rules. Which meant . . .

He slid one shoe off and stepped deliberately inside, leaving the shoe in the doorway, tapping the lights off as the door touched the shoe: old academy trick—if the lock didn't register, the super didn't know if you were in or out.

He could see Lexi through the crack, could see her glance toward his room, smile (an extremely *satisfied* smile, to his way of thinking) and head back toward the admiral's suite.

*Now the kid's in bed, we can all relax? Fine, Cantrell*, he thought, *you do that*.

A flicked switch: the terminal came immediately onLine. A moment's hesitation: Anevai had said it wasn't connected. More lies? or had the Techs come in this afternoon?

A quick check: it had never *been* offLine.

*Why, Anevai?* A moment's regret, but no more. She had her priorities; he had his.

He laid his key-card on the desk and queried the HouseCom for Wesley's location, requested a schematic, punched the key for hardcopy, and as the page slipped from under the monitor, sent a direct to room query to Smith's suite.

An autoresponse message flashed onscreen:
> **To whom it may or may not concern:**
> **I'm here, gentle folk, but ex-cee-ding-ly b-u-s-y.**
> **Don't even THINK about interrupting me.**
> **Leave a message and I might even answer. —Eventually.**
—**If I get a round tuit.**
> **TTFN.**

> **The Wesser.**

Exhaustion struck, and he collapsed into a chair.

It had seemed so simple. 1) Call Wes. 2) Go and talk to Wes. 3) Get this mess straightened out with Wes before the admiral hauled him up to the ship tomorrow. Now . . .

He pulled the map from the tray, folded it several times and tucked it into his belt pocket. He'd need it to find Wesley's room—when and if Smith answered his messages. He sighed and began to type:

*Sir, I've been thinking about our discussion this afternoon and I'd like to meet with you before breakf*

He stopped. Even if he sent this out over the in-house network, Cantrell would know he'd attempted to reach Smith, whether or not he succeeded. But if he simply disregarded the message, went to Wesley and—

*"Sh-sh-sh. Full house, Jacks high. Now shush, that's* Ridenour's *room. We don't want to wake him up. Wouldn't want him to hear us."*

Anevai? What was she doing out in the hall?

A thump, followed by a half-smothered curse and an even more familiar giggle. Evidently not so tired as she'd professed.

*"Hurry! We're late! We were supposed to be in the barn five minutes ago! Dammit, come on!"*

Outside his door. Outside his obviously-propped-open door. Anevai didn't want to wake him up? Anevai said loud and clear where she was headed?

Like *hell* he wasn't supposed to hear.

TJ opened the door, stepped aside to let Lexi in. "What took so long?"

She avoided his eyes. He knew her too well and her talk with Stephen had disturbed her more than she cared to admit. She hadn't thought about Tony in a long while, and not all the memories were pleasant ones. "We had a little talk."

"Boss-lady said not to let him see you."

Normally the implied rebuke would bother her. Right now . . . she shrugged. "Seemed like the thing to do at the time."

"Lex?" He took her by the shoulders, turned her to face him, and lifted her chin to study her closely. His tone softened. "Rough one?"

"No. Not really. He pulled some old strings, is all."

"You okay?"

"Fine."

A quick hug, and release. "Get the kid put to bed?"

"Going through his door, at any rate." Some of the haze lifted from her mind and she could see beyond her own concerns. "Teej? What's wrong? This is more than my disregarding orders."

His turn to shrug. "Nothing much. Boss-lady and I aren't seeing quite eye to eye on a few things. Nothing we can't straighten out."

Personal, then. Perhaps Stephen had been more right than she in his assessment of what was happening in here: she'd never quite understood the relationship between the admiral and TJ. In either case, she knew better than to pry.

"Go on to bed, darlin'. I'll mind the store," TJ said. "And don't worry about Ridenour. He's done all right today."

She paused at the doorway and said in a low voice, "Better than you know, Teej. Better than you could possibly know."

The voices were well down the hall now. Stephen ventured a look through the shoe-propped opening. Anevai—with a man he didn't recognize. Anevai in a stained fur-lined jacket and faded, well-worn jeans, her black hair a single long braid down the back.

*Shut up. Ridenour will hear.*

He'd heard that one before. Comments designed to force him into taking offense—into officially unjustifiable actions.

In other words: bait.

But Anevai? —Just one more seeming-friend sent in to set him up?

Cantrell had been manipulating him back there: he knew that; it was her job, the way it had been Danislav's job, though Cantrell seemed to take a touch more personal interest in the assignment. He didn't happen to appreciate that manipulation or the unrequested interest, but if she was telling the truth, if these people *were* up to major illegal activities, and Wesley Smith was involved, he *should* be arrested.

On the other hand, if *Cantrell* was lying . . .

Dammit, *someone* was conning him: Smith, Cantrell, Anevai—maybe all of them; and suddenly Anevai's little game out there assumed a very unchildish importance in that equation.

He waited until they had disappeared around the corner, counted to ten (several times) as he jammed his foot back into its shoe. He knew of only two ways down: the wide open central staircase and the lifts to the exits at the far end of the building. With his luck he'd meet Anevai as he stepped out. Either option advertised his whereabouts; Anevai was expecting him to follow. It wouldn't be polite to disappoint her. But, dammit, he'd like to choose the time and place.

And there *was* another way down. A way no one *rational* would be looking.

A deep breath, a dash down the hall to a skidding halt at the corner—

—and a moment's dismay as he stood there, breathless and feeling a crazed desire to laugh as his door clicked shut behind.

He'd left the key-card on the desk.

As Bijan would say, *Only you, Ridenour.*

"Hold on a minute, Corey," Anevai said softly; and retraced their path to peer around a broad-leafed plant and over a shale-edged pool toward Stephen's room.

Nothing. But she'd heard—

Suddenly she saw him: not on the wide spiralling staircase, not headed down toward the lift, but levering himself up onto the edge of the third-level feeder-spring.

"What in hell—" Corey said, peering over her shoulder.

She didn't answer, just held her breath in helpless dismay as Ridenour sprinted along a very narrow, very slippery, irregularly curving aqueduct—

—three stories above the atrium floor.

"C'mon, Ridenour," she muttered, "you're almost— *Shit! —Ridenour, look out!*"

His forward momentum checked, his foot slipped, and he disappeared from view in a slow-motion, tumbling dive.

"Ridenour!"

Corey's hand on her arm stopped her.

"Don't be a fool!" Corey hissed in her ear, pulling her toward the exit. "If he *is* hurt, you want to be caught with him? Bad enough you yelled. Better hope he didn't hear you."

She jerked free. "And what if he *dies*, Corey?"

"All the more reason not to be here. I'll check for him when I come back."

"I can't believe you—"

He grabbed her arm, held a finger to his lips. She listened. Heard a stumbling *thud*, a soft curse. And felt her mouth twitch in an almost-smile, while Corey hauled her toward the door.

Ridenour had beaten the odds again.

### iii

Cantrell had a mouthful of toothpaste when a once-familiar knock sounded on her bedroom door. She shook her head at his foolishness, but a tap on the wall with her foot completed the pattern he'd begun.

Her image grinned frothily. *Who's being foolish now, Loren Cantrell?* she thought. The grin faded as a reflected glow caught her eye.

She'd considered the large bouquet in her sitting room a peace offering until finding that *thing* on her pillow. The flowers were native to HuteNamid, the bioluminescence was not. Nor was the technique which created that internally generated glow the subject of any of P. J. Carlson's 'Net papers. On the other hand, 'Hononomii's flowers' were a frequent occurrence in Paul's in-system notes and memos.

Invitation? Or a warning there were things happening here beyond her right to inquire? Her bedroom had been secured, a lock he had somehow gotten through to leave that thing on her bed. She hadn't told TJ about *that* little trick. —Yet.

Well she'd certainly never find out standing in her bathroom with a mouthful of toothpaste while Paul twiddled his thumbs out in the waiting room.

But when she entered her bedroom, towelling her face and hands dry, she found him already there, idly thumbing through the novel she'd left by the bed.

She looked from him to the door and back again, one eyebrow raised.

"TJ let me in," Paul said, disgustingly smug. "He said to tell you Lexi's back."

"Oh, he did, did he? And did he let you in earlier, too?" She pointed with her chin at the glowing flower.

He shrugged noncommittally. Waggled his eyebrows.

"Some bodyguard. Maybe I ought to trade him in on a new model."

"Sometimes old models work better," he said softly, oozing in her direction. "Especially when they know all the owner's habits. If you didn't want him to let me in, you shouldn't have answered the way you did." He paused to lay the book back on the table. "It's a good book. Remind me, I'll introduce you to the author."

The book was a local publication. A detective novel.—

She slung the towel over her shoulder and leaned against the door frame as he started toward her.

—The author was P. J. Carlson.

As he came within arm's reach, she raised a hand and placed it firmly on his chest. He stopped short, hands quiescent at his sides.

Easing the touch into a caress, she asked, "And what of this model? Has it developed any new habits?"

He grinned. "Care to find out?"

She gripped his sleeve and turned him toward the bathroom. "Shower's in there."

The grin widened. "Going to join me?"

"Make it cold, Corlaney. You and I are going to talk."


Cloud shadows skidded across the meadow path he and Anevai had taken only a few short hours before, the trees' green foliage turned silver in the moonlight.

From deep in the portico shadow, Stephen waited, rubbing his sore elbow, while two figures ran stride for stride down the pathway to the barn.

Not an elegant move, and far from a clean landing—several staggering steps back from a suddenly-there edge and a fall to his backside would *not* gain him meet-points for originality—but he was alive and without major injury.

Which was, he thought, more than he deserved. *Next* time, he'd take—

The two figures disappeared into the barn. He took a deep breath and stepped cautiously out of the shadows—

—and stumbled back as lace snapped at his throat and wrists.

Wind. *Lots* of wind which bypassed his shadowed nook, wind that drove those clouds racing overhead to make eerie shadows underfoot. He forced his pulse under control, eased his breathing, then sprinted for the barn, focussing on the path, refusing to acknowledge the wind or the turmoil of his senses.

But gravity rapidly gained the advantage. His knees began to shake, his steps grew uncertain, and he discovered that running on a maximum-efficiency track was very different from running planetside-au-naturel. No matter the moon was bright: there were treacherous dips in the soil, unseen rocks and plants.

On the third near-fall, he slowed his pace, panting and blinking a sweaty film from his eyes. He rubbed an unsteady hand across his face, threw a look back the way he'd come. Strange, he'd thought 'night' would be dark, but it was bright in its own way . . . there were no absolute shadows. You could see—

Fear lent him strength, and he sprinted again, this time for the sheltering bushes beside the barn, well away from the door. But he counted it made too soon. A knee gave, the bushes broke his fall, and he lay still for a moment, rubbing the pain away and working desperately to slow his gasps after air.

Voices, through the pounding pulsebeat. Several voices— from a glassless window three meters above the ground. He crawled from one wind-tossed black lump of bush to the next until he reached that window.

There *was* a meeting in progress, and from the loud debate escaping that opening, perhaps Anevai *hadn't* been bait and they *didn't* know he was there.

A male voice he didn't recognize: "—onomii to happen to the rest of us? We *must* cut all ties to the Alliance. Let them have their fancy buildings *and* the damned 'Net that goes with them! We don't need them anymore, and if they won't go away and leave us alone, we'll give them a free ticket to hell!"

"Enough, Nayati." He didn't immediately recognize the new voice either: it held a note he hadn't associated with it previously. "As you all know," Anevai's voice continued, "because of the presence of our *guests*, father couldn't come tonight. But I speak as he would if he were here. We must try every possible route toward *lawful* isolation, perhaps even eventual independence. But we must keep in mind, not all the People *want* that independence. And I believe we *can* deal with spacers like Stephen

—maybe even Cantrell, from what my father says—without endangering . . ." Her voice trailed off uncertainly.

"Endangering who, Anevai?"

"You know damn well what I mean."

"But, I don't. How can you expect us to—"

"Damn you, Hatawa." So low, he almost missed that. "The Cocheta."

"Yes." A very satisfied sound. "That's what I thought you meant."

A mumbled expletive, presumably from Anevai. A heart-stopping crash above his head: a trap-door come loose in the wind and banging against the side of the barn. He reBooted his heart, sought to pick up lost threads—

"—bargain we must. We're a part of the Alliance 'Net and nothing—"

"Not *all* of us, *olathe*," Nayati interrupted her.

"Not all of us—what, cousin?" Caution in that tone.

"*We* are no longer a part of that precious 'Net of yours."

A pause. Then Anevai, her voice little more than a whisper: "*What have you done, Hatawa? What the* hell *have you done?*"

He closed his eyes, straining to hear. No longer a part of the 'Net? So the admiral hadn't lied. God, what had Wes gotten himself into? They *had* to be talking about his System. Did he *know* what they were doing with it?

The voices sank until the wind-rustled leaves drowned them out. A shiver ran up his spine, a being-watched feeling like the corridors of Vandereaux. A quick scan: nothing but shifting shadows of leaves, bushes and grass. He hunched closer to the wall, blocked off the distraction of the wind with a hand over his outer ear, straining to hear the muffled debate between gusts.

". . . much have you taken off?"

"I don't know. I've got a—fairly—complete record in the Libraries."

"You *fool!* You stupid, egocentric—don't you realize what you've—"

The sound of flesh meeting flesh interrupted her.

Stephen started up, heard Nigan Wakiza's voice say *That's enough of that, Nayati*, and sank back down. Nothing he could do about it anyway.

Nigan continued: "You had no call—"

"—Damn right he hadn't." Anevai's voice: cold and sharp.

"You listen to me, Hatawa, you *ever* pull that on me again, you'd *better* be prepared to use it!"

His feet were growing numb. He shifted position, froze as something snapped above the sound of the wind. Had he or Something Else made that noise?

A shadow loomed. He jerked back and shoved against the building to dive around the creature, but it grabbed him, threw him up against the barn. His head cracked against the wall, and the moonlight gave way to stars—

"I can't really see how that's any of your business, *Adm. Cantrell*. I came here because I chose to. I haven't any obligation to justify that choice, so long as I earn my keep. Has Council voiced objections to my output?"

"Of course not, Paul. Don't be ridiculous." Cantrell was exasperated at his willful obtuseness. "One doesn't complain about the bill on award-winning merchandise. It's not Council asking. It's me. *I* want to know. A man like you doesn't turn down every ThinkTank in the Alliance, planetary and station, to commit lifetime to a brand-new colony world without damned good reasons. Reasons that may help my understanding of the situation here, help my understanding of someone I thought I knew."

He said nothing, his face hard.

She leaned forward in her chair. "Paul, *talk to me*. You always said the ThinkTanks would be the death of the Alliance. I *agreed* with you. We were going to change things. And just when I'd reached the stage where I might begin to make a difference, you disappeared."

A muscle bulged in his jaw and he muttered, "As I recall, I said the death of *science*, admiral, sir."

"*Dammit, Corlaney!*" She threw herself back again. Paul didn't even blink.

TJ's voice (over the com—*not* in her ear) asking Was everything all right, reminding Corlaney he was listening.

And, lest Paul should forget, sitting just beyond the closed door.

She drew a deep breath. "Fine, TJ. Thanks." And verified with a more personal bio-signal. Then: "It took me nine years—nine God-damned years, Paul,—to track you down. Nine years and seven security upgrades. I thought you were dead.

When Lance and Larry disappeared and there was still no word from you, I was certain of it.''

His eyes dropped and she paused, giving him the opening. Hoping that after all this time there was some sane reason for what he had put her through. But if a reason did exist, he wasn't offering it.

''Damn you, Corlaney,'' she said softly, ''they were your friends, too.'' No reaction. ''I finally found you, alive and well and transferred to an undistinguished frontier ThinkTank—a transfer the Alliance Council thought best to keep secret. Better to have Paul Corlaney disappear into a nova like a good little legend than to have it known he'd committed to a Recon—''

''You've got it all wrong, Loro. It was my idea.''

''What *idea?*''

''*I* didn't want my transfer on the 'Net, and the Council was good enough to agree.''

A hand struck his face sharply once, twice . . . a third time hard enough to bounce his head off the wall . . . again. A new bump to match the one sprouting on the other side of his skull.

Symmetry—how nice.

An angry voice spat in his ear, ''Wake up, Spacer-man, you got this far on your own, damned if I'll carry you the rest.''

Stephen blinked. His ear was cold . . . wet. . . . The spitting voice, he thought, disgusted, and reached up to wipe that repulsive wetness off, but something grabbed his wrist, forced the hand painfully back down.

Pain. He'd dislocated his shoulder again. —No. That was this afternoon. It was night now. That was the blackness surrounding him. That and a large creature crouched over him.

The creature struck him again; then grabbed his lapels, jerked him to his feet, and shook him until he was gasping for breath. Fabric ripped and a button snapped free. He struck out blindly, indignantly knocking the hand away.

''*Dammit! That's an expens—*'' A heavy arm across his chest thrust him back against the wall, driving the air from his lungs. His knees gave way, something very cold—and very sharp —pressed against his throat, and of a sudden, getting his knees cooperative again seemed very useful indeed.

''Don't get cute, Spacer-man.''

He swallowed hard, and with that peristaltic movement the sharp point—God! a *knife?*—pricked the skin painfully. Slow damp trickled down his neck, and his head cleared in an adrenalined instant. The pressure eased slightly, and he whispered, "I wouldn't dream of it."

"All right, Spacer-man, move. We're going inside for a friendly little visit. Keep your hands up, palms out where I can see them, and we'll get along fine. Make one misstep, and you're so much animal fodder."

He recognized the voice now—

The blade pressed harder into his throat and the trickle grew to a steady flow. "You hear me, Spacer-man?"

—*Nayati.* He closed his eyes. The arm pressing against his chest hampered breathing, made answering next to impossible. The blade's pressure increased, the trickle became a stream and he gasped, "I . . . hear you!"

The blade left his throat and he opened his eyes on the shadows surrounding him, wondering which was Anevai. She'd be one of this faceless crowd: the bait always was.

It was the academy all over again: the false friend, the faceless tormentors behind the hard-voiced leader—the knives were different, but not the fanatical animosity: it was really quite unbelievable that Recons *and* spacers could so thoroughly despise him.

Funny. A ghost-laugh wasted hard-won breath. He was on the verge of knowing why, and might not live to tell—

—if anyone cared to know. But others knowing didn't matter.

"*Shut*—"

*His* knowing did.

"—*up!*"

This time, the *back* of the hard-knuckled hand bounced his head off the wall and he wondered, in a detached way, which would break first, the wood or his skull. In an equally detached way, he wondered at his own calm. But somehow, simple pain, even death, could be dealt with—

—so long as you *knew* that you were dying. His life had been so full of uncertainties it seemed only fair that—

"I said *move!*" Nayati jerked him away from the wall and shoved him toward the barn door. His shoulder throbbed, having taken the brunt of his fall against the barn wall. He rubbed it, tried to adjust the brace through the cloth as he staggered forward. Without thinking, he reached toward the pocket in his belt.

A hand jerked his collar from behind, stopping him short of the doorway.

"Hands, Spacer-man! Keep them where I can see them!"

Slowly, so as not to startle this hot-tempered Nayati into action they would both regret, he held out the slim pillbox.

The hand released his collar and plucked the box from his fingers. Nayati examined it carefully. Holding it at arm's length, he pried at its lid with his knife tip, never taking his eyes from Stephen's face. The knife slipped, scraped the delicate cloisonné surface. Stephen closed his eyes: he'd saved his personal indulgence credit for two months for that antique.

A hand gripped the lace at his throat. "Open your eyes, Spacer-man." Nayati was holding the box in front of his nose. "*You* open it. One of us gets blown to hell, we both do."

He slipped the catch and gently lifted the top. Nayati took it, looked into it—

—and began to laugh. Stephen clenched his jaw and said nothing as the Recon nonchalantly tossed the box into the darkness.

"Hands up." A jerk of Nayati's shadowy head. "Move!"

He sighed and raised his arms as high as the brace would comfortably allow, doing his best to ignore the pain the movement caused: that, too, would pass.

*"Higher, damn you!"*

His own temper flared. He'd had enough of this brand of idiocy for a lifetime. Had had enough before he'd ever left Vandereaux Station.

Another shove.

"Damn *you*, 'Buster! That's as high as it goes!"

He turned to face his tormentor. Nayati grabbed his collar, whirled him inside with a jerk which pulled his coat off one shoulder and sent a second button flying.

The button bounced off the railing and hit him above the eye. He began calculating the odds of that happening, doing his best not to think about what might come next. Nayati's fist twisted his jacket, thrust between his shoulders driving him up against the rails—

—a move which caught him off guard, but not the brace.

Designed to protect the shoulder from ordinary shocks, it wasn't proof against outright assault. Infinitesimal gears spun, translating the motion of the arm to the far side of his body. Overtight bands cut painfully into his ribs—

*It's not supposed to do that!* he thought, and panicked as the brace tightened again and a vicious twist sent the final button spinning a fuzzy, twinkling path through the dark: comet amidst the stars exploding inside his head.

His knees buckled, and he stopped thinking, tried only to stay awake: as long as he was awake, he wasn't dead.

Nothing else mattered.

Nayati yanked the jacket down, pinned his arms to his sides. The wide belt cut into his stomach, and the brace contracted again, driving the last remaining air from already laboring lungs.

*"What the hell . . . ?"* Nayati's voice rang in his head as his knees dissolved and he collapsed to the ground, senses fading in and out: sickening montage of light and sound.

# iv

"Why, Paul?" The weariness in Loren's voice scraped raw nerves bloody. He'd never heard that tone from her; certainly never expected to be the cause of it. Had youthful fervor given way to mature realism even in her?

Little he could do to help her this time: her loyalties had too many claims ahead of his now.

What had he been thinking of to call her in the first place? To agree to—no, *force*—this meeting? He'd kept clear of her all these years for very sound reasons; yet from the moment she'd entered the system, he'd acted like some overhormoned adolescent.

Even now, it was a major effort to keep his mind off . . .

She was standing at the open balcony door. The baffling screen had to be engaged: outside, branches whipped; inside, her silk robe drifted in a gentle breeze. Moonlight glinted in her eyes, off the tips of her lashes, her silk-covered—

—God, he wanted to—

"You know what I think, Paul?" Somehow, the tone, the words didn't quite fit the image. "I think there's a hell of a lot more going on in this private Eden of yours than is in the 'Net.

More even than the records Sakiimagan gave me. You want to know why?''

Discord in paradise: he *wanted* her to drop the whole subject.

"I see it, Paul, feel it all around me. Sakiimagan, his people—yours: all the right elements—and no results. Stagnation. It doesn't add up, Corlaney. And you know where the greatest discrepancy lies?''

He shrugged, not really caring.

"It's you, Paul.'' She sat down, leaned toward him. "Once I found you, made the link with P. J. Carlson, I tracked down what you've put out on the 'Net since you got here. I was curious what HuteNamid had that no other 'Tank did, what work was in progress here that could possibly tempt you. Do you know what I found?''

He scowled at her. What did she expect him to say? She had the records. Dammit, she could *see*, couldn't she? Why would anyone choose to live elsewhere, once they'd seen this place?

"Paul, the—shit—there's no other word for it—you've put out from here you could have written in your sleep. It sounds impressive, it might even have sparked lesser minds to new insights; but it's the chaff of what you worked on twenty-five—*thirty*—years ago. Where's your real work? Where's the work that created *that?*'' She gestured toward the flower. "How far have you taken it? Is it more than aesthetics? And how much of that work was Hononomii Tyeewapi's?''

His heart skipped a beat. "God. Give the woman a flower . . . What makes you think *I'm* responsible for it?''

"Don't try to be funny, Paul. The only thing to hit the 'Net out of HuteNamid worth a damn is that paper of Smith's and *that* was written in such a way that the experts glossed right over it. Only a damned schoolboy saw it for what it was.''

"Did he? You want answers? How about giving a few of your own?''

"That one—yes. Damn right he did. You can imagine how crazed the 'experts' in the 'NetAT must be right now: enough to listen to the kid, enough to send him to the source. You may also imagine how delighted they're going to be when they learn the theory is alive and well and in a Recon/researcher partnership. They'll put Smith away for the rest of his life! —Is *that* what you want?''

*  *  *

From this angle, Stephen was nothing but a dark lump at Nayati's feet, the sheen of his clothes all that differentiated him from surrounding shadows.

Anevai watched in frustrated impotence from the side door. As a professional spy, Ridenour made a great CodeHead. He'd had his chance—dammit, she'd given him every opportunity to catch up with her and Corey and bloody well *ask* what they were doing. But he'd snapped at the bait like a fish in spring. . . . Damn him.

It was a blasted lynch mob. Had been before she ever got to the barn. Nayati had set her up, set Stephen up. She wished now she hadn't told Corey to take the 'Tube back to the Condos before she'd scoped the situation.

Nayati jerked Stephen's arm: vain attempt to haul him to his feet.

"Nayati, that's enough!" she shouted, loud enough to be heard over the wind, loud enough to be heard across the distance between them—and loud enough to tell him she was mad as hell.

"*Nayati!*" She stepped outside the barn, hoping to draw Nayati to her, hoping to keep him, and Ridenour, outside. Inside had become Nayati's domain.

Nayati looked around, his face harsh and cadaverous in the moonlight, Stephen hanging limp as death from his grasp.

"Let him go, damn you!"

Nayati's grip tightened, a no longer limp Stephen throwing his head back in silent protest, (Dammit, that was Ridenour's bad arm!) and she wished desperately for her father's authoritative presence.

But Nayati surprised her. He bowed mockingly and stepped back, holding up empty hands as the spacer collapsed, his back heaving, a twist of iridescent blue holding his arms at their awkward angle.

"Watch him," Nayati ordered Nigan, who was standing quietly to one side. "If he moves, knock his brains out."

Nayati stalked toward her. Nigan, with a worried look, motioned to the others to watch Ridenour, then followed Nayati.

"Blast it, Hatawa," she said as he stopped just out of arm's reach, "you're totally out of line!"

"Hardly."

"Did Nigan tell you what happened today? He promised me he would."

Nayati shrugged.

"Your actions do you no honor, Hatawa. Ridenour was hurt before you attacked him—and you armed, no less."

"Stay out of it, Annie! This scum's the key. If you can't see that, go back to your stories and your toys; you don't belong here." His face assumed a fanatical glee in the moonlight. "He's Cantrell's, Annie-girl, and he's going to get Hononomii back to us! We've got ourselves a fuckin' hostage!"

"Are you out of your *mind?* Adm. Cantrell's ship is sitting up there with the ability to blow us to hell three times over, and you're talking *hostage?*"

"Anevai's right, Nayati." Nigan put a hand on Nayati's shoulder. Thank the gods, at least one of them was still thinking. With Hononomii gone, she'd been afraid nothing could restrain Nayati's temper.

"What are you doing here?" Nayati hissed. "I told you to stay with him!"

Nigan said, voice lowered, "He's not about to make much trouble, the shape you left him in, is he? —Keep your voices down, both of you. Dammit, he can hear you! —What makes you think he's anything but expendable, Nayati? Use your head. Cantrell will call our bluff. You've got to let him go—before he hears anything more!"

"Let him hear! You claim he's no good as a hostage? Fine! We'll kill him! Show her *we're* not bluffing."

"What good will that do? Get us all up for murder, it will. Get the Alliance Council—and our own—on our backs, and it won't help the Project one damn bit."

"He's right, Nayati," she said. "For all we know, they could be hearing us right now."

Nigan nodded. "Maybe we should all get out of here and . . ."

"Don't be an ass," Nayati interrupted. "If he's bugged, where are his reinforcements? He can tell us what's happening to Hono, and how much the Alliance knows. And we've *got* to know that. Hono used the *'Tap* to call—"

"—Gods, Hatawa," she hissed. "Shut *up!*"

"Let them hear! Don't you two see it yet? The spy's a 'Netman. *You're* the one who keeps insisting he knows what he's talking about. And he's *Cantrell's*, girl. We can *use* that to put pressure on her—on the whole damn 'NetAT." A scowling glance toward Stephen. "But first, by all the gods, he's going to talk. I might not have their fancy juices, but I can sure as hell make him sing like a bird."

"If you keep on, he won't be able to sing like anything." She was sick at her stomach. This blood-thirsty creature was not her cousin—was nothing *like* her cousin. "Just back off, Hatawa! And get the hell out of here. I'll get him inside—clean him up. See if I can cover your ass one more time."

Without waiting for his answer, she worked her way through the silent group clustered around Stephen. He hadn't moved since Nayati let him go . . . and didn't twitch when she bent over him.

"All right, Ridenour, enough's enough. On your feet."

His head raised slowly. Feral eyes, molten silver in the moonlight, gleamed at her out of the shadowed face.

She rocked back on her heels, startled, wondering for a moment if he was entirely sane. She'd been hoping to reason with him, convince him she was on his side and justify Nayati's actions to him. Now . . .

"Stephen . . . ?" Features half-seen in the shadows, shifted. Pain, anger, . . . fear . . . she felt those herself, had no sympathy to spare for his. "Well, *damn* you too, Ridenour," she said, not certain whether he even heard her. "You *could* have minded your own business."

A spark of white from the shadow that was his mouth: lip-lifted snarl. He heard her all right; and she let him hear all the bitter disappointment she felt.

"I was ready to trust you—work with you—now you pull this stunt. You had to take the bait, didn't you, Spacer-man?"

She laid a hand on Stephen's arm; but he jerked away, coming up hard against the barn with his good shoulder, wrenched himself to his feet with an effort she felt in her own knees.

Delicate silk pulled in shreds from the rough wood siding as he reeled back. Blood, black as the indigo shirt in the moonlight, seeped where large splinters pierced deep into muscle. Nayati jumped behind him—probably to stop Stephen's imminent escape, she thought sourly. But she didn't comment. It was probably just as well: that hold prevented Ridenour from collapsing again.

A second recoil when she reached to free him of the ruined coat. But Nayati held him ruthlessly steady while she unfastened the wide belt and eased the sleeves off over his hands. His arms fell free, his breath caught and he swayed heavily in Nayati's grip.

She dropped the jacket, grabbed his right arm and hitched it around her shoulders. Nayati stepped back to Nigan's side, the others gathering behind them.

*"Go on,"* she hissed. "Get the *hell* out of here! You've done damn well enough!" A choked breath from her side. A peculiar choke she'd heard before. "Shut *up*, fool! You pick the damnedest times to laugh!"

The choke ended in a hissed intake of breath as she yanked Ridenour unceremoniously inside. As they passed into the dimly lit interior, she whispered angrily in his ear, "You really blew it, Spacer-man. I hope you enjoy lying in the bed you just made."

The arm around her neck tensed as he strained his head up and she got her first good look at his face. If only Sakiimagan could see him now. Her elegant escort from dinner was gone. Swollen, bruised—blood trickled from nose and mouth, ran a steady stream from a small, deep cut above one eye, creating a sticky film he made no effort to blink clear.

But those dark-rimmed spook-eyes twisted her guts. Gods! Those eyes couldn't lie. Ridenour *couldn't* know what he'd gotten himself mixed up in.

*C'mon, Spacer-man say,* say—anything—*anything at all, give me any explanation, anything to go on. Tell me why and I'll intervene on your behalf. Gladly!* She *wanted* it to be simple curiosity, *wanted* him to be innocent of duplicity. *Wanted* him to be . . . but Stephen's head drooped again, without a word, only a ragged breath.

She dropped him onto one of the bales, grabbed his shoulder to steady him as he swayed. He looked up, not at her, but beyond her; and past another choking cough, whispered, "I don't think they heard you, Tyeewapi."

Someone behind her, his arrival all but masked in wind-sound, laid a second steadying hand on Stephen's shoulder. She whirled. Nigan. Behind him, Nayati and all the others. Nigan motioned with his chin for her to move away and she followed that order. Better him than Nayati.

"Hello, Nigan." Stephen: pleasantly conversational. "Better

watch her. She throws a mean roll. —But you know that already, don't you?''

She saw her own concern reflected in Nigan's eyes, but there was nothing either of them could do. Ridenour was crazy. Such tactics would gain him nothing with Nayati.

There was nothing she could do to stop either of them; not here, anyway.

She headed for the side door.

"Go to your father now, girl, and I promise you, Ridenour's a dead man. Behave yourself, and he has a chance. —If he cooperates, a good chance."

A stiff-backed, slow-motion about-face informed Nayati, and everyone else, what she thought of his tone and his tactics; and gave her ample time to compose her face. "You dare . . ."

Her voice cracked.

Nayati's cold smile widened. **His** eyes flicked to the others, seated now in a rough circle on the floor. Nayati's own Council, his own power. So there it was: open defiance of her father's authority. And if he dared that—

Ridenour was *her* responsibility. If anything happened to him—if Nayati killed him—*she'd* be held accountable. Which meant her *father* would be held accountable: *Alliance* law, not the People's law, and Cantrell administered Alliance law. Cantrell could arrest Sakiimagan, have him removed from office. *Then* who would control Nayati, who, if he continued as he was going, could ruin them all with that ship up there?

*Dammit, Ridenour, why couldn't you have kept your nose out of our business?* And aloud, "Then ask him only what you need to know, cousin, for your sake, as much as his." And seeing the obstinacy in Nayati's face, "Dammit, man, just find out about my brother, then leave the bit-brained CodeHead alone. He's here under false pretenses and Cantrell's orders. Right now, *she's* wrong, not us."

He sauntered toward her, slipped his hand around her waist and pulled her to him. "You admit, then, that I was right about the Spacer-scum?"

Nayati's voice was incongruously low, seductive; his hips pressed against her, moving slowly, insistently. She saw Stephen's eyes on them, his face expressionless until he caught her watching him. An infinitesimal lift of his lip, more eloquent than words.

Fools! Both of them certifiable card-carrying idiots! Nayati had no idea the stakes he was playing for, and Ridenour—who knew what Ridenour understood? With an effort, she kept her feet firmly on the ground, her knee out of Nayati's hyperactive groin and Nayati's knife out of Stephen Ridenour's skinny neck. *Someone* had to keep their head.

But keeping one's head was difficult when Nayati smiled his approval of her implied acquiescence: that chilling, other-Nayati smile, and when that other-Nayati pressed his lips painfully on hers: a deep, rude kiss that made her gag.

That other-Nayati murmured against her mouth, "Anything to please you, my lovely Annie. All right: no more than it takes." And laughed aloud as she jerked away. "No more than it takes to get the truth *and* Hono back! Am I right?"

Nayati's 'council' muttered emotionless, blood-chilling agreement. She shuddered, backed slowly toward the side exit, no longer angry. Terrified. Nayati was crazy. They were all—crazy.

*"Annie?"* She paused, breathing hard, and Nayati motioned toward Bego's stall with his chin.

She shook her head, slowly at first, then emphatically. "No way, Hatawa. I'm not sticking around for the privilege of watching you beat the shit out of a helpless man." She spun on her heel, had her hand on the latch:

*"Anevai!"*

Over her shoulder, she cried, "You *win*, Hatawa. I won't go to my father, but I'm *not* staying here either!"

"You leave, girl, and he's dead in thirty seconds."

A slow turn back. A glance at Stephen slumped on the hay bale: eyes closed now, filthy, bleeding, sullen. *Damn you, Ridenour. Why'd you have to go crazy on me, too?*

But as that thought crossed her mind, Stephen raised his head, blinked and looked around him: puzzled, as though he'd forgotten where he was. His pale eyes widened, he looked very young and very frightened as his eyes flicked from Nayati to her and back to Nayati moving purposely toward him, that knife of his out and ready.

He swayed; Nigan's hands on his shoulders held him upright. His bruised and swollen mouth tightened; spook-eyes, no longer young and frightened, but full of hatred and stubborn anger, narrowed as they looked straight at her.

She dropped her head and ducked through the bars into Bego's stall.

Paul leaned against the window frame, looking out across moonlit landscape: familiar and beloved sight now, and yet so different from the world he'd almost committed to all those years ago. . . .

*(". . . sure Ylaine and I will miss you, Paul. But it's just not working out here . . .")*

This meeting had been a mistake. How could he tell Loren to go away and not ask him for reasons? How could he tell her that his decision to come to HuteNamid had nothing to do with her Recon fetish?

Because the Recon issue *was* hers, much more hers than his. He'd never had her drive, and after the Council's orchestration of his own life, he had little hope for affecting anyone else's.

"I tried everywhere: 'Tank-hopped for three—I don't know, maybe it was even four years, I lost count. Everywhere the same: hatred and resentment so deeply entrenched, nothing would change it. And I was sick of it. But here, on the most biologically rich planet we've ever found— Dammit, I'm *tired*, Loro," he said to her reflection in the window, "tired of fighting. I just wanted a chance to *live* what I believed."

He turned and walked over to her chair, holding out his hands. A moment of hesitation, then she took them, warm and dry contrast to his own sweaty palms, and met his eyes steadily.

He said carefully, "It's been so damned long, Loro. I don't ask you to forgive my silence. I never meant to hurt you—I simply didn't know what I *could* say without betraying Sakiima's people and their desire for privacy, so I reckoned the kindest thing I could do was let you forget about me."

She watched him with unblinking eyes. She'd changed over the years. Once, he could predict every thought she had. Now, there was a remoteness he no longer trusted.

That was why it had been imperative for him to meet her. He was the only one who knew her well enough to know if the old Loro still existed. Only he knew her well enough to sway her to HuteNamid's point of view. Only he—

"That, Paul Corlaney, is the biggest pile of bullshit I've ever been handed."

He stared at her, silent and unbelieving, angry as he'd never been before with anyone; certainly never with Loro. He pulled away, but she kept her hold on his hands and used that leverage to stand up and meet him eye to eye.

"So the kindest thing you could do was let me forget about you, was it? —You're too damned conceited to think anyone could forget you, let alone someone you've had in your bed. Forgive your silence? —Hell, you were just too damned scared to finally admit to me where you were after you were too damned lazy to write in the first place. And you can't talk to me now because you don't know me anymore and it's not your secret to tell? —Lord! That one caps them all! You don't want to say anything, because you don't want the goddamn responsibility. If you didn't trust me, you sure as hell wouldn't have said the word *betray* within my hearing, let alone my Security Voice!" She tapped behind her ear: reminder of TJ's presence. "Don't try to fool me, Paul Corlaney, you're in this up to your eyeballs, and you're figuring to tell me, one way or the other, just so long as *you* don't have to take *personal* responsibility for the telling."

"Going to take me up to the ship next, admiral?"

"If necessary. —Paul, lie to me now, and I assure you, we're through—in every way. I've got a young man on my ship right now who deserves more support from down here than anyone seems ready to give him. Hononomii Tyeewapi may be paying with his sanity—possibly his life—for this planet's little secrets. Does the phrase *Dena Cocheta* mean anything to you? Who is Nayati Hatawa? Where is he? Why do these people want to break out of the Alliance? Is it all of them? Or only Tyeewapi's small faction?"

He ground his teeth.

"Dammit, Paul, you know they can't do that! This world's too rich—ultimately too well placed for future expansion—for the Council to leave it alone entirely. They haven't troubled themselves with it before now, but bring it to their attention this way and you can bet they'll notice. For God's sake, Paul, *help* me find an answer that'll give these people whatever it is they're after and still satisfy the Council, before it's too late. What's going on here? What's Smith into—and what do *you* have to do with it?"

He rested his shoulder against the balcony door and stared out across the moonlit mountains. "Not all of what you say is true. I'm not the Enemy, Loro. Absolutely, I'm not. I've talked with Sakiimagan—I'll talk with him again. But it's the People's show. I'm only along for the ride."

"What 'ride,' Paul?"

He swallowed—hard—and dropped his head, the anger gone, leaving a great nothingness in his gut. "Loro, I'm asking you to trust me on this: old karma, my dear, and damned unfair. I want to stay here, and to go up to that ship of yours would jeopardize my whole relationship with the *Dineh* . . . *Dena Cocheta* is nothing but a kid's code phrase—Nayati's crowd uses it—and Nayati's only a hot-headed, spoiled kid. The People just want to stay clear of Alliance Politics—same as me. You won't learn a damn thing more under Dep; there's nothing else I *can* tell you. If you can't believe that, tell me, dammit!" To his utter disgust, he found his voice shaking with the intensity of his emotions. He was behaving like the damned school-boy! And still he found himself pleading, "I can't take much more of this, Loro. Not from you. On again—off again. Hot—cold. Dammit, woman, I'm too old!"

The hand he'd reached out to her trembled. Clenching it into a fist, he spun away, barely controlling his urge to put that fist through the window. That thought cooled his temper more effectively than ice water in his face. He consciously relaxed his hand.

A rustle of silk behind him. Dark eyes reflected in the glass door.

On an embarrassingly unsteady breath: "Loro?"

Silently, she put her arms around him. With a shuddering breath, he turned and buried his face in her shoulder. And as her hand brushed his hair, her voice whispered in his ear:

"Come in and get him, TJ."

# V

Moonlight winked off the crystal button as Nayati slowly turned it between two fingers. The button had fallen inside Stephen's shirt—at least, that was where Nayati's knife had found it moments ago.

"ZRS. *S* for Stephen, *R* for Ridenour. —What's the *Z* for, Spacer-man?"

But Stephen was apparently no more inclined to answer that question than any of Nayati's others, and his silence elicited a similar response.

Anevai buried her head against the mare's warm neck and concentrated on those buttons which had so fascinated Wes at dinner. It was really too bad about that coat. It didn't deserve the treatment it had received—thanks to its owner's stupidity. The idiot could have had the decency, the basic sense, to put on something a little less—fluorescent—before going spying in full-moon light.

Not only a stupid spy, an ignorant one.

He didn't know what Nayati was talking about, for all Nayati's insistence to the contrary. Those eyes didn't lie, no matter what the mouth below them did.

But even that had ceased to respond. Not a sound out of him for ages. He was awake, his eyes were wide open, but there was no one home: vaporware for brains, just like the Wesser figured.

An angry snarl, the sound of flesh meeting flesh, and gurgling, choked laughter that dissolved into gut-wrenching coughs. *Dammit—*

"*Nayati, stop it!—*" She ducked past the mare and flung herself onto the fence. He turned, startled. She launched herself straight at him. He slipped and she used that momentum to pull him down and over, rolled to her feet and dived at him again, low and hard.

Not the first fight between them, though never so earnest, and she knew his weak spots; but she was too tired, her reflexes too slow. A sweep of Nayati's arm threw her staggering into the stacked bales. Loose hay slipped beneath her moccasins and she scrambled for balance, suddenly terrified that Nayati would trap her with his greater strength and weight. Suddenly terrified for her *own* life as much as Ridenour's.

"Nayati. Enough." Nigan's voice. Cool. Calm. The voice of Reason. A voice that so far had kept Stephen alive.

Terror ebbed as Nayati moved away. One step. Two, and three. She found her balance, swept her hands across bales of hay—

—until one hand encountered cold metal. A hay-hook (touch recognized it) left carelessly in the stack: someone would catch hell for that. But not from her. Not today. She leaned against the stack, striving to look more winded than she was, eased the hook free, then grasped its wooden handle.

A deep breath; a whirling attack—

—and instant realization that Nayati was ready, the battle already lost. He caught her hook-bearing wrist in one hand, her waist in the other, and twisted her backwards until she was sure something was going to break. But she refused to give in, refused to accept his assumption of power any longer.

For a moment, only her harsh breath and his broke the silence. Then:

Loud thump of flesh on flesh. The hook dropped from numb fingers. Nayati eased the pressure, and they both turned toward the source of that thud.

Nigan: standing over an unconscious puddle of Stephen Ridenour, rubbing his knuckles and wincing. Nigan, who shrugged and said, "Sorry. He was trying to escape."

He was cold. That fact registered above all others. Perhaps it was the familiarity of the sensation: he was always cold.

He remembered, with detached fondness, the thick robe Loro had given him one of his first nights aboard her big ship. The *Cetacean* was always colder than Vandereaux Academy, and Vandereaux had always been colder than—before. That robe was waiting for him right now, in his room, in the building with the waterfall. He wondered, in a distant sort of way, if he'd ever see that room again. It wasn't really all that bad. He wouldn't even mind the window being open—

—Not much, anyway.

Something hit him. His head snapped sideways and his body, being attached the way it was, followed. He fell *thud!* into something hard and prickly, his arms twisted awkwardly beneath him.

His arms hurt. But then, he hurt all over.

This hurt he understood. Someone hit you and you hurt. You fell down and played dead and eventually They left you alone. Fighting never helped. There were always more of Them than of you. It had taken a while, but he'd learned that truth.

It was the knives that were strange: he was frequently confused by such issues, but he didn't believe civilized people used knives. Especially not to cut up kilocred shirts. But he might be wrong.

He could well be wrong. After all, he'd known supposedly civilized people to do worse, albeit not with knives.

There were Voices. He thought maybe there'd been Voices for a long time, but he didn't remember for sure: he'd quit paying attention when the Voices kept asking questions he either couldn't answer or didn't understand. He'd learned that truth too: Basic Survival Postulate: Ignore Them and Eventually They Go Away.

Most of the Voices were gone. He was not sure when, but now there were only two left. Two and a sometime third.

*"Give it up, Nayati. He's gone. VOSsed for sure. Even if he knows anything, he can't tell us now."*

That's right, Nayati. Listen to him. Shouldn't waste your time on a VOSsie . . . Never waste time . . . Never enough time . . . But who's gone . . . and where did he go?

*"Get your hands off me, Nigan!"*

Nigan? But he's dead. Cooky's roll got him good.

*"Dammit, Nigan, Hono's as good as dead, and they're going to—"* The angry voice broke off with a sound very like a sob. Poor Nayati. What's wrong? Nigan? Are you there? Don't let Nayati cry . . .

*"But if you kill their boy here, Hono's gone for sure."*

The stifled sobs made him want to cry, too. But if he did, They would hit him again. They always did unless he played dead. But who did Nayati want to kill?

Their boy? Could They mean *him?* Did he belong to Someone now? But why did Nayati want him dead? He didn't want to be dead. Not now. Not if Someone wanted him.

He lay very still, curled on his side and wished not to be dead. Something squeezed his chest, hurt his throat. He coughed. He tried not to, dead things didn't cough, but he couldn't help it.

*"Nayati, please, let's go. He's coming around now. He'll manage all right on his own . . ."*

Something nudged him in the ribs, and when he played dead, kicked him hard enough to make him cry out, never mind he knew better. The angry Voice ordered him Wake up! but he ignored it, wishing it to go away.

But it didn't. A hand grabbed the Thing that was hurting his chest. He waited hopefully. Maybe They would take it away. But They didn't. They pulled on it like a handle and dragged him up.

Maybe the Thing *was* a handle—like the handles on the rodent cages in the labs. That's what They called him, so maybe They put a handle on him because he was too big for a cage. He didn't remember Them doing that, but he frequently forgot things.

He bit his lip and didn't say anything. Kept his eyes shut real tight. But his back was against something solid and scratchy and when They let him go, things poked holes in his back so he wouldn't fall over.

He didn't even fall over when They hit him and made his nose leak again. He thought of the holes getting poked in his back and wondered if he'd leak all over when they pulled him off.

*"Look at me, spacer! I know you're awake! I have a message for your Adm. Cantrell!"*

Angry Voice confused him. He wasn't Spacer—was he? Wasn't that why They were hitting him?

Adm. Cantrell: that was Loro. She gave him the robe. Angry Voice had a message for her. This was Important. Stephen forced his eyes open, tried to focus on the dark, angry face in front of him. But he couldn't. It was too close and his eyes kept crossing.

*"Listen to me, spacer-man."* And even more angrily, the grip on the handle shaking him till his teeth rattled in his head: *"Listen to me! You tell her this is Payment in Kind for Hononomii. You ought to be able to remember that, Academy-scut. Repeat after me: Payment in Kind."*

He laughed at that—a rather poor laugh, but an honest one. This Nayati didn't know what Payment in Kind was—

The Hand struck again. *"Repeat the message, dammit!"*

—but he sure wasn't going to tell *him* that.

*"Nayati, for the gods' sakes, stop it!"*

A new Voice. Not Nayati. Not Nigan. Memory supplied a picture behind tightly closed eyelids: warm, dark skin, black braid and laughing brown eyes . . . and blue fur. But this Voice wasn't laughing. This Voice was distressed. It needn't be. He was all right.

To show her, he made the effort and got the words out, no matter they weren't true. He'd lied before, so God already hated him.

*"That's right,"* Nayati said, *"and there's more where this came from, Spacer-man. We're through playing games with the Alliance. We don't need them and we don't want them. You got that?"*

He couldn't find the breath to answer, but he nodded.
*"Good."*
Then: *"Cut him loose and let's get out of here. —C'mon, Annie."*
*"No!"*
A sound of scuffling. Hands fumbling at his bonds. His arms fell free and he cried out as swollen hands struck the hard ground. He couldn't help it.
But this time, there was no answering blow. Only the sound of a door closing.

"Dammit, Hatawa, let—me—go!"
Anevai set her feet and jerked, throwing her whole body into it this time—
—and found herself on the ground on her backside as Nayati released her. She scrambled to her feet and tackled him, fists flying. He fell back and she got in several good blows before Nigan stepped in and hauled her off.
"It's over and done, Anevai," Nigan said in her ear as Nayati levered himself back onto his feet. "Let it rest. Let's all get out of here—leave Ridenour to Cantrell's people. We're in enough trouble as is."
Nigan, who had talked sense all along. Nigan, who had seen the opportunity to end the senseless torture and taken it . . .
It was sense he spoke now. She knew that and still wanted to smear Nayati's face into the ground. She said through her teeth, "Has nothing to do with Ridenour. Has to do with smart-ass fools treating me like a piece of meat. —That's the first and last time, Hatawa."
Nayati's mouth was bleeding. He dabbed at it with the back of his hand, examined the moonlit dampness, then said to her, "When you start acting like a Human Being again instead of a spacer-traitor, we'll talk. Until then, keep your mouth shut. You're a part of this—as much as Nigan is—as much as I am."
She snorted and turned back toward the barn.
"Where the *hell* do you think you're going?" Nayati yelled.
"Where do you think? We *can't* leave him there. That's a surefire way to bring Cantrell down on us all. You go ahead and hide. I'm going to go find out if there's anything left to salvage."
"Annie!"
She whirled. *"Don't call me that!"*

He walked toward her, she backed away, never mind Nigan's hand on Nayati's arm. Nayati stopped. Looked at her, looked at Nigan.

"You've both gone soft in the head over this spy." And to her alone: "I could have given you the universe, love. But you've opted for the wrong side." He shoved his hands in his pockets and turned to go, paused and pulled out his right hand and opened it, revealing a spark in the lowering moonlight.

"Here, Annie-girl." He tossed the spark in the air, caught it and cast it into the ground at her feet. "A souvenir of tonight."

He turned and left, Nigan following at his heels. She wondered why Nigan had stayed, why he was staying with Nayati even now. Perhaps because he, too, saw his friend evaporating in front of his eyes and it was the only way he could see to save him.

At her feet, the spark caught her eye. She leaned over and picked it up.

*ZRS* winked at her in the moonlight.

# vi

Stephen waited until he was certain they were gone, then began bringing his mind back into focus, step by step, the way he'd learned years ago, simultaneously taking assessment of the bodily damage.

Not too bad. He hurt, naturally, but not enough to bother the meds with. It was difficult to see. Possibly that was because one eye was swollen nearly shut, and something wet had run into the other. He was sitting on the floor with his back to the stacked hay. If he were to get on his feet, he could get over to the com and call for help—just to get him back to his room; he could handle it from there.

That seemed reasonable.

If he could get to his feet.

Reaching up with his right hand, he dug his fingers into the hay for leverage. He closed his eyes, breathing deeply, thinking of the gym, Coach Devon's bark, and one more pull-up—

—and cried aloud as the effort seemed to rip him apart. He didn't open his eyes; the view from inside the lids was alarming enough. He grasped blindly for handholds to keep him on his feet, terrified of losing his balance: he couldn't possibly repeat that move. Not knowing the consequences.

Worse than he'd thought. Somehow, somewhen, Nayati must have gotten his ribs. That was interesting: he'd never had a broken rib.

*Drip . . . drip . . . drip . . .* during a lull in the wind.

Water. He licked dry, cracked lips and squinted through the dark interior, searching for the source, wondering in a vague, detached way how it could be safe to drink, in such a dirt-ridden place, then decided it wouldn't make much difference.

*Drip . . . drip . . . drip . . .* but there was no wind now. That buzz was in his head.

A push away from the hay in the direction of the sound. Several staggering steps had him up against the wall with force enough to dislodge the tools stacked and hanging there. He grabbed their hangers for a handhold.

*Drip . . . drip . . . drip . . .*

He leaned against the wall, searching for the source of the drip—

—and started drifting to the floor. First the knees gave, then his grip on the hangers. He dragged the wall, delaying that downward slip, desperate to stay upright and awake.

His knees hit the ground, then his hands. The ground was wet here. That was interesting. He lifted cool mud to his face, contemplating falling down flat and letting that cool damp invade the rest of him.

But he might drown. Possibly that was not such a good idea.

He listened again, heard the plop of water and sent that muddy hand toward the source: a bucket, by the feel. And nearly full. He clasped the edge with both hands and slid it across the mud, never minding the slosh. Leaning against the wall for balance, he buried both hands as far as they would go, brought handfuls to his face, only vaguely aware of things floating in the water.

He licked the water from his lips, afraid to lean over, afraid to bury his head in the coolth, no matter what instincts screamed.

"Stephen?"

He froze. Had he really heard that whisper from outside?

"Stephen!"

Another double handful of water in his face and through his hair: desperate attempt for coherency as the side door banged open.

Moonlight streamed in silhouetting the slim figure. Fringe fluttered in the wind. His uncertain grip on the bucket gave way. The bucket tipped. Water soaked the ground around his knees.

*"Stephen? Was that you?"* The whisper barely pierced the roaring in his ears. Anevai: somehow, he wasn't surprised.

He grasped the wooden post at his side and pulled himself up, heedless of splinters and hardly aware of his ribs this time. Perhaps they weren't as bad as he'd thought.

Hay rustled. He blinked cold water from his eyes, tightened his hold on the post, as Anevai passed his shadowy haven to the hay bale where she'd left him. She knelt, picked something up. She swore softly, threw it down, and wiped her hand on her jeans, all the while scanning the shadows.

*"Stephen, are you here? Dammit, Spacer-man, answer me!"*

"Welcome back." The grittiness in his own voice startled him.

She whirled.

He said, "I wondered when you . . . would . . ." A gut-wrenching cough doubled him over. Anevai took a step toward him, and he raised his hand to stop her. "Stay right there." His throat felt as though it was coated in the prickling dust floating all around them. He coughed, gasped after breath.

"For the gods' sake, Stephen, let me . . ."

"*—Said . . . stay there!* Don't need . . . help. Don't want—"

He coughed again, tasted copper, and the shaking hand he put to his mouth felt moisture.

Another step. She was close enough now he could see her face. "Stephen, please, let me . . ." But he didn't want to see, didn't want her pity . . . didn't even want the friendship she'd ostensibly offered, before she'd played Their game.

"All I want . . ." He forced the words past a swollen, constricted throat. ". . . is . . . explanation. Sit down." He gestured toward the bale he had occupied earlier with a mocking sweep of his arm he immediately regretted, a pain he refused to acknowledge. "Make yourself—comfortable. . . ."

Her eyes narrowed and she didn't move. "Which version, Spacer-man?"

*"Dammit! I want the truth!"*

The barn canted. He staggered, caught himself against a support beam, felt a blow to his shin as Anevai cried, "Ridenour, look out!"

Reflexive twist around the post scraped his hands raw, but kept him on his feet and put the beam between him and—

—no one.

He glared at her.

She nodded toward the straw at his feet. He followed her gaze to an odd hook lying half-submerged in the hay and straw.

"I'm all right, damn you!" Her hand dropped, and on that same surge of adrenaline, he said: "Just a few simple answers, and I'll leave. No incriminations, nothing. I won't even mention your participation in what happened here tonight."

Her chin rose. "Why? Why won't you tell them?"

He shrugged. "Call it payment. Payment for favors owed." Good an explanation as any.

"For what? Getting you away from them? Nigan did it."

"Fine. I'll cover both of you." He didn't give a damn either way. "But—But after this, we're quits—even. I don't owe you. You don't owe me."

Her lips tightened, then she nodded, once, emphatically.

"Why did you come back?"

"I thought you had that all figured."

*"Why?"* His voice broke on that, but he didn't care.

*"Because I was worried, you idiot Spacer-scuz!"*

"Why should you care?"

Her scowl deepened.

He said dryly, "Never mind . . . If you want to check and make sure I get back alive so your lover won't be accused of murder, I'm sure I should thank you."

"Damn you, Ridenour, that's not . . .''

His breath caught again. This time he knew why, fool that he was. "Not fair? I suppose it isn't. After all, you did try *so* hard to stop him, didn't you?"

"If I'd argued with him you'd be dead now! Besides, why should he leave you in any better shape than Cantrell left Hononomii?"

That Name again. He waited. Hoped. When no explanation seemed forthcoming, he asked heavily, "Who *is* Hononomii?"

Her eyes were deep, unreadable shadows in the moon's silver spotlight. "You mean to tell me you don't *know* who your precious admiral turned into mental jelly up on that ship of hers?"

*"Dammit, woman, who is he?"* His voice broke and he didn't care. The need for reason outweighed everything else as the barn

began to dance around him again. If he was going to die on this planet, he was going to know why. "What the *hell* are you talking about?"

"He's *my brother*, Spacer-man, and Nayati's best friend. And your darling Cantrell took him up to that ship of hers and ran some kind of experiments on him and fried his brain. Is that what you want to hear, Dr. Ridenour? Shit, I bet you don't even deserve that title."

He winced. That struck too close to the truth. "Anevai, please, I—"

"Well, congratulations, Spacer, you finally managed to say my name right. Does that mean you're dropping the act? With Wesley, too? You had him so excited . . . I'll give you this, Spacer-man, you're good. You fooled us all today—even Wes. This is going to kill him."

The room dipped around him, faded in and out of focus along with her words. He didn't want to hurt anyone; particularly not Wesley Smith. Whatever Wesley might be involved in, he'd been nothing but kind to a ridiculously out-of-place Del d'Bugger.

All he wanted now was to get out of here and back to the sensible world of *Cetacean*, where people didn't try to cut your throat in revenge for people you'd never heard of. Up there people hated you or they used you, but they didn't turn around afterward and look at you with concerned brown eyes.

And if going back up there meant that they arrested him and wiped his brain clean . . . maybe they'd take the rest along with it and he wouldn't have to remember the warm brown eyes either.

"Out of here, Tyeewapi," he muttered, "Q&A's over. Now *get out!*"

"And leave you to make it back on your own? Fat chance, Spacer."

"*I said, get out!* I don't *need* your help. I don't *want* your help. I've made it on my own just fine for years, I damn sure don't need you now." His voice broke, breath increasingly hard come by. If she delayed much longer, he *wouldn't* be able to make it. "I told you: no incriminations. As far as I'm concerned, *you* were never here, and even Dep can't make me say it was your fists that did this. You want Nigan cleared—all right, you get one free. As for the others, as far as I'm concerned, you, Nayati, and your whole fucking planet can go to hell. Now, *get out!*"

Never taking her eyes from him, she backed toward the door. At the door, she whispered, "You may not believe this, Ridenour, but I'm sorry this happened. I'm truly sorry."

She turned and fled into the darkness.

For the next several minutes, he stared after her. Not that he expected her to return. He simply had no alternative goal. He'd run out of adrenaline and out of the ability to care.

God. He'd been such a fool.

Why *had* Anevai come back? He rubbed a hand across hazed eyes, but it didn't help. Didn't clear his vision. Didn't clear his head or clarify confused memories.

She'd said Nigan had stepped in; maybe there'd been nothing she *could* do.

Perhaps she *had* come back to see if he was all right. It didn't really matter. At least this way, she would warn Wes and Wes would be gone, *wouldn't* be arrested. Wouldn't have his brain picked until it was cold and empty. . . .

And *he* wouldn't have to face Wesley with what he really was, and what he'd done, telling Cantrell.

Anevai; Nayati: they were Cantrell's problem. Wesley was his: Wesley and the 'NetAT. Whatever Wes had done, he shouldn't be forced back to Vandereaux system. *He* was already owned by Council—by Alliance: Wesley wasn't. Why waste a perfectly good life? *His* should be enough, dammit! He could work with the 'NetAT. Have everything he'd ever wanted. Have more than he'd ever *dared* dream of—

—before this place.

His supporting arm quivered. If he could just get back to the complex, get a hot shower, a little sleep; he could face the admiral with some composure.

A filthy hand wiped across hazy eyes came away wet: blood. Better if he could eliminate some of that, too. There was always the KwikHeal in the emergency kit he'd been required to pack: re-gu-la-shun, as Briggs had said. That was in his room, and the stuff *did* work; in an emergency, it was even marginally better than bleeding to death. He shuddered, wondering if he could possibly apply it to himself, and clamped his jaw on chattering teeth. To keep extraneous issues out of the equation—for Wesley's freedom? Damn right, he could.

But first, he had to get back to the complex. On his own. Somehow.

He looked toward the stairway to the terminal, the world spinning more ominously with every move of his head. Blood pressure. Internal bleeding. He knew the symptoms. Intimately.

He moved his foot. Something hit his shin. He stopped. Looked down.

A wooden handle rested against his leg. A wooden handle attached to a very sharp metal hook. A metal hook that was wedged beneath his toe.

He thought, *I really shouldn't leave that there. Someone could get hurt.*

Some unknown time later, he was still staring at his foot, the buzz in his ears growing louder, more persistent. He might be concussed. Maybe he'd hit his head on something. It certainly hurt enough.

Why had that fellow Nayati wanted to hurt him? Who was Nayati? Who was Hono'omi? But that hook shouldn't be left down there. He was quite certain of that.

He bent over and grasped the handle, then tried to straighten up, but the point was still stuck beneath the soft sole of his shoe.

Perplexed, he considered the dynamics of the system involved. He was calculating the relative merits of lifting his toe, (with its associated risk of losing his balance and falling on his ass) and letting go to stand up, step back and bend over again, (with its risk of altitudinal pressure changes—and falling on his ass) when a sudden wave of dizziness swept over him—

—and he fell on his ass.

He lay absolutely still for a moment; waiting. Waiting for his sight to clear, waiting for the pain to abate. *Waiting for a damn miracle! Well admit it, Stephen Ridenour, it's not going to happen, so move your butt!*

His legs were twisted uselessly under him. He'd never get up till he straightened them out. A roll onto his side to free his legs, to maneuver his right arm where it could lever him up—

—A new stab of pain: sharp, distinct. Not the ribs this time, but close.

A sudden attack of rationality: the hook. He tried desperately to heave himself clear of it, but abused muscles refused to be pushed again and he collapsed heavily.

He felt the hook's bite, felt it slip deep into flesh, felt the warm blood flow, each as a separate, well-defined sensation, and wondered distantly why it didn't hurt more.

And thought, *What an absurd way to die.* . . .

# vii

*The moon is rising, its silver magic flooding the landscape. He is standing on the cliff's edge, the valley a black lake beneath him. The edges of the world draw closer. He has seen this before. Knows its power.*

*He is alone. Utterly, totally alone. He is not afraid. He has always been alone.*

*He lifts his face to Snegurochka's light. A warm breeze, like a million tiny fingers, caresses his body. He holds his hands up to welcome her.*

*For one glorious instant, he feels her love surround him. For one glorious instant, he is one with Winema and all the universe. For one glorious instant, he is Alive.*

*In the next instant, the caressing breeze transforms into invisible sleet cutting trails through his skin and freezing into blood-red icicles.*

"Nayati reported to me over an hour ago, *nituna.*" From across his office desk, Sakiimagan's stony gaze turned on her. For the first time, she understood why it made everyone squirm. "And his version differs from yours—substantially."

But she refused to squirm. She'd tracked him here to his office for this pre-dawn inquisition and refused to give in to his tactics, taking mental notes, instead.

"And you accept Nayati's word above mine?"

"Why weren't you here? Did you think I would allow such actions to continue? The purpose was to expose a spy. To embarrass the admiral and the Alliance, to put them in the wrong—*not* to give her ample cause to arrest yet another of our people."

"I told you: *Nayati* wouldn't let me leave. If he's caused problems beating the hell out of Stephen, how do you think the admiral would feel about murder?"

"And *you* took such a threat seriously? What sort of fool have I raised?"

"I'm no fool, and I *know* Nayati. This wasn't Nayati, I tell you. Whoever he is, he came very close to killing Stephen Ridenour ostensibly to force him to tell what's happening to Hononomii. Don't you see? Stephen didn't *know* anything, didn't even know who Hononomii *was*."

"And when did he say that?"

"When I talked to him after. I believe him—and so would you, had you been there."

"You asked this Ridenour about your brother? After I expressly forbade it?"

"No, I didn't! *Nayati* asked him. Stephen asked me. Possibly he was curious to know why he was being cut into pieces!" Sarcasm crept in. She did her best to curb it. "Please, Dad, can't we sort this out later? Right now, Stephen needs help—badly. He was mad as hell when I left, but I'm not at all sure he's strong enough to—"

"If you don't mind, girl, stick to what you are sure of. Did you ask Nayati about the conversation he had with your brother?"

"Don't you understand? There wasn't *time*. By the time I got there, Nayati had them all riled up talking about fried brains and experiments, and then Stephen—"

"And afterward? Did you ask your cousin about your brother at that time? Surely there was ample opportunity then—for a concerned sister."

"No. I didn't. Frankly, I was a bit more immediately concerned about Ste—"

"I think, possibly, that it would be very good for you to stop mentioning that young man." Her father's voice had never sounded so remote. She wondered if Stephen's safety could possibly be worth the wedge it was driving between her and her father.

"*Why* do you—" His expression challenged her. She looked down at hands clenched into fists on her lap. "All right—*Yes*. I *like* him, but I'm not stupid. Stephen's a spy: he's *supposed* to be attractive. Wouldn't be much use if he couldn't make people like him, would he? But that's not why I feel we should get the EMTs down to the barn. If he—"

"Forget about the barn. The matter has been taken care of."

A foreboding twisted her gut. "What do you mean?"

"As I said. *You* created a situation, and I have taken the necessary steps."

If Paul had the clear conscience he claimed, he was sound asleep on the couch outside her door by now, despite TJ's watchful gaze.

Somehow, Cantrell doubted it. She pounded the lump from her pillow and punched it up under her ear, cursing softly.

*"Guess I don't have to wake you up, do I?"*

"What do you want?" she growled back at the voice in her ear.

*"Ridenour's missing."*

"I thought I told Lexi to see him to his room."

*"According to the HouseOps, he's still there. By physical check, he's not."*

"Get in here."

*"Paul?"*

"Bring him with you."

She was pulling her robe on when TJ slipped through the door with Paul in tow.

"For God's sake, man," Paul was protesting, "the kid probably went off with one of the girls. Give him a break."

She glared at him, and he held up his hands, mocking defeat. "Hey, excuse me. Seemed logical."

She allowed the chill she felt to creep into her voice. "Keep your mouth closed, Corlaney. You don't know Stephen Ridenour at all. —TJ?"

"This—" TJ pulled a keycard out of his pocket. "—was on the desk. The terminal was on." He handed her a sheet of paper. "This was left on the screen."

A print screen of a half-finished message to . . . "Smith?"

"Sleep of the innocent."

She stared at the implied defection. "I wish I could count on that."

"Question is, did he go of his own accord?" TJ tapped the sheet, glanced significantly at Paul. "This would indicate not, don't you think?"

Paul looked from TJ to her, brow puckered. Apparently convinced this was no joke. Reached out a hand. "May I see it, Teej?"

She nodded, forestalled TJ's question with a signal as she saw defeat replace the sarcasm in Paul's face.

Paper crackled. Paul smoothed the sheet out, licked his lips, and said tonelessly, "Check Anevai Tyeewapi."

"She's the one who put us on to this." Paul looked up at them sharply and TJ elaborated. "Surveillance spotted her going into her father's office, contacted me and I told them to monitor."

"I thought I told you not to—" She began, but TJ interrupted her.

"Not this time, Loren. —CentralSec discretion."

Central Security override of her orders. He had the right —though he'd rarely used it.

"So what did you find out?"

"Nothing. We couldn't *hear* a damn thing. And we don't know why."

She didn't need to think, required no time to consider. "Arrest them. *Quietly.*"

"Already gave the order, admiral."


"Stephen's not what bothers me, dad," Anevai said frankly, having no time left to mince words. "*He* was doing his job. It's Nayati. He's getting totally irrational—"

"Nayati says Ridenour knows far more than he's telling."

Knows: that sounded like Sakiimagan did not assume Stephen was dead.

"*Nayati says*—and Nayati would know, wouldn't he? Dad, *listen* to me! Nayati's cracking. There are times I don't think it's Nayati at all. For that matter, what happened to Hono? I'd like to have been there when he attacked that security man. That's not like *him*. He could have redirected the questions. Why fly off the handle? Could he be—cracking—the way Naya—?"

"That's enough, girl! Now you malign your brother the way you have your cousin! Your presence here will simply bring further complications. I've ordered all those who took part into the villages—"

"You haven't heard a word I've said, have you?"

He frowned. "I want you to go now. *Cetacean* Security could arrive here at any moment, though the screen *is* functional, for all you failed to ask."

"I'm not going."

"I don't recall the matter was open for discussion, young woman."

"I won't go." She stood up. "If Stephen lives up to his word, —and I'm *going* to give him that chance—he's not going to say anything, and I'd simply be implicating myself."

"And if Ridenour is incapable of making a statement?"

"I honestly hope that's not the case. When I left him, his *life* wasn't an issue. I came here hoping you would see the sense in helping him, not in saving him. If—circumstances—have made it otherwise, my presence here or in the villages will make no difference."

She started to leave, turned on a thought. "What did you do, dad? Tell Nayati to complete what he'd started?"

"Is that what you think?"

"I don't know what to think anymore. You sent me there, believing Stephen was a spy. How did you know he wouldn't be followed? How did you know I wouldn't be immediately arrested? Did you even care?"

"Of course I cared. The idea was to put Cantrell in a Position."

"And now that that 'position' has been reversed? What's Nayati? The Scapegoat? Are you using his fanaticism to focus Cantrell's attention on him?"

"Don't be ridiculous. Nayati's foolish and headstrong, but understandable. I might yet bring the admiral to that understanding . . . provided *you* don't attempt to convince her otherwise. Can't you see that we can't afford to be generous to this Alliance spy? An insignificant spy *you* allowed to hear things that now *make* him significant?"

"*I* allowed . . . ?" She caught herself: no sense explaining one more time, if her father was determined to see things that way. "Sir, as my father, I love you and as the selected leader of the People, I respect you, but I don't understand you anymore. I don't understand why you're not listening to someone who knows things you haven't been in a position to see. Stephen isn't a bad man. I honestly believe Cantrell isn't a bad woman—although *I've* not been in a position to make such an evaluation of her. I do believe it's high time you started listening to someone other than Nayati Hatawa. *Nayati* threatened me when I sought your judgment on his actions. Nayati adjusted 'Net records you expressly forbid him to touch—'' Sakiimagan leaned forward, but she refused to let him ask that question. ''You might be willing to excuse him for that—I'm not. I *know* the dangers of what he's done, better than you—better than Wesley. You get angry at me, at Stephen, even at the admiral, but never Nayati. Ask yourself why. Ask yourself why Nayati did these things, then ask yourself why Nayati is so certain Hononomii will *Be all right*. and then refuses to justify that claim. I *think* I know the answers—''

''Why? What *did* Nayati say to you?''

''*You* ask him, Father. I'm through playing middleman for you. Perhaps if you see Nayati—perhaps if you talk to Nayati—you'll see what I see.'' She twisted the doorknob. ''By the way, I didn't ask if the screen was working because I didn't have to. I checked before I came.''

Without looking back, she walked out of the room—

—and into the arms of *Cetacean* Security.

*He is dying, and no one knows, no one cares.*
*He is alone, but that is as it should be.*
*Softness surrounds him. The soft touch of death.*
*He is no longer alone— The white wolf has come for him . . .*

The first hint of dawn touched the rugged terraces. Behind her, the admiral was speaking softly into her private communicator. Guards protected the doorway. And Dr. Paul (What was he doing here?) was half-sitting on the desk.

They'd taken her father to another room of the Science Complex. No formal charges; just a simple, *Adm. Cantrell would like to ask you both a few questions.*

Stephen must have talked. In a way, that was a relief: it meant he was still alive. But he'd promised . . . Anevai supposed she shouldn't be upset; she was, after all, guilty. Of exactly what, she was too hazy on Alliance law to know, but she was sure she'd find out.

The admiral leaned back in her chair, crossed her ankles and laced her fingers across her flat stomach.

''You left us rather early last night, Ms. Tyeewapi.''

*Well, this is it*, she thought.

''Where did you go?''

*Ask your damned watchdog, admiral, ma'am.*

"Come, girl, don't waste everyone's time."

"I don't think I have to answer that." Keep it cool. Collected. Confident.

"Oh, you're wrong there, young woman." She was out of her league: Cantrell's tone was an ice storm to her snow flurry.

*She knows anyway.*

"I went to see my father—in his office—*then* I went home."

"Where were you at 0220 this morning?"

*You mean to say, you don't know, admiral? —But let's see you prove it.*

"In bed, ma'am."

"And if I say you were seen leaving this building?"

"I'd say, that's quite impossible, and ask to see your proof. If I've taken up sleepwalking, I'd like to know it."

No mention of Stephen. Where was he? *What* had he told them?

She tried not to fidget as Cantrell, silent and strangely ominous in her lack of expression, studied her from head to foot and back again.

"What do you think of your new researcher?"

New researcher? Was she still pretending Stephen was legit? "In . . . what sense do you ask, ma'am?"

"Do you think he'll get along with the people here?"

"I—I don't see why not." She laced her fingers together, clenched them tightly. "Why do you ask?"

"Just answer my questions, girl—and you might keep in mind, that with our sensor equipment, you may as well answer. Save us all time and effort. You seemed quite taken with him—and he with you. Were you, perhaps, with *him* last night?"

*What's going on here, admiral? You've seen the bruises. —Haven't you?*

She glanced over at Paul, hoping for a sign, but his face was as noncommittal as Cantrell's.

"Pay attention to *me*, girl. How do *you* feel about Stephen Ridenour? You, personally. Do you care what happens to him? Do you care whether he stays or not?"

"Dr. Paul?" She looked desperately toward him, a look he avoided. *Et tu, Dr. Paul?*

"How would you feel if he showed up dead?"

She couldn't claim total surprise, not after the interview with her father, but the straight-forwardness of the question startled her. "But he's not . . . couldn't be . . ."

Perhaps it was lack of sleep, perhaps the missed breakfast, but Adm. Cantrell and Dr. Paul seemed to be drifting away: her vision growing oddly dark around the edges. She glanced toward one, then the other; the changing depth of field made her horribly dizzy.

Someone stepped behind her, grasped her arms to steady her. Dr. Paul's voice in her ear urged her to sit down. She thought she even heard him say *If you know anything, Annie-love, now's the time.* But perhaps that was only the buzz in her ears.

How strange. Was this what 'faint' felt like? God! She sounded like Stephen. Poor Stephen. Poor, crazy, mixed-up Stephen who'd never petted a cat. Could he really deserve to be dead? She bit her lip; discovered the pain helped clear her head.

She brushed Paul's hands away. "No, Dr. Paul. I'm all right. —Please, ma'am. He's *not* dead, is he?"

"I don't know."

"What do you mean, you don't know? Where is he?" Finding no answer in Cantrell, Anevai turned to Paul, who shook his head infinitesimally.

Frantically back to Cantrell: *"Where is he?"*

Cantrell was holding something in her hand. Something that sparkled as she rolled it between her fingers. Something security must have found in the pocket of the coat they'd taken from her.

Cantrell tossed the button on the desk top.

"You tell me."

# viii

*He hears the voices from deep in the valley below; or is it high in the mountains above? He does not know; but with them lies salvation. With them lies hope.*

*He tries to scream, but he cannot. He has opened his mouth to Snegurochka. His throat, his lungs—his heart are hers.*

*And they are ice.*

"Dammit, get that thing over here!"

"I'll kill them for this!"

"You'll have to get in line, Corlaney. —What the hell took you meds so long?"

"Sorry, admiral. Only got the call—"

"Never mind. Just move it."

"What the *hell* is that?"

"Where? Dammitall, Corlaney, don't touch . . . *Shit! Get something to stop that!*"

"God! I didn't think he had that much left in him."

"I *knew* I shouldn't have let you come. —Get him temped, then to the 'port! Damned if I'll trust him to any downworld surgeon. —Briggs, have Lexi meet us there with that girl."

"*No!*"

"Shut up, Corlaney. —Briggs, Anevai Tyeewapi's under arrest until you hear differently from me, *personally*. I'm calling a full investigation team down. We're going to find out who did this and why."

*The voices fade.*

*From beyond the mountain, Etu rises, golden and glorious. The flames of the alien god leap out, consuming Snegurochka. The white wolf fades.*

*He is blinded by the searing beauty of Etu.*

*The flames lick at him, melting the ice that is his flesh, and he cries out in agony—and ecstasy.*

The boy's scream ripped through the barn and Paul Corlaney's nerves. He knelt beside Ridenour, holding clamps and bottles as per Cantrell's instructions, (*Here, Corlaney. Keep your hands out of trouble.*) while the MedTechs connected Stephen to the portable Life Support Unit.

Several transfusors, thrumming in unison, pumped fluids into the boy, replacing the blood which soaked the straw around him, filling the collapsed lung. A broken rib had gotten the lung. Paul had no idea what that *thing* had gotten when he moved it. (*Damn fool! Never trust first aid to a biologist!*)

But Ridenour's color had already *up*graded to deathly pale, and within moments, he'd be sealed in the LSU capsule for transport to the shuttle, Loren having made it perfectly clear he wouldn't be entrusted to Tunica's facilities. Paul considered that a mistake, knowing the locals, but when had she ever listened to him?

Ridenour was quiet again, that single scream his only sound since they'd found him lying face down in the straw. They had him stripped, ready for the LSU, bio-seal sheen on the ragged hole in his side. The blood-covered hook, as well as what was left of Ridenour's clothing, lay in transparent bags by the door awaiting Security's testing.

Messy business. Stupid wasted effort.

Loren, rapid-firing instructions to the chief surgeon aboard the *Cetacean*, gave one final order, turned the com over to the senior MedTech and hurried across the barn to go down on one knee on Ridenour's other side and asked quietly, "What brought that on?"

He shook his head and looked down at the boy's battered face. "I don't know. No one touched him. He seems okay now."

The thermal blankets and heated base of the LSU worked together, slowly bringing Ridenour's temperature up. The EMTs moved away; one to confirm the critical SedaMist jelling solution with Dr. McKenna before sealing the LSU, the others to ready the hover cart.

"Who 'them,' Paul?" Loren's voice was low, private . . . and furious.

"What?"

She said through her teeth, "You said, I'll kill *them*. Who's *them?*"

"Lord, woman, it was an expression! *I* don't know who did this!" He kept his voice at the same low level she'd used, honestly confused. No way was this Nayati's work—or anyone else he knew. Far too messy.

"But you have your suspicions, don't you, old *friend*. What was *your* job? Keeping the boss occupied? Making sure no one got here until too late?"

"Dammit, *no!*"

She dropped her head. Looked up several heartbeats later, deep shadows around her eyes making her expression impossible to read. "Paul, I don't know what part you played in this; maybe you didn't expect it to go this far, but if you know who . . ."

"I don't. But I swear to you, I *will* find out. If you can keep your investigators to a dull roar for a day or two—"

"You're not serious!"

"Loro, these are my friends. I can get to people and places none of your people can. Just give me a little time. Go ahead with the search of the barn and surrounding area, but don't pressure the Tyeewapis yet—for God's *sake*, don't!"

She scowled at him. Ridenour muttered something and tried

feebly to move, but he was fastened to the litter, and the tubes now assisting his breathing made speech impossible. Loren reached under the thermals for the boy's hand.

"God, he's still freezing!" she muttered, then called softly, "Stephen? Can you hear me, son?"

The stirring stopped and the blanket wrinkled as Ridenour tried to close his fingers around hers. Loren smoothed the blanket gently out of the way and laced their fingers.

An action which sent a chill through *him*. Admiral Loren Cantrell had too damn much power to afford maternal instincts.

Without looking up, she said, "The girl goes up with me."

"No! Blast it, Cantrell, you're thinking with your glands!"

"Don't challenge me, Paul. You haven't the authority, nor anything else it takes. Don't presume on our *acquaintance*. I'll leave you here—even grant you time, but I won't leave the prime suspect in your hands. She's going up with me. If her story checks out, she'll be back in a day or so."

"And if the same thing happens to her as happened to Hono-nomii?"

The meds returned. Loren relinquished Ridenour's hand and brushed his hair back before she rose and pulled Paul away with her.

"What the hell do you know about Hononomii Tyeewapi's condition—and how?"

"I told you: people here tell me things. Face it. You don't know what happened to Hono." Bait: he was grasping at damned frail straws. "You don't know *why* it happened. But she *is* his sister. If the reason is medical . . . there's a chance you could destroy her as well."

"You're the geneticist, Corlaney. You're the one who plays chemical games. Is that why you're frightened for her? What have you done to Sakiimagan's two kids? Who else have you done it to?"

His heart stopped as he realized that logical conclusion too late. "Dammit, *no!* I didn't *do* anything. I'm trying to help you. If the People know she's up in that ship with you and running the same risk Hono did—and lost—you *know* they'll band to-gether and refuse to cooperate with anyone, let alone a spacer admiral and her pet—whatever."

"You presume far too much, Corlaney."

"I call it as *they'll* see it, Loro, as you'd know if your head were clear. It's the way *anyone* would, seeing you right now. Please—leave Anevai here."

The meds sealed the dome over Stephen and began replacing the interior gasses with the carefully balanced semifluid which would rapidly solidify, surrounding him in protective gel until he reached the *Cetacean's* sick bay. It curled about the boy's spare torso, absorbed into the damaged tissue, coating and cushioning the rest.

They moved out of the way as the meds placed the LSU capsule on the hover cart and headed for the Tube terminal lift. He grasped both Loren's hands, preventing her from following.

"Promise me you'll let Anevai stay . . . at least until Ridenour can tell us what happened. If he points the finger at her, I'll back you one hundred percent—I want the bastard that did this as much as you do. Maybe for different reasons, Loren, but every bit as much. Just wait, dammit!"

She raised an eyebrow and glanced down at her hands meaningfully. He released them reluctantly, fearing everything lost.

"All right, Paul." That agreement surprised him. Suddenly he wasn't sure he wanted it. It was too easily attained. "I'll give you until Stephen makes his statement—or until it's determined he *can't* make one. My people will confine their attentions to this area. The animals will be transferred to one of the barns in the valley for care, but everything else remains until their investigation's completed. You will, of course, remain under full Security observation."

"For my protection, naturally."

"Let's say, I don't care to wake up one morning and find myself—or you—disappeared. You say people here tell you things. Fine. I'll believe you. But did Sakiimagan bother to tell you I know about your little 'Net editing system? That I know about the cooperative projects? That I know you and Smith have both worked extensively with Hononomii Tyeewapi?" She paused, smiling grimly. "You might just consider how much these people have *not* been confiding in you, rather than congratulating yourself on how much they *have*."

She headed for the stairs. "Bottom line, Paul, you're the best shot I've got right now. On the small possibility you're telling the truth, I'll guarantee the girl's immunity, but she's going up to the ship with me."

He opened his mouth to protest but she overruled him.

"The topic's not open for debate, Corlaney. Right now, she's the only one on this entire planet I've heard pure unadulterated truth out of. She goes with me." She glanced back at him. "Coming?"

He watched her disappear around the corner. Felt exhaustion hit like a blow between his shoulders as her energy deserted him.

*I'm tired, Loro.* God. Had she even heard him?

# VI

## i

All her life, she'd dreamed of visiting the station; of seeing her world from space; of witnessing personally what she'd seen only in pictures. Now, that dream was coming true.

But at what cost? To her? To her People?—

Anevai glanced back at the LSU capsule bobbing gently in its stabilizing web.

—At what cost to Stephen Ridenour? Had he beaten the odds for the last time?

Across the shuttle's central aisle, the admiral was talking steadily into her private com. *Don't cause trouble. Trust her*, Dr. Paul had said when he informed her she was to go with Cantrell. *Material witness*, so they said. *Cooperate*, Paul had said. And earlier: *She's a mediator . . . a good person to have on our side*.

So much, so very much depended now on Dr. Paul's assessment of Cantrell.

Cantrell looked up, caught her watching, nodded acknowledgement, and returned to her MC readout. Cantrell spooked her: in some ways, the admiral was too much like her father. They both excelled at hiding their thoughts, both saw events on a scale she could in no wise comprehend, and both fought with equal passion toward their own separate goals: her father perceived a destiny for his people in which the Alliance played a minimal part—if any part at all. If she understood what her father had said, Cantrell had her own goals for Alliance in which HuteNamid could play a *significant* role.

She didn't know which of them (if either) was in the right. She did know who had the power at the moment. She also knew what could happen if her father tried to use Wesley's System to usurp that power. She might not understand the intricacies of interstellar policies, but the potential NSpace chaos was more than enough to convince her they had to find another way.

And oddly enough, with Nayati going crazy and her father growing mindlessly autocratic, she was less afraid of Cantrell than of her own people. Much as she'd rather be back home, she was increasingly convinced that the only way they were going to discover the truth about Hono was to see him, and that the only way to survival, let alone autonomy, was to play the admiral's game in good faith.

*She's a mediator. When you run interference . . . you can't afford surprises—from either side.*

*Some*one, some*time*, had to stop playing games.

In the back of the passenger section where the LSU floated, three of the MedTechs (all Recon) from the SciCorps hospital wing watched the readings coming from that unit as though their lives depended on it.

They probably did.

What had really happened to Stephen? Her father had said he'd been 'taken care of.' A beating could be explained: tempers out of hand, a provoked attack. A disappearance—not as Nayati's hostage, but a complete (she shuddered) elimination of evidence—could be attributed to Ridenour's own carelessness on a new world: accidental death. This . . .

She shuddered and shut down that memory. It was hard to think in terms of cosmic consequences, remembering that corpselike body. She wondered if *any* secret could be worth putting a human being into so desperate a fight for life, especially someone as ill-equipped to wage the battle as Stephen Ridenour.

Then she remembered feral eyes in the moonlight; a twisting flight off an aqueduct; dogged stubbornness against personal weakness; and the universal enchantment of her hard-headed friends. Perhaps not so ill-equipped after all. Perhaps if anyone could come back from the dead, it would be her stubborn almost-friend.

She turned back to the window and more stars than she'd ever imagined. All her life she'd dreamed of this flight. Now all she could do was pray she'd one day be going home.

"Stephen?"

The beautiful wasted hand, held captive in padded restraints, twitched.

*"Stephen."*

Another twitch. This time of a blue-veined eyelid.

*"Stephen!"*

Slowly, dark lashes pulling gummily away from SedaGel-filmed cheeks, dull eyes opened. More slowly still, those eyes turned toward her. Bloodless lips formed words without sound. Too-prominent veins pulsed beneath her fingers as Cantrell took his cold hand in hers and leaned into Stephen's line of sight.

"No, Stephen," she said firmly. "Don't try to talk. Just listen. You're safe now. You're aboard *Cetacean*. Dr. McKenna's taking you into surgery soon. Next time you wake up, it'll all be over and you'll feel infinitely better."

"N–n–n . . ." His head flopped to the side. "No s–surg . . . n–no an–n . . . nesthy . . ." His voice faded, his head stilled.

A cough: small, quickly stifled. Another. SedaGel seeped from the corner of his mouth, residue from lungs not yet clear of the healing liquid. Cantrell signalled the MedTechs and they suctioned a third time, triggering a coughing fit which left Stephen weaker, but breathing more naturally.

"Don't worry about the surgery, son. You'll be all right. You're safe, now. We have Anevai Tyeewapi in custody, and we'll have the others responsible for this soon."

He gulped for air repeatedly, trying to speak.

"Later, Stephen."

"L–Lo–ro. . . ." More gasping breath than word as the meds steered the gurney toward Surgery's decon room.

"Just a minute," she said. If it was that important to him . . .

"Not—An–n–nv's —f–fault. Own—" Difficult, getting the words out past the drug haze, but his eyes begged her to understand. She took his hand again: touch seeming more reassuring to him than anything verbal.

"Don't worry about her, either. She's safe."

"*Not*—her . . ." His eyes squeezed shut and tears leaked from them. Exhaustion, pain, frustration, —perhaps a bit of each. "Ad—mer'l. D–don't . . . hurt like . . . H–hon . . . mi."

Like *Hononomii*? What did Stephen know about young Tyeewapi?

"Stephen, I won't hurt her. I hear you: she's not responsible. Is that what you need to know?"

Icy fingers flexed weakly. Another gasp for air: "Have . . . mes–s–s–sage . . ."

"Message for whom, Stephen? Me?"

He nodded, a barely perceptible lift of the chin.

"N–n'ati says . . . p—ayment . . . kind for . . . H–hon–n–mi."

"Stephen, what was that? Payment for what?"

"Admiral, please. He must go in *now*."

The meds were only doing their job, and Stephen had virtually succumbed to the sedative dripping into his vein anyway. She stepped back and watched the door slide shut behind the gurney.

Seated in the corner of the waiting room, TJ Briggs observed the gurney's exit with mixed reactions. While he had nothing against the kid personally—yet, —he *didn't* like the effect young Ridenour was having on Cantrell. For the first time in their long association, she was showing signs of real fatigue: total burnout, mental and physical, and was making decisions he frankly didn't understand, motivated by reasons he increasingly suspected.

Leaving Paul Corlaney on HuteNamid was downright stupid. Convenient that Corlaney knew only enough to keep him off the ship. After twenty years here? Not bloody likely. Not the Paul Corlaney he'd known. Half an hour under Deprivil and Corlaney would provide every key they needed to unlock every closet on the world below. But instead, the admiral put limits on her investigation team and left *Corlaney* in charge of questioning Tyeewapi.

Then there was this too-damned-personal interest she was taking in this kid. Ridenour was not some innocent bystander caught up in local politics. He'd had no business being out there. He sure as hell hadn't any business setting up assignations with Smith.

Cantrell walked slowly toward him, muttering under her breath, met his deliberate scowl and froze. Her quirky brow flew up. She frowned and crossed the room to where he was sitting on the arm of the couch. He removed his foot from the seat, tacit invitation for her to sit down.

She settled sideways, saying abruptly, "Make it fast, Briggs. I'm short on time."

But Briggs refused to be rushed. He took a slender knife from his pocket, flicked it open, and eased a bit of dirt from under a fingernail. Sliding the knife through his fingers, he let it overbalance and fall, stopped it with a last minute, two-fingered catch. "He's a real nice boy."

"Mm-hmm."

The knife made another dive off his knee. "I knew another real nice boy once. Name of Lawrence."

"You got a point to make, Briggs?"

"Might."

"Get to it. I have work to do."

"Lance was smart, too—maybe too smart. He went downworld once, never came—"

"Dammit, Briggs. You think I'm trying to replace my son? God! You and Corlaney ought to compare notes. You'll be accusing me of incest next!"

She jerked to her feet, walked the length of the lounge and back. He let her pace, let her grapple with the implied criticism in her own fashion.

Finally, she dropped back onto the couch and after a long silence said: "I won't lie to you, TJ, and say my personal goals aren't involved here." She stretched her arms and back in a bone-cracking arch, then relaxed against the back of the couch. "Paul doesn't matter. I know you disapprove of my leaving him down there, but HuteNamid will be out of the 'Net for another week after today's transmit, and if he wants to play detective for a few hours, I'm willing to oblige him. Who knows? He may just be able to influence Tyeewapi in ways I can't possibly."

Briggs opened his mouth to protest, but held it back when she raised her hand.

"What can he do, TJ? We have him, Smith, and the governor all on tight, round-the-clock surveillance. By the time we hear Stephen's story, we might not need Paul at all." She leaned forward until all he could see was the back of her head. "As for my feelings toward Stephen, I don't think that's anyone's business but my own. Stephen's far more vulnerable than Lance ever was and too damned unique to lose.'' He heard a quiet laugh then. ''Lance was so blasted cocky, any hint of protecting him and he'd have laughed in my face.''

''Not cocky, Boss-lady, —proud. And so's Stephen Ridenour.''

Silence. A *long* silence. Then a sideways glance up at him. A half-smile.

''Thanks, TJ.''

''Any time, Boss.'' He flipped the knife closed and shoved his hands into his pockets. ''Shall we get back to work, admiral, sir?''

She stood up, clapped his arm on her way to the door. ''Let's go.''

## ii

''Hey, Paul, have you seen Anevai or Stevie this morning?''

Paul saved down the memo he'd been working on (for what it was worth: his concentration had been blown all morning) and turned to the door of his office . . . and an appallingly cheerful Wesley Smith.

''I've been waiting for them to show for over an hour. We were supposed to have breakfast together and . . .'' Wesley squinted at Paul for a moment, then: ''Paul, what's the matjyter?''

He'd been dreading this moment. Smith was a Researcher, and that meant Paul's problem. Sakiimagan had made that clear years ago.

''Wesley, come in and shut the door, will you?''

''But—''

''Just do it, Wes. Please. Don't argue.''

Wesley looked puzzled, but complied willingly enough, sitting on the edge of the chair. Typical: Wesley *never* seemed content to stay put for long—not at someone *else's* request.

Of a sudden, he realized his carefully planned speech wasn't going to work. He took a deep breath and plunged. ''There's no easy way to tell you this, Wes. Stephen's back on *Cetacean*.''

''*Why? What did you do to him?*'' Wes jumped out of the chair and stood over him threateningly.

''What a lovely impression you have of me,'' Paul said sourly.

"I didn't *do* a damn thing! *He* did. Now sit down and listen to me."

Wesley looked rebellious, but sat down anyway.

"He had to go up. He was hurt last night—"

"*What! How?*"

"Dammit, Wes, if you don't shut up, I won't tell you a damn thing. —We don't *know* precisely what happened. It was down in the barn—"

Wesley's mouth opened—

"—*I said, shut up!*— It seems that Nayati was right this time. This Ridenour's a plant . . ."

"No." Wesley's hands were over his ears, and he was shaking his head violently. "No, he's not."

"Stop acting like a child—"

Wesley's fist slammed the top of Paul's desk, scattering pencils and paperclips. "Dammit, Paul, you think I can't tell? You think I don't know what he is? Sure, he's a Del d'Bugger . . . but *so what?* I've been expecting one."

"So what? So he's been primed. Taught all the right words. He's not the one you've been waiting for."

"Bullshit. I know, Corlaney. *I know.* He's not here because of what someone told him. He figured it out himself. I'll guarantee you no Vandereaux prof primed him."

"None of which has anything to do with the fact that he followed Anevai down to the meeting in the barn last night and got himself caught."

"*Caught? —By whom?*"

"Who do you think, Wesley? Nayati wants to know about Hono. Wants *him* back as much—no, dammit, *more*—than you want Ridenour: he's got a damnsight more of his life invested in his cousin. Things evidently got a bit out of hand and—"

"I'll kill him." Even-voiced. Matter-of-fact.

"No, you won't. It's *not* Nayati's doing. We found Stephen in the barn this morning and—"

"How bad is he, Paul?" Wesley deflated. Lost his edge entirely. He sat slumped, elbows on knees, staring at the floor.

Paul rose to his feet and placed a hand on Wesley's shoulder.

"Not good, Wesley, but I think we got to him in time. While I haven't heard anything from Loren yet, I have no reason to believe he won't pull through. Dr. McKenna's as good as they come."

But Wesley refused to be mollified. He pulled away and went to the door.

"Wes, remember: if he'd minded his own business, if he'd been your man, nothing would have happened to him."

One hand on the door, Wes paused, said without turning, "No difference, Paul. It makes no difference what-so-ever. Whatever chance brought him, Stephen Ridenour belongs here." He jerked the door open, turned then, his face hard. "And I intend to see that he stays."

"May I come in?"

Anevai masked her surprise. She wasn't at all certain she was ready to deal with this interview yet. Hours had passed since *Cetacean* Security left her in this small room with its tiny bed and private bath cubicle. Exhausting, sleepless hours.

"Of course, admiral." She gestured toward the small room's single chair. "Won't you sit down?"

"Thank you." Like a friend dropping in for a visit.

But Loren Cantrell wasn't a friend. This was *her* ship, the room *she* had assigned to a 'material witness,' and while the admiral relaxed in the deeply cushioned seat, the 'material witness' remained standing, ready to 'witness'—

—she hoped.

Cantrell smiled at her, a smile she felt no inclination to return. The smile changed to a worried-seeming frown. "Please, Anevai, sit down. This isn't an interrogation."

*Like hell*, she thought, but settled on the bed all the same, drawing her legs up under her, forcing her tired spine stiff, wishing she were more alert.

"You look tired. Haven't you slept?"

She shrugged.

"Is the bed uncomfortable? The temperature too low?"

Cantrell was fishing. Damned if she'd admit she was worried sick about a stupid spacer-spy.

"Claustrophobia," she said abruptly. "I miss my mountains."

"Oh." Cantrell raised a dubious eyebrow, but continued smoothly. "I'd like to express my appreciation for your cooperation in coming aboard. Your input as a witness to the events—"

"You exaggerate, admiral," she interrupted. "I spoke with my father . . ." Who'd ignored her presence in the room.

". . . to let him know where I'd be and that I had agreed to go."
As if there'd been a choice in that matter either.

"Nonetheless, it proved effective. Another Official Complaint
such as he filed for your brother . . ." Cantrell paused, apparently waiting for her to comment. What did she expect? Resentment? But how could she resent her father's indifference to her
situation when it was a situation she herself had created? She
could *wish* for his *understanding*, but resent? She had neither the
right nor the inclination.

Cantrell shrugged and continued: "Another complaint of that
nature would definitely look bad on *HuteNamid's* records, particularly under the circumstances, and I don't care to see Hute-
Namid's reputation blemished. It has far too many excellent
qualities—such as yourself."

"Please, don't waste time on all this, admiral. How is Stephen? Is he going to be all right?"

The admiral *seemed* to take no offense. The admiral said quite
conversationally: "I trust you'll understand my curiosity, but
. . . Why? Why do you care so much if a spacer you met only
a few hours ago lives or dies?"

"I thought you said this wasn't an interrogation, admiral."

"This isn't an official question. It's personal curiosity. I'm
asking as one friend of Stephen's to another. I'd like to know
what this gesture means for him and his future here on HuteNamid."

"*Future here?* He has none, admiral. Never meant to have,
we both know that. You *say* this isn't an interrogation. And
yet—" She met the admiral's eyes for an instant. "We *are* being
recorded, aren't we?"

Those dark eyes didn't waver. "Yes, we are. But it goes
directly into *my* Security files. Which means only I use it—if
it's used at all. And my disclaimer is already logged. I've already
said it's not official—therefore, it's not legal testimony in a court
of Alliance law."

She studied her folded hands, noted scratches, bits of dirt that
had survived her scrubbing brush. Thought of the blood-stained
clothes the *Cetacean* fatigues had replaced. Cantrell's people had
those clothes, ultimate proof of her very personal involvement.

She *wished* she knew her rights more clearly. *Wished* she knew
if the admiral was telling the truth. But some*one*—some*time* . . .
She said in a low voice: "What makes you think I'm his friend?"

"You must realize you're in an exceedingly vulnerable position. A position from which you could find yourself a detainee—even on trial for murder, should Stephen fail to recover—and yet your composure would indicate a clear conscience, possibly even an expectation that Stephen will uphold that assessment if he recovers. Your expressed concern has been for *his* welfare without mention of your own. If friendship for Stephen doesn't motivate you, then what?"

"I wonder if you could be . . ." She shifted her gaze to the foot of the bed, tried to think. "Admiral, I . . ." She gulped, then tried again. "Admiral, if I cooperate with you—tell you what I know—will I . . ." A glance up encountered a hard, unyielding face. "Admiral, I don't w–want to be questioned under D–deprivil. Can you understand that? You t–told my father that Hono had a b–bad reaction. I—I'm scared of having that happen to me, too. Would you . . . ?"

Another glance. Still no yielding. If she could just be sure she would be allowed to tell *her* story *her* way . . .

After a long silence, the admiral said, "I'll tell you honestly, Anevai, if I don't have to run a probe on you, I won't. I *wouldn't* have on your *brother*, had he dealt honestly with me. I much prefer voluntary cooperation—in all matters. Does that help?"

It would have to. She was aboard *Cetacean* now, and only beginning to comprehend how thoroughly Cantrell's world the ship really was. Like the view of HuteNamid from the shuttle, such power had been an intellectually acknowledged reality, but until she was actually here, on this ship, she hadn't realized how utterly helpless she *could* be.

Back home, when all was said and done, she could simply disappear into the forest where she could survive the rest of her life free and happy. Here . . .

Here, there was nothing she could do to prevent Cantrell from using her any way she cared to. So she sought an answer that would satisfy both the curious admiral and her own sense of right. "There're lots of reasons I'd like to know. If Stephen dies, *real* friends of mine might be in very real trouble. I'd like to keep the record straight. What they did to him might've been wrong, but they thought it justified—and they *didn't* try to kill him!"

"You're certain of that?"

"I told you—Stephen was just fine . . ." Unwillingly, she

flashed on that corpse-like figure in the LSU. "Well, some fairly nasty cuts and bruises—but I've seen worse and he was functional enough to argue—vehemently—when I saw him last. —And by that time, everyone else had gone."

"Who is 'everyone,' Anevai?"

"Sorry, admiral. I'm not about to answer that one cold sober. —At least not yet."

"Meaning you might eventually?"

She set her jaw. Said nothing.

"Fair enough. Who knows? That particular piece of information might yet prove superfluous: and it's unfair, isn't it: expecting you to betray your family and friends? But what of your own involvement? Is self-defense one of your 'many reasons' for concern?"

Anevai began pleating the bedspread in precise folds, staring at her hands through a blurring film.

"I don't know if you can believe this, admiral, but it's not, really. Whether Stephen lives or dies, I'm partly responsible for his being here and I can't forgive myself for that. No matter what else I might or might not have done, I lured him down to the barn, knowingly. There's no way that I can forgive myself for my part in . . . whatever happened to him."

A half-dozen tears fell on her hands. She smoothed the blanket and surreptitiously wiped the dampness away, then blinked her eyes clear and *really* met Cantrell's eyes for the first time since the admiral had entered the room.

"It's not that I think what *he* did was right or honorable. A *spy* doesn't deserve sympathy. I just don't see why—" She blinked, and the tears began in earnest, bitten lips and clenched fists notwithstanding. "P–Please, admiral, how bad is he? C–can't you just tell me if he's still alive?"

Cantrell's indifference helped Anevai stifle her tears. She hated to cry under any circumstances; in front of this thoroughly controlled woman, it was doubly embarrassing.

She bit her lip, sniffed, and rubbed a hand across her face—hard. A light pressure on her shoulder, and a dark-skinned hand holding a handkerchief appeared in front of her. She accepted it in a wad, shook it out—

—and something dropped free, hit her leg. As she wiped her face dry, she searched the cover underneath her, felt sharp-edged hardness beneath her fingers, and carefully withdrew it.

*ZRS*. She looked up at the admiral, hoping for an explanation, wondering if she meant her to have it back.

Blank-faced, the admiral said quietly, "I have talked with Stephen. He went to great pains—quite literally—to clear you of responsibility for his condition. *He* doesn't blame you. Not *even* for the part you've admitted to."

More tears threatened, but she forced them back. "Thank you, admiral.

I didn't mean to distress you. Stephen's alive and in surgery now and ought to be back in form in a few days." A half-smile, a private-joke-between-the-two-of-us smile. "*Better* than before. You know about his shoulder?"

She nodded.

"Dr. McKenna's going to do some repair work whether Stephen Ridenour likes it or not."

She managed a soggy smile of her own and tightened her fingers around the button. "High time, I say."

"Exactly." Cantrell got up. "Now, Anevai, I'm going to leave you. I have work to do. I really only stopped by to bring you up to date about Stephen's condition."

"But I—" She caught herself. Bit her lip. Maybe *Nayati's* wasn't the head that needed examining.

That realization came too late. Cantrell said, "But what, Anevai?"

No turning back now. "Admiral, I've tried to play fair with you; will you at least return that fairness?"

Cantrell said cautiously, "In what way, Ms. Tyeewapi?"

The button's faceted edges cut into her fingers. "Admiral, last I saw Stephen he should have been all right. First aid stuff. What happened? Why is he in that operating room right now?"

A long silence, then: "All right, Anevai. The major damage was a pierced lung and a deep wound in his side that got the liver. Hell of a lot of blood loss. Other than that, I've seen worse in a bar-room brawl."

Her ears were buzzing. She breathed deeply, fought dizziness with anger. "What caused the wound, admiral? Do you know? Have you—got the weapon?"

She knew the personal arsenal of everyone who would have had *any* cause to come into contact with Stephen. If they had that knife, she could betray that individual in an instant.

Cantrell frowned. Looked honestly puzzled. "Why, girl? Why ask that? And why should I answer?"

And would. As Paul would say, there was no excuse for this level of stupidity. She swallowed and said, "Ignorance serves no one, admiral. Stephen did nothing that I know of to deserve death. If he did, someone has some explaining to do. The condition Stephen was in when I last saw him, self-defense sure as hell wouldn't cut it."

The frown deepened. "All right, I'll tell you—though I honestly don't believe it will solve a thing. It was a tool from the barn itself. I believe you would call it a hayhook."

"*A*—" She gave a shout of laughter: relief, hysteria, or honest humor, she didn't know and cared less. "I don't *believe* this."

"You don't believe what?"

"All this—" She spread her arms wide. "—because Stephen's a clumsy tode."

"I'm not amused, girl."

"You should be, admiral. But then, maybe you shouldn't. Because it's *your* fault, sending him down there in the first place."

"I'll ignore that for now; chalk it up to exhaustion. I'll *talk* to you in the morning."

She'd gone too far. Much too far. "Admiral, —*wait! Please!*"

She jumped from the bed, took the three strides to the door in two, and came up against the wall facing Cantrell.

"Admiral, I *saw* the—murder weapon—minutes before it must have happened. It's *Stephen*. Stephen did it, don't you see?"

"Are you implying Stephen tried to kill *himself*?"

"Tried to? Oh, no, admiral. I'm sure, whatever happened, it was an *accident*. Ridenour collects those the way some people collect bugs. I am saying that when I left the barn a very unstable person was standing with a hayhook in the dirt at his feet. A hayhook *I* dropped there, after Nayati—"

"After Nayati what?" Cantrell was listening closely now.

She said in a low voice, seeing not Cantrell's dark face, but a moonlit barn, "I was trying to stop him. He kept asking about Hononomii. He was so angry—there didn't seem any other way." She laughed shortly. "But Nigan did. He belted Ridenour a good one—put him out cold. Nayati *couldn't* expect him to talk then . . .'' She choked: half-laugh, half-sob. "I can't believe it. Poor, dumb space-tode. I can't help but feel sorry for him . . ." Her voice dropped and she said under her breath, "Even though I ought to hate him for what he's done to my family."

The admiral leaned her shoulder against the door and asked, "You continue to amaze me, girl. What precisely do you think *Stephen's* done to your family? To you, personally?"

She left the door, sat on the bed, one knee pulled to her chest, and framed her answer slowly. "It's pretty obvious now that you sent him down to spy on us—probably on Wesley, too—I haven't figured all of that out yet. But one way and another Stephen's turned us all into fugitives or prisoners or—traitors."

"Good lord, girl. Stephen didn't make those 'friends' of yours attack him in the barn; neither did he make your brother attack my security officer. *He* didn't force you up here or make you confess to your part in last night's events."

"Didn't he?"

"You're serious, aren't you?" Anevai didn't waver. The admiral shook her head and said, "All right, Anevai, I'll bite. How?"

"If Stephen had been legitimate—either way: as the researcher he claimed, or the spy he was—none of this would have happened. If he'd been a researcher, he wouldn't have followed me to the barn and wouldn't be lying in there now. If he'd been a real spy, he'd never have gotten caught."

"But is it fair to hate him for being inept?"

"I don't hate him, admiral. But you see, that's the whole problem: he's *not* inept—except at what he insists on doing. He's lied to everyone—and he's a *lousy* liar. Once you know him, you can tell by looking at him whether or not he knows what he's talking about. I saw him with Wesley. Wes has very high standards—at least where it comes to research partners. Yesterday afternoon at the *Watering Hole*, Stephen kept Wes so entertained, he—Wesley, not Stephen—had to be reminded about dinner—*three times!*"

She broke off, out of breath. But the admiral said nothing and Anevai continued with a wry chuckle, "You'd have to know Wesley better—"

"And *you* do?"

Anevai paused, wondering why the admiral would ask that. "Well, —obviously."

"There's no *obviously* about it, Anevai."

"But he's my friend, admiral. Obviously, I know him better than you would, who just met him a couple of times, right?"

Another shake of the head. "You people just don't see it, do you?" Cantrell asked cryptically.

Anevai didn't answer, afraid now what she might have revealed. In weary confusion, she shook her head. "It's not right for me to like Stephen, but—" She opened her hand, looked from the button to Cantrell. "But I do, and I'd *like* to see him before you—do—whatever it is you're going to do to me. I'd like to thank him for—keeping his side of the bargain."

A long pause. Finally Cantrell said, "I'm not going to ask What bargain? Not yet. For now, if you need anything, ask. Don't be shy. Feel free to wander about this deck. You haven't the clearance to go elsewhere, but I think you'll find enough to entertain you. There's a weight room, library . . . you can get the schematic for the area from the computer." She nodded toward the keyboard and monitor built into the small dresser/desk. "Standard 'NetLink Config. Access is limited to *Cetacean's* general library, but that should be enough to keep you entertained."

"You mean, I'm not confined to quarters?"

"Certainly not," Cantrell said. "You're not a prisoner."

*Not yet*, she thought, but felt slightly more inclined to trust when Cantrell raised an eyebrow and said:

"After all, where would you go?"

Cantrell turned to go, and reckoning this cooperation might end without warning, Anevai said, "—Admiral?"

The ramrod back couldn't stiffen, but impatience triggered the sharp turn back, the sharper response, "*Yes*, Anevai."

She had to ask, "May I—may I see H–Hononomii?"

The admiral's mouth twitched—

"Another of your *reasons*?"

"I'd be lying if I said not, and you're not the fool to believe me."

—and she outright grinned. "Thank you for that, Anevai." Anevai blushed. "But—may I?"

"We'll see."

* * *

"Well?" TJ asked the moment the door closed behind her.

Cantrell angled a Look at him. "I'm too old for this. Ridenour'd better be worth it. And if he's trying to pull a fast one on us, or if he's some flunky for Kurt or Shapoorian or whoever, I'll kill him myself."

"What about the girl?"

"Something happened between them. She's—not indifferent to his fate. She's also ours, if we play her right."

"You're certain?"

"More so after I talk with Ridenour."

# iii

*"Stephen?"*

He was floating. It felt like the ZG gym, but he hadn't used the trainer for years, so why was he here? He supposed he should get out: the children probably needed to use it. But he'd have to open his eyes first. And that would take so much effort.

*"Stephen?"*

How odd. Memory supplied a name to the voice, an almost-face; but mostly a feeling. A mostly-safe feeling. A feeling out of place in a Vandereaux gymnasium as the voice was out of place.

What was Loren Cantrell doing here?

Then he recognized the almost-floating-feeling; the smell; the beep that was his heart. Not ZG. Intensive Care. How had he gotten here this time?

"Stephen, can you hear me?"

Of course he could. Why wouldn't he?

"Stephen?"

She expected him to answer. He tried, but his mouth wouldn't work. It was dried shut: tongue stuck to palate, lips to teeth. Disgusting.

Damp sprayed his cracked lips. A tube eased into his mouth, released an awful taste, but after the taste went away, his mouth worked much better.

"H'lo–oh–oh." Well, better, anyway.

A gentle touch to his forehead and cheeks left them damp and cool, a feeling equally out of place. But from the far side of the academy, not Loro's side. He struggled to stop the tears that almost-memory raised. Mama had sent him away, had told him to obey his Uncle Victor who had told him to forget all the befores, which he did. Mostly. Only sometimes the half-memories brought the tears, and the tears brought laughter and threats to *Give him something to cry about*.

That confused him, now as then. If he was crying, obviously he already *had* something to cry about. Why had They felt compelled to supply *more?*

"Stephen? Do you know who I am?"

"L–Loro?"

A velvet chuckle followed that. He liked it when people laughed like that: not loud and mean, but soft, like they wanted you to laugh, too. He ventured a small one of his own, but it didn't work very well, so he shut up.

"Yes, Stephen, it's Loro. Will you talk with me awhile?"

"Sh–sh–sure . . ." His mouth still wasn't working right; but then, his head wasn't working right, either.

That was funny. He was supposed to be smart. That's what the teachers all said when he goofed and they gave him a bunch more work so he wouldn't goof again. Probably the teachers were lying.

*"Stephen . . ."*

But that was okay. Everybody lied, after all.

Papa lied—'cause he wasn't Papa.

*"Stephen?"*

Mama lied—'cause Zivon wasn't happier at Vandro.

Granther lied—'cause Zivon never got to see the stars. Never, ever, ever.

*"Stephen."*

And the Vandro kids lied—'cause they said bad things about Mama and Papa and made him say they were true or they'd hit him. And he was bad because he lied and said *Yes, it's true*. Then they hit him anyway. *They* lied twice. So they were *twice* as bad as he was.

*"Stephen! Can you hear me?"*

"Sh–sh–sure."

Loro sounded mad. Mad people hit you, and he didn't like being hit, so he listened hard. "Stephen, we need to know what happened; who attacked you. Do you remember the barn?"

"B–barn?" No. The barn was long before the attacks. The

barn was before Vandro. The barn was *his* job. Had he forgotten to clean it again?

"Can you tell us who attacked you, Stephen?"

*Pain. Awful pain. 'Go ahead, 'buster-boy, tell. Who's going to believe you?'*

He tried to shake his head, but it was too heavy. "No. No! No! Won't tell! *Won't!*"

"Stephen, it's all right. Relax. Why won't you tell me?"

"C—can't. S—send . . . me . . . back. B—bijan says . . . cut head off and . . . and feed b—bones to . . . d—dogs."

"*Who the hell's Bijan?* Stephen, *where* do you think you are?"

He was scared. He heard the beep that was his heart speed up. Heard the warning sound. Knew the doctors were going to give him something to make the warning stop and someday it would stop beeping forever: Papa told him so. Papa said, Don't fall asleep when They tell you. And never, ever, ever tell about the hats in the cave. But They gave him stuff and made him fall asleep and then he couldn't remember if he'd told about the hats or not and that made him sick and now they were going to get him and Loro couldn't help because Loro didn't know where he was or who Bijan was. Why didn't Loro know Bijan? Everybody knew Bijan. Bijan said he knew everybody, so everybody must know him.

The scared feeling started to go away; the beep slowed. Please, Loro, don't let Them make me fall asleep . . .

"Where, Stephen?" Loro's voice insisted he answer. "Where are you now?"

"H—Hospital?" He was no longer so certain. Didn't Loro know where they were? "P—Please, L—Loro, d—don't wan—na s—slee—"

"What hospital, Stephen?"

"V—van—d'ro?"

"Vandereaux? TJ, check out his academy records. Find out who this Bijan is. —Stephen, listen to me, let's not talk about Vandereaux right now, let's talk about Wesley and Anevai and *Anevai's* barn. Do you remember them?"

"Sure." His mouth was working better now. That was nice. And of course he remembered Anevai. Remembered Wesley. Remembered, as tears leaked.

He sniffed. Made the tears stop so he wouldn't run out.

"Stephen, do you remember going to the barn last night? You followed Anevai and Dr. Templeton. Do you remember?"

"Sure. Who's Dr. Tempton?"

"Never mind, Stephen. Think about Anevai. Why, Stephen? Why did you go to the barn alone, and at night?"

Too many questions. Too many reasons: all confused in half-memories. But Loro was asking. One of those reasons concerned Loro: he could remember that, if not the why . . .

A warm fire. Another touch of this gentle hand. The tears leaked at an insult recalled. An insult made doubly hurtful because it came from the same source as the gentle hand . . .

"Go . . . show L–Loro . . . eyes . . . open."

"What do you mean, eyes open?"

"Good agent . . . eyes . . ."

Like a good agent, he opened his, but: *"Can't see! Loro, why can't I see?"* He tried to sit up, but he couldn't and it hurt. He bit his lip so he wouldn't cry out. But the Hands pressed his shoulders, made him lie flat and Loro's voice said:

"Easy, son. Your eyes are covered. Hold still and I'll get it off. But it's medicated, so don't let me forget to put it back on, okay?"

"Yes, yes, yes! Take it away! *Take it away!*"

Stephen blinked his eyes to such clarity as they could achieve. Admiral Cantrell was seated next to him looking very tired. How long had she been there?

"Iz–z–ever'thin' . . . okay?" He whispered past the raw burn in his throat. He hated tubes. "You look awful."

She chuckled again, a deep rich chuckle. God, he loved that sound. He thought he remembered thinking that before, but couldn't remember when.

"You're a fine one to talk," she said.

He grimaced. "That bad?"

She smiled. "No, not really. Mo patched you up all nice and pretty again. Got that shoulder of yours, too. No more excuses, kid."

Most of what she was saying made no sense. It was increasingly difficult to watch her; his eyes kept drifting, the lids felt heavy, swollen. "Tha's–s–s . . . ni . . ."

"Stephen, don't fall asleep on me yet."

"Iz–zat . . . pro–po—si . . ." His lungs ran out of air. He inhaled and forgot what he was saying.

Her rich chuckle preceded the lightest touch of her lips next to his and she whispered softly, so close her breath tickled his ear, "Don't tempt fate or me, kid. You're picking up more than 'Net information from your friend, Wesley. Some of it could be dangerous. Two more questions, Stephen, then I promise I'll leave you alone."

He nodded, no longer trying to open recalcitrant eyes; they wouldn't focus anyway.

"Who hit you with the hook?"

"No . . . body. Me. Clum–m–m–sy f–fool."

"You're not clumsy, dear. But you were hurt before that, weren't you?"

"M–m–m–hm."

"Who did that?"

He smiled, feeling clever to have caught her: "Tha's . . . three."

And let sleep drift over him.


"I'll kill him! One name. One lousy name. Someone solid to go after so I don't have to pressure young Anevai, and *he* gets technical."

Cantrell threw herself into the chair and burst out laughing.

Briggs grasped her shoulders, scrutinized her closely, (which only set her off again) decided she was basically sane, gave her a pop on the cheek, and perched on her desk. "Has quite a sense of timing, hasn't he?"

"I tell you—" She gasped. "—no court in Alliance would convict me. —Slippery little eel. I'm tempted to throw him back into the pond." She sobered immediately. "I don't mean that, of course." A strained silence, then: "You realize it's my fault he's in there right now."

"Whoa—slow up. Don't go taking blame you haven't earned. You hadn't any real choice, he was the one who—"

"I'm not talking about that, TJ. You heard him. He followed Anevai to the barn last night as a direct result of something I'd said to him not half an hour earlier. Otherwise, his own good sense would have kept him out of it."

Briggs didn't offer *his* opinion of Stephen Ridenour's 'good sense.' "You really think it's that simple? What about the note to Smith? Why was it interrupted and—"

"—and why was it being sent in the first place?" she finished for him. "My bet is we're dealing with two completely separate issues. We'll know more once he wakes up for real. I wish we could justify keeping him partway under while we got his depo."

"Open-mouthed under the stuff, wasn't he?" TJ said. And remembering the kid's RX records: "No wonder he doesn't like tranquilizers."

"He doesn't?"

"Avoids them like the plague."

"That's interesting. I'll keep it in mind. —Did you check out that name—Bijan, was it?"

"One of the students at the academy. A few years older than Stephen. In a lot of the same classes. Scores were nothing to write home about, but something **of a** leader among the other students." A pause to be certain he had her full attention. "His last name's Shapoorian."

Another pause: Cantrell's this time. "As in *Councillor* Shapoorian?"

He nodded. "Mother."

"Good—God. The woman's older than Methuselah! What's *she* doing with a kid Stephen's age?"

"Three years older." She glared at him; he shrugged and relented. "Surrogate: no way she'd carry the kid herself. The father was some sort of math genius out of an Albion station 'Tank. Bit of a scandal when he discovered whose egg his sperm were swimming with. He tried to sue, but got nowhere."

She swore, long and eloquently. Truly impressive. And when even she had run out of expletives: "That's it, TJ. Eckersley's been trying to push through my applications for years, but I never even tried for Vandereaux. Didn't *want* it, thanks. Along comes Stephen's app and Shapoorian agrees to the experiment at Vandereaux because sonny boy was already there, primed and ready for the kill. —Who in hell would condemn a child to a situation like that?"

"Danislav arranged the transfer."

"Maybe. But I think Danislav was counting on the Board to reject it. Any specifics in the Academy records about what the Shapoorian boy might have done?"

"None."

"Not surprised. No one would dare report Shapoorian's kid in Shapoorian's own private academy. Damn. . . . No wonder Stephen's paranoid." She slouched deeper into the chair, scowling. "Mama Mialla couldn't have told him outright, not even she would dare that: the Recon connection is securitied."

"If she told him to give the new kid a bad time and to be on the lookout . . . Bijan could easily have found out. Among other things, one look at that diary of Ridenour's would give him away."

"That accident in the hall; the abandoned book: it's all beginning to make a morbid kind of sense. Once Bijan and his crowd were armed with that bit of information, who knows what all they could do to a shy, unprotected kid?"

"There *was* Danislav."

She glowered up at him. "*You* should've talked to Danislav: you'd know just how ludicrous that suggestion is. I should have said *worse* than unprotected. Danislav was his damned *guardian*. He'd trust Danislav to *see* and *do* something—if what they were doing was wrong. —And once Bijan knew what Stephen was, he'd know exactly what Mama meant by giving the new kid a bad time. Translated, that would mean, Prove Mama's right and drive the 'Buster-boy out."

"And when they couldn't drive him out, and those test scores drew the interest of the 'NetAT—"

"Exactly. What better way to play the altruist than to send the boy on a proving trip—complete with ready-made transfer—to a 'Tank chock *full* of misfits? If nothing else, get him out of sight for a year or two, let the 'NetAT forget about him. But Shapoorian *planned* for him to go through with the transfer. —Do you suppose she really *believes* that crap she spouts? —Put the kid back on a planet and he instantly defects? Naturally: he's Recon, genetically speaking. Couldn't help himself, could he? Great fodder for Shapoorian's views. Never mind it's the first decent treatment he's received since he was a child."

"What about the 'NetAT's involvement?"

"Obviously, the fallouts were real: it wasn't a setup in that sense. They could well be interested, but—"

The AutoCom's pager flashed.

Loren cast him a frustrated look, and said, "Go ahead, 'Com."

*"Message for you from George Maxwell Downey on HuteNa-mid Station Alpha. Will you accept?"*

"Message, 'Com."

*"He requests information on the duration of 'Net black-out and insists on special dispensation for an emergency call to his broker."*

"Dammit, tell him to stop wasting my time! His stocks have the same emergency coverage everyone's do! The 'Net block cannot be lifted for any reason. If he hasn't got the proper forms, we'll send them."

Then, her wicked grin returned and she paged BridgeCom. "Mat? Re: that last AutoCom trans: fax over every remotely relevant form. Tell him to fill them out in—quadruplicate—one for Tunica, one for us to Secure, one for his broker and one . . . and one for just-in-case. Stress *originals*. *Legalities* due to the 'Net being down. —Cantrell out." She chuckled. "That'll keep him busy for a while. —Lord, where were we, TJ?"

"Getting redundant. —Timely interruption. God invented clowns for occasions like this, Boss-lady."

"Believe it or not, I checked his stock records and I think we're doing him a favor. He's lost money on every transaction he's ever made."

"What *are* you planning regarding the 'Net shutdown?"

"Status Quo until I know more."

"Then why the hell don't you go downworld and kick a few butts and find *out* more?"

"Patience, old friend. Patience. I'm working on it. What about those 'Tank transfers? Have you found any connecting factor in the researchers' backgrounds or reasons for coming to HuteNamid?"

He grinned. "Patience, old friend. Patience. —I'm working on it!"

*"Did you hear me, Dad? I said Stephen is out of surgery, and he's going to be all right.—Dad?"*

Sakiimagan's jaw tightened, then he said, "I heard you, Ane-vai."

*"Well, I . . . I guess that's all. . . . Tell Dr. Paul, will you?"*

Sakiimagan glanced at Paul, and said, "If he asks. Tyeewapi out."

*". . . Goodbye, Dad . . ."*

Paul winced as Anevai's strained voice faded out. He had no right to interfere in Sakiimagan's handling of his own children. On the other hand—

"How's Stephen doing, Sakiima?"

Sakiimagan frowned. "That's not funny, Paul."

"Am I laughing?"

"If you think to embarrass me, you won't succeed. The girl blatantly disregarded my orders."

"And that's it?"

"What else is there? Either she respects my leadership, or she doesn't. There's no half way in this matter."

"And what about Nayati's respect for your leadership? He's been erasing 'Net files against your direct orders, murdering Alliance researchers, and yet I don't see you turning him over to Cantrell."

"I didn't turn my daughter over to Cantrell. As to Nayati, we have no proof, yet, that the disappearance of those files was his doing. —Or, for that matter, that Ridenour's condition is."

"Good God, man, what do you need? A signed confession? You said you had no idea those files had been wiped before Loren brought it up. What more has Nayati done that you don't know about? What if Anevai's correct in her estimation of Nayati—*and* of Ridenour? Have you even considered that possibility? Have you even *tried* to confront Nayati?"

"Anevai's judgment is suspect. Her contact with these spacers has obviously warped her sense of perspective."

"In case you've forgotten, *I'm* spacer, born and raised, Sakiimagan Tyeewapi. Have you and your children been warped by your contact with *me?*"

"You know I didn't mean it like that, Paul."

"Didn't you? You know damn well she warned you about Nayati *before* she met Stephen, and while force is one thing—though I can't believe you truly endorse such actions—murder is something else entirely."

"I'm not *endorsing*, as you put it, Nayati's actions. After the admiral has gone, Nayati will receive proper punishment: his actions were uncivilized and embarrassing. But I'll not turn over another of my people to Alliance's brand of justice. As for murder—you said yourself, if Nayati wanted the spy dead, he'd be dead."

"You weren't there. You didn't see the boy. He was well gone before that hook ripped out half his side. I doubt very much he'd have made it back by himself."

Sakiimagan shrugged. "He survived long enough to be found, even with the other injury."

"Only because I—"

"You what, Paul?"

He sighed. "You'll find out soon enough. When the boy turned up missing this morning, I told Anevai to cooperate—she was trying to stall. Trying to save Nayati's ass."

"You? Then it *wasn't* Ridenour. Interesting."

"Good Lord, Sakiima, you could at least have the fatherly decency to want to rip my throat out."

Sakiimagan shrugged. "Had Anevai followed my orders in the first place, she wouldn't have been here to be taken. I can't blame you for responding as you felt necessary. You're not of the *Dineh*."

Paul leaned toward his old friend, puzzled by this heartless chill. "But don't you understand, Sakiima? I *did* it for the People. Because you can't continue this way. You're so convinced Anevai has turned on you, but *what if* she's right?"

"I tell you, it's her imagination. Nayati's hotheaded —yes—but he's young, and while his methods may be questionable, his goals are not. I've lost *one* child trusting your judgment of Cantrell. I'll not lose another."

"Which child? Hono? —There's no proof of that. Anevai? —No proof of that, either."

"I've already answered that, Paul."

"Have you? Dammit, Sakiima, where are the Elders in all this? Who set you up as dictator? —What's happened to you?"

"I'm not; and nothing. I stand where I always have. You know I'm not for total independence, but if it comes to a choice between that and throwing the Project to the Alliance 'Net, then, yes, I'll take secession—and the Elders will back me. A week ago, so would you! What's the matter, Paul? There's more to this argument than one spy's health."

Hard to answer that, when so much depended on it. Paul said slowly, "Three years ago, we began discussing the very possibilities we might have just blown. I'm not talking about throwing the Project to the 'Net; I'm talking about bringing a few key people in on it, same as I always have. The same as you *used* to talk. Wesley's system was the key to that fast, private access to the best minds in Alliance. If Wesley was right about Ridenour, the boy could have been the key to getting that system up and running in months instead of years.''

''And if he's not? If Cantrell's not what *you* think she is?''

''You never even gave them a chance.''

''She never gave *us* a chance. The 'Net's been down since she came insystem.''

''What difference does that make to you? You never use it anyway.''

''It's the power, Paul. Doesn't it make you just the least bit nervous that for the last two days she could have destroyed us all on a whim and *never* have had to justify that act? Or that in that time, her people have pushed mine into violent acts they'd *never* have considered before her arrival?''

''I'm worried, all right; but not about Loren. I'm worried about myself, Nayati, Hono, the whole damn planet. But not because of Loren's actions: she has that power because she *won't* use it on a whim. I've had some—reactions—I can't explain away. If those same reactions affected Nayati—or Hononomii —with *their* youthful tempers, the results might very well be grossly out of character.''

''What are you trying to tell me?''

''I think it's time to find out exactly what happened to your son up there and why. I think the Project can't remain yours alone any longer. Mainly, I think that if we alienate Loren now, we're losing our only chance to remain independent and still tap the minds of the Alliance, and I think we *need* that outside, uninfluenced viewpoint. I think—''

Sakiimagan said abruptly, ''And *I* think, Dr. Corlaney, it's time for you to leave.''

He stood up, using action to disguise his dismay. ''Shall I put in my transfer, then?''

Sakiimagan frowned. ''Whatever gave you that idea, Paul? I meant go. Get out of my office. Give me time to consider what you've said.''

He grinned lopsidedly and held out his hand. ''Thank God! I really believed for a moment you *were* sending me packing—''

Sakiimagan gripped his hand, then steered him toward the door. ''I wouldn't dare, Paul. After the garbage you've published for the last few years, nobody else would have you: you'd end up polishing test tubes in some kitchen or other.''

Paul, at the door to Sakiimagan's office, gestured rudely and left quickly while he still had the final word.

# iv

*(The white wolf looks back—black silhouette against the rising sun—the golden glow echoes in its eyes. Snegurochka is mist, the wolf lives on.*

*(The sun rises. The wolf fades. . . .)*

''No. I won't go. Not yet . . .'' Stephen roused from the dream, discovered the distant murmur for his and shut up. —Fast.

He was alone—except for the viewers. There were always viewers, regardless of where he slept. But this was *Cetacean*, not Vandereaux. He remembered that now. Here the viewers might have some respect for a man's privacy.

But he didn't count on it.

An unsteady hand lifted to his face felt a familiar drag of tubes in the low-G of ICU. He thought he'd seen the last of these damned hospital rooms.

White wolf? What the hell was a wolf? Where had that dream come from? He recalled other dreams and shivered. Heard the monitors protest.

And he thought Anevai Tyeewapi had a problem making up her own stories—

The door opened and Dr. McKenna entered. She looked him over, checked the monitor and said, ''You look okay to me, kid. What's your problem?''

''I—'' He put a hand to his head, confused. Had he said something was wrong? Paged her? She grinned and pointed to the monitor beside the bed.

He smiled weakly in return. ''Sorry. —I'll try to control myself.''

''See that you do. —Seriously, son, how are you feeling?''

''Foggy.''

''You will.'' She gestured to the AutoMed again.

He turned his head slowly, focussed on the readouts, the

medications, recognized some of them. "Shit," he said on a breath and looked to her. She seemed amused. He was glad someone was.

"How's the shoulder feel?"

"Sh—Shoulder? Why . . ." He shifted it around. "D—Different."

"I should hope so. Be careful with it and it should be good as new when it heals. Best if we don't try to accelerate that process too much. Don't want to risk abnormal tissue generation after all the stress it's had over the years. But I'm good. God, I'm good."

"But they said—" If he weren't so tired, he'd laugh.

"Who said what, son?"

But he shook his head. It didn't matter. Not anymore. And why should it surprise him? Just one more lie. One more fabrication to keep him out of competition. To keep him from the one thing he *could* do. The monitor beeped. *Shut up!* he told it silently. And it did. Because he truly no longer cared.

He looked up at McKenna, smiled and said softly, "Thanks, Dr. Mo."

She laid a hand on his and headed for the door. "Any time, kid. Glad to be of service. Now, go back to sleep. Doctor's orders."

*"He's awake, Loren. But take it easy on him, hear me?"*

"I hear you, Mo. Easy as I can. Cantrell out." Cantrell cut her office com and turned to TJ. "—Well? Remind you of someplace?"

He killed the report display and leaned back in the chair. " 'Sometimes, they just leave.' —Isn't that the phrase Tyeewapi used?"

"What do you think, TJ? Am I creating connections?"

TJ cradled his coffee mug between his hands, took a long swallow. "The thing that has always intrigued me about working with you, Loren, is your ability to see what no one else notices. My first reaction was, You're crazy. But now, I'm not so sure."

"Disappearing IndiCorps personnel. Not off the files, but certainly from the settlements. Ever since I talked to Sakiimagan, I've had a feeling about this place. Stephen's presence already had me reviewing the Rostov files for the first time in years. Some of *those* Recons had projects in common with the ThinkTank too.''

''The kid's folks?''

She nodded. ''Among others. But even those researchers still on good terms died. Different world, different situation, but I've got this feeling . . . I wish to God I'd known some of those people—been there to help. There *were* signs. Disappearances, irrational, out of character behaviors. . . . Sound familiar?''

''Very different Recon/researcher relationships.''

''But not early on. Not with some researchers. Not with *some* Recons even toward the end. *Significant* Recons, TJ.''

''You going to tell him?''

''I don't know. Kind of depends on Stephen, doesn't it?''

The journal entry winked out. In its place:

> **Hi, there, kid.**
> **Welcome back to the real world.**

''Who . . . ?'' Stephen muttered, then queried the system.

> **SecOne DProg Chet Hamilton**.

He felt the bottom fall out of his stomach. God. What had he done now?

*Good morning, sir.*

> **Name's Chet, kid.**
> **How're you feeling?**

*Fine, thanks.*

> **Wonderful.**
> **Now how are you really feeling?**
> **It's OK. This is a SecLine.**
> **You can be honest.**
> **By the way, you left out a comma in that last line**.

Stephen chuckled. Talked to this way, the man seemed as crazy as Wes. He felt a twinge of regret, thinking of Wesley Smith; wondering if there was anything he could do to remedy the disaster he'd created. Thinking of Wesley, he answered:

*Like shit, thanks.*

> **Better.**
> **Did you have a good time?**

A good time? A distant memory of a bar, laughter, and a moonlit valley:

*The last hour or so wasn't the most fun I've had in my life, but
the rest made up for it.*
> **Good boy.**
> **Find out anything interesting for the old SecMan?**

He hesitated, not knowing how to answer, no longer certain
of what he'd discovered, now he was back (as Chet put it) in the
real world.

Another memory: this time of the barn. His own thought:
whatever Wes had done, he shouldn't have to go back to Vandereaux system.
> **You there?**
*Yes, sir. I think maybe I did. I*

He paused, wondering if he dare ask. But if he could just
convince Chet he *knew* all there was to learn here . . . keep
Wesley out of it . . .
> **Want to talk about it?**
*Please, sir.*
> **Whenever you're ready, kid.**
> **You know my number.**
*Thank you.*
> **One more thing.**
> **You remember what Cantrell told you about the 'NetAT's
interest?**

Stephen wasn't certain he wanted to hear this.
*Yes.*
> **True, kid. I guarantee, true.**
> **And you've got at least one top recommendation coming
from this ship.**
> **See you later?**
*Yes, sir. Thank you, sir.*

The entrance request lit over the door.
*Must go. Visitors. Thank you again.*
> **Watch those commas.**

With a warm glow uncomfortably similar to what he'd felt
downworld, Stephen pushed the terminal arm to the side of the
bed and tapped the release.

The young man that looked up from the terminal was like,
yet unlike, the Stephen Ridenour who'd boarded *Cetacean* at

Vandereaux Station. No longer quite so reserved, but no longer the anxious kid he'd been down below either. On the one hand, Loren Cantrell welcomed the return of the 'NetAT representative she needed. On the other, well, she'd miss the kid. . . .

"You're looking quite well this morning, considering. How're you feeling?"

His eyes dropped and he blushed bright red. Perhaps not so composed as she'd thought.

"Like a fool," he said. "Other than that, not bad—considering." He gestured to the bedside AutoMed. "I've sufficient painkillers and growth accelerators to cure an army overnight and have them disgustingly happy in the meantime." He glanced up through his lashes. "Admiral, I'm—"

She anticipated him and overrode. "You've nothing to be sorry for. I owe you one, Stephen. I put you in a Position, and you not only rose to it, you damned near got yourself killed in the process."

"I damned near killed myself, don't you mean?"

She pulled down a hydaway and settled into it, placing her briefcase unobtrusively at her feet. "And I suppose you were also responsible for two broken ribs, several dents in your skull, jamming every gear in your brace and putting cuts and bruises over ninety-five percent of your surface area?"

The blush returned. "No. But I was stupid enough to get caught in the first place." His already low voice dropped, but couldn't hide the tremor. "Admiral, what—what did I say when I was—out of it? I can't remember anything. Did you make a tape? I couldn't find anything on ship's records."

She thought of certain comments a reserved young man wouldn't care to admit to having said, would be embarrassed as hell if he remembered, and lied without qualm. "Don't worry about it. Your instincts are alive and well. You didn't say anything you wouldn't have fully cognizant."

"If only I could be sure . . ." His thin voice faded, the worried look remained. *Open-mouthed under the stuff, wasn't he?* TJ's words, echoing her own thoughts. Perhaps it *wasn't* the rather personal trend of his waking moments Stephen was concerned about.

A tapped signal. The AM trank indicator rose. A wait till the change monitored, then she asked quietly:

"Stephen, what is it you're afraid of? Wouldn't it be easier to clear your conscience than carry this load around with you?"

"I don't . . ." He seemed to concentrate on something very far away. "I d—don't know, admiral. I can't remember. All I ever remember is the fear of revealing what I'm supposed to keep—" His eyes suddenly focussed on her, went wide with some deep fear; shifted to the AutoMed and fear changed to resentment. "That's not fair, admiral."

She masked her frustration. "Just trying to help, son."

"Don't call me that." Bitter. Angry. Tired echo of another time and place.

"Fine. Let's keep to business, then, shall we? I need you to fill in some of the details of what happened in the barn. Why don't you just start from the beginning; we'll go from there."

He seemed willing enough to talk. And overall, a simple enough episode, although she shuddered to think of some of the risks he'd taken without a second thought. Further questioning brought out details of the afternoon and his meeting with Smith.

Only one flagrantly unexplained detail. She waited until he was tiring; too tired to notice the slight rise in the trank. Then:

"How, Stephen? How did you happen to hear Anevai's baiting? Those rooms are very well insulated."

His eyes were drooping. He yawned and lifted a hand wearily to rub his eyes. "The door was propped—" His hand dropped. He stared straight ahead, lids no longer drooping.

"Propped open?" She prodded gently.

A hesitation. A reluctant nod.

"Why, Stephen."

"Because I—" And a blink toward the AutoMed. "What the hell. —Because I'd already intended to leave."

"To meet with Dr. Smith?"

Another nod. Tired eyes flickered toward her— "The message?"

She nodded.

—and closed. "Shit." His head fell back against the pillows.

"Why'd you do it, Stephen?"

He shook his head wearily. "Hell, —excuse me, admiral, but it all seems so incredibly stupid now. —I just didn't know who to believe. Who to trust. You wanted him up here; and I *knew* how Wesley hates being coerced—"

"How do you know, Stephen?"

"Lord, admiral, look at his record. You've met him. And he was frank enough about it at the *Hole*. I thought maybe I could clear some things up on neutral territory, that's all." He looked desperately up at her. "Admiral, what's going to happen to Dr. Smith? What have I done to him? There's nothing in the law to cover what they're doing here—is there?"

"What about your own actions? Your own involvement? Aren't you concerned about how this will reflect on *your* record?"

He shrugged. "Won't much matter, will it?" And before she had time to wonder at his meaning: "What about Dr. Smith? What of Anevai and the others?"

"I told you before, Stephen. There's nothing you can do to hurt these people."

"That's not very precise."

"It'll have to do, Dr. Ridenour."

He swallowed hard and said, "Nigan kept me alive, admiral. I honestly believe he—and Anevai—would have stopped this Nayati if they could."

"And you think that exonerates them of all guilt?"

"I—I suppose not. I just promised—but it *does* make them different, and it seems to me that there's little to gain from arresting either of them."

Promised who? Anevai? Had he kept other 'small details' from her? "As far as that's concerned, who gets arrested for what reason in part depends on you."

"I—I don't understand."

"Are *you* going to press charges? The attack was against a citizen—you, not Alliance Security."

The AutoMed beeped a warning. Stephen's hands were shaking, his face white.

"Stephen? What's wrong? —Stephen!"

*Go ahead, 'Buster-boy, who's going to believe you?*

Press charges? Five years ago, he'd have given anything to be granted that option. Now . . .

. . . now, it wasn't worth it. Not against people he'd never see again. Easiest simply to forget that yesterday ever happened.

"Let them go, admiral," he said, "I'm not pressing charges against anyone."

"You're certain? You realize they will likely be brought up

on other charges anyway. That it's not just the assault on you in question.''

''Don't cloud the important issues, admiral.''

''Meaning you're not?''

''Not—'' The monitors beeped . . . ''Not compared with chaos in the 'Net or—'' . . . and beeped again. *Shut up*. ''—or family devotion.''

She frowned: thought, not anger. He hoped.

Eventually, she leaned over without a word, and picked up the security packet. She was leaving, and he still didn't know—

''—One more thing, admiral.'' His voice was hoarse with fatigue. And at her look: *''Please.''*

''Don't beg, Stephen. *Claim* your right to be heard.''

Another beep from the monitor. Not surprising: his heart missed every third beat. Difficult to believe in rights you'd never had. Unkind of her to extend it when she knew it wasn't so. But if she was offering . . .

''When Anevai came back to the barn after . . . she said something about her brother. . . . That you're holding him prisoner and had . . . had f—fried his brain in an experiment. And that she was supposed to—to t—take care of me or else this Hono-something would suffer. I . . . What was she talking about? Please, admiral, don't l—lie to me. I'm so t—tired of lies and half-truths.''

Her mouth hardened, and she studied the blank wall for several moments before saying slowly, ''Her brother's the one who attacked Buck Buchanan the first day here. He had a bad reaction to Deprivil, that's all. He's better now. We'll probably release him as soon as this situation's resolved.''

''And the hostage part? What happened was *my* fault. Not Anevai's.''

''Hardly your fault when you were deliberately led into a trap. She did, you know. She admits her involvement.''

''. . . Led?'' So he'd been right in the first place. ''Ane-vai . . . ?'' She *had* meant him to follow. Meant this to happen. When he'd remembered her attack on Nayati, he'd hoped . . . ''Oh, God . . .'' His stomach, already queasy with drugs, heaved. The AutoMed beeped and instantly compensated. But forestalling the gag-reflex could not eliminate the sickening train of thought.

"Stephen?"

Had Anevai known about him all along? How could she and still act as she had—before? Had Wesley lied? Did *he* know? Did—did Paul Corlaney? Had they *all* conspired to make him trust them so he wouldn't go to Briggs? Bijan had been right all along: Recons *were* crazy. Maybe living on plants made spacers crazy, too. But what did that make him? Was he—

*"Stephen!"*

His heart jolted as the admiral reached out and grasped his wrist.

"Stephen, listen to me. *Tell* me about Bijan Shapoorian."

He flinched. The AutoMed beeped, fought again to compensate.

He murmured, "What . . . what about him?"

"Do you know who he is?"

He swallowed hard. "Not much to tell. He was one of the student Supervisors in my wing. All of the other students . . . looked up to him. He was . . . very . . . opinionated."

"Beyond that. Do you know *who* he is? Who his mother is?"

He grew confused. He didn't *do* politics, and names confused him under the best of circumstances. "You—you mean the councillor? I don't—"

"His mother is the *leader* of the Separatists. Do you realize what a threat to her you personally represented? Still represent? It's all politics, son, not you. Not you at all."

Threat? Him? To a councillor?

"Are—are you saying that B–Bijan was—told to—by his—*mother? Why?*"

"Come, now, Stephen. To run you out. Make you fail. But you didn't, did you? You succeeded beyond anyone's wildest expectations. So what's she got now to support her anti-Recon claims?"

"Nothing . . . I suppose . . ." But: "If it was simply to drum me out, why did they . . . and why did Anevai . . . ? Oh, God. What am I? What do I do to . . . ?" He closed his eyes, rocked back and forth, trying *anything* to avoid reacting, to avoid giving the damned machine another chance to betray him.

The mattress gave beside him, and Loren's—the *admiral's*—grip slipped from his wrist to his hand. The monitors protested briefly as his heartbeat fluttered.

"Stephen?"

But he couldn't look at her. He kept his face rigidly blank as he looked at their hands, and beyond . . .

The blood rushed from his head, making his ears ring, and the monitored sound a steady warning. He heard the admiral speaking to someone—not himself—heard his name, heard the beep stop, but dismissed it as irrelevant.

Nothing else mattered. Nothing beyond that notebook on her lap.

(*"Mama, can I take my book?"*

(*Mama, looking up from her writing-table. Mad. "Don't stutter! And take whatever you want, Zivon. Just hurry up or we'll miss the shuttle."*

(*Himself, clutching the book. She didn't mean his Specials: his shell-rocks, the little Meesha Papa had carved. If she meant him to take them, she'd have packed them in the suitcase by the door. She meant him to leave them for his Replacement. But he told himself it didn't matter. They were all in his book, even if he couldn't draw very good. Meesha, Papa, the kittens—even Mama, though he could never make her pretty like she really was. But the shells made of stone were in there—fossils, Papa had called them—and maybe at Van'dro they could tell him how to find them on the 'Net. Maybe they'd let him write to Papa and tell him what they were. Maybe . . .*)

"Where . . ." He swallowed, tried again: "Where did you get that?"

"From someone who'd waited years for you to ask about it."

Stephen thought hard. Who . . . ? "Danislav?"

She nodded.

"Have you . . . have you read it?" he asked with a detached, rather morbid curiosity.

She nodded again.

"Oh, —God." He longed to turn away, to hide in the safety of the bed and the pillows. To give in to the chemicals which would bury his senses—

—and should have, by now.

"Damn you . . ." he whispered. Then: *"Damn you! You had them shut it down!"* His voice caught, spiteful of his efforts to control his ragged breathing. "Damn you!"

"Damn me all you want, son," the admiral said evenly. "You're not getting the chance to run this time. I don't know precisely what Bijan Shapoorian said to or about you. I could wish, frankly, that you hadn't quit keeping the diary. You lost something very important the day they attacked you."

"I never said—"

"—You lost the sense of perspective the truth can give. Bijan, like his mother, is an ignorant fool. The truth about you is in that diary, not in his boogie-man tales. Danislav told me to keep that in case you asked for it. Well, I'm not waiting for you to ask. I'm giving it to you now, and it's up to you what you do with it. *I* think you ought to read it. And re-read it until you recall the boy who wrote those words; the boy, his parents and his world. Once you've got that down pat, I'm going to call up the Security files on Rostov-on-Don—yes, son, there are files: SecOne and for good reason—but I'll call up those files and let you read them. It's not precisely legal, but it's a judgment call I'm making and I will pay the consequences, if any. Gladly. Because you *must* understand, Stephen. Because Rostov is—"

"*Admiral, —don't!*" He was frankly terrified: of what she was asking him to do and of the information she was about to reveal. Securitied information it could mean his life to be privvy to, never minding she claimed responsibility. It would still be information in his head. Information he wasn't supposed to have.

"Rostov is dead," she continued firmly.

Dead? What did she mean: dead? Planets didn't die. Weather equipment failed. Biological breakdown sent the planet back to the way it was before.

"A full-scale revolution destroyed everything. Everyone's dead."

Nevyah was dead. Dead was a blackened lump with empty, staring eyes. Dead wasn't blond hair and warm arms and a deep voice that called him 'son.'

". . . reasons for that revolt are still a mystery . . ." She was lying. The people left. Mama and Papa and the Replacement had a life elsewhere; he'd *seen* the letter.

And Memories couldn't die. Wasn't that what Lexi had said? *No matter where you go . . . they're always with you?* ". . . removed entire system from the 'Net while top security teams investigated. . . ." But Cantrell had nothing to gain from lies;

not any more. ". . . more details in those SecFiles. Details you might, with your firsthand experience, help us to understand. Details we must understand soon, because they *might* have bearing on the situation on HuteNamid. But you can only help if you care enough to remember."

He *didn't* want to remember. Hadn't *wanted* to remember for years. Remembering hurt too damn much.

"Do you understand me, Stephen? Do you understand the importance of our mission here—beyond Smith's theory, beyond any records problem, even beyond your position with the 'Net-AT. —On Rostov, *something* drove the peaceful, loving people in your diary to appalling acts. It could be happening here. That's why I'm risking my career giving you those files. That's what *I'm* risking for you and for HuteNamid and for the Alliance. Are you willing to risk your self-induced ignorance?"

Self-induced?

*("Can't I go home? You don't want me here, the others don't. Please, Uncle Vic—"*

*(His head ringing. Picking himself off the floor and pulling himself back into his chair, the stink from Danislav's cigarette choking him.*

*("I told you* never *to call me that!"*

*("Sir." Feeling sullen, angry, but mostly very, very tired. "Please let me write to my father. See if I can't go home—just to work for them. I'm big enough, now, I can—"*

*("You can't."*

*("But, if you authorize—"*

*("My authorization has nothing to do with it. Your parents aren't there anymore."*

*("How . . ."*

*("Rostov's gone off-link. Catastrophic systems failure—"*

*("Are my p–parents dead, sir?"*

*("Don't interrupt! There was no budget to restore, so they shut it down—relocated everyone."*

*("Th–Then, my—my p–parents aren't—"*

*("Stop stuttering! Of course not." A paper thrown across the desk to him: a personal transmit from his father. To Danislav, not to him. Never to him. "They've relocated—started a new life with their* real *son. There's no room in their lives for a bastard now, and they certainly don't want to be reminded*

*of—past indiscretions. So forget home, forget all those stories and get your butt in gear and make something of yourself . . .")*

He'd tried to be good . . . like Mama told him. To make Mama proud of him so she'd let him come back home. Only Mama never knew. She'd sent him away because he was Bad and now she was dead. There was no Mama to go back to. No Papa.

He pulled his hand free, hesitated, then reached for the book. His hands trembled so he could barely hold on to it.

A page fell out, drifted slowly to the bedcovers. He stared at it, at the careful scrawl that once was his. —An appalling sketch of a fossil from all angles and with measurements carefully noted. He'd never found the answer. Had never been able to tell Papa what it was. Now he could find that answer—

—but there was no Papa to tell. Not anymore.

He picked up the page and tucked it into the proper spot with a hand no longer trembling. He clutched the book to his chest, and slowly bent his head over it, a choked swelling in his throat: memory of tears held back years ago and now they would never be shed. There'd been too many shed since and he had none left.

The weight lifted from the side of the bed. A remote corner of awareness registered a touch to his head, his shoulder—a quiet order before the lights dimmed and chemical tranquility began drifting into his body.

He didn't fight. Still cradling the book, he lay back against the pillows and let the chemicals take over entirely.

*"Yes, Paul, what do you want?"*

Bloody little bastard, Paul thought. About time you answered. "Wes? Where the hell have you been? I've been trying to reach you all day. I *needed* you at that meeting, dammit."

*"My business, Corlaney. What do you want?"*

"I've got news for you, but damned if I'll tell you, if you insist on being an ass."

*"If the news is that Stephen's all right—I already know. If it's anything else, at the moment, I don't give a shit. You're not exactly high on my list right now, Paul, and I'm busy. Is that all?"*

"No, it's *not* all!" Paul caught his temper before he threw something hard and damaging at the inoffensive office com.

"The Tribal Council and I would like to know if there's a way to trace precisely what's been transacted via the 'Tap."

*"Yes."*

"So when can we have it?"

*"Oh, I don't know. I'm pretty busy right now. Sometime next year, I suppose. If nothing more important comes up."*

"You—"

*"Of course, if Stephen were here, he could have it for you in . . . ten . . . maybe fifteen minutes. But then, Stephen's not here. —Is he, Paul?"*

"Damn you, Smith."

*"Glad to be of help, Paul. TTFN."*

Cantrell asked without taking her eyes from the window: "Did you get a chance to watch the tape?"

Briggs dropped into the chair beside her and grunted his affirmative. Watched Ridenour reach for the water glass with a shaky hand. Then: "I hope you knew what you were doing, Loren. It's a hell of a time to run experiments on the Council's fair-haired boy."

"Fair-haired boy, my ass. If they cared so much about him, why'd they ever subject him to that— What was I supposed to do, TJ? Let years of psychoses color what happened to him down there? If he's to be of any use to us—any use to *himself*—he's got to put what he's endured into perspective."

"And the Rostov information?" The thought of that conversation on record made him queasy enough. That she would even consider following through . . .

"I told you I might."

"You *said* you might tell him a few facts. Turning him loose with security records is something else altogether."

"If he's ready to hear, I want all the help I can get. If Stephen could help us pin down what happened on Rostov . . . I wonder why no one's tried it before."

"Maybe they have."

She glanced up at him. "Maybe they have. Let's hope we have more luck."

*"—Admiral?"*

Stephen: his query automatically transferred to the observation galley from Cantrell's office. She tapped a transmit clearance.

"Yes, Stephen? Are you ready for those Rostov records?"

The boy twitched. Looked around him nervously. "—*T—thank-you, no. Not yet, anyway.*" Kid was showing more sense than Loren. "*Did you say Anevai Tyeewapi's onboard* Cetacean?"

Loren grunted. Said under her breath, "I should've expected this." To the 'Com: "Yes, Stephen. She is."

Stephen closed the book and held it to his chest, his face thoughtful now.

"*Do you think— Is there any chance you could convince her— Would she be willing to t—talk with me? Af—after what I did?*"

Loren blocked transmit and glanced up at him. "What *he* did. Always his fault, isn't it?" And to the com: "I'm certain we could arrange it." Another glance his way. "She asked earlier to see you."

"*Wh—why?*" Not happy to hear that. Made the kid shifty-eyed nervous.

"To thank you."

Wide-eyed, unfocussed stare. A whispered: "*F—for wh—what?*"

"For keeping your side of the bargain, so she said."

"*Oh,*" he said, and seemed to relax again. "*May I see her?*"

"Are you certain that's what you want?"

Give the kid credit, he didn't answer right away. He at least appeared to reconsider. Then nodded. "*I'm certain, admiral. And I . . . I'd like to know if there's any reason I shouldn't tell her . . . tell her where I . . . what I am.*"

"God!—" It was out before Briggs could stop it. *Sorry*, he mouthed to Loren, but she shrugged and said:

"—I'll have to think about that one, Stephen."

"*Admiral, if I can use it to make her understand—*"

"I'm not saying No outright, boy, but allow me time to con-sider—"

"*What harm could it do if she knows I'm Recon myself? It's certain to become common knowledge soon enough.—Bijan Shapoorian knows, and as soon as it's to his advantage, he'll broadcast it over the 'Net, won't he? So why can't I use it first? For HuteNamid's sake, admiral.*"

"I said I'd think about it, Dr. Ridenour! I'll let you know. Cantrell out!"

The boy signed off quietly and returned to his book.

"Surprisingly calm, isn't he?" Briggs said. "Wonder if he knows something we don't."

"I suspect," she said drily, "he knows he's right and, for some odd reason, he still trusts me to know he knows."

"How's that?"

"It's time to put the cards on the table."

"For God's sake, woman, not *all* the cards!"

"Meaning Rostov?"

"Damn right, I mean Rostov."

"If that boy *mentions* the word Rostov to her, she's away for life, and Stephen Ridenour right along with her."

"You going to tell him so?"

"And *challenge* him to call my bluff? Not bloody likely. Besides, you saw his reaction when I told him the files were SecOne. He won't tell her *anything*."

"You going to okay the visit, then?"

She sat back, steepling her fingertips, tapping the index fingers together. "I don't know, TJ. I really don't know."

A puzzled look crossed the young man's bruised face. He searched through several pages, turned carefully to the very beginning, turning a page at a time, still with that confused look.

Sudden realization. "You didn't give him the translations, did you?"

Loren shrugged. "See if he can read them himself, first. Then, we'll see."

"That's plain cruel, Cantrell."

"Depends on how you look at it."

"And telling him his folks were dead? Does that depend on how you look at it, as well?"

"He'll never know differently."

"Turned psychic, have you? You don't know that, Loren."

She looked squarely at him then. "Kinder than the lie he's been living with for eight years, now."

"What are you talking about?"

Without taking her eyes from the screen, she reached for a file, handed him a single sheet. "I found this in that diary."

It was a copy of a communication to one Victor Danislav . . . From Stefan Ryevanishov.

''Where was it? Why haven't I seen it? Wasn't mentioned in his files.''

''Don't know. This was slipped into the cover of the diary—''

''Into?''

''The seam in the leather cover had been split and this slipped into it. I don't know how the kid got his hands on it. —Read it.''

> **Dear sir:**
>
> Thank you for the update on Stephen's progress. I'm more convinced than ever that we did the right thing in sending him to you.
>
> The rescue lift has been successfully completed. Ylaine and I look forward to our new home with our new son. He's a beautiful boy, Victor, blond hair, dark eyes and bright—very bright. But don't expect to get him away from us, too. He's mine. All mine. You'll have to make do with Stephen.
>
> As for Stephen, let this newest act of God complete the severance between us. Since any further contact might jeopardize his future and gain us nothing, I will not give you our transfer destination and please, sir, do not use your very substantial abilities to deduce that information.
>
> Tell Stephen to be good and follow your wise counsel in all things . . .

''Et cetera, et cetera, et cetera,'' Cantrell finished for him. ''Lying bastard. Stefan Ryevanishov never wrote that letter, and all these years, that boy's had to live with that.''

''So why did *you* lie to him?''

''Because, in a way, Danislav had the right idea. He can never go back there, never find his parents. Kinder by far to make a clean break. Let him get on with his life.''

''Is it?''

As though the boy could sense their conversation, he slipped his fingernail along the inner edge of the leather, looked surprised at the opening, as though he hadn't expected it to be there. He pulled the original out and spread it flat with very shaky fingers.

The bruised mouth began to tremble, and those shaking fingers caressed that lying paper. But the mouth steadied, the fingers did, and then deliberately tore the paper in half.

"Is it kinder, TJ?" Cantrell said. "Absolutely."

# V

The girl looked decidedly nervous. To Cantrell, shepherding Anevai Tyeewapi down the rimway to the lift, this was not a welcome sight. She needed her wits about her, dammit.

Yesterday, Stephen had put his diary aside and gone back to reading journals. He'd not asked again to see Anevai Tyeewapi. Neither had he asked for the files on Rostov. He hadn't said much of anything to anyone. She hoped Anevai's visit would shake him out of that lassitude.

In the lift, the girl pressed into a corner and stood silently, eyes closed, hands gripping the balance bars. They eased to a halt, she got out and waited for Anevai to join her, which she did a deep-shaking breath later and stumbling a bit in the low-G of H3Deck.

"Are you going to be all right?" she asked. Anevai nodded, but: "If you want to call it off, you can. You're not obli—"

"*No*. I—I'd like to see him, admiral. It's just—" The girl looked down at hands that shook, stuffed them into her pockets, and smiled wanly. "We didn't exactly part on the best of terms."

"If you have *any* doubts, get rid of them before you go in there, or don't go in at all. I'll be honest with you—I don't like this. Stephen Ridenour has some real problems, problems he's trying to work through to help you and your people, and he seems to think talking to you is the way to do it."

"Then we both want the same thing and there's no problem, is there?"

"Not necessarily. Handle this wrong, girl, and everyone loses."

"What is it you'd like me to do?"

She smiled. She'd hoped the girl would have the sense to ask. "Two things. First: hear him out—no matter what. That won't be easy: he's not always good at expressing himself. But listen, and I think you'll understand."

"And the other?"

"Don't lie. Whatever else you do, don't lie to him. He's never had a friend that hasn't turned on him—not because of anything he does, but just by being born. But he doesn't realize that. He thinks he makes people hate him and, frankly, he expects it."

"But—"

"I'm not asking you to like him; just listen. *Really* listen. Then if you choose to leave and never see him again, just be honest with him about *why*. If you can't promise me that, girl, you can go back to your quarters right now. On the other hand, give me your word, and I'll trust you to keep it."

Anevai was on her way: the admiral had promised.

Stephen adjusted a pillow under his elbow, then rested both hands on the notebook in his lap, amazed at his own calm.

But for once in his life he knew what he needed to do and he was absolutely certain he could do it. Anevai already hated him; he'd told Cantrell it was one of his 'special talents.' Making Anevai fear him, at least fear what he could *do*, would be as easy: he'd had excellent instruction in that area, too.

Not precisely what Cantrell had hoped for, he was sure, but it was the best he could do with what he was willing to use. The diary she'd based such hopes on had accomplished nothing: he remembered no more about Rostov than before. The memories he did have were nothing remotely like his experiences on Hute Namid: overall, they were memories he was more content without. And for that nothing gained, she'd compromised his freedom with what she'd already handed him without his consent.

Cantrell wanted answers. Had deliberately forced his cooperation when she revealed that information—limited as it was. He *needed* no more.

On the other hand, if Rostov's people *had* died, there was no doubt in his mind what was responsible: bigotry. Bigotry of the sort that had turned Zivon Stefanovich into Stephen Ridenour in far more than just name; bigotry which had its roots in the Council Cantrell represented. That being the case, it served both Cantrell's needs and his to alienate Anevai from him, and send her to *Cantrell* for a solution to HuteNamid's problems.

*His* obligation was to Smith; and he needed Anevai to carry a message to Wesley. Needed to convince Anevai that he understood Wesley's system; that he could counteract any move Wesley made on the 'Net; that he was taking the matter up before the 'NetAT and would use that ability to catapult himself into a position of power from which he would know every move Wesley made on the 'Net. Let her tell Smith as long as he behaved himself, he would be free here on HuteNamid.

He might even be able to pull it off. He knew the games now, the admiral had helped him see that much, though he doubted that had been her goal. If his success threatened Shapoorian, he could use that leverage along with his limited knowledge of Wesley's system to gain the obscurity he desired. It was all in the game, and he'd have no compunction whatsoever about lying, cheating, or manipulating the 'Net, if it meant keeping Wesley free of the Shapoorians and their ilk.

He could see what Cantrell was after. Could even understand, after a fashion, her desire to preserve that which existed on HuteNamid and was willing to help her achieve that end.

Because Wesley was him. Or what Stephen Ridenour should have been. At some base level, their minds worked alike: why else was he the only one to understand Wesley's system? Why else did he feel this unique camaraderie with another individual? Why else did he feel this driving need to protect Wesley?

Because Wesley was no more prepared to play the Council's ugly games than Anevai was. That was *why* God had created so corrupt a being as himself. *He* was totally capable of doing what Wesley was too good to do. *He'd* spent a lifetime learning to play these games. He could do it—

—and do it with no conscience at all.

But only if he was certain Wesley hated and feared him. He'd never carry it off if he thought he'd meet Wesley on the 'Net, or imagined that Wesley might regret his leaving. He didn't *want* Wesley to like him, didn't want the least suspicion that Wesley was his friend. That was a weakness he could in no wise afford.

Which meant—

The entrance request beeped. An image flashed on the monitor. He pushed the button to release the door and said, "Come in, Ms. Tyeewapi."

Anevai looked at the floor, the wall—any place but at him. Not that he cared exactly, but it *was* rather disconcerting to have people look elsewhere because the sight of you made them want to vomit.

"Pretty awful, am I?"

"*No!* Not at all!" She met his eyes at last: brown warmth conjuring a memory sternly suppressed. "It's not that, Ste—Dr. Ridenour. I just feel so . . ." Brown eyes disappeared; a visible shiver touched a part of him he wished dead.

Unfortunately, it wasn't, quite. "A–Anev–ai?" He said the name carefully, needing to get it right, needing—just for a moment—to see those eyes smile. And holding out his hand: "Won't you sit with me awhile? I'm bored silly already, and Dr. McKenna's refusing to let me up for several more days."

She moved over to his bedside, but she didn't smile—"Why? You don't look so bad to me."

—and ignored the hand. It trembled, showing undesirable weakness, and he let it drop back onto the covers. "Tyrannical doctors. I'm feeling better than I have in years and they're saying I'm falling apart at the seams."

Anevai giggled: a sound that sent a warmth through his gut one instant—

She said, "I suppose they could be right. I understand they stuck that arm back on, but I imagine it'll be pretty loose until the glue sets."

—and a chill down his spine the next. No more time to waste.

"How come they're not keeping you tranked? Seems to me they'd let you sleep through all this." She bit her lip. "I'm sorry, Stephen. I've no . . ."

He answered calmly, seeing the first step toward his goal and taking it. "I have a bad reaction to most repressants. Deprivils are virtually useless, and tranquilizers invariably make me physically ill, which require *more* drugs to stabilize the rest of my system."

Intent frown: her response right on cue.

He pursued the subject. "So instead of being sensibly senseless, here I sit, totally useless, increasingl—"

"Stephen Ridenour, you shut up right now! You're not useless."

Right on the itinerary.

Anevai said sternly, "For a smart man, you certainly can be stupid."

Mistake.

He glanced away from her and down at a notebook lying on his lap. His hands trembled noticeably on its disreputable cover. The monitors beeped.

He made them both stop. Step two:

"I'm afraid my intelligence has been . . . somewhat . . . over-rated, Anevai. That's one of the—"

"You sure fooled Wesley, then, Spacer-man. . . ."

Wrong response. Why couldn't the damned girl follow the script?

". . . *He* thinks you're God's own answer to his prayers."

"Yes . . . well . . . that was part of my job here. I was supposed to impress him. I . . . I was to check out *Harmonies* and either link it in with 'Net theory or discredit it altogether."

A sudden sway; an abrupt collapse onto the edge of his bed, one hand to her head. Dismayed, he touched her arm. "Anevai?"

She brushed his hand away, glanced sideways at him and said, "Do you mean to tell me you're nothing but a *Del d'Bug man?*"

He nodded. Her tone held all the contempt he could ask.

So why did it have to hurt so damned much?

"Then what in hell were you doing down at the barn? Why didn't you just tell Nayati *that*, for the gods' sakes?" Laughter that hurt, that he held himself firmly from resenting. "My God, you idiot spacer-man, why let him do this to you? He wouldn't give a *damn* about investigations into Wesley's little computer games!"

He stared at her, shocked that *anyone* could take that *game* of Wesley's lightly. Even an ignorant Recon should know better than that. He said through a constriction in his throat, "Nayati never asked me why I was there. I don't really think he wanted any answers. I—I think I was a convenient way to send a m—message to Adm. Cantrell. S—secondly, if you think W—Wesley's involved in some little g—game, you're in—c—credibly naive. That s—system of his could undermine the 'Net and take the Alliance with it. And th—third—"

This was not going well. His insides were churning, the damned monitor was beeping steadily: its warning bell Cantrell's price for turning its blood chemistry control off. He picked up the diary as something solid and real, and hugged it to his chest, his hands trembling so hard now he could scarcely retain that hold. But he thought of Mama's scolds and forced the stutter away. "I've allowed you to believe another lie, Anevai, and . . ."

He lost it then. He'd kept from saying it, denied it to himself and everyone else for so many years now, the words just wouldn't form.

"Stephen?"

He stared at the bed cover, knowing he was failing utterly at this ultimate test and not knowing how to pull it out. But when she reached for the bedside com, he clasped her wrist and said quietly, "No. Don't. I—I'm quite all right. Besides, there's no need. I suspect we're being watched right now."

She glanced around. "Recorded?"

"Probably."

"Then are you sure you should tell me this deep, dark secret?"

"The admiral gave her permission before she agreed to this meeting."

"Got to get Mama's permission to do everything?"

"Not everything, no." Resentment flared. His breathing rate increased and the monitors beeped a warning. "Anevai, will you please just listen to me? I—I don't know how long I'll last . . ." Yet another beep: more insistent this time.

"Well, what's so effin' important, Spacer-man?" Pushing. Always pushing for straightforward truth. And something in him responded to that, a response he couldn't afford.

"Well, c'mon, Spacer-man. Speak up so I can get the hell out of here."

"Anevai, *please*, don't . . . I—I mean . . . *Dammit, Tyeewapi, don't call me that!*" He made a frustrated sweep with his left arm, sending the notebook flying to the floor, scattering pages all over, as the first real pain he'd felt since waking radiated from his shoulder. He gasped, clutched his arm and fell back into the pillows, eyes clamped tight against the revolving room.

A calm voice issued from the walls: Dr. McKenna. *"Another outburst like that, Ridenour, and we'll put you in a freefall body float for the next week. Understand?"*

He frowned and nodded.

"Stephen, are you okay?" Anevai. With brown-eyed sympathy. He'd see it if he opened his eyes. He squeezed them tighter shut.

The shoulder throbbed. God, how stupid could he be? That damned diary—

—That damned diary held information on who and what he was. That damned diary held top security information. That damned diary was lying open in front of the very person he was trying to get off this ship and down to Wesley—

He dived for it—

"Gods, Ridenour!" Anevai grabbed Stephen, shoved him back up against his pillows, then followed his distraught gaze to the notebook scattered on the floor. She knelt, began gathering the loose pages. Pages full of childish pictures and awkward script.

*"Dammit! Give it to me!"*

She looked up into a white, angry face. Well, that was gratitude for you.

"Here." She slammed the notebook shut, crumpling pages every-which-way, and tossed the lot in his general direction.

A one-handed stop kept it from sliding off the other side of the bed, and steadied it on his lap. Then began a page by loose page check, his fingers smoothing each sheet carefully before slipping it into place.

She headed for the door in disgust. Stephen Ridenour had problems, no doubt about it, but Anevai Tyeewapi wasn't the one to fix them. She hit the release on the door. —Nothing. Slammed it with her fist. —Still nothing.

Evidently Adm. Cantrell did not share her opinion. She scanned the room again, remembering a promise made: *Hear him out . . .*

Evidently, Ridenour wasn't through talking yet.

She looked back. "Stephen?"

He continued collating.

"Stephen?" She tried again, a bit louder this time, but still he didn't answer. Order restored, he worked his way under the covers and turned on his side, that stupid notebook tucked in with him.

The tode probably figured she'd try to steal it.

She walked back to the bed and sat on the edge, deliberately staying at his back. If he was so anxious to talk, he could damn well trouble himself to turn over.

"Stephen?" She reached out, touched his shoulder. Tense. Hard as stone. She tried to pull him over. "Stephen?"

He jerked away. She folded her hands in her lap, wondering how to undo—whatever it was she'd done; unsay—whatever she'd said. *Handle this wrong, girl, and everyone loses.*

"Stephen, I'm sorry. I truly am." And a bit sourly, under her breath: "Whatever it was I did."

A breath: long drawn and shaky. Finally, he muttered, "God, Anevai, go away. Just leave me alone, can't you?"

"No, Stephen, I can't. I promised Cantrell I'd hear you out."

His head flew up at that, though he still didn't face her. "*God dammit! She had no right!* She had—no—" His voice caught on something very like a sob and he whispered, "Dammit, get out of here!"

He settled his head on the pillow again.

"Stephen?" He *was* hurt. "Please, Stephen, you're making me feel like a scuz. Granted, I may be, but won't you let me—"

"C–consider yourself—absolved. I've—said all I had to say." His breath caught again. "Please, just *go!*"

She stared at that obstinate back, her gut twisting inside her, wondering what she should do. Hono, Nayati, Wesley: all the young men she'd ever dealt with were so simple: if they were depressed, you listened; if they were out of line, you bashed them; if they were sad or lonely, you hugged them.

Then she remembered Stephen in the bar. At dinner. By the fire. Could he really be all that different? What had he said? *Where I've been five* hours *would have left me so far behind I'd never have caught up.* And he'd been in that place since he was a child. Had he ever had *anyone* to listen to him? to bash him?

He'd never held a cat. Had anyone ever held *him?*

She reached out and touched his head. The monitors protested wildly, but not a sound escaped him. He reminded her of nothing quite so much as Bego when, with escape impossible, he stood stiff-legged and trembling beneath her hands. Worse, far worse than he'd been when she first arrived. Then he'd been aloof. Now he was just plain scared, and, after what Nayati had done to him, after what she herself had done, she couldn't blame him.

She gently stroked his hair and along his back to his shoulder. The shudder gave way to steady tremors, and she let her hand rest quietly until the monitor's warning stopped, then added a light but insistent pressure.

"C'mon, Spacer-man,—"

"D–Dammit, don't—" A choked bark of bitter laughter. "Go'way, 'b–'buster."

Suddenly, remembering what that choked laughter disguised, she knew. Suddenly, a whole lot of crazy made sense. *Don't call me that!* How many times had she heard that and dismissed it as anger the way she felt about his calling her 'buster—

——Pictures: fourlegged critturs. Script: awkward handwriting? Or nonstandard alphabet?

Cantrell had said . . . *listen and you'll understand.*

She hoped she'd finally heard.

She eased the pressure on his shoulder, patted it gently, then let her hand rest there: simple, undemanding, human contact.

"Stephen, you don't have to talk; just listen. I think maybe I've been assuming some things that just aren't so. I think maybe this wasn't your first time downworld—just the first time in a long time. I think maybe I've said and done some things that have hurt you very much. I think maybe a lot of other people have done the same thing. Some maybe even meant to hurt you. But I didn't, Stephen. I didn't *mean* to hurt you—not even when I thought you were a spacer. Not even when I thought you were a spacer-spy. But you aren't, are you, Stephen? You know what I think? I think you aren't spacer. I think you're Recon—just like me."

# vi

"TJ?"

*"Here, Admiral."*

"Are they *still* at it?"

*"Yessir."*

"Stephen behaving himself?"

A long hesitation.

*"Yessir."*

"Something you want to say?"

*"Nossir."*

All right, TJ, have it your way. "Call me when they break it up; I've some details in those Tunican records I need to discuss with you."

*"Yessir."*

Cantrell flipped the com off. She had a dozen-and-one odd jobs and trivial shipboard problems before her, all of which required attention before she went back downworld. Problems she could resolve in less than an hour—

——if two lousy kids would just go to sleep.

\* \* \*

"Wait a minute, Stephen. What are you talking about?"

He blinked at her as visions faded into the present. "Sorry," he said, "Sometimes I forget . . . Gymnastics. Fifth gravity level?"

"Oh. I know a little about that: I've seen the 'Net coverage. I always thought ZeroG would be fun to try."

He smiled hesitantly. Perhaps he could share something *good* of his world as well. "Stick around awhile, and—and as soon as they let me out of here, I—I could take you there. Show you some . . ."

"They have one on this ship?"

He nodded. "Of course. ZG's mostly for EVA training and such, but they've got some of the equipment." And remembering a day not so long ago, "*Excellent* equipment."

She smiled obligingly, but when she spoke, her voice held little or no enthusiasm. "That'd be fun, Stephen, but you said you were at fifth? Were you any good?"

So much for sharing. "I—" His thoughts drifted. "I'd just been designated Vandereaux system's fifth level all-around when this challenge came up and—"

A hand touched his arm, shocking him back to *Cetacean's* sick bay, and brown eyes brimming with unshed tears.

"Gods, Stephen. That was you?"

*NewsVids.* Sometimes, he truly hated the 'Net.

"Shit. Anevai, I didn't mean to drag all this up. It's ancient—"

Her fingers closed around his and squeezed. "If you stop now, Stephen Ridenour, I'll pull your plugs and you'll deflate all over the room like a balloon."

He shrugged, strove to match her humor with nonchalance. "As you've guessed, all did not go well. The idea was to add this move to my routine for my first inter-system meet." He dropped his eyes, not wanting to face her. "Unlike the VRDs, I did *not* complete the maneuver on my first try and did not make history by being the first to use the move in competition. I blew it—royally—and a lot else. I'd been watching the tapes from second level and didn't adjust my timing adequately for the gravity change: got up too much speed. I—missed the final catch—tried to break my momentum on the side oval—that's when the shoulder got it. It wouldn't have been so bad, but the three who were supposed to be spotting me—"

"Spotting . . . ?" She seemed to grapple with the term, then: "Oh, my God . . ."

He shrugged a second time. "It was rather, uh, messy—and put me permanently out of competition. I still work out some, but it's not . . ." Stephen swallowed hard, remembering the hospital . . . Coach Devon's visit . . .

*("Dammit, boy, how could you? After all the warnings—"*

*(Himself, thinking the drugs were confusing him, keeping him from understanding. "H–How c–could I what, s–sir? Wh–What did I—"*

*("Sir? What happened to Dev? Or isn't that good enough for the Star Image? You too good for us all? Too good to use spotters trying a new move? God-damned irresponsible—" Devon turning an angry face to him. "Have you any idea where this leaves the team? Trev can no more replace you than—"*

*("But—" He couldn't think straight, couldn't be hearing right.*

*("Well, your 'too good' has ruined any Olympic hopes you had, boy. You'll be lucky to walk again, let alone fly.")*

That had been the first he'd heard of the extent of the damage. Of course, walking was never an issue—that was basic health care. Surgery, had it been required, would have been covered. A shoulder replacement? To create a gymnast who could never compete? What had truth mattered, after that?

Dev had finally sat down and asked, in the old way, What the hell went wrong—as if it had been another miscalculated landing.

He remembered staring at the foot of the bed, the pattern of the blanket's folds more real than his Coach. Remembered every detail. A shout—real or in his head, he didn't know; the sudden realization he was off-vector; the looks on the faces of his would-be spotters—

—They were laughing; as his shoulder snapped, as his back struck the side bar and—

"What did you tell him, Stephen?"

"I told him I blew it, just like he said. That I was arrogant enough to think I could do it."

*"Why?"*

"Why not?"

"They could have killed you, bit-brain!"

He almost laughed at that. "If not then, some other time.

Can't you see, Anevai? They didn't *want* a Recon representing Vandereaux. Eventually, that truth would have come out. Important people were following my—career. They couldn't afford to let me stay active in the sport.''

''Oh, gods, Stephen, how could anyone even consider . . .''

He laughed shortly. ''You know, it's actually rather funny. All those years, I told Danislav I was limping around because of falls in the GPlus gym, and he never . . .''

After a moment, Anevai said, ''Gods, Ridenour, don't you *ever* finish a thought? *Why* did you lie? Why not rat on the rats?''

He shrugged and looked away. His throat constricted. He coughed, sensed unnatural relief of that irritation and realized they'd reinstated the AutoMed, decided it didn't matter, not even if they tranked him. What difference could it make? He'd already revealed more to Anevai than he'd ever have believed possible.

A glass touched his hand. He accepted the water and sipped slowly, thankful for the reprieve. His hand shook with fatigue, spilling water onto the covers. He steadied it with his left hand, sipped again, then closed his eyes and tilted his head back against the pillows, while the water seeped down his throat. ''God, I hate those tubes. You'd think . . . they could invent . . .''

He felt the glass tip too late to stop it. Sensed Anevai's reflexive save and jerked awake. ''Sorry,'' he muttered.

''No problem.'' She set the glass within easy reach, then rose to her feet. ''Stephen, I'd better let you sleep awhile.''

*''No!''* It was out before he could stop it. He couldn't have made his point yet, couldn't remember what that point was. Important. He *knew* it was important. ''Please, Anevai, don't go yet!''

''Good grief, Ridenour, I can come back, can't I?''

''I— Maybe. I honestly don't know.'' He bit his lip, then said, ''Never mind.''

He'd done all he could. He held out a hand. ''Goodbye, Ms. Tyeewapi. Thank you for your—'' Another damned cough. ''—patience.''

She looked at him, at the door, the bedside clock, then: *''Dammit!''* Ignoring his hand, she sat down on the edge of the bed. ''Hey, man, I'll stay as long as you want, okay?''

He didn't answer; the point was lost without a new one to take its place. He reached for the glass again: an excuse not to look at her. Running his finger around the rim, he said, ''I wonder if we could bring some of your water up from Tunica. It tastes so—"

"*Stephen!*"

He looked up at her through his eyelashes. She frowned at him and he felt his mouth twitch to a rueful smile.

"All right, Tyeewapi. You win. I didn't say anything because of Bijan."

"Not him again. How could you let him get his bluff in on you that way?"

"It was no bluff, Anevai." He coughed. His throat was sore, his head hurt from too damn much talking. Too damn much runaway emotion. "I think I knew even at ten that he could do pretty much whatever he wanted and get away with it. No one in that place would chastise Councillor Shapoorian's son. And Bijan told me—he said they wouldn't believe me—that I was at the academy only as a favor to Danislav and if I complained, they would send me back to a Recon world."

"What's so bad about that?" she asked.

His eyes dropped to the diary, knowing there was no way to answer that without sounding the fool, but seeing no way around the question. "He—he said they wouldn't send me to—home, but to another—settlement where they'd beat me or sacrif–f—" He couldn't finish that one. It was too stupid.

Now.

"And you *believed that?*"

"Bijan—took things he'd read and twisted them. Turned them into orgies and sacrifices . . ."

"But—shit, Ridenour, you're anything but stupid. There *must* have been something else—"

"There were nightmares."

(*Crawling under the fence, using the bushes for cover. In the distant pen, obatsi milling. There—that was Miloshi. Papa had lied.*

(*Darting through the brush. A window—*)

He clenched his arms around the diary and rocked back and forth, staring straight into the past. "There were screams . . . blood flying everywhere and—and something being held down on a table, kicking—and screaming—and . . ." He looked at her defiantly. "I could *remember* that."

She eyed him narrowly. "And can you remember *where* this

sacrifice took place? Are you *sure* it wasn't some kind of animal?"

"Well, yes, it was." But:

*(His inarticulate screams joining the creature's. His fists beating a protest on Papa's shoulder. And Papa saying: "It's God's purpose for him, Zivon. We overlooked him last year, but the herd's too small and he's no good for breeding . . .)*

"I know—now," he said, embarrassed and still, even after all these years, shaken. "It's all written in the book. I snuck into the slaughterhouse one day—caught hell for it, too—and something went wrong. At least, that's what Pa—m—my father told me after it was all cleaned up and I quit screeching. But at the time, in such contrast to the station life, it—it seemed . . ."

His throat constricted. Too many years. Too many drugs and tests and orders. Too much of Bijan's brand of terrorism. All he'd remembered was that Miloshi was his friend and that his Papa and the others had cut him into little pieces for stew.

She shook her head, justifiably bewildered. "That's plain nuts, Ridenour. You're crazy—VOSsed for sure."

She didn't mean it literally. He knew that, and yet . . .

And yet, he hadn't touched anything like stew in twelve years. Even the thought made the AutoMed beep a protest and pump neutralizers into his stomach.

He stared at the covers, shivering, seeing a fuzzy black face and curly grey mane . . . and cold staring, sightless eyes, and finally said, mostly to himself, "That's . . . what I'm afraid of."

Anevai's hand sought his, pulled it away from the notebook, tightening when he failed to respond. "Stephen, I don't mean that. You're *not* crazy. Not now. For all I know, you might have been once, but you're not now. Hear me?"

His focus drifted up to her face, and she repeated firmly, "*Hear me, Ridenour?* You're not crazy!"

His mouth twitched again. This time, he wasn't sure why. "I—I hear, you, Tyeewapi."

Cantrell leaned back from her desk and stretched, glanced at the time. 3010 in the goddamn morning and those two were still at it.

She tapped her personal.

"Teej?"

A pause: *"Yes, Boss-lady?"*

"Any end in sight?"

Another pause: *"Can't see how they can go much longer. Two tired kids, Loren."*

"Yeah, well. Forget the meeting. It'll wait for morning. Go on to bed when they're through."

A *third* pause.

*"Thanks, Boss, but I don't think I'd better."*

Lord, she was too tired for riddles.

"Don't think you'd better *what?*"

*"Go to bed."*

There was something in his voice that came through—something about having one of these things in your head for years made you able to tell. She tried not to anticipate:

"Important?"

*"I—think so, Loren. Enough I don't think it should wait till morning. I might lose the thread."*

"Good enough. Call me when they're through."

*"Sorry, Boss-lady."*

"Yeah. Right."

A choked breath escaped from the pile on the bed. Anevai hesitated at the door, turned back uncertainly. Damn. *God's retribution* . . . No god would warp a whole life that way.

What sort of people gave their children so frightening a heritage?

She headed back for the bed. She didn't care what he'd said, she wasn't leaving yet. Stephen was curled around a pillow, eyes open and staring at the wall. She reached out to him, then pulled the hand back uncertainly. Every time she touched him, he flinched away.

Spook-eyes flicked, followed that movement, slid up over her face and circled back to the wall inches from his nose. A breathy excuse for a chuckle reached her. "You too, Tyeewapi? Always wondered what it was about me. Funny, I thought it was the fact I was Recon. . . ." The whisper faded away into silence. What the hell was he talking about?

"Ridenour?" She made his name a demand for his attention, not allowing him to wallow in whatever bog of self-pity he was mired. Spook-eyes drifted listlessly around to her again. "What was that all about?"

A shrug; an equally listless drift back to the textured wall.

"Dammit, Ridenour, *look at me!*" She grabbed his shoulder and pulled him around. He gasped and twisted away. "Shit," she said and released him, afraid she'd hurt the shoulder. "I'm sorry, Ridenour."

The bitter look focussed squarely on her now. His voice, when he spoke, was harsh with a confused mixture of emotions. "For what? Touching me? Sorry if I—soiled your hands."

"Is that what this is all about?" His loud silence provided answer enough. "Well, you've certainly wasted a great deal of energy, haven't you? If I had a problem with getting my hands dirty, I wouldn't touch Bego, now would I?" No change in the pale, stubborn face. "Dammit, Ridenour, *say* something!"

"Funny how there's always a—good reason. Thanks for not hurting me, Tyeewapi. Now, would you mind getting out of here?"

"As a matter of fact, I would."

"Well, do it anyway. Good-night." Nose back to the wall. Right back where they'd been when she'd first come in the room. Then she thought of what he'd said. A guardian who denied their kinship, classmates who hated him, his earlier fear her touch would somehow contaminate him . . .

The other students left the academy on holidays; Stephen had extra classes. The other students partied on Vandereaux Station on weekends; Stephen studied. Day in and day out. Yet he spoke of that situation without bitterness, without rancor. It was simply the way his world was ordered.

And he believed, somehow, it was the life he had earned: if he'd worked harder, been smarter, he wouldn't have had to do the extra work. He actually believed that if he'd done well enough to earn vacations, his so-called sponsor, Danislav, would have taken him into his home, made him a part of his family. He couldn't see that Danislav ignored him because he was too hot to invite into his home: he would *sponsor* a Recon boy in the academy, but he wasn't about to give him a home.

*Sorry if I soiled your hands.* "Gods, Ridenour," she murmured. He didn't twitch, the monitor didn't beep, not even when she put her hands on his shoulders and pulled him up into her arms.

He came easily enough, but didn't respond, not even when she wrapped her arms around him and pressed her cheek against the top of his head as it rested unresisting against her neck. She refused to be discouraged. Refused to explain her actions and convince him of her sincerity. He either believed her or he did not.

An eternity later, a hand crept around her waist, another joining it when she didn't object. A single, tiny shuddering breath was the only sound he made. He relaxed against her, his light hold slowly closing. It never achieved what she would term a decent hug, but it was a start. She stroked her fingers gently over his sweaty hair; he murmured something about smell and tried to pull away. She tightened her hold and said in his ear, "Shut up and deBoot, Ridenour."

A long time later, Stephen's arms tightened and he stirred restlessly. She winced and gently extricated herself from his grasp. His eyes, red-rimmed and puffy, blinked open. He murmured something unintelligible and reached for her hand again. She stopped him with a touch on his wrist and stood up. "Time for both of us to get some real sleep, Stephen."

He appeared disoriented, time slipping sideways on him as it had more than once in the past hours. He caught her wrist. "B—back—later?"

"You betcha, kiddo."

His teeth closed on a trembling lower lip. It would do him good to cry, and cry hard. But he didn't. The lip stopped trembling; his grip relaxed, slipped away, and she headed for the door.

"Anevai?"

She turned back, met eyes working to stay open as he struggled to say something. Finally, eyes dropped and he murmured, "Just, . . . thank you."

She waited for him to look at her. When she had his attention, she smiled and said, "That's what *friends* are for, Stevie-lad. G'night."

"G'night." He echoed. And on a whispered breath as the door slid closed behind her: "F—friend."

# vii

*"Admiral?"*

Who—? She tapped the 'Com ID: *Anevai Tyeewapi!*

"Yes, Anevai?"

*"Admiral, may I come see you—right now? I realize it's late, but—it—it's important."*

Fatigue waged a quick, highly unsuccessful battle with curiosity.

"Of course, Anevai. I'll send Briggs to escort you here. You're calling from . . ." She checked the readout. ". . . just outside Stephen's room?"

*"Yes, ma'am."*

"Well, stay there. He won't be long."

She cut to the central 'Com and flagged TJ.

*"She just left, admiral."*

"I know. Bring her here, will you?"

*"Sure 'nuff."* An audible yawn from his end. *"You want me to listen in? or take off and come back later?"*

"Listen in."

*"Right, Boss-lady."*


"What are you saying, Anevai?" Following stream-of-consciousness from a mind as tired as her own and far less orderly than her own was difficult under the best of circumstances. Conditions, Cantrell thought wearily, were far from optimal. "You think Stephen should talk to your father? If so—"

"No! Not at all. Stephen wouldn't—couldn't. But—he said you were taping us and now I'm glad you did. I think you should make my father watch it—and Paul and Wesley. *Make* them understand—we've got to work with you in this."

Cantrell shook herself awake. The girl had come to sense—a great deal of sense. "In what, Anevai?"

"I can't answer that. I will say, HuteNamid has more than an extremely rich environment, but the *sociological impact* of some of our projects could be far more destructive than anything Dr. Paul worked on before he came. If the Council could keep *his* work off the 'Net while the sociologists did their impact studies . . ."

"What are you talking about?"

"You know, admiral. The longevity virus. The Council shut that project off—"

She hadn't known. "If HuteNamid's projects warrant it, I *will* work for the isolation you all seem to want—and my influence isn't small in such matters. But I can't make that judgment until I know what those projects are, can I?"

"That's why you've got to show dad that tape—you've got to convince him not to try to convince the Council alone. That—that a Recon *can't*. That chaos in the 'Net is *not* the answer. Please, admiral."

"I can't promise anything, Anevai, but I'll view that tape. I'll do what I can."

The 'Com blinked.

*"Sorry if I'm interrupting, Boss-lady, but are you free yet?"*

*Not* like TJ to get pushy. She threw Anevai a questioning look.

The girl said quietly, "That's all I had to say, admiral."

"Anytime, Teej."

"If that's all, admiral," Anevai said, starting toward the door.

Cantrell nodded. "Good night, Anevai. And don't worry overmuch. Any father responsible for what you are, I can work with."

"Good night, admiral." At the door she paused, brushed a hand through her hair. She muttered, "I must be . . ." And Cantrell wasn't surprised when the girl turned back: the girl made a habit of second—and third and fourth—thoughts. "Admiral, will you swear to me you used nothing but Dep on my brother?"

*That* surprised her. "I won't *swear* to anything, girl! But, as a matter of medical record—you can look it up—no."

She thought for a moment the girl was about to say something else, but the door opened and TJ entered. Anevai nodded good night to them both and left before the door slid shut.

"So all the HuteNamid researchers received direct communiques from Sakiimagan immediately prior to requesting transfers?"

"So it would appear, admiral. —Scuze me." TJ reached past her, swung the keydrawer to face him and pulled up a file. "That'll give you everything I found—dates, names—personal letters: Sakiimagan's to local IndiCorps reps, generally within a month of transfers being filed."

"None of the letters? Any proof they were directed to the researchers?"

"None other than coincidence. But I don't believe in coincidence on this scale."

She thought a moment. "Where was Paul when he received his?"

"That's a cute one. He was hopping at the time—all over the galactic map. My guess is at least one letter chased him through three different 'Tanks before it finally caught up with him."

"How do you figure?"

"Once you know what to look for—" He clicked on a file, then sat back to watch her reaction.

"Shit. —Rostov?"

"You've got it."

"Who was his contact there?"

He tilted his head at her expectantly. She didn't even bother to check the file. "Stefan Ryevanishov."

He nodded.

"Good God. What was he doing there? Why haven't we known before now he was working—"

"Because he wasn't. He wasn't there officially. Claims he was visiting relatives." TJ shrugged at her look. "Hey, I just report the official record. *I* don't know why he was there. Why don't you ask him?"

"I intend to do just that, soon as we finish up here." She sat back and folded her arms. "Looks like Stephen Ridenour isn't our only source for—" She broke off, staring at the screen.

"Loren?"

Her eyes flicked toward him. "Anevai Tyeewapi's calling." She flipped the com on. "Yes, Anevai. What is it that couldn't wait till morning?"

The girl appeared on the screen, apparently ready for bed. TJ said *sotto voce*, "Much as I appreciate the view, admiral, do you think we should tell her the vid's on?"

Anevai evidently heard him, blushed, though not overmuch, and grabbed a towel from the floor. *"Sorry."* Said with a grin which rapidly sobered. *"I'm sorry to interrupt you, admiral, but it's been bothering me since I left and I don't think—"*

"What *is* it, Anevai?"

*"I was just wondering if it would be possible—I know it's asking a lot, so please don't be—"*

"What do you want, girl?"

"*You said you gave my brother nothing unusual—that his reaction was unusual.*"

"That's right."

Her young face assumed a very mature determination. "*Then may I see him? —Please, admiral. Not this minute, but before you go to my father. It's* important!"

Good—God. What would the girl ask for next?

"Hono? Can you hear me, brother?"

No answer. Not even so much as a flicker of recognition. Anevai looked toward the door where the admiral stood watching, and hoped for reassurance.

"I can't tell you," Cantrell said, with no sign of remorse in her tone or expression. "Sometimes he talks and acts quite normally. Sometimes—he's as you see."

She turned back to her brother, gripped both his hands until her knuckles turned white. Using her best imitation of their father: "Hononomii Tyeewapi, you answer me! This is Anevai. I'm your sister, and if you don't pay attention, I'll kick your butt all the way home!" Beyond Hono's broad shoulder, she saw the admiral exchange surprised glances with Briggs and Fonteccio, but she continued in the same tone. "You know I can, brother; you might be older than I am, but you're not half as mean. *Now talk to me, dammit!*"

A flicker of an eyelid. Hono's brown eyes met hers. An endless instant later: "Anevai? Annie, is that really you?"

She hated that name. *Hated* it. But it was the sweetest sound she'd ever heard.

"Yes, Hono." Her voice broke. She steadied it, released his hands to grasp his shoulders. "It's me, brother. It's really me."

His sudden lunge nearly got him killed: Briggs' weapon was out before she yelled: "It's all right!" She wrapped her arms around Hono. He hugged her as he never had before, hugged her till she feared for her ribs. But she relished the pain the way she relished the hated nickname. While Hono might not be well, he *was* at home upstairs.

But *something* was locking him in. If she could only—

She pulled back far enough to watch his face. Getting a fistful of hair in each hand, she forced his attention.

"Hono, what happened? Are you okay?"

"I—" Desperation in his eyes, in the fierce grip on her arms. Something he wanted to say and couldn't. His eyes began to drift, his head to sway. She let him go on for several moments, then asked, speaking in the old tongue:

"Hono, where are you? What's happening?"

A slow smile. "Flying." Lips barely moved, forming ancient Athabascan words. "Flying with my Cocheta. On and on and . . . Gods, Anevai, it's beautiful, so very beautiful."

A chill down her spine. "Why, Hono? Why are you flying with your Cocheta?"

"Because Nayati told me to. Sister, it's to protect all of us, don't you understand?" A pause, then: "What are you doing here? Are we still on the starship? Sister, go to him before you reveal our secrets. Go!" He pushed at her, making her stagger. "Go! *Go!* Go to him so he can protect you! Protect your Cocheta!"

She backed away, anger dispelling the chill: anger at Nayati for what he'd done to Hono, anger at her brother for letting him do it; anger at her father for treating her warnings with ridicule.

She paused face to face with Cantrell and said, without hesitation, certainly without lingering doubts, "I still believe it would be best for you to deal with my father. Tell my father I'm done with his leadership if he doesn't act now. Tell him Nayati *is* responsible for Hononomii's condition. Tell him that comes directly from his *son*, not his—*impressionable young daughter*. You tell him that *his son* told me to go to Nayati, not *for* protection, but to *get* protection—for me *and my Cocheta*. You tell him—remember what I said about Nayati's balance. Tell him Nayati has disobeyed him in the Libraries just like he did with the 'Net. And finally, tell him either *he* deals with you, or *I* will. Nayati's gone crazy and I'm not having my home, my people, and my friends destroyed by some eons-dead *lunatic!*"

Cantrell leaned back against the door frame, her arms folded across her chest, and said calmly, "Why don't *you* tell him?"

# viii

"Gentlemen, I've brought you here to view a tape. Before you ask, it has been edited, but an edit for the sake of efficiency, not deception.'' Cantrell slipped the tape into the slot built into the Science Complex conference table. "If you wish to view it in its entirety, I might be willing to make it available—under certain conditions.''

"Loren," Paul broke in. "For heaven's sake, cut the theatrics. What's this all about? I thought—"

"Bear with me, Paul."

*Eons-dead lunatic, the Tyeewapi girl had said. And her brother is 'flying with his Cocheta.' More of Nayati's 'code words,' Paul? Or something more you're not telling me?*

"How is he, admiral?" Smith asked, his eyes anxious. "Is he really going to be all right?"

At least one of the three cared enough to ask.

"I won't lie to you, Dr. Smith, it was close. *Very* close. But, yes, Stephen's quite well, considering. —You'll see for yourself in a moment. —Unless there's something you'd like to add?" She looked at Paul and Sakiimagan, but neither spoke.

*And what of you, Sakiimagan Tyeewapi? What is this Library your nephew has been playing games in that is as significant to your daughter as the 'Net?*

Somehow, she didn't think it was the Tunica public.

*Do you care?*

She started the tape.

Anevai lifted the cover off the dice. A pair of fives. She looked up and shrugged an apology, "Sorry, Stevie-lad."

"*N* . . ." Stephen hiccuped. "Scuze me. . . . Not again! 'S not fair! There's—a s–s–syz–zz–iss–tm. *Know* there is."

Stephen's voice was bright and energetic, if occasionally interrupted.

It really *wasn't* fair, though not the 'it' His Royally Drunken Nibs meant. Here she was, virtually sleepless for days because of him, struggling to stay awake and concentrate on this dumb game, and he had the nerve to complain about her winning.

He could at least have the decency to be humanly asleep at this late hour. But no. Nothing would do but that he learn Truthercon and nothing would do but that he learn to play it *now*.

Why had she ever mentioned the stupid game?

All day yesterday working with Cantrell editing that tape. Too hyped last night to sleep. After a morning spent with a restless and irritable Stephen, Anevai had convinced Dr. McKenna to let his nibs out before he unplugged himself and walked. At least this way (she'd argued) Dr. Mo was able to lay down the ground rules of his release.

Two of which he'd already broken.

She'd done all she could for everyone involved and now all she wanted was to go to bed and sleep for a week. Not so Stephen Ridenour. *He* was wide awake. *He* was bored.

And so here they were, in his personal quarters, playing a dice game as old as mankind and alcohol, and with as many names as there were civilizations to play it. And she suspected that here they would remain until he won a game. She considered throwing a game, but he was just sober enough he might catch on, and that would start a whole new argument.

She yawned widely, and leaned her head on her hand. "C'mon, Ridenour, I'm wiped, and *you* weren't supposed to have any alcohol, you know you weren't! I let you talk me into this, but it's gone on long enough. I don't want Dr. Mo coming after me in the morning."

He reached across the little lap table they'd been playing on and laid a hand lightly on her wrist, saying contritely, "I'm sorry, An–nen,"—hic—"An–nen–en—hell—*Nev-ya*. I d–don' wan' you t'get inta t–trouble."

He leaned forward conspiratorially, tilting the table, scattering the dice. "I won' tell Mo. 'M okay. Truth—ly. Jus' need more *vot'er*. You ge' me some? Then go t'bed. I be f–"—hic—"fine."

She grabbed his chin, forced him to look straight at her. After a bit of wandering, his eyes focussed on hers and a rather silly grin split his face.

"Gods!" she muttered to herself. *He* was beyond understanding. "Dr. McKenna'll have my hide for sure."

"Nope," he said, shaking his head. Then: "O–o–ohgod. M–mistake." He raised a hand to his head and collapsed into the pillows piled at his back. Dislodged dice bounced off the floor in tiny thuds. "Oops." He leaned over the edge of the bed to pick them up.

"*Stephen!* Good grief, man." She jumped to her feet and caught him before he fell on his head.

She heaved him back up into the pillows. He tilted his head back, grinned at her, and (fair imitation of the indomitable Wesley) said, "Hi there. New in town?"

She plopped him down.

"Heaven save us, you're infected, Spacer-man." His face fell. She immediately added, "And that makes you the nicest Indi-Spacer-man I've ever met. But now, it's time for this pumpkin to return to its patch."

"Wha'ssa pum—umkin?" he asked.

"What I'll turn into if I don't get to bed."

She leaned over to kiss the top of his head: if he insisted on acting like a kid, she'd treat him like one. Caught off guard or in that personal time warp of old instincts—he jerked aside, head thrown back, eyes wild.

"Well, if you insist—" she murmured and lightly brushed his lips instead—

—and discovered she liked it—particularly when his startled jolt failed to knock her teeth out and he actually tilted his head, the better to accommodate her and not like a child. Not at *all* like a child.

A long moment later, she drew away. He was staring straight ahead, the tip of his tongue tracing his lips. He blinked. Looked up at her and blinked again. Lips still slightly parted.

His wide-eyed stare followed her as she edged toward the door. "I knew we'd cure you . . ." She reached behind her to tap the door release. "I—I just didn't think . . . it would be . . ." Her own breathing was none too steady.

She said in a rush, "—G'night, Stephen."

And was out the door and down the corridor before he could say a word.

His mouth was hanging open like a witless fool's: so he closed it.

What in hell . . . ? His hands were shaking, for God's sake! *This is ridiculous. You'd think I never . . .*

He chuckled ruefully, eventually laughing outright, relaxing weakly into the pillows.

The fact was he *hadn't*. Not like that, anyway.

He ought to call her. But he was afraid he would make a fool of himself all over again. He pulled the keyboard off the desk and balanced it on his knees. After three abortive hand positions, (not as sober as he thought) and six attempts to spell *confrere* (He wasn't about to give in and use the 'Checker.) he typed:

*Thanks for the game, confrere, but you left without
explaining your last throw. Was that payment Truth?
or Consequence? Either way, I think I finally won a
round.*
*Till tomorrow, sleep well.*
*Soberly yours: SR.*

Or had he? Somewhere, his plans had gone dreadfully awry.
Somehow, instead of Anevai going back home and warning
Smith, while he and Cantrell returned to Vandereaux, the admiral
was downworld again, and he and Anevai were playing strange
games of chance in his old quarters aboard *Cetacean*, with no
mention of going back to Wesley.

He might have guessed Anevai Tyeewapi would make her
own set of rules. Like she had in this Truthercon. She *couldn't*
have been playing the same game she'd explained to him.

He sent the message, then on a whim, set up a simulation of
Anevai's Truthercon. And won the first three rounds. There *had*
to be a method behind it: the odds were so simple!

So why had he invariably lost?

He strove to recall Anevai's every move in detail, while idly
scanning his way through files under his own computer lock,
looking for chaff to erase: unlike the virtually limitless 'Net
memory, the shipboard computer had a definite max storage
capacity and it wasn't polite to leave garbage in the storeroom.

It seemed odd that every time Anevai had thrown, she'd barely
glanced under the cup to see how the dice had fallen. Her eyes
had always been on his face, regardless of who was throwing. . . .

### . . . VANDEREAUX.TRSPT:

Now *there* was a file he'd never looked at. By the entry date
it had transferred into *Cetacean's* records along with his other
files, so he supposed it was his property. . . . Test scores. Test
scores and those all-important correspondence percentiles that
elucidated those scores.

The file's presence in his personals could mean Danislav was
relinquishing his legal hold, or it could be one final warning
from his sponsor. Students weren't supposed to read their own

files; it wasn't supposed to be psychologically healthy. But could anything be more humbling than what he'd already been through?

Curious, he began reading those records in earnest. Early on, they were as bad as he'd feared. *Worse* if possible. But later—especially for the last three years—If these files really *were* his . . .

"Why didn't they tell me? *Bastards!* Danislav, *you* could have, damn you. Give you a thrill, did it? Watch the 'Buster-boy bust his *butt* in terror? Hope it was worth it."

His hands were clenched, his heart beating loudly in his ears. Dr. Mo would be severely pissed at him if he didn't—

> Hey, kid, bedtime.

An override on his monitor: Chet Hamilton. He knew without even checking.

"Shit," he muttered, then realized Hamilton might have been monitoring sound as well and typed:

*Hello, sir. Didn't know you were there. Sorry for the language.*

Faint laughter—Hamilton *had* established an audio link. But response came via the screen:

> Ha! remind me to teach you some really good expletive deleteds sometime.
> Stuff you don't learn in the dainty a-ca-de-my life.

"I doubt—" he muttered.

**BED!**

"All right. All—" The screen blipped off: Hamilton's override.

*Right*, he thought and flipped the lights off. An unidentifiable feeling drifted over him along with the darkness.

*How does it feel, Shapoorian? How does it feel to have a bastard, Recon 'Buster-boy three years your junior graduate a year before you? And with the highest ever graduate rating?*

Recognition of the feeling. An involuntary bark of laughter, quickly smothered as he pulled the covers over his head and burrowed into his pillows. After all these years:

Understanding. Contentment—

Vindication.

Wesley Smith waved to his Security tail and closed his apartment door. The guard wouldn't do much good if he chose to get out, but they needn't worry about him. Not tonight, anyway. He wasn't about to go anywhere—tonight.

Tonight he had work to do.

He pulled his sweater off over his head and drop-kicked it across the room. Whistling tunelessly, he waltzed into the bathroom, flipped the shower on, parked his elbows on the counter, cupped chin in hand and said to his reflection, "You, my dear, are a genius. *Some* people might think you heartless scum, but we know better, don't we?"

He kissed his finger and touched the tip to his mirror image's lips, kicked his slacks out the door and stepped into the shower.

Cantrell was off making up to Paul. He wished them both luck, sighed, and leaned into a hot, wet massage.

It really wasn't fair, you know, Paul had his admiral Loro—if he didn't fuck it up. Anevai was up there with Stephen Ridenour all to herself. Who'd J. Wesley Smith have?

Nobody, that was who. Even Metzky was avoiding him. Couldn't blame her after the other night. Wasn't *really* her fault he missed Stevie's message. But—*dammit!* If *she* hadn't been distracting him that night, who knew what might have happened?

He should have guessed Anevai would get through to the kid first. She had all the luck. Probably a good thing—he'd never have convinced the kid to talk that way. Never would have gotten around to it. Too much else to discuss.

Watery needles painfully flossed his teeth. He shut his mouth on the reminiscent grin. Anevai had been so disappointed at his initial reaction to Ridenour. He really should have trusted her judgment from the first. Who better than she would know a legit 'NetTech from a fake? And she'd spent the whole morning observing Ridenour.

Fact was, he was too damned tired of ass-kissing academy pretty-boys out to impress the 'NetAT. When he'd seen Ridenour, there'd been no question of his business here. He was a Del d'Bugger—no surprise that—but ass-kissers didn't stand up to challenge the way Stevie-boy had, and Wesley Smith wanted Stephen Ridenour back for reasons that had nothing to do with the damned paper.

For the Del d'Bugger he'd expected, he had a special file squirrelled away, ready to implement the instant a Del d'Bugger went after it.

And a bigger pile of shit had never hit the 'Net.

Damn, he was good. It was an elegant little piece of programming, designed to insert dates and abortive thought experiments throughout the records for the last five years. And would do it so no one could tell the difference. Had nothing to do with the true story behind *Harmonies*, but it was a damned sight more than enough to haze the eyes of someone primed for the job.

It wouldn't snow Ridenour for a micro.

*That* was why he wanted Ridenour back. He didn't give shit about the 'Net. Didn't give shit about retaining rights over *Harmonies*. But Stevie was just too damned good to be wasted on the assholes back in Vandereaux, both inside and outside the 'NetAT.

He finished rinsing his hair, tapped the shower off and stepped out into a stream of warm, drying air, combed his hair with his fingers as the man-made wind whipped it about.

And if anyone wanted to give him grief about Stephen Ridenour, well, he had another program he could implement faster than the other. A program that would teach the 'NetAT to disregard his warnings. A program that would wipe the NSpace DB clean with the tap of a button.

He grinned at his reflection, blew it a kiss and kicked the door shut behind him. He flopped on the bed, propped his keyboard on bare knees, and pulled up his own private 'Net access.

He had homework to do. Seeds had, after all, been planted. Given light, they might even grow. *That* depended on the fertility of the ground upon which they'd been cast.

And that, if Jonathan Wesley Smith was any judge at all, was fertile ground indeed.